The Last of Our Kind

Third in the Buenaventura Series

Gerald W. McFarland

SUNSTONE
PRESS

SANTA FE

Sunstone books may be purchased for educational, business, or sales promotional use.
For information please write: Special Markets Department, Sunstone Press,
P.O. Box 2321, Santa Fe, New Mexico 87504-2321.
Book and cover design › Vicki Ahl
Body typeface › Book Antiqua
Printed on acid-free paper
∞
eBook 978-1-61139-420-7

Library of Congress Cataloging-in-Publication Data
McFarland, Gerald W., 1938-
  The last of our kind / Gerald W. McFarland.
    pages ; cm. -- (Third in the Buenaventura series)
  ISBN 978-1-63293-085-9 (softcover : alk. paper)
  1. Warlocks--Fiction. 2. New Mexico--History--To 1848--Fiction. I. Title.
  PS3613.C4393L37 2015
  813'.6--dc23
                        2015029689

WWW.SUNSTONEPRESS.COM
SUNSTONE PRESS / POST OFFICE BOX 2321 / SANTA FE, NM 87504-2321 /USA
(505) 988-4418 / ORDERS ONLY (800) 243-5644 / FAX (505) 988-1025

The Last of Our Kind

To Matt Grillo:
All the best!
Gerry McFarland

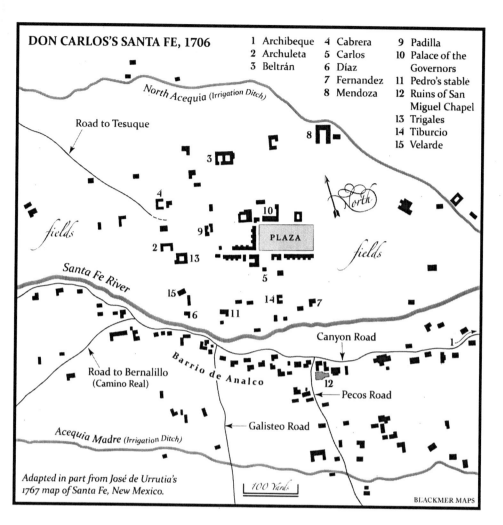

DON CARLOS'S SANTA FE, 1706

1 Archibeque
2 Archuleta
3 Beltrán
4 Cabrera
5 Carlos
6 Díaz
7 Fernandez
8 Mendoza
9 Padilla
10 Palace of the Governors
11 Pedro's stable
12 Ruins of San Miguel Chapel
13 Trigales
14 Tiburcio
15 Velarde

North Acequia (Irrigation Ditch)

Road to Tesuque

North

fields

PLAZA

fields

Santa Fe River

Road to Bernalillo (Camino Real)

Barrio de Analco

Canyon Road

Pecos Road

Galisteo Road

Acequia Madre (Irrigation Ditch)

Adapted in part from José de Urrutia's 1767 map of Santa Fe, New Mexico.

100 Yards

BLACKMER MAPS

Map by Kate Blackmer

Preface

The Last of Our Kind completes the Buenaventura Series trilogy. Most of the events described in the novel take place during a three-month period from April to June 1706. As with *The Brujo's Way* and *What the Owl Saw*, the first two volumes in the series, the story's setting is Santa Fe, New Mexico, a small town on the northernmost edge of Spain's North American empire. Once again the central character is Don Carlos Buenaventura, a powerful brujo whose true identity is known only to a few close friends. The rest of his acquaintances know him as Don Alfonso Cabeza de Vaca, a well-educated young man in his early twenties who is an active member of the Santa Fe community.

Brief descriptions of the main characters and major events that carry over from the first two volumes in the Buenaventura Series to the third may be helpful to readers of *The Last of Our Kind*. In volume one, *The Brujo's Way*, Don Carlos is born in 1684 into an aristocratic Catholic family in Mexico City, a social and religious milieu in which his identity as a brujo, if known, would put him in mortal danger. Initially he recalls that he was killed in his immediately preceding life by his enemy through many lifetimes, a sorcerer named Don Malvolio. But because of the need to suppress any sign that he is other than an ordinary young man, Carlos soon forgets both his past lives and his brujo powers.

He rediscovers these powers, especially his ability to transform himself into hawks and owls, while traveling to Santa Fe, where he is to become the personal secretary to the governor of New Mexico. Once in Santa Fe, Don Carlos again adopts a conventional persona and lives as an upper-class Spaniard whose true identity is known to only one other person, his manservant and friend, Pedro Gallegos. A trip he has to make back to Mexico City turns his quiet life upside down. In a battle to the death with a sorcerer who is Don Malvolio's most powerful apprentice, Don Carlos must call on all his latent brujo powers. Then a chance meeting in Mexico City with Zoila Herrera, a woman trained in Hindu spirituality, is life-changing. He returns to Santa Fe resolved to pursue a new spiritual path. He also enters a friendship with a beautiful young widow, Inéz de Recalde, who becomes his love interest in the next two books.

What the Owl Saw begins with a terrifying dream that convinces Don Carlos that Don Malvolio is once again closing in on him. In his everyday life, Don Carlos loses his job as the governor's secretary and begins a career as a real estate investor. He continues his romantic interest in Inéz and befriends a young Pueblo Indian man, José Lugo, who is studying to be a medicine man. Into this picture comes a trio of itinerant entertainers, a magician (Leandro de Luna) and two alluring dancers (Mara Mata and Selena Torrez), who seem to have access to deeper realms of consciousness that fascinate Carlos. It's possible that they are also agents of his enemy, Don Malvolio. In the novel's final chapters Carlos, Inéz, and José engage in a desperate effort to rescue four kidnapped youngsters, the children of a wealthy Santa Fe merchant couple, Raul and Bianca Trigales.

The Last of Our Kind opens some two months after the successful rescue of the kidnapped children. Inéz, who in the process of the rescue had been transformed by Carlos into many different animals, has been prostrated since her return with a mysterious illness. While it is known that Carlos and Inéz played some role in the rescue, Carlos's ability to transform himself and Inéz obviously remains a secret, and a town Council of Inquiry has been established to determine the facts. The discovery of Leandro's body at the ransom site, and another unidentified body found nearby, leads the council to conclude that Leandro was the kidnapper and that he was killed in a quarrel with his accomplices. The two women entertainers associated with him, Mara Mata and Selena Torrez, were not charged with any knowledge of the crime, inasmuch as Leandro had attempted to poison them prior to the kidnapping.

Carlos, who has been absent from Santa Fe on a wild horse roundup with his Pueblo Indian friend José, learns of the results of the Council of Inquiry's report following his return to town, after which he is plunged into new problems besetting Santa Fe: the increasing threat from hostile Indian tribes, the doubling of the Presidio garrison in response to this threat, the arrival of three inquisitors searching for a brujo (himself) thought to be hiding in Santa Fe, and a spate of burglaries that seem to involve a black dog and the possibility that the thief is a shape-shifter. As in the two previous novels, the story line shifts back and forth between extraordinary events and the everyday life of Don Carlos and his neighbors.

In the course of writing *The Last of Our Kind* I benefitted from the generous assistance of a number of individuals. Once again, as in volume two, Kate Blackmer prepared an excellent map of early eighteenth-century Santa Fe. Helen Wise read the manuscript with special attention to technical details. Janet MacFadyen, Dennis Shapson, and Wilhelmina Van Ness went above and beyond the call of friendship by reading the entire manuscript and making useful suggestions. My wife, Dorothy J. McFarland, brought her skills as a professional editor to bear by undertaking the arduous task of being my in-house editor. Both the novel and I are better for her many interventions.

1

Danger

José noticed them first and called out. "Carlos, trouble ahead!"

Carlos looked up and silently cursed himself for having been so inattentive as to allow the two of them to ride into danger. Instead of being vigilant, he had relaxed in the belief that he and José would not come under attack only two hours from Santa Fe. The April beauty of the landscape through which they were passing, the fact that they had succeeded so well in locating the herd of twenty wild horses that they were driving in front of them, and the steady, soothing movement of his horse, Eagle, under him—all had contributed to his inattention.

But now up ahead, in a stand of cottonwood trees next to a ford in the river alongside which they were riding, were five mounted Indian warriors. Carlos could see they weren't friendly. All five had bows and arrows, and two were readying arrows for an attack. They weren't from any tribe Carlos recognized—not Pueblo Indians, Apache, or Navajo. They were young men, barely more than boys who had ranged far from their homes, probably out for a first taste of warfare that would prove their courage and manhood.

These thoughts flashed through his mind as he considered what to do. Two men against five wasn't the best of odds, and he and José were lightly armed. Carlos had a musket in a scabbard and a knife in his belt, but José, who as a full-blooded Indian was not allowed to bear firearms under Spanish law, had only a knife with which to defend himself.

José, impatient for some sort of response from Carlos—they were drawing closer to the waiting war party with every passing moment—called out again, "Should we make a run for it and let the horse herd scatter?"

The five warriors were on the right-hand side of the road along which Carlos and José had been driving the wild horses. "No," Carlos shouted back, "I'll stampede the herd down the road and you steer them toward the war party from the herd's left flank."

José surely knew that Carlos's strategy gave the two of them the best chance to fend off an attack. Without a word he spurred his mount forward on the left side of the herd. When José was in position, Carlos let out a loud whoop, followed by more cries and shouts that set the wild horses, already jittery at being herded by humans, into a full-fledged stampede, charging forward with manes and tails flying and hooves thundering and making loud screams and neighs—a veritable war party of powerful, four-legged beasts.

The young warriors ahead had apparently not considered they might come under attack, and as the herd of wild horses charged toward them—José had skillfully steered them directly at the grove where the Native raiders had been waiting—two warriors abandoned their position and bolted for the ford to cross the river. Another two were having trouble controlling their mounts as they faced the prospect of being overrun by the approaching herd. Only one warrior, perhaps the leader, held his ground and launched an arrow at Carlos.

Carlos had extraordinarily quick reflexes, and he knew he could evade the oncoming arrow. But he was also a brujo, Don Carlos Buenaventura, and as such he chose to draw on his training as a sorcerer in order to strike fear into the heart of the young warrior. Instead of dodging the arrow, Don Carlos snatched it out of the air and, rising in his stirrups as he and Eagle continued to rush forward behind the stampeding horses, he brandished the arrow in the air and let out a powerful battle cry: "Aaaaeeeeehhheeeaahhheeeehee…!"

The sight of a man who could catch an arrow in flight and who let out such an unearthly scream unnerved the young warrior, and he swung his mount around and followed his four companions across the ford.

Don Carlos turned the shaft of the arrow in his hand until the arrow-head was directed toward the fleeing warriors. By using his brujo powers he could have hurled the arrow with enough force to kill one of the young raiders, but he did not like killing and in the past had done so only when required in defense of himself or his companions. Killing didn't seem necessary in this instance, but he believed he should take some action to discourage the war party from rallying and returning to the attack. So he carefully aimed at the thigh of the boldest of the warriors, who was also the one still closest to him, and hurled the arrow, which lodged in the exact spot he had intended. The warrior, displaying bravery that Don Carlos respected, did not cry out, though he cast a ferocious look over his shoulder at Don Carlos, an attacker whose powers surpassed anything he had ever heard of.

Seeing that the young warriors continued to flee, Carlos and José slowed their mounts, Eagle and Pepper, to a walk in order to stop pressing the wild horse herd forward. This did not immediately have the desired effect, as the herd kept charging pell-mell down the road.

Pulling Eagle up beside José and Pepper, Carlos said, "Getting them calmed down and rounded up again could take a while."

"Maybe not too long," José replied.

"I admire your optimism, but tell me why I should share it."

José nodded toward the herd, which was rounding a bend in the road ahead. "What I see," he said, "is that they've stayed in a tight group behind the stallion. They're not scattering in every direction."

"Okay, but that still doesn't get them to stop."

"I think they will slow down once we're not chasing them. There's a small meadow about half a mile beyond this ford. I'll bet the stallion will decide that's a good place to stop and graze. The rest of the herd will follow his lead."

"I'll take your word for it, José. I saw you win the stallion's trust after we found the herd near Old Man Xenome's sacred mesa. But shouldn't we wait a while before approaching them?"

"Yes, give them at least an hour. We can watch from far enough away that we won't set them off again. Once they've quieted down, we can gently nudge them southward again."

"You're the horse master," Carlos said. "But I'm worried that we won't reach Santa Fe until after dark."

José shrugged. "If we have to stay here tonight, that's what we'll have to do."

They asked their mounts to move forward and they followed the herd from a good distance at a slow walk. As they rounded a bend they saw that the stallion had brought the herd to a halt a quarter of a mile ahead. Many of the horses were still milling around, too excited to graze on the grassy area that was adjacent to the road, but a few mares had settled down and begun to eat. The stallion, spotting Carlos and José, watched them intently. When the two men brought their horses to a halt, the herd's leader began to relax.

Carlos and José sat without speaking for a long time. Except for a nagging concern that they wouldn't reach Santa Fe before nightfall, Carlos didn't really mind the wait. He enjoyed the chance to quietly take in their surroundings as the shadows of trees gradually crept across the valley floor, the river murmured vigorously nearby, and the lofty faces of the Sangre de Cristo mountains to the east, gold with the declining sun, gave a dramatic backdrop to the scene. Carlos observed again, as he had hundreds of times since coming to New Mexico in 1704, now more than two years ago, that the beauty and power of the high desert environment surrounding his adopted home never failed to stir his heart. I suppose, he thought, you could say I am in love with this land.

The pause from actively driving the horses also gave Carlos a chance to reflect on how close he, a Spaniard of the *hidalgo* class, and José, a Pueblo Indian, had become. Only two years earlier he had saved José, then a slender boy, from being hanged for a murder he hadn't committed. He had also, following instructions given by a Pueblo Indian medicine man named Old Man Xenome, become José's mentor in the Shaman's Way, and José had come to live at Carlos's place to take care of his horses and serve as his all-around helper. Despite being José's employer and several years his senior, he deferred to José's keen intuitions about horses. In any case, José was no longer a boy. He was now nineteen years old and everything about him—his broad face, long black hair in two braids that reached halfway down his back, the calm gaze with which he surveyed the scene, and the erect way he sat quietly in the saddle—conveyed a dignity beyond his years.

After more than an hour had passed, José spoke at last. "I think they're ready to be herded again. Let me go forward slowly by myself. If they run away, we'll have to wait longer."

The situation unfolded better than either Carlos or José had any right to expect. As José moved his mount forward, the horses in the herd, almost in a single motion, lifted their heads and then began to meander south on the road to Santa Fe. When José gestured that it was safe for Carlos to follow, he did so, and together they half drove and half followed the wild horses.

It was nearly nightfall when they reached the northern outskirts of the small frontier town of Santa Fe. Lamps had already been lit in some of the three- and four-room adobe houses in which farmers and craftsmen lived. Carlos and José had intended to drive the herd south of town to Rancho Rosón, whose owner, Carlos's friend Raul Trigales, wanted to add the wild horses to a herd he was developing for sale to local ranchers and farmers. But it was growing so dark that Carlos called out to José, "Perhaps we should leave them in the big north pasture that belongs to the Presidio. It was empty ten days ago, and I don't think Captain Posada will mind if we leave the horses there overnight."

José, who was in a better position to see the pasture as it came into view, announced, "I don't think we can do that. The north pasture seems to be full of horses—about forty of them."

14 ———————

"That's a lot of horses that weren't there ten days ago," Carlos said. "And now that I'm close enough, I can see some spotted horses that I've never seen in the Presidio pastures before. What do you suppose is going on?"

"I don't know," José replied, "but we have to go on to Rancho Rosón." And that was what they did, although it took more than an hour for them to drive the herd around the town on a peripheral road and then south on the Camino Real. This route took them past a few scattered farmhouses whose occupants stuck their heads out of windows and doors to see who was on the road after dark. When they finally arrived at Rancho Rosón, four vaqueros came out of the bunkhouse to greet them. After a brief exchange of greetings, the vaqueros saddled their own horses and helped Carlos and José move the wild horses into a meadow next to the main ranch house.

Don Carlos and José then consulted about what to do next. "I'll stay here overnight and possibly longer," José said. "I want to see how the herd settles in. After a day or two I'll ride to town to report to Señor Trigales and return Pepper." (Although Pepper belonged to Pedro Gallegos, who ran a stable for Raul Trigales, Pepper boarded at Carlos's place, where José had been living.) "If," José added, "you see Señor Trigales tomorrow morning, please tell him that we've added twenty horses to his herds, and when you see Pedro, please thank him for the loan of Pepper."

"I'll pass on your messages to Raul and Pedro," Don Carlos replied. "And as for the future, it seems to me that your duties as Raul's horse master will mean that you'll take over here, and I'll have to find myself a new groom and right-hand man."

José nodded, managing to convey regret. "A possible replacement for me might be Orfeo Jiranza. He already works for you as your carpenter and he's been staying at your place while you've been away. But you'll still be without a cook."

"That could be a problem. Ever since Pedro's María moved out and I've had to cook, I've found kitchen chores tedious. But if Orfeo will help with the horses," Don Carlos added, "I'll manage. I'm more concerned about you. Can you continue your studies with Old Man Xenome?"

"I hope so," José replied, in a tone that seemed to indicate some uncertainty. "I'll soon find out whether I can be both Señor Trigales's horse master and an apprentice medicine man."

Don Carlos answered by clapping José on the back. "I hope so too," he said. "For now I'll be on my way. I'm feeling bone weary and eager to get back to Santa Fe. Rest well."

"You, too," José said. "I hope you'll find that everything there is all right. Ernesto, the foreman here, said that a large party of soldiers and other men arrived in Santa Fe while we were away. The cavalry horses in the north pasture probably belong to them."

Don Carlos nodded, took his departure, and made it home in forty minutes. Home! What a nice ring that had to it. He felt warm anticipation as he rode up to the corral in back of his modest four-room house. An oil lamp was lit in the kitchen, and he could hear Orfeo playing the guitar and singing an old Spanish *verso*, one of a seemingly endless number of songs that he knew. Carlos's little dog, Gordo, heard Carlos and Eagle returning and came dashing out of his doggy door and danced around them wagging his tail and yipping in delight. "Hello, old fellow," Carlos said, dismounting and bending down to accept licks on his cheek and hands. "I missed you too."

Orfeo, tall and slender, with narrow hands and long fingers which were agile on the guitar and capable of delicate work at his profession of carpentry, hurried out the kitchen door. "Welcome home, Don Alfonso," he said. (Don Alfonso Cabeza de Vaca was Carlos's public name; his private identity as Don Carlos Buenaventura, a brujo who had lived five previous lives, was known to only his four closest friends.)

"How have you been?" Don Carlos asked.

"I've been fine. José's cousins came for two days and helped me with the house we're building for Dr. Velarde. We've finished the first wing."

"And how is Inéz?" Don Carlos asked. After she and Carlos had returned from rescuing the kidnapped Trigales children two months earlier, she had collapsed with a mysterious illness.

"Pedro said she's feeling much better."

"Good. I'll go see her first thing in the morning."

"Also, several people came by looking for you while you were away."

"For instance?"

"The governor's secretary, Marco Cabrera. He said Governor Peralta wanted to see you. Marco also wants to talk with you. Then Dr. Velarde came by. I think he wants to move into the house we're building, even though the second wing isn't done."

"Let's go inside, Orfeo," Don Carlos suggested, "and you can tell me more while I get something to eat."

"I'll tell you what I know," Orfeo said, "which isn't much. You'll have to get the details from Pedro and Inéz." Following Don Carlos into the house, Orfeo added, "A lot happened while you were away, and I get the impression from Pedro and Inéz that not all of it is good."

2

Home

*D*espite his late return from a tiring trip, Don Carlos started his morning in the usual way, rising before dawn and doing silent meditation for two hours. Gordo, as was his wont, rolled over in the bed he'd been sharing with Carlos and went back to sleep.

Carlos didn't achieve a state of deep quiet during his meditation. Images from the encounter with the Indian war party kept coming back, and when those images didn't dominate his consciousness, speculation about what had happened in Santa Fe during his absence took over. Why had a company of soldiers been added to the Presidio garrison at a time when the barracks were already near capacity? What did Governor Peralta want to discuss? The two of them had never developed a warm relationship, even when Carlos had been personal secretary to Peralta's predecessor, Governor Juan Villela, and Peralta had been the province's vice governor. And recently the new governor's wife, Pilar Peralta, had been going out of her way to exclude him from social gatherings of the town's leading families (principally those of the governor and his top administrators), although Carlos qualified for this circle both because of the position he had held as the governor's secretary and because of his birth into a titled Mexico City family.

While eating breakfast and doing his best to ignore Gordo's begging for a third helping of food — the once-scrawny stray that Carlos had adopted now lived up to his name — Carlos concluded that he needed to stop speculating and gather some facts. From what Orfeo had said, Pedro and Inéz would be useful sources of information. Pedro Gallegos, formerly Carlos's manservant, was now working for Raul Trigales, who owned the town's only stable as well as Rancho Rosón. Pedro would definitely be up at this early hour to feed the horses under his care, and Carlos decided to visit him first. Inéz, who normally cooked for the household of Raul's brother- and sister-in-law, Javier and Cristina Beltrán, was still recovering from her illness and often slept late.

A short walk across several neighbors' fields brought him to the stable, where he found Pedro distributing hay to the horses. "I heard you were back," Pedro said in his laconic way.

"I'm glad to see you too," Carlos replied, amused by his friend's disregard for preliminary pleasantries. He felt great warmth for Pedro, one of the few people who knew that he was a brujo, and a companion with whom he had shared many adventures in the past two and a half years. Pedro walked with a limp, the result of a wound he had received as a soldier in some now-forgotten war, but he was physically strong and solid to the core—eminently practical, thoroughly dependable, and a loyal friend.

"How did you hear that José and I had returned?"

Pedro grunted. "If you drive a herd of wild horses around the west side of town, people notice. Young Clemente Faustino came over at sunup to get the horse his father boards here, and he said you'd gone by their place last night."

"Nothing goes unnoticed around here for long. What else has happened? I can't go away for even ten days without a cavalry troop arriving. José and I couldn't leave our little herd overnight in the Presidio's north pasture. It was empty when we left, but now it's full of at least forty horses."

Pedro shrugged. "Forty cavalrymen, three *hidalgos* on expensive horses, and three Franciscans riding mules arrived the day after you left. There were also two other men, maybe the Franciscans' servants. At Mass yesterday, the senior Franciscan told everyone to come to a meeting on the plaza at noon today. That's all I know. Ask Inéz. She probably knows more."

"I'm on my way to see her next. How is María?"

"My wife is getting bigger every day. I think she might have twins."

"But she's still working mornings for Raul and Bianca Trigales?"

"She doesn't complain. She says women scrub floors until the day before their babies are born, and after that they wrap them in a *rebozo* and go about their work. Women are tougher than men."

Carlos recalled seeing mestizo and Indian women in the market selling their produce with their babies tied to their bodies with long shawls. Still, he thought María could use some help with her own household chores. "What about hiring a girl to help out here?" he asked Pedro.

Pedro made a hand gesture indicating that it would cost money they didn't have.

"Marisol Díaz lives right next door," Carlos ventured. "She's young and capable, and used to taking care of her younger siblings. She could help María around the house and with the baby."

Pedro grunted. "Maybe so, if that carpenter of yours, Orfeo, doesn't snatch her first."

18 ——————

"Something going on there?" Carlos asked.

"Looks like it. I've seen her at the Velarde building site a few times, doing sewing, and singing along with Orfeo. They both have nice voices."

"Ah!" Carlos said without comment, even as he noted that it would complicate his life if Orfeo married and wanted to start his own household. Keeping good help wasn't easy. In the past two months four workers—Pedro and María, José, and a young Indian man named Diego—had left his employ for better jobs. As he turned to go it occurred to him to ask, "Do you have any idea why Governor Peralta wants to see me?"

Pedro shrugged again. "They're looking for places to house the new soldiers. You have two empty rooms. You might have to take in a few soldiers."

"That would be rather inconvenient," Carlos said drily. "Since you and María moved out, I don't have a cook or housekeeper. Even if one of them can cook breakfast for the rest, it will be a nuisance having them around."

Pedro looked unimpressed. "Life is trouble, only death is not."

"Has becoming a businessman made you into a philosopher? But if the priests are right, death will bring a lot of trouble to sinners."

"Men like us, I suppose," Pedro replied, and they broke into the comradely laughter that they so often shared.

After parting from Pedro, Carlos headed off to see Inéz, taking a path that passed west of the Palace of the Governors and continued a hundred and fifty yards beyond to the large house owned by Javier and Cristina Beltrán. He went to the back of the house, knocked, and then tried the kitchen door. It was locked, but he could hear someone moving around inside, so he knocked again more loudly. The kitchen's occupant turned out to be Rita Piño, a short, stocky Pueblo Indian girl with soft black eyes. She had initially been hired to help out in the kitchen when Inéz had left to accompany Carlos in pursuit of the kidnappers of the Trigales children.

Rita welcomed him with a big smile. "Don Alfonso! Señora Recalde will be so happy for your return!"

"I hope so," Don Carlos said, aware that Inéz would have been worried because he had been away longer than he'd originally expected, and that worrying about him tended to put her in a bad mood. "I notice," he added, "that you're locking the door again. Have there been more break-ins?"

The corners of Rita's mouth turned down. "Some silverware was stolen from us this past week," she replied. "You'll hear the story soon. Everyone is very upset."

"Have other families besides your employers also experienced break-ins?"

"Yes, but you shouldn't delay going to see the Señora. She got up a few minutes ago. I'll tell her you're here, and that she can join you in the dining room."

Rita had set out a tray with Inéz's breakfast on it. Don Carlos reached for the tray. "I can take this to the dining room while you go tell her I'm here."

Rita hesitated and then said, "Thank you, but that's not necessary. I will bring the tray when the Señora is ready for it." Aware that Rita might not want a *hidalgo* to do a servant's work, he didn't insist.

Halfway to his destination he was met by Inéz's employer, Cristina Beltrán, who had an amused expression on her face. In the light tone she often adopted toward him she said, "I heard you offer to carry the tray with Inéz's breakfast to the dining room. I keep wondering why you persist in auditioning for a position on the household staff! You should know by now that you don't have to do service to be welcome in the Beltrán home." Dropping her teasing manner, she added, "We are so happy for your safe return, and you're in luck. Raul and Javier are in the dining room. I'm sure they will want to hear about your trip."

The brothers-in-law looked up and greeted Carlos as he entered the room. The only dishes on the table were two cups filled with coffee. Javier gestured to Carlos to pull up a chair, a handsome piece of furniture made by a skilled craftsman, a luxury item found in few Santa Fe houses. "Will you join us for a cup of coffee?" he asked.

"No, thank you, Javier," Carlos replied. "I've had breakfast. I just stopped by to see Inéz and catch up on the news."

Carlos had no sooner sat down than Inéz arrived, followed by Rita with the breakfast tray. The three men rose as one. Taking a seat at the end of the table, Inéz said, "Good morning, all. Please sit. I'm very hungry. Let me eat while the three of you talk."

"Before we move on to other topics," Carlos said, "let me report that José and I reached Rancho Rosón last night with twenty healthy horses that we drove here from the northern mesa area. We had no trouble with the horses, but we did encounter a small war party of Indians yesterday. They fled when we stampeded the herd directly at them."

Concern showed on Raul's, Javier's, and Inéz's faces, but Carlos reassured them. "Everything turned out all right. I would tell you more, except that I can't stay long. I need to report the incident to the Presidio's commandant, and the governor has asked me to stop by his office. So in the little time we have I would appreciate you giving me the latest news." Turning to Raul, Carlos said, "I would particularly like to hear from you how your four dear children have been."

"Physically," Raul said, "they are well enough. But they've not gotten over what happened to them—setting off on a happy journey with Leandro the Magician, whom they trusted, then being suddenly forced off the road, seeing their governess and our groom pulled out of the carriage and killed by men of monstrous size, and then being seized themselves by those monsters, carried off, and left in a pit in a remote mountain cave. As the eldest, Cristofer makes a great show of being brave, and he is brave. But the twins, Carmela and Constanza, have nightmares and break into tears for no reason."

"What about little Anton?"

"That's a mixed story. You know what a carefree, happy child he was. He's a solemn little boy now, and he won't talk about whatever is bothering him. But he does often talk about the angel that rescued them from the cave and spent the night with them. He insists that the angel looked just like Inéz," he added, turning to Inéz and smiling.

Carlos, who had used a sorcerer's technique to give Inéz the appearance of an angelic figure with wings, knew that she was indeed the angel who had helped rescue Anton and his siblings. Since that information could not be disclosed, he merely commented, "I'm sure Inéz doesn't mind being taken for an angel."

Inéz looked up from her breakfast and replied, "Not at all. Anton is a sweet little boy."

"I hope," Raul went on, "that that chapter in the children's lives, in all of our lives, has been closed, now that the Council of Inquiry has presented its report."

"Please tell me about it," Carlos said.

"Except for you and the children, everyone who had testified before the council—myself, the dancers Mara Mata and Selena Torrez, and Inéz—was present, plus the three men from the posse who pursued Leandro south after you and I returned to Santa Fe. I didn't permit my children to attend the session at which the council gave its report because I didn't want them to have any further reminders of what they'd been through. And I was annoyed with the council for having discounted the children's earlier testimony that four giants helped Leandro kidnap them. I believe my children, even though I've never seen grotesque, eight-foot-tall monsters."

"No one," Carlos said, "who saw the huge footprints that Leandro's accomplices left at the murder site could ever doubt that some beings larger than ordinary humans were involved."

"I appreciate your supporting my children's memories," Raul said. "However, the council based its findings on the report from members of the posse that they had discovered Leandro's dismembered body under a pile of rocks at the side of the road, and that they also found the badly decomposed body of a mestizo man on a nearby slope. They believed that the dead mestizo was one of the kidnappers, and no monster—he was only average in height, nothing like the giants the children described."

Carlos knew that he and Inéz had buried Leandro, and that the dead ogre, one of the monsters who had participated in the kidnapping the children, had shrunk in size after he and Inéz had killed him. But he couldn't reveal that information and keep his identity as a brujo secret, so he changed the topic and asked, "What was the council's conclusion about Mara and Selena? Were they thought to have played some role in the kidnapping?"

"Whatever Mara and Selena may have known," Raul replied, "the testimony you and Inéz gave that Leandro had tried to poison them inclined the council to believe that they were not involved."

"So they weren't charged with aiding and abetting?"

"No, although naturally they feel rather like outcasts—Leandro was, after all, their partner. As you know, they moved out of the Tiburcio place they shared with Leandro and now live with Juan Archibeque, who, as a Frenchman in exile here, is also an outsider. He needed governesses for his daughters and hired them. It's an ideal arrangement. Juan gave them work they seem to enjoy and a place to live that's on the far edge of town. As long as they don't come into the center of Santa Fe, which as far as I know they haven't done except for the sessions with the council, they won't have to endure the stares of curious or hostile townspeople."

Before anything more could be said, a groom came into the room. Addressing Raul, he said, "Señor, the Taos traders you've been expecting have arrived with three wagons of goods. They said they hope to see you right away."

Raul stood up and said to Carlos and Inéz, "Please excuse us; duty calls. Javier and I must tend to business. In any case, the two of you will want a chance to talk alone." Javier, who had also stood up, left the room along with Raul and the groom.

Smiling at Carlos, Inéz said, "Rita tells me that you wanted to bring me my breakfast. That's nice of you, but you needn't do her work."

"I hope she doesn't think I'm after her job," Carlos replied and was rewarded with a laugh. He loved Inéz's laugh and was glad she seemed to be in a good mood.

"You were gone a long time," she said, though without any reproach.

"Yes, I was," he agreed. "Once we'd been away more than six days I began to worry. I should have taken an owl's form at night" — Inéz was one of his four friends who knew that he was a brujo skilled at transforming himself into owls and other animals — "and flown here to reassure you that I was all right."

"That's something that never occurred to me. Perhaps next time. I'm glad your trip was successful. But I don't like this story about your encountering a war party. Were you holding back details when you mentioned it to Raul and Javier?"

"Nothing important," he replied. "As I said, I need to see the commandant and the governor this morning, and I didn't think there was time for the whole story."

Giving him a searching look, she said, "You're hiding something. I can tell."

"Perhaps a small something, but before I confess, please tell me how you've been."

"I wish you had come by as soon as you got back. I don't like being the last to hear about your adventures."

"I didn't get back to Santa Fe until well after dark, and I thought it prudent to wait until daytime to visit you."

Inéz laughed. "You, prudent? I appreciate your thoughtfulness, but you know you're always welcome here. Cristina considers the friendship ring you gave me a sign that we are engaged, and she's spread that story among her friends."

"Does that bother you?" Carlos asked. "I hope not. I'm pleased to have the freedom our supposed status as an engaged couple gives us. At the same time, I also want to respect your reluctance to consider marriage."

"Hmmm," she murmured noncommittally.

"If you won't talk," Carlos said, "you might as well finish your breakfast."

"I am hungry," she said, and picked up a piece of toast that had butter and apricot preserves on it. She took a big bite and closed her eyes as she savored its taste. This gave Carlos an opportunity to let his eyes linger on her face—her high forehead, dark eyebrows that arched over striking gray eyes, fine nose, full lips, and strong chin.

"What?" she asked, glancing up and catching him looking at her.

"I like looking at you," he said.

"Look all you want," she replied playfully. "I need to eat."

"It doesn't take a brujo's intuition," he told her, "to see that whatever you did yesterday left you feeling pleased with yourself and very hungry. So what have you been up to?"

"It's a longish story," she said. "And I don't understand why you're stalling about telling me the details of your encounter with hostile Indians."

"I have no intention of holding anything back. I just want to hear your story first."

"If you insist," she replied. "A lot has happened since you and José went off to chase wild horses. Raul has already told you about the Council of Inquiry's report, but you and I both know that they got many details wrong."

"How did Mara and Selena take it? They must have been relieved that they're not going to be charged with anything."

"Relieved not to be charged, but shocked to hear that Leandro was dead, and that his body had been torn to pieces. Mara, as you know, has the unbridled emotions of a child, and his betrayal of them was devastating, and it was only compounded by her grief at losing him. Selena, of course, is made of steel. She sat through the proceedings without showing any emotion, but Mara barely held herself together."

"Did you speak with them afterward?"

"Yes, when the inquest was over. I invited them to walk from the Palace of the Governors back here. Before we were even halfway along, Mara began to tremble, and by the time I got them to my room—incidentally, the first time they'd ever been there—she began to wail. Selena told me to give her a thick towel and let her bury her face in it so she could weep without restraint. It was as if she gave the towel all her grief, and it contained it. And Selena's and my tears too."

"What women do always amazes me," Carlos said at last.

"As it should," Inéz agreed. "It allowed us to release what we had been holding—their shock and grief at the loss of Leandro, and my horror and grief at having seen him torn apart by those monsters. When it subsided, we were calm. I think it helped lift this strange illness I've had off of me. I've been feeling much better since."

"I can see that you're better—you were in such a good mood when you came in the room! But other things must have contributed to that."

"Yes," she said, taking a big bite of toast. "Let me continue. The day after you and José left, about forty cavalrymen and several Franciscans and their servants arrived in town. Along with them were three Mendoza brothers, nephews of Doña Josefina, the Mendoza family's matriarch. It was quite a show—the cavalry entered the plaza in full formation, banners flying, horses prancing, and bugles sounding. It was soul-stirring even to me. I could see the appeal of the martial life, even though I hate anything to do with war."

"I've been wondering what that is all about, but I don't see why it should contribute to your feeling good."

Inéz popped the last piece of toast in her mouth. A little apricot preserve escaped at the edge of her mouth and she dabbed at it with a napkin. "Dearest Carlos," she said, "so impatient, so impetuous, and yet I love you for those qualities, annoying though they can be at times.

"My feeling good is in large part related to the arrival of the Mendoza brothers. The three of them—Antonio, Julio, and Santiago—are potential heirs to Josefina Mendoza's fortune. She's now in her eighties. As you probably know, she was married to the son of one of the founders of Santa Fe, and the Mendoza family received a huge grant of land for the part they played in the town's early history. Josefina's husband died long ago and their son and grandson were both killed during the Pueblo Revolt of 1680. I guess you could say the Mendoza hacienda is a house of widows. There are no male heirs except these three great-nephews. In honor of their arrival, Josefina Mendoza and Governor Peralta and his wife, Pilar, each gave dinner parties last week. From the ever socially ambitious Pilar's viewpoint, events unfolded in a very fortuitous way. The older two Mendoza brothers were smitten by the beauty of Pilar's daughters, Juliana and Victoria, and at Mass yesterday Juliana appeared on Antonio's arm and Victoria on Julio's, the girls well chaperoned, of course.

"This, as you can tell if your travels in the wilds of New Mexico have not addled your wits, left the youngest of the brothers, Santiago, without any local beauty to woo."

"I still don't see what this has with you feeling so good and being hungry for breakfast, unless this Santiago met and began to court you."

"Now you're being silly," Inéz laughed, "and possibly a little jealous too, though it might be good for you to have a rival. No, what happened was

that Santiago noticed Elena Beltrán at Mass and afterward asked to be introduced to her. Having taken up fencing and consequently having lost some
weight, she has become quite striking. Santiago is a handsome fellow with
impeccable manners, so the attraction was mutual. In conversation he learned
about Elena's fencing, and he asked if she would fence with him.

"Elena agreed, but now she's in a panic because she hasn't fenced for
the months that I've not been well. Since I was feeling so much better, yesterday I fenced with her for nearly an hour. I enjoyed myself immensely and was
delighted that I could keep at it for so long. But I'm a little tired today. She's
very eager to get more practice in before the bout with Santiago. Perhaps you
can help her by fencing with her today and tomorrow."

"I'll be glad to help. I, too, need to practice, especially if my favorite
partner in swordsmanship, the beautiful Basque woman Señora Inéz de Recalde, will honor me with a bout now that she's restored to health. Perhaps
she would even join me for a ride in the country and, at some suitably remote
spot, allow me to use my brujo skills to change the two of us into hawks for a
flight."

Inéz's face clouded. "Our time flying together," she explained, "was
thrilling, and I treasure the memory. But I think that the many transformations you worked on me during our journey to rescue the Trigales children—
from hawk to owl to coyote to ground squirrel to bat and I can't remember
what else—contributed to my illness. I was so exhausted—I felt like every
bone in my body had been broken into tiny pieces, and if I tried to stand
up I would collapse in a heap." She paused for a moment, as if recalling the
feeling. "And sometimes," she went on, "it seemed as though I was full of
holes, and there was a kind of rushing noise that something made through
the holes." She shook her head. "Very unpleasant, I assure you. And horrible,
grotesque images kept forming and unforming and reforming in my mind—I
suppose from seeing those monsters, the ogres, and having to kill one."

"Dear Inéz, I'm so sorry you've had to go through all of this," Carlos
said with great sympathy.

"Oh, it's all right," she said quickly. "I seem to be over it now. And the
important thing is we rescued the children. But no more of this! You promised
to tell me about encountering a war party of Indians yesterday."

Carlos took a deep breath. "It happened near that ford on the river
about two hours' ride from here. José spotted five Indian warriors in the trees
ahead."

Inéz remained calm. "Since you're here to tell the story, you must have driven them off. Did you use your brujo powers?"

"I couldn't see any way to send a bolt of invisible energy above the heads of the wild horses without terrifying them, so José and I created a stampede and sent the herd charging directly at the glade of cottonwoods where the warriors were lurking. Faced with the likelihood of being trampled by the onrushing herd, the warriors abandoned their plans and retreated across the river."

"That's it? No sorcery?"

"Just one bit, and for obvious reasons I couldn't tell Raul and Javier about it. I snatched an arrow that was shot at me out of the air, and when the last of the warriors to hold his position against the charging horses saw me do that, even he chose to abandon the fight."

"I'm glad that worked out so well."

Surprised, Carlos commented. "You're taking this much better than I expected."

"Another thought I've had during the many days I've spent in bed over the past two months is that there's no way I am ever going to change you. You're a risk-taker, you're given to seeking adventures that are often dangerous, and it's not in your nature to be reflective or introspective. No, don't protest. I've decided that I must love you as you are or not love you at all."

"So," Carlos asked, "does that mean that you now love me as I am?"

She smiled. "A debate is still raging between the Inéz who thinks she can love you without trying to change you and the Inéz who thinks she can't. Right now the Inéz who loves you just as you are has the upper hand, but I can't guarantee that the meddlesome, anxious Inéz won't surface with a vengeance again. I'm sorry. I can't seem to deal with you without an internal struggle."

"I love both Inézes!" Carlos exclaimed.

"Ha!" she replied. "Answers come so easily to you! I wonder if that's true or simply what you'd like to be true. Perhaps time will tell. But as for now, don't you have to report to the commandant about the war party you encountered?"

"I would rather sit here and watch you eat breakfast."

"You need to leave, but first there is something else I want to tell you. The three Franciscans who arrived with the new troops are inquisitors, and the Chief Inquisitor, a priest named Father Arturo Dorantes, announced at Mass yesterday that a forty-day period of grace is about to begin. He called for everyone in Santa Fe to come to the plaza at noon today so he can explain this forty-day period. So you must attend."

"An inquiry by the Holy Office!" Carlos exclaimed. "That doesn't sound like good news."

"It probably isn't," Inéz replied, "but if you want to see the governor and the Presidio's new commandant, Major Tomé Cortés, and then hear Father Dorantes's address at noon, and still get back here for a fencing session with Elena, we'll have to discuss the matter of the Inquisition later. Go!"

3

Threats

Carlos left the dining room and let himself out the back door. His next destination was the Palace of the Governors. He made his way to the part of the building where the governor's office was located. In an outer room he met Marco Cabrera, who had been his boyhood friend and fencing partner in Mexico City and who was now the governor's private secretary.

"Marco," Carlos said, "I heard you were looking for me. What's on your mind?"

Marco, a handsome young man with a frank, open face, clasped Carlos's hand warmly. "Perhaps you've heard," he began, "that a company of forty cavalrymen arrived while you were away. The barracks are full to overflowing. The governor has directed me to find rooms in private homes for at least twenty of the newcomers. Lucila Archuleta has offered space in the old Tiburcio place, which could accommodate six to ten soldiers. I know that the house you're building for Dr. Velarde is only half complete, but you might, in a civic-spirited gesture, let soldiers occupy the three completed rooms."

Reviewing his options, Carlos appealed for time. "Let me consider what I can do. For one thing, I should consult with Dr. Velarde before making that space available."

"Of course," Marco agreed. "Are you also aware," he went on, "that the soldiers were accompanied by three Franciscans who are representatives of the Holy Office?"

"Yes," Carlos replied. "Inéz just told me that the Chief Inquisitor is going to address all of Santa Fe on the plaza at noon today."

"So I expect we will find out more then," Marco said. "But perhaps I could come by your house shortly after the Chief Inquisitor's address to discuss a personal matter of concern to me? And now you should see the governor about providing rooms for the surplus soldiers, and whatever else is on his mind."

As Carlos was wondering what else Marco and the governor might want to speak with him about, Marco stepped to the door of the governor's office, knocked, and announced, "Don Alfonso is here, Excellency. Would you like to see him now?" A faint affirmative came from within, and Marco opened the door and ushered Carlos into the governor's office. As Carlos crossed the room to shake the governor's proffered hand, he noticed that Ignacio Peralta had made many changes in the décor. His predecessor, Carlos's former boss, Juan Villela, had favored a rather ascetic style. The only decorations on the wall during his long tenure in office had been a plain wooden crucifix and a small replica of New Mexico's official provincial seal. Governor Peralta had replaced the wooden crucifix with an elaborate carved image of Saint Francis, Santa Fe's patron saint. The provincial seal remained in place, but a variety of other artifacts had been added — the battle standards of two New Mexican regiments, a pair of crossed swords, a map with prominently marked locations of Spanish victories over New Mexican Indians, and a Peralta family coat of arms on a plaque that was larger than the province's official seal. On the whole, it was, Carlos thought, an aggressively militant set of choices.

"Welcome home, Don Alfonso," the governor said, indicating that Carlos should sit in a chair across the desk from him. Don Carlos nodded in what he hoped was an agreeable manner and waited for the governor to have his say. At a glance, however, he was reminded of several of the reasons why he did not particularly admire Ignacio Peralta. The man was unprepossessing — short, paunchy, and with a receding hairline. He had a nervous way of drumming his fingers on his desk and he spoke in a reedy, high-pitched voice. In Carlos's estimation the recently installed governor did not have a strong character. Still, both by virtue of being a head of state and at the top of the small community's social pyramid, he was someone it would be wise to accommodate.

"I have a number of topics," Peralta began. "The first concerns housing for some of the cavalrymen who arrived a week ago. The barracks are overcrowded at present. Our province's attorney, Nicolas Archuleta, asked his wife if some of the soldiers could have the use of the Tiburcio place, and Doña Lucila has generously agreed to let them do so. The esteemed Doña Josefina Mendoza has offered to house four of the unit's junior officers. Since you are in the real-estate business, perhaps you might find space for a few of the cavalrymen in your properties, or even in your own house, now that your man Pedro Gallegos has gone to manage that stable that belongs to Raul Trigales."

Don Carlos was glad that he'd had some time to consider what he was willing to do. "Yes," he said, "the two rooms that Pedro and María occupied are unused at present, and I could offer them for two or possibly three men. If I may make a request, however, I would prefer that my lodgers not be strangers. There are three young privates at the Presidio who are old friends of mine — Alejandro Guzman, Luis Madrid, and Gonzalo Navarro. They accompanied me on a trip I made last year to El Paso del Norte and back, and I have friendly feelings towards them."

The governor agreed. "That would be most helpful. I'm sure those three men can be assigned to live with you."

"But wait," Carlos said, holding up his hand. "I can do much more. As you know I am having a house built for Fabio Velarde. Although it's barely more than half complete, I believe he would like to move into the part that's habitable. If so, he would vacate the Fernandez place, the four-room house that I've been renting him. That house could take eight soldiers if they don't mind close quarters."

The governor smiled broadly and said, "That's splendid! Will you tell Marco as soon as you know whether that's possible?"

"Of course." Don Carlos said nothing more, waiting for the governor to introduce a new topic.

"I have asked you here for another reason as well," Peralta began thoughtfully. "I am disturbed by the number of Indian attacks on Spanish people. In the past year, you have been the subject of two such incidents known to me — the hostile warriors you fought while crossing the Jornada del Muerto last summer, and the encounter you had last January with three Indian bandits south of Santa Fe. I commend you for your resourceful response in both instances. There have been too many such episodes in recent years, something that wouldn't have happened in the era when Governor Vargas and your stepfather, General Rodrigo Alvarez, dealt firmly with such threats. Your former employer, Governor Villela, had many virtues, but in my opinion he didn't take a firm enough hand with restive Indians."

Don Carlos realized that what he had to report would only substantiate the governor's feelings on the subject. "Regrettably," he began, "I have to report yet another incident that occurred only yesterday. As José Lugo and I were driving a herd of horses southward, we encountered a war party of five Indians who were lying in wait for us at the ford about two hour's ride from Santa Fe."

Peralta interrupted Don Carlos. "Exactly!" he exclaimed. "The hostile Indians are growing bolder and bolder. What tribal group were these warriors from?"

"None that either José or I recognized, and José, being a Pueblo Indian, would certainly have known if they were Pueblo, Apache, or Navajo warriors."

"How were they armed? We have information that some tribes to the north and east of here are acquiring muskets in trade with the French."

"These were very young men, boys really, and their only weapons were bows and arrows."

"But five against two! How did you live to sit here and tell me about it?"

"José and I stampeded twenty wild horses into the place where the warriors were lurking, and rather than be run over and trampled by a charging herd, they fled without attacking us."

The governor's eyes narrowed. "It seems you respond with great skill in dangerous situations. That makes me wonder whether you would consider accepting an officer's commission in the provincial militia, with the specific assignment of tracking down and punishing Native troublemakers."

Carlos was astonished by the offer. "I'm flattered by your proposal," he replied, "but I am not a military man. All I wish to do is to report this incident to the Presidio's commandant later today and let him decide what actions need to be taken."

"Do you, perhaps," the governor asked, shifting abruptly to another topic, "speak French?"

"I know a little," Carlos replied. "Why do you ask?"

Forming his fingers into a steeple, the governor said, "It's complicated. I assume you are aware of the situation in Spain."

Carlos nodded. "I follow events as best I can."

"So you know that the present king of Spain is French, a grandson of Louis XIV, and that his claim to the throne is contested by his cousin, a Habsburg Archduke of Austria."

Carlos nodded again. "Yes. And half the countries of Europe have taken sides and gone to war over this. But frankly, I don't see how this affects us in Santa Fe."

"Ah," said Peralta. "That's where you're wrong. France has a great interest in its large possessions in North America. The French are moving westward from the Mississippi River Valley and coming into contact with tribes close to Spanish territory, making trade alliances with them and perhaps supplying them with weapons."

"To be used against us?" Carlos asked.

"I believe it's entirely possible," Peralta replied. "And since it's possible, I would like to be prepared."

"So," Carlos said, "having an officer in the provincial militia who speaks French might be desirable. I would think that Jean L'Archevêque, a Frenchman by birth who lives up the canyon east of town, would be an obvious choice."

The governor displayed some annoyance. "I know about L'Archevêque, or Juan Archibeque as he now calls himself. I don't trust him. He was a French soldier who got lost and was captured after wandering into Spanish territory. His loyalty is certainly to France. And besides," Peralta continued with a marvelous lack of logic, "he's taken in those two women who were connected with that horrible man responsible for the kidnapping of the Trigales children and the murder of their governess and carriage driver."

He paused, and Carlos took the opportunity to speak out on behalf of Mara Mata and Selena Torrez, to whom Peralta had just referred. "Let me assure you," Carlos said firmly, "that they had nothing to do with the kidnapping scheme. Their partner and manager, Leandro the Magician, planned it by himself in hopes of gaining a large fortune through ransom. I can say this with complete certainty, because I was present when Señorita Torrez regained consciousness from a coma induced by poison Leandro had given her. He had intended to kill both her and Mara, and he nearly succeeded."

Peralta didn't look entirely convinced, but before he could comment a knock at the door distracted him. His secretary, Marco Cabrera, leaned in and said, "Pardon me, Excellency, but Doña Mendoza is here to see you."

"I'll be free momentarily," Peralta replied. Clearly, one did not keep Doña Josefina Mendoza waiting. Governor Peralta rose and brusquely dismissed Carlos, though not without thanking him for offering hospitality to the soldiers who needed housing.

As Don Carlos left the governor's office, he needed to step aside to allow Doña Josefina to enter. This was the first time that he had laid eyes on her. She was rarely seen in town, even for Mass, though it was rumored that the town's senior priest, Father Benedicto Murrieta, visited her regularly. Carlos thought she might ignore him altogether, but she looked at him appraisingly with her dark eyes. Although she was quite old, she carried herself very erectly and her expression suggested she was not to be trifled with. Her all-black outfit, made of expensive fabric, was in a style that had been in fashion fifty years earlier. Instinctively, he bowed slightly to her. She acknowledged his courtesy with the barest of nods as she stepped past him into the governor's office. Marco Cabrera closed the door quietly behind her. "An impressive lady," he whispered to Don Carlos.

"Indeed," Carlos replied. "And will you stop by my house shortly after one o'clock?" Marco answered that he would.

The Presidio was next door to the Palace of the Governors, and Carlos went directly to the commandant's office. A noncommissioned officer greeted him with cold formality. "Sergeant Roque Camacho at your service," he said stiffly.

Don Carlos replied with equal formality, "Please tell the commandant that Don Alfonso Cabeza de Vaca has come to report an incident of a Native war party's attack on him and a companion yesterday on the road north of Santa Fe."

The sergeant stepped aside and indicated that Don Carlos could come in. "I will announce your visit to Major Cortés."

Major Cortés entered the room a moment later, a short man with hard eyes and a brusque manner. No social courtesies for the major, such as extending a hand in greeting. He moved to the topic at hand without delay. "What's this about a war party not far north of Santa Fe?" he asked.

"Yesterday afternoon my friend José Lugo and I were driving a herd of wild horses southward on the Camino Real. As we approached the ford that is about two hours' ride from here, we saw a war party of five Indians waiting in a small stand of cottonwoods ahead."

Cortés interrupted Carlos's account. "How were they armed?"

"Bows and arrows only."

"How did you know their intent was hostile?"

"Several were fitting arrows to their bowstrings."

"How were you and this Lugo fellow armed?"

"José is a Pueblo Indian who adheres strictly to the prohibition against

Indians carrying firearms. All he had was a dagger. I had a musket and a dagger."

Cortés looked Don Carlos up and down in a skeptical way. "What did you do to avoid being captured or killed?"

"We used our horse herd as a weapon. They are wild horses, so it didn't take much shouting to set off a stampede, which we steered into the grove of cottonwoods where the war party was waiting. Rather than hold their ground and be trampled by the horses charging at them, they turned tail and crossed the ford in great haste."

"Did you fire your musket?"

"I managed to wound one of the raiders in the thigh," Carlos said, phrasing his response in such a way as to evade saying just how he had inflicted the wound.

Cortés grunted. "Exactly when did this all take place?"

"Late afternoon yesterday."

"You should have reported the incident at once, rather than the next day," Cortés said sharply.

"The process of rounding up the horses delayed our return. I didn't get back to Santa Fe until well after dark."

"So these five Indians have had plenty of time to get away. What tribe were they from?"

"Neither José nor I recognized them as Indians of a tribe — Apache, Navajo, or Pueblo — known to us."

"I assume you were away with your horses," Cortés said, "when the party of soldiers under my command, accompanied by three Franciscans and three colonists, arrived last week. The soldiers are here specifically to protect Spanish settlers from hostile Indians. The Franciscan priest who arrived with us has particular duties to fulfill in Santa Fe by virtue of his position as a representative of the Holy Office, but he also has a mission to the pueblo settlements north of here. A squad of my soldiers will be escorting him there. I will ask Sergeant Camacho to take four of those men and investigate the ford where the incident you have just reported took place."

Sent on his way by Major Cortés with what he took to be an uncalled-for instruction to be more prompt in reporting incidents like yesterday's encounter, Carlos walked across the plaza and returned home. He let himself in through the seldom-used front door and went down the hallway to the kitchen. Gordo looked up from where he was resting next to his doggy door, which gave access to the path that ran past the back of the house. "How are you, old friend?" Carlos said, reaching down to scratch the little fellow's head. Then he heard an odd sound from the other side of the room near the hearth. He looked over and saw another dog with a color pattern identical to Gordo's—all white except for a black patch around one eye. This dog, obviously a female from the fact that she was nursing three puppies, watched him with an apprehensive expression. Carlos asked, not expecting an answer, "And who might you be?"

Gordo's doggy door was available for his use at all hours of the day, and in a place like Santa Fe with many stray dogs, it was always possible that one of these strays would take advantage and invite him- or herself into Carlos's kitchen. However, something told Carlos that this female had an established relationship with Gordo. "Are you responsible for these puppies?" Carlos asked Gordo, who, in a most uncharacteristic response, put his head down between his front paws and looked contrite. "I'll deal with you later," Carlos announced. "Right now I have more pressing business."

Carlos got a plate of leftovers from the pantry, divided them into two parts—half in a bowl, and the other half on a plate—and put the bowl down for Gordo and the plate near Gordo's female guest. The mother dog, who was almost as skinny as Gordo had been when he first put in an appearance two years earlier, stood up and began gulping down the leftovers. This, Carlos decided, indicated that she didn't have a home where she received regular meals. "Three soldiers and four stray dogs added to the household in one day," he muttered to himself. "That's what I get for feeling sorry for myself because I had almost no housemates."

But there was business to conduct, and there was still some time in the morning to do it before the meeting of all town residents that had been called for noon. He quickly ate a bowl of cold chili and a piece of cornbread and hurried out to look for Fabio Velarde. Luck was with him; he found the young doctor in the kitchen of the Fernandez place, the house he'd been renting from Carlos while waiting for his own house to be ready to occupy.

After exchanging greetings, Carlos asked, "Have you been wondering if you could move into the completed wing of your new home while Orfeo finishes the other half? Orfeo said he thought you might want to."

Gesturing for Carlos to sit down, Fabio replied, "Yes, I'd like to do that. I've had six chests made that can be used both for storage and as seating. I've also acquired a few Indian rugs and blankets, so I'm about ready to move in. This house, and the furnishings you provided, has been completely satisfactory, but I would like to occupy a house of my own."

"Ah," Carlos said, pleased. "The timing couldn't be better. Since the arrival of that new cavalry company, the Presidio's barracks are overflowing, and the governor has asked me to take some of the extra soldiers as lodgers in my properties. If you're ready to move out, they could move in."

"I don't have any appointments this afternoon. If Orfeo can help me, I believe I could have all my personal belongings transferred to the new house before dark today."

"Splendid!" Carlos exclaimed, relieved that Dr. Velarde's move was working out so well. After conversing with him about a few details, Carlos excused himself. He made a quick stop at his house, greeted Gordo, and saw that the mother dog was back in her previous spot with her puppies. Then he continued to the plaza, which, although it was not quite noon, was already jammed with people, more than he'd ever seen there before except possibly on fiesta days. Latecomers were streaming into the square. He saw Inéz and Marco Cabrera standing together and talking on the opposite side of the plaza, but he didn't try to push through the throng to join them. He contented himself, upon catching Inéz's eye, with a friendly wave in their direction.

4

Afternoon

Precisely at noon the chapel bell began to toll and Father Dorantes, a tall, thin Franciscan with gray hair, emerged from the chapel. He mounted a three-foot-high platform with railings on two sides that had been set up adjacent to the near wall of the chapel. He signaled for silence and then, in a strong voice that carried well across the plaza, he began to speak.

"Indios, mestizos, Spaniards! Citizens of Santa Fe, the city of Holy Faith! I have already addressed some of you at Mass in different groups, but I would that you in Christ—that we—be all one. My purpose in being here, in speaking to you as I do, is to bring back those who have fallen away from this holy unity. Today is the first day of a forty-day period of grace during which any of you who have blasphemed by showing irreverence toward God, or have practiced any form of witchcraft, are urged to come forward, confess, repent, and receive forgiveness for your sins. The purpose of the Holy Office through the agency of the Inquisition is not to punish, except for those who refuse to confess and repent, but to restore individuals and the community of Santa Fe to a wholesome and holy relationship to God and His Church. But," he said, his voice rising and growing darker, "those who do not acknowledge their sins or who have knowledge of witches and blasphemers and do not report them to representatives of the Holy Office will be punished!"

He paused before continuing in a more modulated tone. "Long ago, when the Spanish came to this land, they brought with them the light of the Christian faith. But, brothers and sisters, the members of the Inquisition know well that practices of witchcraft, practices of affecting the soul of another through magical means, persist among some who would claim to be Catholics. All of you need to understand that many practices that seem innocent are not. If you have toyed in the slightest way with old charms and potions, incantations and magic, whether with the intent to heal or to curse, to incite passion or to kill passion, you have had, whether you realize it or not, intimate relations with the Devil!"

Carlos, who was listening to the colors and cadences of Dorantes's voice more than the content of what he was saying, followed the growing intensity in the priest's voice and even, to a certain extent, was carried away by it. "What is the difference," Father Dorantes was saying, "between pagan spells and incantations and the act of praying to God to heal a sick person or lighting a candle in church with a special intention in one's heart? Don't be deceived into thinking there is no difference simply because both pagan and Christian practices make connections between this world and supernatural realms. Only those prayers addressed to the One True God, or to Our Lord, or to Our Blessed Mother and the saints, will lead to eternal life in the bosom of our Savior. But to call on dark spirits and pagan deities or to employ magic is the Devil's way and the path to death and eternal suffering in Hell!

"So I exhort you, examine your consciences, look closely at your thoughts and deeds, and if you find the least fault in this regard, confess and repent. Likewise, examine the behavior of your neighbors. Is there anyone who is known to practice these evil arts, under the cover that they are innocent and harmless, even benign? Now, and throughout this forty-day period of grace, is the time to confess and be restored to the unity of the Christian faith.

"My fellow members of the Holy Office, Brother Gustavo and Brother Inocente, are here to offer guidance and counsel, and Father Benedicto and I stand ready to hear your confessions any time, any day. Do not wait! Do not risk eternal damnation!"

At the Franciscan's mention of Brother Gustavo's name, Carlos snapped out of his half-attending trance and became inwardly fully alert. He had heard that name before, and it had been spoken by his old enemy, the sorcerer Don Malvolio. The scene came rushing back, and successive images replayed themselves in his mind.

Two months earlier, in the course of attempting to rescue the Trigales children from their kidnapper, the magician Leandro de Luna, Carlos and Inéz had overheard a lengthy exchange between Don Malvolio and Leandro. As they listened, they learned that Malvolio had sent Brother Gustavo secretly to Santa Fe to ascertain whether the *hidalgo* Don Alfonso Cabeza de Vaca was actually the brujo Carlos Buenaventura. Brother Gustavo was evidently a sorcerer with unusual powers, for he had taken control of the mind of a wolf and had confronted Carlos in the street outside his house one morning at dawn. Though Carlos had sensed that the wolf was some sort of spirit animal, he had not used sorcery to drive it away, and as a result Gustavo had concluded that Carlos was not a brujo. The mere presence of the wolf, however, had had a powerful effect on Carlos, leaving him shaken and disoriented.

Carlos's mind now fixed itself on the implications of one of Malvolio's associates being here in Santa Fe. Among other things, it raised the possibility that Father Dorantes, as the chief representative of the Holy Office, also had sinister reasons for bringing the Inquisition to Santa Fe.

Carlos's memories and speculations blotted out the scene around him as Dorantes, having concluded his address, descended the steps of the platform. Carlos recovered himself in time to see Dorantes disappear into the chapel with two other Franciscans following in his wake. One was very young and slender, the other stocky, bald, and considerably older. Carlos was convinced that this latter brown-clad brother was Brother Gustavo. His aura was ominous: dark as a thundercloud, but briefly illuminated with flashes like sheet lightning.

Troubled by what he'd seen, Don Carlos turned and walked back to his house to wait for Marco Cabrera. By the time Marco knocked on the kitchen door, some twenty minutes later, Carlos had regained his equanimity and greeted Marco as though nothing had upset him. "Come in!" Carlos said, nudging Gordo out of the doorway so that Marco wouldn't trip over him.

Looking around, Marco observed, "You seem to have a new dog, and puppies too."

"They arrived today without giving prior notice. I'm not sure what I'll do about them," he said, guiding Marco to a bench on the far side of the room from the puppies.

"You will have quite a houseful of guests if three soldiers move in too," Marco said, taking his seat and stretching out his legs.

"True enough," Carlos shrugged. "You'll be glad to know that one place I own, the Fernandez house, will be available for other soldiers by nightfall today. Its present occupant, Fabio Velarde, is moving to his new home. The Fernandez place is a partly furnished four-room house. It ought to accommodate upwards of nine men, admittedly under rather cramped conditions."

"I don't think they'll mind at all. At present they're sleeping in the Presidio's courtyard. I'm sure they'll appreciate having a roof over their heads."

"Can I leave it to you to report to the governor and the Presidio commandant on these arrangements, and show the soldiers assigned to the Fernandez place where it is? The location of my house is well known to my friends Alejandro, Luis, and Gonzalo. Do you have any idea how long they'll be staying with me? Is a Presidio garrison nearly double its former size going to be permanent?"

"I have no idea how long this will last, and that's part of what I wanted to talk with you about. It's a topic I didn't feel free to broach in the outer office of the governor's suite." Marco took a deep breath and went on. "Before I describe what worries me about the present situation, let me ask you a question. What were your impressions of the changes Governor Peralta has made in his office?"

"Very militant—regimental battle flags, crossed swords, a map on which Spanish victories over Pueblo people were prominently marked."

"Yes, very militant indeed. I believe that Governor Peralta is trying to recapture the glory days of Governor Vargas and your stepfather by emulating their vigorous campaign to restore Spanish control in New Mexico in the 1690s. I think he wants his administration to be distinguished by a policy of repressing Indian resistance. Hence the additional soldiers under the command of an unusually tough officer, Major Cortés."

Though he privately agreed with Marco, Carlos ventured support for Peralta's argument. "But don't you think that Peralta's concerns have some grounds? The number of Spaniards in New Mexico is very small. We're vastly outnumbered by the Natives, both the mostly pacified Pueblo people and hostile raiding tribes, Navajos and Apaches, among others, that surround us on every side. One could argue that Peralta is simply doing his job, charged as he is with preserving our safety."

"You're right, of course," Marco replied, "and I admit that I may have misjudged him. When we first met, he struck me as passive and indecisive. But of late he's launched several major initiatives that may produce more problems than they solve."

"Specifically what?" Carlos asked.

"For one thing, practically doubling the size of the Presidio garrison seems logical in the light of the recent attacks by Native raiders, but the trouble is that we have been in the midst of a drought and last year's harvests were skimpy. Even though the two hundred new settlers who arrived earlier this year brought foodstuffs with them, the supplies available locally are barely adequate to meet the town's needs. The arrival, at the governor's request, of forty cavalrymen has strained the limited stockpiles of foodstuffs. It's all very well and good to have Cortés and his men tracking down and punishing war parties, but people's anxiety about having enough to eat is something that driving off hostile Indians won't alleviate."

"I see your point," Carlos agreed, "and having to lodge members of the garrison will only remind them that there are more mouths to feed. And apropos of new additions to the town, where do you see Father Dorantes and his fellow inquisitors fitting into all this?"

"Ah, yes, the Inquisition. I'm sure you know how it operates," Marco replied. "The object is to strengthen orthodox beliefs in a community, but I worry that it is just as likely to be divisive."

Carlos commented, "I share your concern. If your neighbor has an old grudge against you, you will be afraid of being denounced, charged, presumed guilty, tried in secret, and sentenced at a public ceremony, an auto-da-fé. Everyone will live under the shadow cast by these possibilities."

"It saddens me," Marco said. "I've been in Santa Fe only a few months, but I read the reports received by the governor's office and I keep abreast of what's going on in the Town Council. I feel considerable affection for this place, and I'm worried that the combination of an increased military presence and the Inquisition's activities will upset what is a fairly harmonious community."

Carlos sighed. "I'm glad to know how you feel, even though I don't see what we can do for now except keep a watchful eye on events as they unfold. Please, let's keep in touch."

Marco agreed earnestly and said, "I appreciate this chance to speak frankly. Now I'd better get back to the office. Governor Peralta is strict about not being away from the office during business hours."

They both rose. Carlos saw Marco to the door and was left feeling thoughtful. It was a few minutes before he remembered that he had promised Inéz he would return in the afternoon to coach Elena in fencing. He went to his bedroom, changed into his leather fencing shirt, and retrieved his sword from its place in the corner. He checked the horses in the corral on the south side of his house. Apparently, while Carlos had been out during the morning, José had brought Pedro's Pepper back from Rancho Rosón and had exchanged Pepper for Inéz's Alegría. Carlos was pleased. During the months that Inéz had been ill, Alegría hadn't gotten enough exercise. He supposed that José was going to Tesuque Pueblo to visit Old Man Xenome.

Hurrying a little now, Carlos walked across the plaza toward the Palace of the Governors. As he looked down the street toward the Presidio, he saw a small party—Father Dorantes in his brown habit, mounted on a mule, and a dozen cavalrymen—starting north on the road to Tesuque. As Carlos watched, Dorantes turned in his saddle and looked back in Carlos's direction. Carlos could read nothing in the priest's face.

Carlos continued on his way to the Beltrán house, which was one of the largest in Santa Fe. Its two central patios were surrounded on all sides by verandas that provided cool shade for the summer months that were not far ahead. Carlos's destination was the courtyard that contained a well-groomed thirty-foot-long fencing strip. He knocked at the front door and was greeted by a female servant who showed him to the patio where Elena and Inéz were waiting.

He was momentarily taken aback by Elena's appearance. She had on one of Inéz's fencing suits. It was, in fact, one that Inéz had worn many times when she and Carlos had fenced in the first months after her arrival in Santa Fe a year and a half ago. Those memorable bouts with Inéz, who was a superb left-handed fencer, had been suffused with erotic energy, memories of which came rushing back when Carlos saw Elena, once a plump young woman who could not have fit into Inéz's clothes, presenting her now-trim figure in the snug fencing suit. "I see, Elena," Carlos said, "that your fencing master has decided you are ready to wear the outfit of an advanced student."

Elena, not displeased in the least, replied, "Not quite worthy of the word *advanced* as yet, but perhaps you can help me move beyond my beginner status."

Inéz, having taken note of the appraising look that Carlos had given

Elena's figure, pushed him a little further. "You should tell her how well the outfit suits her, Alfonso."

Carlos had the grace to blush. "You are ravishing, Señorita," he said with a little bow. "This Santiago Mendoza fellow will be hard put to keep his mind on fencing when he comes for his match with you."

"Will you two stop it!" Elena exclaimed. "I need your help with fencing much more than I need flattery!"

Carlos asked Inéz what she had noticed in the way of weaknesses in Elena's skills that he could coach her on. "She has trouble parrying a high inside thrust that is directed at her chest," Inéz said, imitating the gesture. "Also, she often fails to block an attack on an inside low line below her sword arm."

"Let's work on both of those situations," Carlos proposed, "starting first with a defense against an attack on an inside low line." Motioning to Elena to move to the center of the fencing strip, as he did likewise, he called out, "On guard!"

With only a slight pause, Carlos initiated an attack and scored a hit below Elena's sword arm. Stepping back, he said, "Again!" Once more he scored a hit and called "*Touché!*" After two more repetitions with the same result, he suggested that she attempt the same attack on him. "Watch how I parry your thrust, and next time try to duplicate it."

Three times she attempted to attack but did not come even close to scoring a hit. "How did I parry your efforts?" he asked.

"Somehow you managed to block my approach by contacting my blade with yours."

"Excellent! Now let's try the same exercise in slow motion. I will attack, and you will parry my thrust by contacting my blade with yours." Still, Elena couldn't quite manage to do it.

"Turn your blade a little," Inéz called from the sideline, "in anticipation of creating contact as Don Alfonso moves forward." She demonstrated with a stick she had picked up.

"Let's go at it even more slowly," Carlos proposed. This time Elena managed to parry Carlos's attack. Repeating the process again and again, they gradually increased the speed of the exchange until after twenty minutes Elena was successful at a much faster pace.

"Very good!" Carlos declared.

After pausing for only three minutes, they resumed fencing with the focus now on parrying high inside thrusts. This time they started in very slow motion, with Elena on the attack observing how Carlos deflected her thrusts. Then they reversed roles and gradually increased the speed of their exchanges until Elena began to gain confidence.

"Good," Carlos said. "Would Elena's fencing master suggest that her pupil and I attempt a few free-style exchanges?"

"I wouldn't stand a chance against you, Don Alfonso," Elena protested.

"To even things out a little," Carlos suggested, "why don't I call out a defensive action that should be taken for each move I make?" This they did with some success. Then Carlos urged Elena to go on the attack, telling her that in each instance he would call out precisely what he did to avoid a hit. Time and again he parried her attacks. "Bounce forward using your feet rather than your knees," he suggested, and after ten repetitions it seemed she was able to move forward in a fast, fluid way.

Should I, he wondered, allow her to score a hit as a way of giving her encouragement?

"Don't you dare go easy on me!" Elena burst out.

Carlos turned to Inéz and asked, "Did you notice that?"

"Yes," Inéz replied. "She read your mind."

"I did not!" Elena protested. "I'm no mind-reader."

"Then how do you explain a statement of yours that quite accurately addressed something that was going through my mind? Don't underestimate your capacity to read people's intentions. Intuitions are invaluable in fencing. The action can be so fast that you don't have time to mull over what your opponent is going to do next. I'll tell you a secret. Much of my success as a fencer comes from correctly reading my opponent's intentions."

"Another key to success," Inéz added, "is repetitive practice of various moves until they are knowledge your body has, responses you make without having to think about them. But let's leave it at that for today. I congratulate you, Elena, on making excellent progress. If Don Alfonso agrees, let's get together for another lesson tomorrow."

"That would be my pleasure," Carlos declared. "But before I leave, tell me about these house break-ins that Rita mentioned to me this morning."

Inéz matter-of-factly reported that two days after Carlos and José had left to bring home wild horses, José's sister Ana Lugo, who was working as a house servant for Bianca Trigales, noticed that a porcelain plate was missing from the chest where it should have been stored. Everyone had been thoroughly puzzled. "Then," she continued, "there was an incident the day before yesterday that involved Elena."

Elena, with a frown, said, "I told my parents that someone had crept into my bedroom that night and woke me up as he jumped out the window. But I didn't tell them everything, because they would worry even more than they already do about my safety. It was nothing, really."

"I wouldn't say it was nothing," Inéz said, "but I've agreed to keep Elena's secret, or the part of her story she wants to keep a secret."

Elena continued. "I was sound asleep and having a lovely dream about a man kissing me on the cheek. Suddenly I half woke up, and I realized that there was someone in my room and that that person had actually kissed me. I rolled over and looked toward the window and saw the figure of a slender man, a man not even as tall as me, slipping out the window. I got up, went to the window, and looked out in every direction. The only thing moving on the street was a black dog running toward the plaza with a bag in its mouth."

Inéz picked up the story from there. "Later Saturday morning Rita noticed that one place setting—a knife, fork, and spoon—was missing from the chest where the silver is stored. She reported it to Cristina, who instructed everyone to lock the doors and gates at night, and to latch all the windows also. Elena told me about the man in her bedroom, but she made me swear not to worry her parents by telling them that he had kissed her."

"Actually," Elena added, "I didn't feel a bit frightened. It was a sweet, loving kiss."

"Very strange," Carlos commented. "This thief is certainly a bold fellow. Then again, his conduct toward Elena, though improper, was done in a gentle way that suggests he meant her no harm. Curious."

"I don't have anything more to report," Elena said, "so I'll leave you two to yourselves while I go and change."

Elena left the patio and Carlos turned to Inéz. "There is something you need to be aware of," he said. "This noon, when Dorantes spoke on the plaza, he mentioned that one of his fellow inquisitors is named Brother Gustavo." Carlos paused and Inéz looked at him blankly.

After a moment Carlos went on. "Don't you remember the exchange we overheard between Malvolio and Leandro when we were hiding on the Chupadera Mesa? Malvolio said he was in charge of the Inquisition at El Paso del Norte, and that someone named Brother Gustavo, who was assisting him there, had been working with him for many years."

Inéz blanched. "No, I don't remember. All I remember is how frightened I was. Are you saying that Malvolio said he was a priest?" That he was connected with the Holy Office? How can that be? And are you trying to tell me that the Brother Gustavo who is here is an associate of Malvolio's?"

"That's exactly what I'm saying. What I am afraid of is that Malvolio—and yes, he is a priest, and a leading figure in the Holy Office—is using the Inquisition to try to track me down."

"Oh," said Inéz, turning away from Carlos and going to sit down on one of the benches under the veranda. Carlos followed her and sat down opposite her.

"Yesterday at Mass," Inéz said thoughtfully, "Dorantes announced in his sermon that rumors had reached the Holy Office in El Paso del Norte that witchcraft was being practiced here in Santa Fe. He and his fellow inquisitors, he said, had come here to protect us from all such 'devilish machinations,' as he put it. So it's you they're really after?"

"I think they're after Carlos Buenaventura, but I believe that Alfonso Cabeza de Vaca is not under any suspicion, and we need to keep it that way. We must exercise great caution. Among other things that means we should attend Mass regularly and behave like good Catholics."

Inéz briefly made a face, which seemed to restore her good humor somewhat. Then she thought of something else. "Oh," she said. "Ana came home yesterday from the Mass for Indians practically in tears. Apparently Dorantes addressed them in severe terms, warning them against heresy. She was very worried about José and his connection with Old Man Xenome."

"Tell Ana not to worry about her brother. José is a full-blooded Pueblo Indian, and more than a century ago Indians were removed from the Inquisition's jurisdiction. José can't be investigated or punished by the Inquisition for practicing his people's traditional religion."

"I'll tell Ana," Inéz said. "That much is a relief, anyway."

"Also," Carlos added, "he won't be in town much, now that he's decided his job requires him to live at Rancho Rosón."

"If he won't be living at your place anymore," Inéz asked, "who will help you with your horses and cook for you, not that José ever did much of the cooking?"

"I hope Orfeo will move in and take care of the horses."

"That still leaves you without a cook and house servant." Inéz stood up and gestured to Carlos to follow her. She was walking a little in front of him and she glanced at him over her shoulder. "I suppose you'll try to hire some pretty young woman like Marisol Díaz?"

"No," he replied, trying to turn Inéz's allusion to his weakness for attractive women into a joke. "I've been looking around for an elderly Indian woman with a possessive husband to cook and clean for me. So far, I've had no success."

Inéz seemed to appreciate his attempt at humor and smiled at him. They had reached the front hallway, and she let him out the door, saying no more but giving him a kiss on the cheek.

Carlos walked back to his house. He entered by the kitchen door and found José sitting next to the kitchen table and absent-mindedly petting a puppy that he was holding on his lap. His face was inexpressive. Carlos asked, "What's the matter?"

José gave him a piercing look. "I keep forgetting that you can read auras. I'm trying to get over some bad feelings."

"What caused these bad feelings, José?"

"I was on my way back to Santa Fe after visiting Grandfather Xenome when a party of twelve soldiers and a Franciscan stopped me. The sergeant who was in charge was mean and insulting. He wanted to know how an 'Indian boy' — he kept using the word 'boy' — could be riding such a fine horse as Alegría."

"What a —!" Carlos exclaimed, using a vulgar word that slightly shocked José.

José went on. "I tried to tell him that I worked for you and Señor Trigales and that Alegría belonged to a friend of yours who let me ride her. I don't think he believed me. Then he asked me where I'd been.

"I said that I was returning from Tesuque Pueblo. Then the Franciscan asked what business I had been doing at Tesuque. I told him that I had visited relatives. 'And who are these relatives?' he asked. His manner was friendlier than the sergeant's, but knowing the Franciscans' dislike of medicine men, I didn't want to mention Grandfather Xenome, so the only names I gave him were Rubén and Lázaro.

"The priest also asked me whether I was a Catholic. I remembered what you once told me about dealing with Spanish people. 'Be a good Catholic by day,' you said, 'and keep your Pueblo religion a secret,' or something like that. I told this priest that I had been baptized and went to Mass whenever I was in Santa Fe. 'I will look for you when I say Mass,' he replied. He didn't insult me like the sergeant had, but I still felt threatened."

"What an unfortunate encounter," Don Carlos said sympathetically. "But don't worry if Father Dorantes learns that you're studying to be a medicine man. The Inquisition's authority doesn't extend to full-blooded Indians like yourself."

"Not even if they've lived in a Spanish settlement all their lives, as I have?"

Don Carlos wasn't totally certain, but he decided to speak as though he was. "I believe you're safe. Don't worry. Can you stay for dinner tonight? Perhaps Orfeo can teach us some more *versos*. Singing together will make us all feel better."

"Thank you, but I want to ride on to Rancho Rosón tonight. I have horse work there and no wish to stay in a town with these Spanish newcomers I met on the road today. I have one bit of good news, though. When I got back to Santa Fe, I stopped at Señor Trigales's house to tell him that the herd we captured is doing well, and he gave me a young mare from his stable named Viva for my own. I'll leave Alegría with you and Eagle and Pepper."

"Did you tell Raul Trigales about the treatment you received from this sergeant and the priest?"

"There was no need to involve him. Spaniards are often rude and abusive to Indians. They see us as their inferiors. Besides, I was ashamed."

"Ashamed! That's terrible! You have nothing to be ashamed about."

José looked down. The puppy in his lap had begun to squirm and cry, so he put it down and it walked a wobbly walk over to its mother, who was nursing the rest of her litter. Finally, José spoke. "I was ashamed because I had no power and had to humble myself. What I really wanted to do was to hit them with a blast of the invisible energy your brujo powers give you. Then I was ashamed of myself for feeling such anger and hatred toward that sergeant and the priest. Hating goes against everything Grandfather Xenome is teaching me about the Old Ways."

Don Carlos clapped José on the shoulder. "I am not doing any better than you at not hating those men. I'm very angry on your behalf. But we must act in a wise way. They could make a lot of trouble for us if we crossed them. On the whole, your idea to spend most of your time at Rancho Rosón makes a lot of sense. The chief losers will be Gordo and me. We'll miss having you around."

"Rancho Rosón is not far away. You can always visit me when you take Eagle out for a ride in the country."

"Now there's a happy thought," Carlos said. "Let's go to the corral and you can introduce me to Viva before I see the two of you on your way."

5

Thievery

After José left for Rancho Rosón late Monday afternoon, Carlos and Orfeo helped Fabio Velarde move his possessions from the Fernandez house to his new home. Carlos was satisfied that the place was ready to be occupied. Although only one wing of the courtyard house Orfeo was building was finished, it was the larger of the planned-for wings and consisted of three rooms: a bedroom, a kitchen, and a general-purpose *sala* (main room). A rough shed and small corral at the back provided shelter and turnout for Fabio's horses.

After he had helped Fabio move, Carlos returned to his house, set up a box in the corner of the kitchen for the mother dog and her puppies, scolded Gordo thoroughly for the trouble he was causing, and checked the two back rooms of his house to see that they were ready to become living quarters for three soldiers. There was only one bed, but he supposed one or two of the men could sleep on the floor, using blankets and whatever bedrolls they brought from the Presidio for mattresses. He made dinner for himself, Orfeo, and the dogs—he still wasn't completely reconciled to saying "his dogs" in the plural. Orfeo had a very gentle touch with the puppies and volunteered to make a place for them and their mother in the hayloft. "Don't count on Gordo not to sneak them back in the house the first time he gets a chance," Carlos warned, and they had a good laugh at the thought.

Not long after he and Orfeo finished the post-meal cleanup, Don Carlos's new houseguests—Alejandro, Luis, and Gonzalo—arrived. They all sat around the kitchen table, and Carlos and the three soldiers entertained Orfeo with stories of the long trip they had taken together the previous year from Santa Fe to El Paso del Norte and back. They recalled it as mostly a good time despite a few harrowing episodes, including their having to battle an Apache war party on the return trip. Carlos was amused to see that the three young men habitually fell into extended and highly repetitive discussions of subjects about which they disagreed. A year later they were still debating whether Jorge, the boy Carlos had at least temporarily saved from becoming a compulsive gambler, would be able to break his habit permanently. Gonzalo was of the opinion that he couldn't. Repeating the same words he'd used earlier, Gonzalo insisted that Jorge would remain a slave to his addiction. Alejandro was more optimistic. Carlos was glad to be able to report that when he'd last heard, Jorge was still on the straight and narrow.

After breakfast on Tuesday, Carlos saddled Eagle to go for a ride. As they entered the lane heading north from his house, he noticed a group of five men near the center of the plaza beginning work on a construction project. Curious, he rode into the plaza and approached the workers. One man, Cristobal Montoya, was a mestizo farmer with whom he'd had some dealings. Greeting Montoya, he asked, "What are you building?"

"Ah, Don Alfonso! We have been hired by the inquisitors to construct a platform. It's to be ready for the end of the forty-day period of grace Father Dorantes announced yesterday. Then it will serve as the place where men and women sentenced by the Holy Office will be given a final chance to repent their sins. If they don't, they will be punished here for all to see."

"A most unhappy prospect," Don Carlos responded. "I trust the inquisitors are paying you for your labor."

"Yes, a little," Montoya replied. "But, as you might imagine, I would rather be working in my own fields."

After commiserating with Montoya, Carlos rode to Rancho Rosón. He found José working with horses from the herd he and Carlos had rounded up. He watched the process for a while before returning to Santa Fe in the early afternoon, when he went to the Beltrán house for another session of fencing practice with Elena.

Today he put her through a longer session and pressed her to achieve a higher level of skill. She was willing and a fast learner, though still no more than an advanced beginner. He was amused at himself, and he said as much to Inéz. "I feel," he told her, "like a doting parent who wants his child to perform well."

"Interesting," Inéz remarked, "that Elena is bringing out your parental side."

"Perhaps it's also because as of yesterday I became a father."

Inéz gave him a shocked look and said, "I hope you're joking!"

Raising his hands in a calm-down gesture, he said soothingly, "I should have explained that my house has become a foster home to a mother dog and three puppies that Gordo brought home. Four weeks from now I'll be imploring all my friends to take one of the puppies."

"It serves you right for leaving the doggy door open day and night," Inéz commented in a sharp tone, letting him know that she was annoyed at him for teasing her on such a subject.

In his final preparations for Wednesday afternoon, Don Carlos put some careful thought into what to wear to help chaperone the fencing session between Elena and her guest Santiago Mendoza. He found himself wanting to make a good impression on Santiago, and for that reason he chose the formal daytime outfit—dark, elegant, and understated—that he used to wear when he had worked at the Palace of the Governors as the governor's private secretary.

A maid admitted him to the Beltrán house and showed him into the patio with the fencing strip where Inéz, Elena, and Santiago were waiting. He noticed that Inéz was wearing one of her best daytime dresses. For her part Elena was well turned out in the fencing costume Inéz had loaned or given her. Santiago was also in fencing attire, an expensive black outfit with gold trim across his shoulders and down the sides of his legs. He had a slim but strong-looking body and an attractive face—a broad forehead, high cheekbones, and a somewhat pointed chin. He and Elena, both of them eighteen, made a handsome young couple.

The two young fencers began their bout, and Don Carlos followed their exchanges with great interest. Santiago was taller than Elena and had longer arms, giving him the advantage of a longer reach. He was also the more experienced fencer. Consequently Elena lost point after point, although Carlos was proud to see that she forced Santiago to work hard to score hits, using to good effect the defensive techniques on which he'd drilled her for the past two days. As the bout progressed Carlos noticed that despite Santiago's greater experience and physical advantages, his movements seemed to arise from calculation rather than instinct. Also, Elena seemed to be in better condition than Santiago, a surprising circumstance given that she hadn't been fencing for many weeks.

Eventually, Elena broke through and scored a hit on Santiago. She cried, "*Touché*!" but then lowered her sword and gave him a severe look. "Did you let me win that point?" she asked.

His slight hesitation before saying "No" seemed to indicate that he had eased up on her.

"Don't you ever give me less than your best!" she said emphatically.

Santiago looked surprised. Inéz leaned over and whispered to Carlos, "He is probably unaccustomed to women his age being as assertive toward him as she just was."

"If he's worthy of her," Carlos replied, "that will make her all the more attractive to him."

As Carlos and Inéz were having this exchange, Elena was saying, "It's getting very hot in the patio. Why don't we finish our bout when one of us has seven more hits?"

They resumed fencing, and it seemed to Carlos that Elena was making an energetic effort to go on the offensive. Although she lost point after point, in fact seven straight points, on two exchanges she managed to attack with such vigor that she drove Santiago back nearly all the way to his end of the fencing strip. After the seventh of Santiago's successes, the two combatants bowed slightly to each other and Carlos and Inéz applauded and called out, "Well done!"

Just then Rita entered the patio with tall glasses of iced tea, and Inéz invited Elena and Santiago to join her and Carlos at a table set behind a vine-covered trellis that created some cooling shade. Swirling tea in her glass, Inéz announced, "The clinking sound you just heard is the last of the ice we stored in the cellar in February. You have both earned a refreshing cold drink."

From that point the conversation drifted pleasantly for a time. Then Santiago complimented Elena on her fencing, and she replied that she hoped to become much more skillful, though she had no hope of ever matching the abilities of her two teachers, Inéz and Carlos. Santiago instantly sat up straighter and asked with considerable animation, "So is what I've heard true—that Don Alfonso is the best fencer in all of New Spain, and that Señora Recalde is nearly his equal?"

"We would never say such a thing," Carlos replied mildly, "though it's true that I have had a very successful career so far, and when I'm in good form, I make for a challenging opponent. But my fencing master, the incomparable Don Ignacio de Tortuga of Mexico City, always told me that every competitor, no matter how skillful, eventually meets an opponent who is either better or luckier."

"Dear Alfonso," Inéz said, "you are much too modest. You know very well that you've never been defeated in a bout, and at age twenty-one you are scarcely ready to retire."

Santiago looked astonished. "You are only twenty-one! I would have thought you were at least five years older."

"People often assume he is older than he actually is," Inéz said casually, though she knew that he had lived five previous lives as a brujo and brought at least some of his past-life experiences to his present life.

Directing a question to Santiago, Don Carlos said, "Permit me to ask how it is that you and your brothers have come to this remote and unprepossessing outpost of the Spanish empire when there is a war in the Old World that involves nearly all of Europe's great powers? That would seem to offer many more opportunities for adventure or for distinguishing yourselves than anything to be found in the high desert and mountain country of New Mexico."

Santiago's face grew serious. "The chief reason we came here from Spain is because of our great-aunt's situation. Doña Josefina has no male heirs except the three of us. She asked us to come to Santa Fe to discuss what may be done with her estate, which includes large plots of land here and also significant properties in northern New Spain, all of them received as land grants to her father-in-law. She seems undecided whether to split her fortune three ways or to leave it to a single heir only. I don't know how she will make up her mind, since none of the three of us has a wife or a male heir."

Don Carlos was thinking that the obvious answer was for one of the brothers to marry and have a male child at the earliest opportunity. Inéz seemed to read his mind and shook her head ever so slightly.

The party broke up soon after Santiago asked Elena if they could meet for another bout in a week. She agreed; Santiago went off; Elena excused herself to change, and Inéz and Carlos stood up and walked through the house to the front door. He turned to Inéz and said, "I'm feeling a need to go off for a night in the mountains, possibly to our Sacred Pool, and practice my brujo skills."

"Please be extremely discreet about that. You know the inquisitors would like nothing better than to discover you are a brujo. As for your trip, I wish I could come too. I would like to talk with Elvira, who advised me in love," she added, smiling at the memory of the friendly skunk she had met near the Sacred Pool. "Shouldn't she have had her litter by now? Last fall she told me she thought she was pregnant."

"April would be the time when most skunks around here have litters, and I don't see why Elvira should be an exception. It always seemed strange to me that she thought she might be pregnant in the fall."

"Give her my greetings, if you see her," Inéz said lightly, brushing her cheek to his in farewell.

Carlos went home, saddled Eagle, and made good time northward, reaching the cutoff from the main road to his and Inéz's favorite spot half an hour before dark. He tethered Eagle in a grassy area and walked the final hundred feet to the pool, which was fed from both a hot spring and a mountain brook.

For a time, Carlos simply sat. The events of the past few days had left him, he realized, tense and unsettled. There was the matter of the confrontation with the war party, the necessity of explaining it to the bureaucratic and military powers, the disruption of the peaceful status quo in Santa Fe with the arrival of newcomers, the chilling realization that one of them was connected to Don Malvolio, and the disturbingly bad treatment of José. Even the addition of a mother dog and three puppies and three soldiers to his household had jarred his routines. He had continued his practice of meditation, but it seemed to have done little to restore him. He was in need of relief.

He spent the rest of the night in the brujo's world. Transformations had always been his most extraordinary skill and he used the techniques that he had been taught nearly two centuries earlier by his long-ago master, Don Serafino Romero, to change himself into owl form and fly around over the moonlit landscape. Toward morning he spotted Elvira, Inéz's skunk friend, walking about followed by five little skunks. Changing into skunk form—a visit from an owl would have alarmed her no end—he tried to engage her in conversation.

"Perhaps you remember me," he said. "I came here last fall with a woman friend of mine."

"Yes, I remember her. She was very nice."

"My friend, whose name is Inéz, sends her greetings and wonders whether you have a message for her."

"I do have something I'd like to say to her, but it's a rather private matter that I prefer to tell her in person."

"I'll pass that on to her, but it may be a while before she can get here. She's been quite ill and is only now, in the past week, feeling at all well."

"I'm glad she is better," Elvira said, "but I need to say good-bye now. It will soon be daylight, and I want to get my brood back to the nest by then. They're getting harder to keep under control all the time."

Dismissed, Carlos went back to where Eagle was tethered, sat in meditation until the first light was visible in the east, and then rode back to Santa Fe, arriving in mid-morning.

The sight that greeted him made him wonder what was going on. Approaching the town from the north, he had a view that encompassed the homes of the town's most important residents—the Peraltas, Cabreras, Mendozas, Beltráns, Archuletas, and Trigaleses. Every house had three or four soldiers stationed around it. Carlos's first thought was that hostilities had broken out between Indians and the Spanish, or, even more improbably, between the Spanish and an invading French force that Governor Peralta seemed to fear. What the devil—? Carlos thought. He rode to the stable next to the Beltrán house and handed Eagle into the care of one of the family's grooms. "Is anyone home?" he asked.

"Yes, Don Alfonso. I believe everyone has gathered in the *sala*."

Carlos went to the front door, knocked, and was admitted by a maid. He found Cristina and Javier Beltrán and Elena and Inéz seated at a table. "Are we at war with somebody?" Carlos asked.

"I gather you haven't heard the news," Javier replied. "The burglar struck again last night, not once, but twice. The soldiers guarding various houses are the governor's response to requests from several families for protection."

"Not from us," Elena burst out.

"Please be patient, Elena," her mother gently rebuked her.

"This is a total overreaction because one of the homes that the burglar invaded was the Peraltas'," Elena replied.

Don Carlos appealed for more information. "Please tell me the known facts in some semblance of the order in which they occurred."

The Beltráns and Inéz looked at each other, and Inéz asked, "May I try?

"I was up early to start making bread," she said, "when Nina, the Archuletas' cook, came to the kitchen door. She was out of breath and very agitated. She said she had been working in their kitchen and heard the front door close. She was surprised that anyone else would be up at dawn, so she went to investigate. She opened the door, looked out, and saw a black dog running down the street with a bag in its mouth. Then she went to the chests where the family stores its best dinnerware and found that a goblet, which was a wedding present to Lucila and Nicolas, was missing. She woke Lucila and Nicolas and told them what had happened. Nicolas dressed and went to the Presidio to report the theft. Nina came over to our place to ask if we were all right."

"Could the supposed bag the dog had in its mouth have been the goblet?" Carlos asked.

Inéz gave him an incredulous look. "A dog entered the house, opened the chest with the goblets in it, took one out, and ran off with it? That's preposterous!"

Carlos didn't feel like arguing, though he had the beginnings of a theory about how the dog was involved. "You said there were two break-ins. What about the other?"

"The second apparently happened earlier in the night, but it wasn't reported until an hour ago."

"What was stolen in the earlier break-in?" Carlos asked.

"Apparently nothing except a kiss, but that has caused a bigger uproar than the theft of property. Juliana Peralta's personal maid reported that Juliana had seemed very nervous when she got up in the morning. Juliana's mother became suspicious and questioned Juliana until she confessed. She said that the previous night she had been sound asleep, and she had been awakened when she felt someone's lips pressing against her cheek. Juliana, as we all know, is an avid reader of romantic novels, and naturally she often had dreams of being kissed. But this was not a dream. She woke up enough to know that it was a man who was kissing her. 'No! No!' she whispered, 'You must stop!' The man ran to the window and jumped out of it. Juliana said she hadn't wanted to report what had happened because she was afraid her mother would accuse her of encouraging him."

"Now that she's getting a lot of sympathy and attention," Elena said tartly, "you can bet her story will grow more elaborate."

"Elena!" her mother said sharply. "I know you don't like Juliana, but you should be more charitable. It must have been a frightening experience."

"Did she seem frightened when you went over to the Peraltas' to express your sympathy an hour ago?" Elena asked with some skepticism.

Cristina shrugged. "I admit that she seemed more worried about what her mother would say than about the invasion of her bedroom."

"So how was it decided to have soldiers guard private homes?" Carlos asked, bringing the conversation back to the matter at hand.

Javier replied, "Some of us—Salvador Cabrera, Nicolas Archuleta, and I—gathered at the governor's office after news spread of last night's break-ins. Governor Peralta was beside himself. He pounded on his desk and shouted, 'We must do something to protect our wives, daughters, and property from this scoundrel!' It was his idea to have Major Cortés assign soldiers to guard people's houses. He is also considering sending Major Cortés's men to search every house in the Barrio de Analco on the assumption that the thief is from the Indian and mestizo part of town."

"I don't like that at all," Carlos said. "Just because our neighbors are poor, we shouldn't assume they're the thieves."

"Hmm, yes, very good point," Javier agreed.

"We shouldn't assume anything," Inéz added. "Almost nothing is known about the thief, except that he's very bold, he can find his way around the homes of the wealthy in the dark, he doesn't take much in any single attack, and he likes to kiss sleeping young women."

"Just Juliana," Cristina said.

Elena opened her mouth and then closed it. Finally she said, "Mother, you must keep this a secret, but the man who entered my room also kissed me."

Cristina gasped. "How could you not tell me?" she said angrily.

"Neither my honor nor my person was ever in danger, Mother. I didn't want you and Papa to worry."

Don Carlos, fearing that a heated exchange between mother and daughter was about to ensue, quickly stepped in. "Are we certain," he asked, "that the intruder was a man? The items taken, especially the goblet and the porcelain plate, scarcely seem like things a male thief would take. Wouldn't a man be more likely to steal money or jewels?

"And then," Carlos continued, "there's the strange matter of the black dog. Both the Archuletas' maid and Elena say that when they looked outside for the thief, the street was empty except for a dog running away. In both cases, a black dog," he said meaningfully.

"Yes," Elena said, "that's very strange."

"You're making this sound like some sort of witchcraft," said Javier. "That doesn't make me feel any better."

"I wouldn't leap to any conclusions, Javier," Carlos cautioned. "In the end there may be a simple explanation. Besides, now that guards have been stationed around many houses, the thief is unlikely to risk another intrusion."

"No troops are stationed around your place," Inéz said teasingly.

Carlos laughed. "That's the virtue of having nothing in the house worth stealing."

The general laughter that followed broke the previous tension, and Carlos was soon able to leave. Inéz followed him to the stable, and while the groom retrieved Eagle, she said, "You have some ideas about the thief, don't you?"

"Not his or her identity, but the two sightings of a dog running down an otherwise empty street after the burglaries incline me to believe that we're dealing with a shape-shifter."

6

Dorantes

Friday morning Ana Lugo came to Don Carlos's house to say that he was invited to dinner Saturday evening at the Trigales's.

"Is it a special occasion?" Carlos asked.

"Yes. Father Dorantes is to be the guest of honor, and Señora Trigales has asked Inéz to supervise the meal preparations and to join the dinner party once everything is going well."

"Did Inéz give you my message," Carlos asked, "that you needn't worry about Father Dorantes investigating your brother because he wanted to be a medicine man?"

"Yes," Ana replied. "Inéz said you told her that the Inquisition has no authority over Indians. But Father Dorantes still frightens me. I'm glad José doesn't live in Santa Fe any more."

"If I may ask—do you know why your employers are hosting a dinner for Father Dorantes?"

"The Señora said that Señor Trigales's grandfather and Father Dorantes's grandfather knew each other in Spain."

"Ah," Carlos replied, accepting this explanation but still not seeing why he was included among the guests.

During siesta early Friday afternoon Carlos stopped by to see Inéz. "Do you know," he asked her, "why you and I are invited to this dinner?"

"I'm invited because Bianca wanted to make the best possible impression on Father Dorantes by serving a special meal. As a reward of sorts for my services, she invited me to be a member of the dinner party. I said I didn't want to do that unless you were present also. She said she would be happy to have you at table."

"How do you feel about this, Inéz, really?"

"I didn't want to have anything to do with Dorantes, but then it struck me that the better part of wisdom might be to respond in a welcoming way."

"And you're not worried about me sitting across the table from him?"

"No. You're the best-educated man in Santa Fe, and unless he's incapable being charmed, I think you will make a good impression on him."

"And?"

"And? I admit I have another motive. I think this dinner party will give you a good opportunity to meet Father Dorantes in an intimate setting. You may learn more from doing that than watching him from afar when he's giving sermons."

Carlos had to agree, and he had to admit that he was interested in engaging Father Dorantes in conversation. There might be a risk in doing so, but if he was careful and played the role of a gracious *hidalgo*, all should go well.

Saturday evening, at a fashionably late hour, he arrived at the Trigales's residence, a large house west of the plaza. A servant answered his knock and showed him in. Bianca Trigales came to greet him in the front hallway and steered him to the big *sala* that served as a dining room and social area. Carlos had fond memories of dancing a variety of dances there of a type he was quite certain would not have won Father Dorantes's approval.

It was a small party—only Raul and Bianca Trigales, Bianca's sister Cristina and her husband Javier Beltrán, Father Dorantes, Inéz, and himself. As Don Carlos entered the *sala*, Father Dorantes was admiring one of the two Trigales family portraits that hung on the walls. "I'm very impressed," Dorantes was saying, "that your grandfather was able to persuade Diego Velázquez to paint his portrait."

"The story my grandfather always told," Raul replied, "was that Velázquez found my grandfather's face of great interest. Indeed, I believe Velázquez used my grandfather's face in another painting, though I don't know its name. And I must acknowledge that my grandfather paid a substantial commission for this portrait."

Dorantes laughed appreciatively, revealing more warmth than had been evident in the two previous times Carlos had seen him.

Raul turned to Don Carlos and introduced him as a local businessman, formerly private secretary to Governor Peralta's predecessor, and also well known as the most skilled fencer in New Spain and New Mexico.

"Ah!" Father Dorantes exclaimed. "In my youth I enjoyed fencing a great deal, but that is twenty years in the past. My own skills have atrophied completely; however, if someone locally offers you a challenge, I would like to see the bout."

Don Carlos was about to say that his most challenging opponent was Inéz, but he wondered whether a Spanish priest would approve of a woman acquiring such a skill. He nodded and replied, "Before moving here from Mexico City, I used to fence under the tutelage of the great master Don Ignacio de Tortuga. Marco Cabrera, the governor's secretary and the son of the vice governor, was also Don Ignacio's student, and Marco has begun to practice here with me. If we regain our skills sufficiently so as to not embarrass ourselves, we would be pleased to have you observe us."

Bianca Trigales intervened with an invitation to everyone to be seated, and the soup course was served.

Raul Trigales took the initiative in steering the conversation to the several connections that existed between him and Father Dorantes. "Our grandfathers," he said, "were boyhood friends who grew up in Salamanca and moved to Madrid after studying law at the University of Salamanca. Their sons, our fathers, also entered the profession of the law."

Father Dorantes picked up the story. "By the time I had to settle on a profession, practicing law had become a family tradition, and my father and grandfather expected me to follow suit. I tried to fulfill their wishes and completed a law degree at Salamanca. I don't regret those years. They serve me well in my present position in the Holy Office. But I found that my conversations with friends who were studying theology interested me more than my courses in the law. Once I completed my law degree I traveled with one of these friends to the Franciscan Monastery of Saint John the Evangelist in Toledo. After many years of further study I was ordained there as a Franciscan priest."

"My story is similar," Raul said. "My father and grandfather also wanted me to be a lawyer and to stay in Spain, but I had more interest in the world of commerce. Then in several of her letters my sister-in-law Cristina, who was living here in Santa Fe, urged Bianca and me to join her and Javier and seek our fortunes in New Mexico. Even though this is a remote outpost of Spanish colonization, Javier and I believe the town and the surrounding area have great potential."

Through the meal itself, the talk touched on many topics — the climate of New Mexico, the problems of an economy in which hard currency was scarce, and the hopes that Raul and Javier had for their business raising and selling horses to farmers, ranchers, and other newcomers to the region. Father Dorantes praised the Trigales's wine and drank more than one glass. Don Carlos remarked later to Inéz, "I was surprised at how normal the whole dinner-table conversation was. And Father Dorantes seemed genuinely interested in those ordinary subjects."

Father Dorantes also seemed genuinely impressed with the quality of the meal. "This leg of lamb Basque style with mushrooms," he exclaimed, "is extraordinary! I hope you will pardon me for having assumed that the cuisine on the farthest reaches of Spanish settlement would be more modest, but these dishes would win high praise at dinners in Madrid."

"Señora Recalde is the secret behind our fine dining here in Santa Fe," Bianca said with a smile. "The only trouble is that my sister Cristina claimed her as cook and hostess for her household before Raul and I arrived in Santa Fe. So we can't have her permanently, but my sister lets us borrow Inéz to cook for us on a special occasion like tonight."

After dessert Bianca excused herself. "I promised the children," she said, "that I would tell them a story if they're still awake, which they almost certainly are."

Inéz also excused herself. "Father Dorantes, it's been a great pleasure to meet you, but I must get up before dawn to start breakfast preparations, and if I don't leave now, I will be a very sleepy cook tomorrow."

Cristina said, "Please excuse me too, Father Dorantes. My daughter is too old for bedtime stories and I don't need to be up as Inéz does before dawn, but I sense that you gentlemen would like some time together to discuss religious and political topics of importance in Santa Fe. I'll walk home with Inéz and hope to see you socially again, if your duties permit."

Once the women had left the room, a young Pueblo Indian woman servant appeared and distributed glasses of brandy to Father Dorantes, Raul, Javier, and Don Carlos. Raul Trigales raised his glass and said, "Welcome, Father Dorantes."

After inhaling its vapors and letting the liquor roll around in his mouth, Father Dorantes declared, "This is excellent brandy. I must admit again that I never expected to share so many fine things in this frontier outpost."

"We may be engaging in small deceptions," Raul said. "Señora Recalde's cooking and this brandy are scarcely typical fare in Santa Fe. We reserve them for special occasions." Father Dorantes nodded in appreciation and Raul went on, "But your mentioning that our town is a remote place leads me to ask what brought you and your colleagues to travel so far from the Holy Office's headquarters in New Spain—unless that's an improper question?"

"No, not at all," Father Dorantes replied. "I arrived only recently from Spain as a replacement for a Franciscan who died last year. The Chief Inquisitor for New Spain, Father Aurelio Abascal, had that same week received a report of witchcraft and sorcery in Nombre de Dios; so, joined by his associate Brother Gustavo, we traveled to Nombre de Dios to investigate this case. Our investigation there led us to continue on to El Paso del Norte. Then Father Aurelio was summoned back to Mexico City, and Brother Inocente was added to the tribunal. He is young and inexperienced, but he is well educated and thus able to serve as our scribe and record-keeper."

"And Brother Gustavo?" Carlos ventured.

"A most valuable member of the tribunal," Dorantes replied. "He grew up in the town of Morelia west of Mexico City, and in his youth he observed many examples of witchcraft among his neighbors."

Dorantes's mention of Morelia gave Carlos a start, since in his immediately preceding life, which would have overlapped Brother Gustavo's youth, he had been born a full-blooded Tarascan Indian in Morelia. The coincidence, if it was that, of Brother Gustavo being from the same place was unsettling.

Carlos returned his full attention to Dorantes, who was saying, "When Brother Gustavo came of age, he went to Mexico City and contacted the Holy Office with the intention of aiding its work. Seeing the young man's potential, Father Aurelio guided him, first into the Franciscan Order and later into assisting the Holy Office's investigations."

Raul intervened to say, "That's very interesting, but you broke off the story of your travels at the point that you'd reached El Paso del Norte, still a long way from Santa Fe."

"So I did," Dorantes said. "Straying from the main topic is a habit of mine. Thank you for keeping me from wandering too far afield, though before I share a few details about our present investigation, I'm going to follow another aside. I earnestly want to convey the fact that the central purpose of the Inquisition is a positive one, to preserve the unity of the One True Church. Too often, I regret to say, the Inquisition's work is seen solely as punitive, which it is not at heart."

Raul nodded, but he carefully went on to disagree. "Still," he said, "your words at Mass and at Monday's gathering on the plaza did strike fear into some people. One of my Indian servants came home from Mass distressed because she has many friends in her pueblo who use potions and Native chants for healing and other purposes."

"Ah!" Father Dorantes replied. "She is laboring under a misconception. I hope you will assure her that the Holy Office has not had jurisdiction over indigenous people for more than a hundred years."

"I will pass your assurances on to her," Raul said.

"On Monday," Dorantes went on, "I spoke in some detail about the use of charms, potions, and pagan spells to warn everyone that seemingly innocent practices can draw their users into commerce with the Devil. Only prayers and intentions placed before God, the Blessed Virgin, Our Lord, and the saints can serve to safely connect this world and the supernatural. Powerful forces are involved, and those that are not of God should be feared."

"Yes," Don Carlos said, "but don't you find it necessary to distinguish between cases according to their gravity?"

"Yes, definitely," Dorantes replied. "The tribunal sometimes has to examine cases of fairly trivial transgressions. Such a case occurred in El Paso del Norte. A mestizo woman came to us and accused one of her neighbors of having laid a curse on her. This neighbor, she said, had picked up an ant and crushed it by rubbing it between her fingers, all the while casting an evil eye in her direction. At once the woman felt pain in her back that was so severe she couldn't stand up straight. The inquisitors led the accused woman to see that her intention to cause pain to her neighbor was morally evil, and thus required repentance and a resolution to mend her ways. She complied, and her punishment was relatively light. This can be seen as an example of folk magic. The neighbor's act was effective because she was drawing on a superstition she and the mestizo woman had in common."

"Then," Raul asked, "is there no such thing as true magic in which the practitioner uses the agency of the Devil to achieve his purpose?"

Father Dorantes now spoke with more force. "There definitely is true magic, as you call it. Just as we Catholics believe prayer can make a connection between our world and a heavenly world, so too magicians, sorcerers, and Devil worshippers believe in existence of a lower spiritual realm that can be exploited to affect the world of our daily life. Enlisting the aid of dark spirits can lead to humanly impossible acts. Individuals capable of such acts are of special interest to the Holy Office."

"But these instances are rare, aren't they?" Raul asked.

"Yes," Dorantes said, "but they must be treated with the utmost seriousness, and they must be eradicated by bringing to bear all the power at the Holy Office's command."

"Was the case that took you to Nombre de Dios of that magnitude?" Carlos inquired.

"It was. A sorcerer had used his powers to bewitch all the villagers in a mountain town and had enslaved them to his will. He was reportedly capable of superhuman acts, such as leaping over a house, and he was said to cast bursts of invisible energy that would knock someone down who was standing twenty or more feet away from him."

"Astonishing!" Carlos exclaimed, though he had intimate personal knowledge of this sorcerer, whose name was Mateo Pizarro and who had been Don Malvolio's apprentice. In fact, Don Carlos had killed Pizarro after a battle that lasted for many hours. Curious to know how Dorantes would describe what happened next, Carlos asked, "Were you able to end this sorcerer's activities?"

"No, or more accurately, it didn't prove necessary. By the time Father Aurelio and I arrived in Nombre de Dios, this sorcerer was dead. We have every reason to believe that he was killed by another sorcerer. There was some evidence that this second sorcerer went north from Nombre de Dios to El Paso del Norte."

"So that is why you went to El Paso del Norte," Raul said, "a place with little else of significance to draw the Inquisition to it."

"Yes," Dorantes replied. "We found no trace of the second sorcerer, but it was in El Paso del Norte that I first witnessed something for which there was no ordinary, natural explanation."

"Can you tell us about that?" Raul asked.

Father Dorantes seemed to hesitate before answering Raul's question, but his passion for his subject moved him on. "My colleague Brother Gustavo and I," Dorantes said, "were told by Father Aurelio to apprehend and question an old mestizo woman who was reputed to be a witch. We went to the hovel where she lived. Brother Gustavo, who has more experience than I in such matters, told me to stay outside in order to be safe if she resisted arrest. He said he intended to surprise her by bursting in the door without knocking. He did just that, and instantly I heard terrible screams — inhuman screams, I would say — coming from inside. Then a bat flew out of a window on the side of the house.

"A few minutes later Gustavo came out the door looking very odd. He caught his breath and said, 'If you go inside, you'll see the old woman's clothes lying in a heap. She refused to come with me voluntarily, and when I tried to seize her, she changed herself into a bat and flew out the window.' We entered the hovel, and I saw her clothes piled on the floor as though she had stepped out of them in a single act."

The conviction with which Father Dorantes told his story produced a breathless silence. In a respectful voice Carlos commented, "That story certainly exemplifies the power of the invisible world as it manifests itself in our world."

"The invisible world," Dorantes repeated. "That's an apt way of putting it."

Javier Beltrán, who was more comfortable with the visible world, spoke for the first time. "But don't you think, Father Dorantes, that most of the troubles of the world are caused by human conflict or natural phenomena rather than supernatural agency? There are many such examples in Santa Fe life—three years of drought, and the recent attacks by Indian war parties—that don't require sorcery to explain them."

"Yes, of course," Father Dorantes agreed, "and the same is true in the larger world. The unity of the Church has been broken by various Protestant schisms, which have led to decades of religious wars between Christians of different beliefs. Spain has remained a strong pillar of the Church, expanding God's kingdom by bringing the true faith to the New World, and God blessed Spain for this with great wealth in gold and silver from these new lands. But now Spain itself, and most of Europe, is divided over who should be Spain's king—Philip of Anjou, a Frenchman who was hastily crowned by his grandfather Louis XIV, or Archduke Charles of Austria, a Habsburg, as all of Spain's kings have been for the past two hundred years."

Dorantes paused. "And thus," Carlos added, "we have a war over the Spanish succession."

"Do you see the outcome of this war," Javier asked, "as having a direct effect on us as Spaniards in New Mexico?"

"Yes, I do. If the Habsburg alliance loses, I believe the Spanish Empire will be weakened. The French will have a freer hand in North America, and if Frenchmen control commerce with the Indian tribes of the interior, it could have dire results for New Mexico's economy. Therefore I see strengthening the Indian people's ties to Spain as very important, and part of my mission here, which is not too different from my work as an inquisitor, is to visit nearby pueblos in order to bring all New Mexicans, whether Indians, mestizos, or Spaniards, into the arms of the Church."

Father Dorantes sat back in his chair. The expressions on Raul's, Javier's, and Carlos's faces were serious and thoughtful.

Finally Carlos took it upon himself to speak. "What you've told us is both informative and thought-provoking. I, for one, feel privileged to have heard your explanation of your mission in New Mexico and Santa Fe." Javier and Raul nodded in agreement. Father Dorantes smiled, evidently pleased with the way his words had been received. Raul thanked him for his presence, chairs were pushed back, and the men said their goodbyes.

Carlos, walking home alone, was thoughtful. On the whole, he mused, the situation was better than he had expected. True, the Inquisition had come to Santa Fe because Father Aurelio (whom Carlos knew to be Malvolio) believed the brujo Carlos Buenaventura was to be found there. And Brother Gustavo also believed this, but what he had seen through the eyes of the wolf had convinced him that Don Alfonso Cabeza de Vaca was not a brujo. So, as he had told Inéz earlier, Carlos continued to believe that in his identity as Don Alfonso he was beyond suspicion. And, he thought, although the Inquisition was bound to stir up trouble, Father Dorantes did not seem to be pursuing any agenda other than the unity of belief of Catholic Santa Fe. As far as Carlos himself was concerned, all might be well.

7

Uncertainties

$\mathcal{S}$unday morning Don Carlos went to the Beltrán house in order to escort Inéz to Mass. Elena and her parents were standing next to Inéz in the entry hall, obviously intending to join Carlos and Inéz on the short walk to the military chapel in the southeast corner of the Palace of the Governors. (Both of the town's former places of worship, the parish church and the San Miguel Chapel, had been destroyed in the Pueblo Revolt of 1680 and had not yet been rebuilt.) Carlos greeted the Beltráns and Inéz with a few comments on the success of the dinner the previous evening and repeated the praise that Father Dorantes had lavished on Inéz's skills as a cook. To her he said, "You're looking particularly well this morning. I'm glad to see that last night's efforts didn't seem to tire you."

"Yes, I'm much better," she replied. "I thought I might be exhausted, but it's such a beautiful spring day that I want to get out. We can stand at the very back of the chapel, in case I feel tired and we need to leave."

Signs of spring were everywhere. Trees wearing their new leaves were a luminous green in the morning sunlight. Beyond the plaza, Carlos could see that local farmers had plowed and planted the fields adjacent to their small houses. Lambs that had been born in the past few months were grazing next to their mothers. As parishioners converged from every direction, Don Carlos, who always liked to observe women dressed in their Sunday best, said to Inéz, "How do women know what they know?"

"That's an obscure comment. Know what?"

"Well, last week all the women who attend the late Mass—Bianca Trigales, Regina Cabrera, Margarita Posada, the three Peraltas, Pilar, Juliana, and Victoria, and even the youngest of the Mendoza widows, Doña Josefina's granddaughter-in-law—were wearing dresses of heavy fabric with long sleeves and had wrapped themselves in thick shawls."

Inéz shrugged. "It was chillier last Sunday; of course, they dressed more warmly."

"But today is not that much warmer," he observed. "My point is that without any way of knowing what other women were going to wear—I'm obviously rejecting the idea that they sent their maids around to inquire—they all emerged from their houses in nearly identical outfits, varying somewhat in color, but lighter in weight."

"Don't you prefer this?" Inéz replied. "I know you appreciate dresses that show off women's figures. And all those women have very nice figures that today's fashionable narrow waistlines and tight bodices put on display."

"I..." he started to protest.

"Don't be silly," Inéz said. "You have my permission to look all you want."

After Mass they lingered on the plaza. Raul and Bianca Trigales approached them, and Bianca struck up a conversation with Inéz about the spring dresses women were wearing. Raul had something else on his mind. "I haven't had a chance, Don Alfonso, to thank you sufficiently for helping José with that herd of wild horses. I went to Rancho Rosón yesterday and was impressed with what fine, healthy animals they are. José says the stallion is a very special horse, and I agree. He will bring a good price in the future."

"I'm sure," Carlos began, "I don't need to point out that José has an unusual ability with horses. The fact that he somehow convinced that stallion to come with us, bringing the rest of the herd with him, was truly remarkable."

Raul nodded but then shifted the conversation to another concern. "I'm confident that the horse business will pay off in time. But at the moment I haven't rebuilt my capital from the blow that ransoming my children dealt me. I still can't repay you and Inéz for the money you contributed."

Without hesitation Carlos replied, "That's not a concern for Inéz and me. And speaking of that precious quartet of your children, here they come."

Sure enough, the four Trigales children were approaching, accompanied by two young Pueblo Indians, Diego Campos and Ana Lugo, who worked for Raul. Nodding toward Diego and Ana, Carlos commented, "It looks as though the early stages of that particular romance are progressing well."

"So it would seem," Raul replied approvingly.

The youngest Trigales child, Anton, ran ahead of his older brother and twin sisters and went directly to Inéz. She bent down and gave him a hug. Once she released him from her embrace, he took hold of her skirt and looked up at her with an adoring gaze. "He's convinced," his older brother Cristofer announced, "that Señora Recalde is the angel who rescued us from the cave where the monsters had left us."

"She certainly is angelic," Don Carlos replied to Cristofer, "but angels usually appear only to children, and they certainly wouldn't show themselves in broad daylight to all these adults."

Cristofer nodded seriously, and Carmela took the opportunity to ask, "Papa, can Ana and Diego take us to Don Alfonso's house to see the puppies?"

Raul hesitated. "That is for Don Alfonso to say."

Before Carmela could appeal to him, Don Carlos said, "It's all right with me, Raul. But I think it's only fair to warn you that all baby animals are adorable, and these puppies are no exception."

"I haven't promised the children anything," Raul said with a smile. "Go along," he told his offspring, who immediately grabbed Ana and Diego by the hand and headed off across the plaza toward Carlos's house.

"Puppies, lambs, green leaves — isn't it nice that spring has come and life in Santa Fe has returned to normal?" Carlos asked.

"Normal?" Raul said with a shake of his head. "I wouldn't put it that way. I thought Father Dorantes made quite a convincing case last night that we live in unsettled times."

"I stand corrected," Carlos said.

Gesturing toward the soldiers who could be seen down the street standing guard around his house, Raul added, "What better example of those unsettled times here in Santa Fe than the presence of soldiers on guard? I feel as though we're in some sort of military camp. I suppose I should feel safer for the governor's having ordered these protective measures, but they strike me as excessive, and they aren't good for business."

"How so?"

"I am a merchant who lives by trade. I need as many customers as possible to buy my wares. Yesterday's Saturday market was poorly attended, and my employees made fewer sales than usual. The highly visible presence of Spanish soldiers kept many Indian traders and customers away. They don't see Spanish soldiers as protectors; quite the opposite, and, given past experience, their suspicions are justified."

Don Carlos considered telling Raul about the bad treatment José had recently received from the Spanish soldiers accompanying Father Dorantes to the pueblos, but he held back. That was José's story to tell.

He gazed at the surrounding scene, the colorful attire of the women gathered on the chapel's steps, the Trigales children skipping happily across the plaza, a variety of local residents—Pueblo Indians and mestizos—quietly conversing around the edges of the square, and, despite Raul's words, he appreciated the pleasantness. But he sensed that Inéz was tiring, so he excused himself and took her arm to escort her home. As they walked along, he asked her, "Suppose the plaza this morning could be read like a book. What feeling does the scene convey?"

Inéz glanced around, looking thoughtful. "It's very pleasant," she said. "But I think there are dark undertones."

"So you sense it too. As we turned away to walk you home, a feeling of something dark washed over me. I glanced back, and the auras of all the people, whether they were the wealthy men and women in handsome spring outfits on the chapel steps, or the common folk around the plaza, seemed to be clouded, as if they were under a dark shadow."

"Hmmm," said Inéz. "From what Javier told Cristina and me about your after-dinner conversation last night, most of the world is worse off than we are—all we have are marauding Indians and soldiers on guard everywhere. But I agree with you that people here are putting up a good front on the surface, and trying to hide other feelings. Javier also said that Father Dorantes talked last night about his work with Brother Gustavo, and about their coming here in search of a sorcerer. Doesn't that bother you?"

"I still believe that Brother Gustavo has crossed Don Alfonso off his list. And Father Dorantes has no reason to be suspicious of me. I plan to keep things that way."

"I doubt that you'll manage to avoid drawing attention to yourself," Inéz remarked. "You're too prone to be reckless—and don't deny it. I've seen your risk-taking side all too often."

Carlos loved the give-and-take of conversations with Inéz about his character, and with evident good humor, he said, "Why won't you use a more positive word for my behavior: bold or courageous?"

"Incorrigible is more like it," she replied, responding in the spirit in which he'd spoken.

Turning serious again, Carlos told her, "I do have worries, Inéz. Quite a few, if I allow myself to think about them. But now that your health is improving my personal life is almost all positive."

"What about your finances, if I may ask about something that's not my business? Raul still hasn't been able to repay that large sum you gave him from your nest egg to help ransom his children."

"In fact," Carlos said, "I gave him nearly every last peso in that nest egg, as you called it."

"Then aren't you short of cash? And by volunteering to let eight or nine soldiers occupy the Fernandez house, you won't have any rental income from it."

"True, but on the plus side of the ledger, Fabio has given me half the price we set for his new home, and that puts more than enough in my coffers to keep Gordo and me in beans, cornbread, and cheese. But I think the very visible military presence in town is unsettling everyone."

"It all starts at the top," Inéz declared enigmatically.

"Dearest, now it's my turn to ask for an explanation."

"When the head of state, be it a king, a prince, or a governor, is sick, the whole kingdom comes down with a cold."

"Are you saying that Governor Peralta is ill?" he asked incredulously.

"No, and I'm sure you know what I mean."

"Yes. When Governor Villela was our leader, he radiated confidence that security would be maintained and that the town could master the economic challenges it faced. As a result, all of us could enjoy our daily lives. But Governor Peralta, by the very act of ordering soldiers into the streets, conveys a disturbing message that all is not well."

"And," Inéz added, "he wants us to believe that he's in control, when in fact he isn't."

"I think you're right, Inéz. I'll have to talk with Marco Cabrera to learn what he's seeing from his vantage point as the governor's secretary."

"I'd be interested too. But—on a happier note—I haven't had a chance to tell you that the Recalde Fencing Academy has another student."

"Oh? Who's that?"

"Ariel Padilla. Yesterday afternoon she came by with legal papers her father had drawn up for Javier. After she'd delivered them to him, Cristina brought her to the patio where Elena was practicing some fencing moves under my direction. Ariel stayed to watch. Before long, she said she hadn't realized that women fenced, and she would love to learn. Elena was delighted. Of course, Ariel was not dressed to fence, but Elena insisted that that problem could be remedied.

"They went off to Elena's bedroom, with me tagging along feeling like the older sister. They had such fun, and I did too. Ariel took off her dress and tried on Elena's extra fencing suit. We all laughed. Elena is bosomy, and Ariel is just the opposite. Also, Ariel is very slender, not skinny, but willowy, and Elena is heavy-boned and broad-shouldered.

"There was lots of laughter as they tried to adjust the suit to fit Ariel. The result was baggy in places, but it served the purpose, and the two of them practiced fencing for a while. They're going to get together again tomorrow after Elena's maid alters the suit to fit Ariel better."

Elena and her parents, who had left the post-Mass gathering of the town's social leaders, caught up with Carlos and Inéz in front of the Beltrán house. "Won't you come in for lunch, Don Alfonso?" Cristina inquired.

"Thank you," he replied. "But I need to go to Marco Cabrera's house and ask him some questions that are better discussed when he's not at his office in the governor's suite."

"Understood," Cristina said, "though surely you can wait to hear what Elena overheard Juliana Peralta saying this morning."

"I'm all ears. I wouldn't want to miss it. I noticed that Elena, the Peralta twins, and the three Mendoza gallants were engrossed in conversation after Mass, under the watchful eye, of course, of Pilar Peralta and the youngest of the Mendoza widows, Doña Marta."

"Yes," Elena said. "But as to that conversation, it wasn't an exchange so much as a monologue by Juliana. Her story of the intruder in her bedroom has gotten more dramatic and her role more bold in the past three days. As she tells it now, she awoke from what she thought was a dream of being kissed to find a man standing beside her bed. She cried out, 'Go away or I'll scream!' This, she claims, frightened the burglar and he made for the window, but the scarf he'd wound around his face caught on a hook in the frame. As he was freeing himself, Juliana says she got up and shoved him out the window."

"That is quite an expansion of her original account; doubtless mostly a fantasy, though I wonder," Carlos said, "whether the detail that the intruder was wearing a scarf as a sort of mask might not have some truth in it."

"The Mendoza brothers were hanging on her every word, telling her how brave she was. Victoria, I think, is jealous of all the attention her sister is getting, because she declared that Juliana *should* have screamed. If she had, help might have come and the intruder might have been caught."

"And did you say anything?" Inéz asked.

"No, I scarcely get noticed, except by Santiago, of course. After all, I'm a merchant's daughter and the governor's daughters and their rich Mendoza friends—again, except for Santiago—see themselves as socially superior to me."

Don Carlos, who in his youth as the heir to his father's title of marquis had once moved in such circles in Mexico City, knew exactly what Elena meant. He contented himself with saying, "Their snobbery impoverishes them."

Vice Governor Cabrera's large house was only a short walk away. Don Carlos knocked at the front door and was admitted by a servant who directed him to the *sala* to wait for Marco. Marco soon ducked into the room from the front hallway and greeted Carlos warmly. "Don Alfonso, I'm glad you stopped by. I wanted to speak with you after Mass, but you left before I could get to you. How is your friend Inéz?"

"She was tired, Marco, and that's why we didn't stay longer, but she is feeling much better. We both noticed that you were speaking to Ariel Padilla. She's a very engaging young woman. When I was your predecessor as the governor's secretary, I sometimes had to deliver documents to her father's law offices, and she was often there greeting his visitors."

"Yes," Marco said, "that's how I met her. She doesn't have a mother to take her into society, so she doesn't attend many social gatherings, although that doesn't seem to bother her. What impressed me is that she seems to be familiar with many legal issues. Apparently her father has encouraged that interest, even though she could never enter the legal profession."

"Did Ariel tell you that she and Elena Beltrán are being tutored in fencing by Inéz?"

"Yes," Marco replied, "she did, and I wanted to talk with you about that. When both of us still lived in Mexico City, you and I used to fence at Don Ignacio de Tortuga's studio. But I haven't fenced for more than a year now, and I'm completely out of practice. Could you find time to fence with me, not that I expect to be much of a challenge for you?"

"By an odd coincidence, I was going to propose that we fence. I too am badly out of practice. But what prompts your sudden interest? It wouldn't have something to do with Señorita Padilla, would it?"

Marco looked down at his shoes as though embarrassed. Finally he admitted as much. "I would like to get to know Ariel better, but to maintain proprieties we would need to be chaperoned, and she doesn't have a female relative who could do that. But if we fenced at the Beltrán house, either Inéz or Señora Beltrán could supervise our rendezvous."

"Excellent idea," Carlos replied. "As for fencing with me, would this afternoon be convenient? You can bring your fencing suit and swords to my place and change there. We can go to the old Tiburcio place, which has a good fencing strip in the patio. The house won't be occupied at this time of day because the soldiers who are being quartered there will be out on maneuvers."

"Maneuvers on a Sunday? How unusual."

"Indeed it is." With a meaningful look, Carlos added, "A lot of unusual things are happening of late. If you like, that's something we can discuss during a break from our bout."

Lowering his voice, Marco replied, "I would like that, and doing so would be more suitable there than here."

Toward the end of siesta, Marco arrived at Carlos's house, changed into his fencing suit, and accompanied Carlos down the path to the Tiburcio place, where Inéz had first lived in Santa Fe. As Carlos had expected, none of the current residents were home.

As he entered the house and walked through the front hall to reach the interior patio, Carlos was assailed by a rush of memories from the time nearly two years ago when he and Inéz had engaged in intense fencing bouts there, and also, more recently, from the occasions when he and Inéz had been entertained there by Leandro, Selena, and Mara, who had briefly rented the house. He pushed these memories aside as he entered the patio and put the bottle of wine and two glasses he had brought along down on a table. "This," he said, "is to refresh ourselves once we've revived our skills at fencing."

Since Marco had said that he was badly out of practice, Carlos suggested that they do simple warm-up exercises that their long-ago master Don Ignacio had taught them. These consisted of one fencer going on the attack while the other limited himself to defensive maneuvers. After ten such exchanges, they reversed roles. Soon Marco was gaining confidence. "My muscle memories are coming back," he announced.

"I think that once they're learned they're never entirely lost," Carlos replied.

At Carlos's suggestion they next went through a series of drills in which they focused on particular situations — initiating a high thrust and then parrying a high thrust; initiating an attack on the chest area and then parrying such an attack; initiating a low lunge and then parrying the same. At the end of many repetitions, Carlos said, "We're making progress. Let's try free exchanges." Here Carlos's great superiority to Marco was clearly demonstrated. Time and time again Carlos achieved hits without Marco making a single one.

"Ah!" Marco exclaimed, breathing heavily from his exertions, "you remain truly masterful."

"But Marco," Carlos replied, "you're already regaining some of your former competence. I'm sure you would easily prevail in a bout with a beginner like Ariel, if that's your goal."

"It is my goal," Marco admitted. "I wouldn't want to be bested by a woman. That would wound my pride."

"Then," Carlos said with a laugh, "be sure you don't fence with Inéz. She is very skillful, and though I win our bouts, she tests my skills more than any man I've ever known. But enough for now. Let's have some wine and speak frankly of things other than fencing."

Once wine had been poured and they had raised their glasses in a toast to friendship, Carlos asked, "I wonder whether you felt, as I did today, that the underlying mood of the townspeople is far from happy."

"I did, and it's no surprise, given the presence of soldiers guarding the houses of the rich and powerful. My opinion, which I trust you'll keep in confidence, is that placing round-the-clock guards at certain houses may not have been the wisest course of action."

"But what would you have had Governor Peralta do, Marco? Quite a few voices were being raised to demand that he do something."

"I'll grant you that, and I'm not altogether unsympathetic to his situation. The threat to property, and most of all the fact that the intruder entered his daughter's bedroom, has rattled him. He's supposed to be in command, and he can't even protect his own daughter."

"Juliana seems to be taking it well enough. It's been an adventure for her."

"After the fact, perhaps. I suspect she was terrified at the time, and she has created this romantic story to cover up how scared she was."

"Returning to the governor," Carlos said, "do you think he's more unnerved now than he was the other day when I reported the encounter José and I had with an Indian war party?"

"Allow me," Marco replied, "to give you a long and rather indirect answer." After taking a sip of wine, he began. "I've noticed quite a change in Peralta in the months we've worked together. At first he seemed uncertain and without direction. Then he struck on the idea of launching a military response to the Native raiders and to the threat of French encroachment from the east. As it happened, Cortés's unit was on patrol in northern New Spain and could be diverted to help secure Spanish control in this area.

"What he didn't foresee was that Father Dorantes and his fellow inquisitors would arrive at the same time as these additional troops. The prospect of an Inquisition on top of the presence of extra soldiers has stirred people up and raised unanswered questions—why were all of them here in the first place, and how much of the town's supplies would be needed to feed them? Now people have to worry about the correctness of their own personal behavior, and that of their neighbors, under threat of punishment. And they were already uneasy on account of the burglaries—not ordinary ones, but surrounded with mystery. So when the thief struck again, the governor—and yes, I would say he was unnerved—ordered guards to be posted outside the homes of the wealthy. What worries me is that if he reacts so aggressively to a small event, might not another incident provoke a more extreme, possibly quite rash, reaction on his part?"

"It might, indeed," Carlos replied. "But I hope you're wrong."

"I hope so too. All you and I can do is to wait and see. Let's meet again next Sunday afternoon to fence. I enjoyed fencing with you today. Physical activity is the best antidote to mental anxiety."

That evening Don Carlos's three lodgers got in very late. It having slipped his mind that they were out on maneuvers, Don Carlos asked them how they had spent their day off.

Gonzalo groaned. "Day off? What day off? Cortés had us riding around the countryside from dawn to dusk."

"To what purpose?"

"We're not sure," Luis replied. "Alejandro says Cortés is trying to toughen us up for a hard campaign. Gonzalo thinks he's out to frighten the Natives."

"That's what we did," Gonzalo said. "We rode to three pueblos—Tesuque, Nambe, and San Ildefonso. At each place he had us line up in formation. Then he had the pueblo's leaders call all the people together in the village plaza. Then he gave an address in which he said that we would help protect them against mounted raiders from other tribes, and he urged them to cooperate with us. But it sounded to me like he was warning them not to make trouble."

"But you left out an important fact," Alejandro objected. "The only troops who went with Cortés were those of us who've been on garrison duty for the past year. We've gotten soft. He wants us to be saddle-hardened. That's what a good officer would do."

"Hmmpf!" Luis said. "Cortés may want us to be battle-ready, but he's a mean man, and that doesn't make for a good officer."

"Mean or tough?" Alejandro asked. "Just because we don't like missing our day off doesn't prove that he's mean."

"I say he's mean," Luis insisted.

Soon, in their usual way, the three soldiers were going in circles, repeating their points almost word for word. Don Carlos found their way of relating amusing, but it wasn't long before he excused himself to go to bed.

8

Stones

As April became May the weather in Santa Fe became especially pleasant—warm, but not too warm, at least for a time. Local residents gradually grew accustomed to seeing soldiers guarding six of the finer homes to the north and west of the Palace of the Governors. And if one stayed on the south side of the Santa Fe River, where Indian and mestizo locals generally lived, there was little sense of being in the middle of an armed camp.

In time, therefore, the spirits of Santa Fe's residents revived. Farmers sang as they worked in the fields that were scattered throughout the town. Participation in Saturday markets returned to normal. The soldiers surrounding the houses of Santa Fe's first families relaxed a bit and began to flirt with the Indian servant girls who worked in the places the men were guarding. Even Father Dorantes, who had taken it as his special mission to say the Mass for the town's Indian residents, allowed himself a smile when he noticed that attendance was increasing every Sunday.

Governor Peralta, perhaps feeling that the town deserved a celebration, declared Saturday, May 1st, a special feast day, *La Fiesta de San Felipe y Santiago*. The town's musicians brought their guitars, violins, bugles, flutes, and drums and played dances and songs. Under other circumstances, the platform that the Inquisition was having built in the plaza would have had a forbidding aspect, but in the spirit of celebration the revelers incorporated it into their fiesta and the musicians used it as a stage from which they played dances and songs. Following long-standing tradition, members of the great families—Peraltas, Cabreras, Mendozas, and Archuletas—joined the town's humbler folk on the plaza and the two groups mingled, a custom that affirmed a measure of solidarity among all Santa Fe residents, regardless of class and ethnic differences.

The sun smiled on Carlos's personal life as well. Raul and Bianca Trigales took two of his puppies as birthday gifts for their twin daughters, and when José made a quick visit to town and expressed an interest in having Nana, the mother dog, and her remaining puppy as guard dogs for Rancho Rosón, Carlos gladly gave them to him. Gordo, however, missed his canine friends and moped around the house for a week before finally regaining his normal good spirits.

Most important of all from Carlos's viewpoint, Inéz's health continued to improve. The two of them frequently strolled around town, engaged in brief fencing bouts, and, on Inéz's day off, took Eagle and Alegría for short rides in the country. Carlos and Marco Cabrera practiced fencing once a week, as did Elena and Ariel with Inéz as their tutor. Carlos noticed that the three women—Inéz, Elena, and Ariel—sometimes went off together to some unknown location for an activity that they told him was to remain a secret. Whenever he asked what they were up to, their eyes smiled in a conspiratorial way and they laughed behind their hands. "You may never find out," Inéz told him.

"Then again," Elena teased, "we may let you know some day."

He was quite content to be mystified, if pretty women were the source of the puzzle.

Only a few shadows lurked at the edges of this scene. Soldiers were still ever-present on guard duty outside the homes of the wealthy. Major Cortés continued to order squads of his cavalrymen to accompany Father Dorantes on visits to nearby pueblos, a practice that Don Carlos felt was unduly provocative. And Elena, poor Elena, was never invited to the dinner parties that the Cabreras, Peraltas, and Mendozas gave for each other, despite Santiago Mendoza's complaints to his aunt, Doña Josefina, that it was unfair that Juliana and Victoria Peralta, in whom his elder brothers were interested, were present, while Elena Beltrán, whom he particularly liked, was not. "The Peralta girls are there because their parents are invited to dinner," Doña Josefina would remind him. "But Señor Beltrán belongs to the merchant class." That seemed to place the issue beyond discussion. Fortunately, Doña Josefina raised no objections to Santiago visiting Elena at the Beltrán house for fencing lessons, as long as he could claim that he was being tutored by Don Carlos. "Don Alfonso at least has an aristocratic background," she said with some satisfaction.

This relatively serene scene was shattered on the night of May 5th, when the town's now-notorious thief brazenly broke into two homes that had been left unguarded.

The thief's first target was the most startling. This was the residence of Captain Tito Posada, second in command at the Presidio garrison. No one, including Posada's senior officer, Major Cortés, had ever considered the possibility that the thief would trespass on the property of the military out-post responsible for defending the town. "Outrageous! Unthinkable!" Cortés shouted angrily upon learning that the thief had entered the Posadas' apart-ments and had taken one of Señora Posada's gold-rimmed bowls from the chest in which it had been stored. Since the set to which the bowl belonged was used for special occasions only, its absence might not have been noticed for some time had not the thief left the lid of the chest open. Precisely how the intruder entered or left the Posadas' apartment was not known.

The thief's second target interested Carlos more. Some of the circum-stances surrounding this break-in offered clues, albeit minor ones, to the thief's identity. This burglary took place at the home of Horatio Padilla, the town's only lawyer in private practice. His daughter Ariel was awakened by someone who had softly stroked her arm and then kissed her on the cheek. Startled, she burst out, "Who are you?" The intruder moved quickly to an open window and jumped out. Ariel told her father that she got up, went to the window, and looked down the street. A waning moon gave some light outside, and she thought she saw the shape of a dog running away with something in its mouth. Upon investigation, Ariel and her father found that a silver soup spoon was missing.

These two break-ins jarred the town's leading citizens. By mid-morn-ing a group of them assembled at Governor Peralta's request in his office. Don Carlos was a bit surprised that he had been asked to attend, though he assumed that this was because Marco Cabrera, as the governor's secretary, had been responsible for issuing invitations. He now found himself standing in a room packed with government officials (Vice Governor Salvador Cabrera and Provincial Attorney Nicolas Archuleta), representatives of the military

(Major Cortés and Captain Posada), two priests (Father Benedicto and Father Dorantes), Antonio Mendoza, who was the eldest of Doña Josefina's nephews, and three men besides himself drawn from the town's business and professional class: Horatio Padilla, Raul Trigales, and Javier Beltrán.

Governor Peralta asked Horatio Padilla to report what his daughter had seen that morning.

"Another dog!" the governor exclaimed, when Padilla had finished his account. "Just as in the case of Señorita Beltrán."

"Witchcraft may be involved," Father Dorantes said in an ominous way. "I can't divulge any details, but that's consistent with an accusation that led me to come to Santa Fe."

Father Benedicto evidently did not know about the bat incident Father Dorantes had witnessed in El Paso del Norte, and he did not consider that the involvement of dogs suggested witchcraft. He said, "There are many dogs in Santa Fe, Father Dorantes, and even if we are talking only about a black dog of the type Señorita Beltrán saw, there are dozens. I'll wager that if we stepped outside now and looked down the street in both directions, we would see at least one black dog."

The expression on Father Dorantes's face suggested he might be remembering something. "A thief that turns into a dog..." he said to no one in particular. Then, very forcefully, he declared, "This person must be found! Use all necessary means to search every household in which a black dog is known to live!"

"That would be nearly a hundred houses," Nicolas Archuleta said, "even if we're limiting these searches to the Barrio de Analco."

Don Carlos was relieved that Father Benedicto, the parish priest and a weighty voice in such matters, spoke up. "I would advise against imposing searches on the residents of the Barrio, especially on Indian households," he said. "I well remember the wariness and, yes, the anger of our Pueblo Indian neighbors toward the Spanish when we first returned to Santa Fe in the 1690s. I fear that we would reawaken those feelings if such intrusive measures were taken."

"Then what alternative would you propose?" Governor Peralta asked.

"I could ask the church sexton, a fine old man, Mateo Suarez, to compile a list of all the households that own black dogs. He lives in the Barrio de Analco and knows the district well. Father Dorantes and I could then accompany Mateo to those houses and explain that a black dog had been seen carrying off stolen goods. We would be careful to say that the owners themselves were not under suspicion, but that we need to ask them to help us search for things a dog might have brought in."

Major Cortés—rather surprisingly, Carlos thought—supported Father Benedicto's suggestion. "Usually," he said, "I am inclined to take the most forceful possible actions; however, in this case, which involves our very numerous Indian and mestizo neighbors, it is important to maintain their friendship."

With relatively little further discussion, Father Benedicto's proposal received the unanimous endorsement of those present.

Later that afternoon, Don Carlos joined Ariel, Elena, and Inéz to practice their fencing at the Beltrán house. Before they could start, Ariel announced that she wanted to tell them additional details about the thief's intrusion into her father's house. "I didn't share these with my father or anyone else," she said, "because I don't want her to be caught."

"Her?" Inéz asked. "Are you sure?"

"Yes. Let me give you a fuller version of what happened. It was a very warm night, so I wore only a sleeveless chemise to bed and left the window open. I was awakened by someone stroking my arm so gently that at first I thought it was simply a cooling breeze that had come up. When I realized that it was someone's hand touching me, I was afraid and pretended to be asleep in hopes that the person would leave without my having to scream. But instead of leaving, the thief kissed me softly on the cheek. I stirred, as though I was only now waking up, and the intruder pulled away and went to the window.

"It was dark in the room, but I got a glimpse of the thief in the moonlight. She pulled off some sort of loose dress she had been wearing, tucked it under her arm, and stepped onto the windowsill. I know it was a she because I could see her breast. Then she jumped out the window.

"I got up and hurried to the window. When I looked out, I saw a dog on the ground below gathering a sack in its mouth. I said, 'Wait!' It eyed me for a moment and then trotted off down the street. I've always been unladylike, and my thought was to follow the dog. I picked up a robe, put it on, climbed out the window, and ran down the street after the dog. It stopped and looked back at me, as though it was tempted to wait for me to catch up. Then it turned and ran away. I couldn't keep up, and besides, the rough ground was painful to run on barefoot."

"What a story!" Elena exclaimed.

Ariel held up her hand. "There's one more detail. When I got back to my house, I found a long scarf lying on the ground beneath my bedroom window. The fabric was of good quality wool, finely woven, but it was old and ragged around the edges, and it had been carefully mended. I thought it must belong to a poor person. I decided right then that I didn't want to catch this girl, both because she's a woman and the men in our circle are being so pompous about protecting their ever-so-weak daughters and wives, and because she's poor and hasn't been greedy about what she's taken — a goblet, a silver place setting, a porcelain plate, and a soup bowl and soup spoon."

Elena reached over and put her hand on Ariel's arm. "I feel the same. I kept telling everyone that the intruder was gentle in a sweet way. If the intruder is a poor girl or woman, I wouldn't want her to fall into the hands of the authorities. Men can be so annoying! Don Alfonso excepted, of course," she said with a smile.

"Don Alfonso can be plenty annoying, on occasion," Inéz remarked. "But he may be our only hope of finding this woman and keeping her safe from the authorities."

"Me?" he asked. "What can I do?"

"I think you know," Inéz replied, "and this is no time to be modest. You once suggested that the thief who kisses young women and then seems to be replaced by a dog is a shape-shifter. You might be able to spot her among Santa Fe residents."

"How could you do that?" Elena asked, giving Carlos a questioning look.

Carlos wasn't ready to tell Elena and Ariel about his training in the Brujo's Way, but he believed he could safely tell them something close enough to the truth to serve his purpose. "Ariel, Elena," he said a bit sternly. They both looked at him attentively. "I'm going to tell you something I hope you will promise not to tell anyone else.

"This," he said, leaning forward and speaking as though he was delivering an important confidence, "is one of the secrets of my success as a fencer. Years ago my fencing master taught me to detect an opponent's intention by reading his aura. That's a field of light that surrounds all of us. When an opposing fencer is about to make a move, there's an anticipatory shift in his aura that indicates the nature of the move. Obviously, if I can see what's coming before my opponent has actually begun to move, it's to my advantage."

"How will that help you spot this thief?" Ariel asked.

"I think I see," Inéz said, trying to make a bridge to what Carlos was getting at. "If we're right and the thief is a shape-shifter who can take on the form of a dog, then Don Alfonso needs to find a local resident whose aura is that of a shape-shifter. There can't be many in a town the size of Santa Fe."

"What would a shape-shifter's aura look like, as distinct from mine or Ariel's, for example?" Elena asked.

"I gather you accept the existence of auras and the possibility of seeing them," Carlos said cautiously.

"Yes. When those two entertainers, Mara and Selena, performed at private parties here and at Uncle Raul's, I sometimes saw a glow around their bodies during that dance called *Duende*. I think from what you just said that I was seeing their auras."

"Excellent insight!" Carlos replied, genuinely impressed.

"The question," Inéz reminded Carlos, "was what would be distinctive about a shape-shifter's aura."

"I haven't seen many, in fact, only three, so it's difficult to generalize. But there is something different about them. I would think that if I saw another one, I would recognize it."

Elena looked a little dubious, and even Carlos wasn't entirely sure.

"Enough for now," Carlos said. "It's time for you two victims of this female thief's kisses to get to work. Inéz and I will do our best to come up with some drills that will further your training."

Later, once the practice session had ended, Inéz walked Carlos to the door while Ariel and Elena stayed behind to change out of their fencing suits. "Do you have a plan?" she asked, looking at him appraisingly. "Or is this aura test another case of your improvising as you go along?"

"I always have a plan. I love plans," he replied. "The only trouble is that many of my plans don't achieve much, and others fail altogether. If you get a chance, come to the plaza Saturday and watch me watching for a shape-shifter."

Inéz nodded. "I understand. On market day the plaza is crowded with nearly everyone who lives in town and many from out of town. I guess that's as good a place to start as any."

As Saturday morning neared, Carlos decided that his preparations were almost complete. He hadn't told Inéz his whole plan, which was to set up a blanket on the south side of the plaza not far from his house. He possessed a fairly large collection of crystals and semi-precious stones that he had acquired over the past two years during his explorations of the Santa Fe area and on his trips to and from Mexico City. Many of the specimens he had found himself, and some of the more unusual ones he had obtained through bargaining with Spanish and Indian traders. His interest in them was in some way related to his sense of different kinds of power in different landscapes; each kind of stone, as he held it in his hand, seemed to have its own distinct energy, a vibration he could attune himself to and, in some obscure way, align himself with. He did not know what, if anything, the power of the stones could 'do,' but he knew there were folk stories about stones having properties similar to healing potions or love potions.

What he had told Inéz was that he would spend the day at Saturday market looking in a general way for a shape-shifter. What he had not told her was that the attractive display of stones he was setting up was specifically designed to catch the attention of a shape-shifter, and that in doing so he was dabbling in the very waters of superstition and folk belief that the Inquisition was on the lookout for. It was a risk, he knew; but he felt the power of the stones, and he believed it would bring the shape-shifter thief to him.

Accordingly, early Saturday morning, after doing his usual meditation practice, Carlos went to the hallway that ran through the middle of his house and began sorting through the semi-precious stones he had stored there. He selected stones from nearly a dozen different varieties and placed three to five specimens of each in bags.

As market day was getting started, Carlos enlisted Orfeo's help in carrying the bags of stones from his house to the near edge of the plaza. He laid out two blankets to claim his spot, and after three round trips to his house, everything was in place.

To maximize his opportunity to watch unhindered, he asked Orfeo to deal with most of the customers while he, Carlos, sat at the back of the display. He suggested that Orfeo bring his guitar and sing a few of the New Mexican folk *versos* he knew as an additional attraction to Carlos's display.

Carlos studied the plaza. It was early on market day, but many vendors had already taken positions near Carlos on the plaza's south side, and others had set up their wares on the north side and on the square's west end adjacent to the chapel. The east end was where the *parroquia*, the parish church, had once stood. No new buildings had been constructed there, and as a result the plaza's eastern side, which was more than a hundred yards from its western edge, was poorly defined, cobblestones simply giving way to fields in which the first green sprouts of spring corn were beginning to show.

Orfeo had begun to sing as Don Carlos settled down behind the display. The plaza was filling up with shoppers of all types—Spanish, mestizo, and Indian—who were preparing to bargain for items available at this time of year: root vegetables, hardy greens, chickens, goats, a piglet or two, hides, bushels of pine nuts, jewelry, and many varieties of woolen goods. Carlos had no competition in offering semi-precious stones, and he supposed that the uniqueness of his display would draw some attention.

He was pleased with the visual appeal of the many types of stones that he had in his display. Some, like the clear quartz crystals, were two or more inches long; the amethyst crystals were smaller, but some pieces of rose quartz were as large as a fist. The garnet crystals were mostly about the size of a kernel of corn and were still embedded in chunks of matrix. His examples of tourmaline, some pink and edged in yellow-green, and some others that were very black and larger, were eye-catching. There was a pile of turquoise nuggets and some pieces of agate that were smooth and beautiful. All of these varieties Carlos had arranged in two rows along the front edge of his blankets. He kept one more group of stones, a handful of fire opals that he had bought from a Zuñi jeweler, in a separate spot by his side at the back of the display.

As Don Carlos had hoped, the novelty of his display and the beauty of Orfeo's singing attracted many viewers. Quite a few of them asked Orfeo what he wanted for this or that crystal or stone. Carlos's main purpose wasn't to make a profit, so he had instructed Orfeo to respond to inquiries by asking what the buyer was willing to offer. Because coinage of any sort was in very short supply in Santa Fe, most customers preferred to barter. One man offered a chicken in exchange for three pink tourmalines and a small bag of pine nuts for five garnet crystals. Carlos almost told Orfeo to turn down the proffered chicken, whose fatalistic stare in his direction convinced him he didn't want to kill and eat the poor creature. Then he remembered that Caterina Díaz, a tenant in one of his rental houses, had just started a flock, so he told Orfeo to give it to Caterina in return for a few eggs now and then.

That exchange taken care of, Don Carlos settled down into himself and shifted his attention from his everyday way to seeing to his brujo vision. What he was looking for was the specific peculiarity of a shape-shifter's aura, which he could not describe but thought he would recognize. What he saw was less the definite physical appearance of the persons passing by and more a kind of moving veil around the body that extended out in varying degrees and in varying degrees of brightness. Some were light, some were dim; some were streaked, some were clear; some were dense and seemed almost opaque; a few were frankly dark, and these Don Carlos found he did not want to look at very closely.

After a time, he pulled himself out of his half trance and returned to his normal way of seeing. He had counted on the fact that few if any members of Santa Fe's wealthier families would attend market day. Shopping for their households would be done by servants. Sure enough, Ana Lugo, who worked for Raul and Bianca Trigales, came by with a basket of root vegetables. She chatted briefly with Don Carlos, but from the look on her face he could tell that she was puzzled to see him in the role of a merchant manning a booth on the plaza.

His luck with avoiding socially prominent townspeople ran out when Governor Peralta's twin daughters and the two elder Mendoza brothers, chaperoned by their widowed cousin Doña Marta Mendoza, paused by his display. Juliana Peralta, whom he knew from many social occasions, seemed amused to see Don Carlos in a mercantile capacity. "Don Alfonso," she said in an arch manner, "I thought you were investing in real estate. Is this yet another new career?"

This jibe was difficult to answer without making matters worse. "I have a secret purpose," he replied.

Doña Marta, a severe-looking woman in her mid-forties, was openly critical. "A man of your social status should not appear in public as a street merchant. That should be left to your servant, this guitarist."

He had already stood up, a matter of common courtesy when conversing with the Doña Martas of the world. "Ordinarily I would," he said, and then, not satisfied with this response, he leaned close to Doña Marta and whispered, "Please don't reveal my purpose. But for your ears only, I will say that this display is an effort to entrap the thief who has been breaking into our homes. I'm sure you're sympathetic with that goal."

She gave him a surprised look, and the young people in her party waited for her to say something. When she didn't reveal what Don Carlos had said, they lost interest and moved on. Doña Marta followed in their wake.

The next visitor was Brother Gustavo. Don Carlos had noticed the Franciscan across the plaza earlier, talking with three Indian men. During his exchange with Juliana Peralta and Doña Marta, he had lost track of Brother Gustavo's whereabouts. Suddenly he was standing next to Don Carlos's display and staring at him. Taking the initiative, Don Carlos addressed him. "Good morning, Brother Gustavo—a beautiful morning, wouldn't you agree?"

Brother Gustavo gave Don Carlos a sharp look and asked, "How did you know my name?"

Don Carlos felt a most unpleasant sensation in the pit of his stomach and had a mild attack of vertigo, but he steeled himself not to give any sign of the effect that close proximity to Gustavo had on him. "I had dinner not long ago with your colleague Father Dorantes," he explained. "He spoke highly of you."

"And who are you?" Gustavo asked.

This, Don Carlos knew, was disingenuous, since only a few months earlier he had been approached by a wolf sent by Gustavo, who controlled the animal's mind from a distance and could see what it perceived. That, of course, could not be acknowledged, so Don Carlos replied, "Pardon me for not introducing myself. I am Don Alfonso Cabeza de Vaca, formerly secretary to Governor Villela, but now a real estate investor."

"And also a street merchant," Gustavo observed with a question in his voice.

"Only for today, aided by my young friend, in an effort to dispose of many stones a previous occupant of my house left in a storage area." Wanting to steer the conversation away from the stones, Carlos said, "Did I understand Father Dorantes to say that you grew up in Morelia?"

Gustavo frowned. "I am glad to have left it," he said darkly. "What connection do you have with Morelia?"

Don Carlos was surprised at the blackness of the emotion in Gustavo's response. Unable to refer to his previous life in Morelia, he merely said, "None, really. When I was growing up in Mexico City, one of my Jesuit tutors taught for a year at the university in Morelia."

"Jesuits!" Gustavo replied disapprovingly. "All head and no heart."

"My tutor was a scholarly man, that's true," Don Carlos replied. "But, since you are from Morelia, I wondered if you know that several Santa Fe residents—Manuel Gómez and Magdalena de Ogama, among others—are Tarascan people from Morelia."

"No, I don't," Gustavo said. "How do you know that?"

"I've lived in Santa Fe for more than two years. In such a small town there are not many secrets."

"We will have to talk again," Brother Gustavo said. He turned away and walked off. The man has no social graces, Carlos observed to himself. He watched the Franciscan as his figure retreated across the plaza. Once again he noticed Gustavo's ominous aura, dark like a thundercloud, though with flashes resembling sheet lightning illuminating it from within. But this time Don Carlos saw a detail he'd previously missed. The bursts of light were concentrated almost exclusively around Gustavo's head. His power is mental, Don Carlos thought. But there was no sign that Brother Gustavo could read auras, which Carlos found reassuring.

Nevertheless, he felt physically unsettled by his encounter with the Franciscan, and he staggered slightly as he returned to his seat at the back of the display of stones. Orfeo noticed and looked up. "Are you all right, Don Alfonso?" he asked.

"There was something underfoot," Don Carlos said with a dismissive gesture. "I turned my ankle."

Ten minutes of sitting quietly, watching the passing crowd and listening to Orfeo sing, restored Carlos's equilibrium. A Pueblo Indian woman approached the display of stones and, ignoring Orfeo, spoke directly to Don Carlos. "I have a neighbor in the pueblo who is jealous of my good fortune in having three sons," she said. "Do you have a stone that can protect us against her jealousy?"

In Don Carlos's mind there was a moment of hesitation; was it wise to suggest that a stone might have magical powers? Moreover, he had no direct knowledge of such powers. Nevertheless, he took the plunge and began to invent freely. Picking up an amethyst crystal, he said to the woman, "Amethyst is often called the protective stone. How large is your family?"

"Five—my husband, me, and three sons."

"Then take five small amethyst crystals, make little pouches for them, and wear the pouches around your necks. That may help."

"I have no way of paying you."

"Do you have hens that are laying?" The woman nodded. "Then bring me five eggs when you have a surplus. My home is the first house down the street behind me. Just leave them for Don Alfonso. There's no rush."

She looked startled to learn that he had the honorific title of Don, but she readily agreed.

A mestizo man who'd overheard Carlos's conversation with the Indian woman stepped up as she left. "My brother-in-law injured me. He has moved away from Santa Fe, but I still hold a grudge."

Don Carlos looked directly at the mestizo. "First, I suggest you go to confession, confess your grudge, and ask to be forgiven for it. But I will give you something that will help you forgive your brother-in-law for injuring you. Take this garnet crystal," he said, putting it in the man's hand. "Make a pouch, and put it in your pocket or wear it around your neck. It will help to heal the wound in your heart."

A small crowd had gathered. A young Pueblo woman called out, "What stone helps with unhappiness?"

"Several stones have qualities that might help," he replied. "Agate is said to be a peace-loving stone, and you might benefit from sleeping with one of these agates under your pillow. Smoky quartz crystals, often called transformation stones, are said to absorb black thoughts and change bad feelings into good feelings.

"But," he continued, warming to his subject, "I've always liked the story associated with watermelon tourmalines. According to one ancient legend, the first tourmalines lived in the earth and were opaque and dull, either black or brown from the soil, but one of them somehow managed to travel up into the sky and to pass through a rainbow, where it picked up the rainbow shades of pink, yellow, and green. From then on tourmalines were widely regarded as having many positive traits, conveying to those who possessed them peace and joy, truly a happiness stone."

Don Carlos's attention was drawn to a young Indian man who was standing at the edge of the small crowd. His face was inexpressive but Don Carlos sensed that he hoped to speak privately with him. From the fellow's clothing, Carlos judged him to be a poor man. Don Carlos asked Orfeo to take over negotiations with anyone who wanted to acquire one of the agate, smoky quartz, or tourmaline pieces he'd been showing to onlookers. He then stood up, stretched, and walked over to the young Indian man and said, "Did you have something you wanted to ask me?"

The man lowered his eyes before whispering, "I have a problem I don't want anyone to know about. Will you please keep it a secret?" Don Carlos assured him that he would not reveal this secret.

"My name is Estefan Chacón. My heart desires a girl who lives in another pueblo. I believe she likes me." He paused.

"Then what's the problem?" Don Carlos prompted him.

"Every time I'm with her I become unable to speak of my feelings."

"The perfect stone to give her as a gift," Don Carlos suggested, "is rose quartz. Not only is rose quartz often called a love stone, but it is said to free the tongues of shy lovers, giving them the courage to speak of their love." Taking a piece of rose quartz from his pocket, Carlos said, "Carry this stone in your hand when you wish to speak with her. When you have told her of your love, give it to her. She will like it. See, it is almost heart-shaped."

"I can't pay you. I don't have money or anything to trade," Estefan replied, his face stiff. "I heard you tell a woman that some of your stones cost two reales each."

"I was saving this one for a special situation—a gift for you. Take it. It's yours for free."

Estefan tried unsuccessfully to express his gratitude. But Don Carlos understood and shooed him away with the words, "You've said enough. Just put it to good use. That's all I want in return."

By mid-afternoon the crowd was thinning out. Don Carlos was disappointed that he hadn't made any progress toward identifying a shape-shifting thief. He and Orfeo had begun to pack up when he became aware of a tiny mestizo woman bent over the small pile of opals that he'd kept at the back of the display. "May I help you?" he asked.

When she stood up, she appeared to be very hunchbacked. Her old face was creased by deep lines, but her black eyes were bright and alive. "I noticed," she said, "that you didn't offer these opals to anyone. Why was that?"

He invited the old woman to sit down, which she did. "I was waiting for the right person," he replied. "Would you like to hold them?" She looked, hungrily he thought, at the small flashing stones. "Here," he said, offering them to her. "Take them in your hand. Perhaps they will speak to you."

Don Carlos slipped the opals into the woman's open hand and they both gazed at them. "The opal," he told her, "is known as the water stone, because it plays with light the way water does. It is as changeable as water is when it moves. Flashes of color come from it, and the colors change, too."

He studied her lowered face. A hunch that came straight from his brujo intuition led him to set aside all discretion. "I'm hoping," he said softly, "these opals will help me identify the thief who stole things from the homes of the rich."

The woman gave him a questioning look. "How would they do that?"

He returned her look. "I believe," he replied, "the thief is a shape-shifter who changes from human form into a black dog. I think shape-shifters would be drawn to a gemstone with a changeable nature." Then he took a bold leap. "You have a shape-shifter's aura," he said. "It's like a cloud, a swirling mist that churns about, constantly changing its shape."

Neither confirming nor denying what he'd said, she replied, "If you can read auras, you're a most unusual Spaniard. Those Franciscans, the inquisitors who just arrived here, are unable to read auras. If they could, think of all the witches, sorcerers, and shape-shifters they could catch!" This thought seemed to amuse her, and she let out a short burst of laughter.

"How did you learn that these Franciscans can't read auras?" Carlos inquired.

She ignored his question and asked, "Have you seen all three of them?"

"Yes."

"The Chief Inquisitor wields the power of the Holy Office, but the inquisitor whose aura might interest you more is Brother Gustavo."

"And why is that?" Don Carlos asked.

Again the old woman answered his question with a question. "Is the thief you're after a woman?"

"I suspect so. And a black dog is often seen leaving the scene of the burglaries."

"I share your suspicion," she said. "But a girl who can turn herself into a black dog will be very difficult to catch."

"Are you, perhaps, that girl, as you called her?"

The woman didn't laugh out loud, but her body shook with deep laughter. "I wish I were! Once upon a time I could have done as she's doing, but I'm no longer able to—my powers have weakened."

"Then perhaps she's your daughter or granddaughter?" he suggested.

"If she were, I'd be proud of her."

"Most of Santa Fe's important families are angry with her," Don Carlos said. "She may have stolen only a few material things, but she's invaded the privacy of their homes and the bedrooms of their daughters."

"Perhaps she's mocking them?"

"You mean she's saying to them, 'Ha-ha, you can't catch me,' and they've been unable to?"

"That may be what they think, but I believe all she's done is take a few things that she wants. Maybe you should be asking why she wants those particular objects."

Don Carlos was puzzled. "How can I find out why she wants what she has taken unless I catch her? And how am I supposed to do that?"

"To catch a dog, you need to become a dog," the old woman said, again shaking with silent laughter.

Don Carlos closed the woman's hand around the opals and said, "Take them. They're yours. I hope we will meet again."

"Perhaps so, or perhaps not, Don Alfonso," she replied.

"You know my name; will you tell me yours?"

"My mother named me Manuela, but that won't help my enemies find me because I don't live here." She stood up and, before Don Carlos could ask where she lived, she turned and shuffled off across the plaza.

Don Carlos finished putting the remaining semi-precious stones in bags and was folding up his blankets when he was approached by a middle-aged Pueblo Indian woman wearing the dress of a housemaid. "Are you Don Alfonso Cabeza de Vaca?" she asked.

"Yes. What may I do for you?"

"Nothing for me, but I ask you to accept this message from my mistress." She handed him a single sheet of paper, folded down the middle, and without waiting for him to read the note, she turned and strode off. Don Carlos opened the note, which was written on expensive paper and was addressed to him in firm, elegant handwriting. It contained one sentence only: "Doña Josefina Gutierrez y Mendoza requests the favor of your presence at her hacienda tomorrow morning after Mass."

9

Stirrings

On Sunday, as was his custom, Carlos accompanied Inéz and the Beltráns to Mass. After exchanging greetings, they started for the chapel. Carlos and Inéz were in the lead and Elena and her parents close behind. "What's wrong with Elena?" Carlos asked Inéz in a whisper.

"She's disappointed because Santiago Mendoza didn't come by to escort her to Mass. She's convinced that Doña Josefina is keeping them apart as much as possible."

"That may well be," Carlos observed. "Doña Josefina comes from a social class that thinks a merchant's daughter is not a suitable match for a man from an aristocratic family."

"Are we sure the Mendozas are a noble family? What titles did the Mendoza men have?"

"None in the direct line of her husband. Their claim to high standing in Santa Fe comes from having been among the town's earliest settlers and from the grants of land they received as a result. Of course, the Mendoza men served in the provincial military and were rewarded with high ranks, but not noble titles. But Doña Josefina's brother-in-law, her nephews' grandfather, held the title of marquis, which Antonio has inherited upon the death of his father."

"I see," Inéz said. After a slight pause, she asked, "Speaking of aristocratic status, I notice that you're wearing your good suit. What's the occasion?"

"I have received a summons to visit Doña Josefina at her hacienda after Mass."

Inéz exclaimed, "That's the most interesting news I've heard all morning! I'm very curious to hear what she has to say."

"I'll give you a full report."

All the talk among the town's leading citizens after Mass was about the two recent break-ins. "They can't catch this burglar soon enough for me," Regina Cabrera declared. "As long as he's at large, one is constantly worried about him striking again. And although I'm grateful to the governor for taking measures to protect us, it's a nuisance to have soldiers posted outside every door."

"I heard that a dog was involved again," Lucila Archuleta said, "this time in the break-in at Horatio Padilla's."

"They should round up all the black dogs and shoot them!" Victoria Peralta said.

"That's much too harsh," Elena replied. "Many people love their dogs!"

Don Carlos was sure that Victoria's retort—"Say what you will, but at times it's necessary to act decisively"—reflected her father's views.

Not wanting to hear any more talk about massacring black dogs, he stirred restlessly. Inéz took pity on him. "Let's excuse ourselves. I want to get home to see how luncheon preparations are going, and you mustn't linger here when you have an appointment." Ever the soul of discretion, she didn't mention who his appointment was with, a name that would definitely have become fodder for gossip and speculation.

Once they reached the kitchen door of the Beltrán house, he brushed Inéz's cheek with his and continued on up the hill to Doña Josefina's hacienda. Despite being a one-story structure, it was an imposing house, said to have eighteen rooms, larger by half than any other private residence except the Beltráns'. Though Carlos had lived in Santa Fe for more than two years, he had never before seen the Mendoza house at close range. Even last fall, when he could see from a distance that craftsmen were doing renovations to prepare the place for the Mendoza women's return, he had been too preoccupied with other concerns to visit the site.

A heavy-set man, one of the few black servants in town, answered his knock and showed him to a room off the front hallway. The Mendoza family's wealth was clearly in evidence. The walls were adorned with the kind of objects that would have been found in the homes of rich families in Mexico City but were rare in the remote frontier town of Santa Fe. Carlos's eye was caught by an oil painting of a falconer with five of his falcons. On the same wall was a small mirror in an elaborate carved polychrome frame, and on the opposite wall was a large rug in soft colors with an intricate floral and leaf pattern that Carlos felt certain was Persian.

He stood waiting for Doña Josefina. She entered the room quietly, the rustle of her silk dress the only sound that accompanied her approach, and held out her hand for Don Carlos to kiss, which he did with a bow. The dress she was wearing was similar to the one she'd worn when they'd met briefly at the governor's office—fine silk, all black, and in a style fashionable many decades earlier. To this she had added a dark red scarf, which reflected a touch of color onto her pale skin.

She sat down and gestured for him to sit in a chair a few feet opposite her. Without further preliminaries she said, "You're a strange one. In passing through El Paso del Norte, I learned from your stepbrother, the commandant of the local garrison, that you were the heir to the title of marquis, but that you transferred the title to a young nephew. And yesterday, according to what I heard, you were selling goods on the plaza like a common street merchant."

This was said as a statement, though it was clear that it contained implicit questions.

He replied carefully. "Shortly after I arrived in Santa Fe, I found that I was comfortable with a life in which wealth of a material sort is not necessary, and my father's title also seemed unnecessary to my happiness. However, I know that if I wished to return to my old life, my wealthy relatives and many friends among the social leaders in Mexico City would help me reassert my claims to a high status."

"Somehow," Doña Josefina observed drily, "I suspect you never will. I admire you for choosing to be an outsider. In some people that would be a sign of weakness. In you, I believe, it's a sign of strength. But that's not my main reason for inviting you here. I am worried about the youngest of my great-nephews."

"Is it because he is attracted to Elena Beltrán?"

"I would prefer that he was courting the daughter of family with a higher social status, but that's a minor issue. The problem is that I don't see what's to become of him. His brothers are socially adept members of their class, and already they are proud and masterful. They enjoy commanding servants and anticipate glory through military endeavors. Santiago is more… sensitive. He doesn't like to insist that servants show deference, and he's not inclined to pursue military adventures."

"Would it be so unfortunate," Don Carlos ventured, "supposing he and Elena developed a serious attachment—by no means a certainty, given that both of them are perhaps too young for such a thing—if he were to marry a merchant's daughter?"

"I don't find them so young, at least not Señorita Beltrán. I married when I was not yet sixteen, younger than she is."

"Let me approach the question of status. In Mexico City I had some friends whose fathers had both wealth and titles. Then there were those whose fathers were not wealthy, but had a title. And lastly, there were those who had no titles but were very wealthy."

Doña Josefina understood. "I see where you're headed," she said. "To have a title without wealth puts one in the position of always trading on the title for favors; a very wealthy person never needs to beggar himself in that way."

"Precisely. And while Javier Beltrán belongs to the merchant class, and lacks the social status of, say, the Peraltas, he owns the second-largest house in Santa Fe. I think a bigger obstacle than the Beltráns' status is that Elena is very headstrong. Santiago might not be comfortable with that."

"I," Doña Josefina said, "am very headstrong. That seemed to suit my husband fine." Don Carlos met her direct gaze. "It is a pity," she went on, "that you do not have a sister, Don Alfonso. She might be a suitable match for Santiago."

Carlos smiled. "I have two sisters," he said, "but alas, one is married and the other is in a convent."

Doña Josefina smiled in return. "Yes. Let us go on to another topic. These Franciscans, Father Dorantes and his fellow inquisitors, worry me. Those of us who went through the Pueblo Revolt know what terrible consequences can come of antagonizing our Pueblo Indian neighbors. I understand from my great-nephew Antonio, who was at the discussion of how to respond to the latest burglaries, that Father Dorantes proposed using force to search the homes of the Barrio de Analco's Indian and mestizo residents."

"Most unfortunate," Carlos said with some feeling.

"I am glad that we agree," Doña Josefina replied, "and I was pleased to hear from Antonio that even Major Cortés, who is usually in favor of applying the iron fist, didn't support Father Dorantes's proposal.

"Did you know," she continued, "that New Mexico's political leaders have not always been so narrow-minded? You're familiar, I trust, with the kachina figures in Pueblo Indian religious life, the deities who are represented in their rituals by masked dancers." Carlos nodded, and Doña Josefina went on. "Two governors in my time here in Santa Fe not only made no effort to repress kachina dances but actually encouraged them. In 1637, when my husband brought me and our infant son from Spain to Santa Fe, Governor Luis de Rosas invited Indians from nearby pueblos to perform their kachina dances on the plaza. And later, in 1659, Governor Bernardo López de Mendizábal showed his appreciation of Pueblo traditions by issuing a similar invitation to the men from Tesuque Pueblo."

"Wasn't Mendizábal charged with heretical views by the Franciscans of that time?"

"Yes, and by the Inquisition too. The Inquisition was a horror, searching for witches under every bush. I do my Catholic duty, but perhaps some of my thoughts are less than orthodox."

"As, I'm sure, are mine," Don Carlos said.

"There's another thing about Father Dorantes," Doña Josefina went on. "I suspect he doesn't understand that, in Santa Fe's history, ethnic boundaries have been less rigidly observed than farther south in New Spain. The presence of so many mestizos in Santa Fe offers clear evidence of intimate relations between Spaniards and Indians, and some of those mestizos have won respected positions. In 1680, the lieutenant governor of New Mexico was a mestizo named Alonso García. I knew him and his Indian mother and viewed him as worthy of the post."

"I'm certain I would have felt the same way," Don Carlos agreed. "But to get back to your original concern about Santiago, is there something I can do in regard to him?"

Doña Josefina nodded approvingly. "Ah, yes. Would you be willing to take Santiago in hand? Perhaps tutor him in fencing, take him for long rides in the country, and introduce him to some Native people, men and women, to help him better understand the Indians and their way of life? Whichever of my great-nephews inherits the Mendoza land grant, he will need Indians to work it, and he will need to know better than to treat them as slaves."

"I would enjoy spending time with Santiago," Don Carlos replied.

"Then we're done for today," Doña Josefina said, rising and again offering her hand for him to kiss. "At least you haven't abandoned your manners along with your title," she said half over her shoulder as she left the room.

Carlos went directly from the Mendoza place to the Beltrán house to give Inéz a report of his conversation with Doña Josefina. "What she told you," Inéz said, "about those governors in the past appreciating Pueblo culture is certainly new to me."

"Yes, to me too, and would be to most of our Spanish neighbors, I expect. People have vivid memories of the revolt and the reconquest, but not many are around who remember a happy episode in Spanish relations with Pueblo Indians from nearly fifty years ago. From what Doña Josefina told me, it seems that in the old days the lines between Indians and Spaniards were not always as sharply drawn as some of our prominent neighbors—I'm thinking of Pilar Peralta in particular—would like them to be now."

"That would seem to make you, because of your close relationship with José and Old Man Xenome, belong more to the old days."

"My bond with Native peoples is deeper than that. You'll recall that in all my previous lives as a brujo my parents were either Indian or mestizo. My soul is at least half Native."

Inéz gave him a serious look. "You've never put it quite that way before." She paused and continued, "We must do something about Doña Josefina's wish that you take Santiago under your wing. I suggest we begin this coming Wednesday. Instead of staying here to practice fencing, let's invite Elena and Santiago to join us for a picnic at our Sacred Pool." Carlos agreed, amazed, as he often was, by Inéz's way of focusing upon what needed to be done and suggesting a means of doing it.

On his way home from seeing Inéz, he reviewed what little he knew of the burglar he hoped to track down. He decided that the scarf she had left behind at the Padilla's might offer some clues to her identity. Accordingly, he stopped at the Padilla residence and found Ariel and her father having lunch. Recalling that Ariel hadn't told her father about finding the scarf, he was momentarily uncertain how to pursue the topic. Improvising, he said, "Ariel, it seems you have an admirer who has asked me to represent his interests, and he wished me to share this information with you alone. I hope," he added, turning to her father, "that you do not feel this offends your parental rights."

Horatio Padilla, a studious and good-natured man, raised his eyebrows, but he replied, "Ariel, you're excused from the table. Join Don Alfonso in the hallway, where he can share this secret."

Ariel stood up with a frown on her face and followed Carlos into the hallway. "If anyone should be offended, it's me," she declared. "What sort of coward is it who doesn't speak for himself?"

"I apologize for using the ruse of a secret admirer so that we could speak alone."

"So now," she told him, "you remove even the slim hope I had that there might be such a man, coward or not!"

"I believe I may say that Marco Cabrera has mentioned to me that he finds you both attractive and interesting. But the matter that requires privacy concerns the scarf the burglar left behind. Would you be willing to lend it to me for a few days?"

"You'll think me odd," Ariel said, "but I regard that scarf as a treasure—an irrational attachment on my part, I'm sure. If I lend it to you, will you return it soon unharmed?"

"I will make every effort to do so."

Ariel went off, he supposed to her bedroom, and returned with a neatly folded woolen scarf. She handed it to him, and he examined it closely. "The fabric seems old and its edges are ragged, but it's been carefully repaired. That seems to indicate that its owner values it."

"I came to the same conclusion," Ariel agreed.

"What puzzles me," Carlos continued, "is that you said it was a warm night. A wool scarf would be hot on a warm night."

"You're right. Why would she have been wearing it?"

"I don't know. But please let me take it for a day or two. Perhaps it will help guide me to its owner."

A look of concern came over Ariel's face. "Please promise me that you won't hurt her."

"My intentions are precisely the opposite," Carlos replied. "I hope to find her before the authorities do."

"Good, and if you can do it with sufficient subtlety, let Señor Cabrera know that he'd better speak for himself soon." She laughed. "But I don't mean that to sound like a threat. I rather like him."

Carlos's next stop was at Pedro's place. Not finding him at work outside, Carlos knocked at the kitchen door adjacent to the stable. Pedro answered the door and stood aside to let him enter. "How did selling the stones go?" he asked.

"I am richer by one chicken and the promise of a few eggs," Carlos said, and I acquired a few bits of information. I believe that whoever is stealing dinnerware from our wealthy neighbors and kisses from their daughters is a shape-shifter, changing from human to dog form as she leaves the scene of her crimes."

"She? Are you sure about that?" It was María's voice, and Carlos turned to see that María, quite advanced in pregnancy, had come into the room.

Handing her the thief's scarf, Carlos asked, "Does this look like a man's or a woman's piece of clothing?"

"Obviously, it's a woman's. Why do you ask?"

"Keep this to yourselves, because the authorities are unaware that the thief left it behind the night she broke into the Padilla house. Ariel Padilla found it but didn't tell anyone."

"Why not?" Pedro asked.

"Ariel doesn't want the thief caught. She believes the person is very poor and hasn't done much harm, despite all the uproar certain people are making about these break-ins."

"That's sweet of Ariel," María said. Carefully examining the scarf, she added, "This scarf has been lovingly mended. I agree with Ariel. I hope she's not caught."

"My feeling too," Carlos said. "If she's caught, her punishment will be greatly out of proportion to her crimes."

"What do you intend to do?" Pedro asked.

"Find her before the authorities do."

"You may not have much time," Pedro said. "The sexton who's making a list of people with black dogs in the Barrio de Analco came by today. He says the list is almost complete."

"I'm going to start my search tonight. It would helpful if you'd let me launch the search from your stable. If María will take care of this scarf until then, I'll be back after dark to set my plan in motion. I hope that's all right with you."

"Of course," María replied. "But you're being very mysterious. Please tell us more tonight."

"You will be privy to the whole adventure," he promised.

Don Carlos was restless, eager to put his plan into effect as soon as it was dark. While waiting during the afternoon, he fenced with Marco Cabrera at the old Tiburcio place. He didn't tell Marco everything he'd learned in his conversation with Ariel, saying only in an offhand way that Marco's name had come up during a visit to her home and that she had seemed interested in getting to know him better. Marco replied that he would like that very much.

After dinner with Orfeo, Don Carlos was cleaning up the kitchen when his three lodgers arrived for the night. "We spent another day riding all over the countryside," Gonzalo complained. "The only difference was that this time we visited pueblos south of Santa Fe. Father Dorantes urged the Indians to be good Catholics and Major Cortés told them he expected their cooperation in suppressing Native raiders. Both seemed to suggest that there would be consequences if their advice was not heeded."

"Cortés and Dorantes are peas in a pod," Luis declared. "Fear is their favorite method of getting what they want from the Indians."

Alejandro disagreed. "That's not so," he said. "Dorantes has friendly feelings toward Indians. The other day when we were guarding the Cabrera house, he came by with two Indians who live in Santa Fe, and he was laughing at a story one Indian was telling. Cortés is harsh with everyone, even his right-hand man, Sergeant Camacho."

Alejandro's statement launched a new debate among the three soldiers as to whether Cortés and Dorantes were more alike than different. Luis stuck by his guns and insisted that Cortés and the Franciscan were alike in both using fear to get what they wanted. Gonzalo granted that they both used fear, but he maintained that Father Dorantes's behavior was not always harsh.

Alejandro agreed, offering an observation that startled Don Carlos for its acuity. "Cortés," he said, "is mean through and through, but Dorantes has two sides to him. In his sermons he threatens us with Hell to get us to behave, but he has a soft side—like a good father, he's stern when that's needed but gentle and loving at heart."

The debate raged on until bedtime without being resolved, but Don Carlos kept thinking about Alejandro's insight about Father Dorantes. Now that Alejandro had mentioned it, Carlos could see that at different times Dorantes behaved in two distinctly different ways—sometimes as the threatening preacher, at other times the kindly father. Was one, Carlos wondered, true and the other an act?

Excusing himself and saying that he was going out, Don Carlos asked Orfeo to keep Gordo inside for the next two hours. "I don't want him following me around tonight," he said. "He'd be all too likely to interfere with my plans for the evening." Gordo looked very disappointed.

Don Carlos walked to Pedro and María's rooms next to the stable. He knocked, and being admitted, he told them what he intended to do and, more important, how he intended to do it. "María," he began, "you know that I am a brujo. What you may not know is that my greatest skill as a brujo is my proficiency at transformations. Tonight, in search of this thief who takes the form of a dog, I am going to transform myself into a dog and prowl about the streets of Santa Fe, especially the footpaths of the Barrio de Analco.

"I'm going next door into the stable to change to dog form. Once I'm a dog, I'd like you, María, to let me sniff that scarf the thief lost during her last break-in. I don't know what I'll discover, but smell has such importance in a dog's world that I think my nose will be more helpful than my eyes in my pursuit of the thief."

"Didn't you tell me," Pedro asked, "that when you changed into an animal, you were able to talk to other animals of the same kind?"

"Yes, although 'talk' is misleading. What I do is project my thoughts and receive the other animal's responses in the same way — in my head, rather than through my ears."

"So," Pedro said, "you're going to ask the dogs you meet if they know about this shape-shifter dog. Why don't you ask Gordo?"

"That's the strangest thing, Pedro. As long as I've lived with Gordo, who's certainly an intelligent dog, he's never spoken a word to me. I may find the same is true of all the dogs in Santa Fe. It's possible that town dogs lose the ability to communicate in the way that animals living in the wild do."

Don Carlos let himself out the door between the Gallegos's kitchen and the stable. He took off his clothes in order to avoid having them draped all over him after he'd taken animal form. Then he imagined the dog he wanted to become, a medium-sized black dog of the nondescript breed that was present in great numbers in Santa Fe. As always, he felt a momentary dizziness and disorientation caused by the sudden shift in his size.

He went to the kitchen door and scratched on it to be admitted. Pedro let him into the kitchen and teasingly reached down and patted him on the head. "Nice doggy," he said. Don Carlos growled softly to indicate that this wasn't play.

María placed the thief's scarf on the floor next to Don Carlos. He lowered his nose and inhaled deeply. Then he lay down and rubbed his head against the soft wool fabric. What happened as he did so was a complete surprise, something he had never before experienced in any of his previous lives as a brujo. An image of the person who had worn the scarf came to him, and the longer he rubbed his face against the scarf and inhaled the scent it gave off, the clearer the image became. He saw in his mind's eye a slender young mestizo woman of middling height. She had slightly rounded shoulders and small breasts, and her hair was straight and black. What stood out about her was that she had a crippled arm and scars on one side of her face.

He stood up, went to the door leading to the outside, and scratched at it. Pedro let him out. His first thought was "Now what?" He knew the thief was a young woman with a crippled arm; that should make her easy to spot. Yet he'd never seen her around town. How could that be?

Perhaps, he thought, some dogs could tell him of having seen a dog trotting along with an object in its mouth, and he headed off to the south, crossing the Santa Fe River and entering the Barrio de Analco. Finding dogs in this part of town was easy. They were everywhere. For the next two hours he sought out members of Santa Fe's canine community. They fell into two types—solitary wanderers, who seemed not to want to be disturbed as they went about their business, and small packs that were prowling around. He soon adapted himself to the usual etiquette of the canine world, which featured sniffing a newcomer's behind. This he found singularly unappealing, but it seemed to be obligatory; the first time he showed reluctance to participate in this ritual he was treated with great suspicion.

What was worse was that none of the dogs he met responded to his inquiries. Either they weren't creatures who could mentally communicate or they refused to do so. Since Don Carlos believed all animals had at least some degree of this ability, he decided that life in a town had dulled them. He could understand if that was the case, because something of the same sort had happened to him many times. When he spent long periods in town he began to lose his brujo powers, and he had to renew them by going out into the high desert and mountain wilderness surrounding Santa Fe.

At no time did he smell any scents that had been associated with the thief's shawl. Discouraged, he started back toward Pedro's place. As he passed a long line of small houses along the south side of the Santa Fe River, he heard a gruff voice. "I hope you're not going to the plaza or beyond," the voice said. "Soldiers from the Presidio who would like nothing better than to shoot a black dog are all over the place."

The speaker turned out to be an elderly male dog named Rufino, whose red coat and snout were flecked with gray. "You're new in town. What are you up to?" Rufino asked.

"I'm trying to locate a thief who's a shape-shifter. She robs the homes of wealthy people across the river and then, as she escapes, she changes herself into a medium-sized black dog."

"What do you stand to gain if you catch her?" Rufino inquired.

Don Carlos, surprised at having his motives questioned, said, "Well, nothing, really, but I'm a shape-shifter myself, and I'd hate to see another shape-shifter get hurt. Besides, she hasn't done that much harm, and she doesn't deserve having the whole Presidio garrison out to get her."

Rufino was silent for so long that Don Carlos began to believe he might not say anything more. Finally he replied. "I can't tell you much about the black dog shape-shifter, except that she passed me twice with something in her mouth. I could have spoken to her, but I didn't think it was any of my business."

"Which direction was she headed?" Don Carlos asked.

"South on the Pecos Road toward the irrigation ditch."

Don Carlos hadn't gone that far south in his search. Damn! He'd been looking in the wrong place, too close to the Santa Fe River. He wanted to continue searching, but the first hint of dawn was showing in the east. He didn't want to be caught prowling around in broad daylight. Thanking Rufino for his help, he crossed the river near Pedro's stable. He heard the sound of boots, and then saw two soldiers coming along a path from his left. Both had muskets, and both had the unsteady walk of drunks.

"There's a black dog!" one of the soldiers cried, pointing at him. "Shoot it!"

Both soldiers raised their muskets to fire, and Don Carlos in dog form broke into a run. Though Pedro's stable was closer, he didn't want to lead the soldiers to it, so he headed for his own house, straight ahead and only a hundred yards away. Before he could reach it, he heard two musket shots, and one musket ball grazed his right hind leg.

Now the two soldiers were running after him. He had a good lead on them, so he ran past the front of his house, turned right on the side facing the plaza, turned right again down the path on the kitchen side, and ducked through Gordo's doggy door, startling Gordo out of his wits. For several minutes Carlos lay panting on the floor before changing back into human form. Gordo, who'd never seen Don Carlos make a transformation, wasn't immediately reassured.

Apologizing to Gordo for giving him such a scare, Don Carlos moved into his bedroom, put on his nightclothes, and climbed into bed. Apparently other soldiers who had been in the area soon joined the two who had chased him, and for the next half hour he heard soldiers in the streets on all sides of his house, calling out to each other, "Keep an eye out for a black dog." These noises woke his three resident soldiers and Orfeo, who was sleeping in the hayloft. Finally one of his housemates—it sounded like Gonzalo—got up and shouted at the soldiers who were prowling around outside. "The only dog here," he told them irritably, "is a white dog with a black spot around one eye. Shut up and go away!" They left soon thereafter. At last Carlos was able to roll over and go to sleep.

10

Dolores

Not having gotten to bed until dawn after his excursion to the Barrio de Analco, Carlos slept late on Monday morning. He was awakened by sounds from the kitchen. Shrugging on a shirt, he went barefoot to the door to the kitchen and found Pedro standing by himself next to the hearth. "I gather you spent the night running around as a dog," Pedro said.

"That's about right," Carlos replied.

Pedro had more to say. "María and I were worried. When I went to feed the horses this morning, I found your clothes. I came over here and Orfeo told me you got in at dawn."

"That's also correct."

"You, or rather the dog you, are the talk of the town this morning."

"What's being said?"

"Why don't you start by telling me what happened?"

"I was returning from the Barrio de Analco. As I crossed the river near your stable, two drunken soldiers came down the path on my left. I took off at a run, and they both fired their muskets at me. I ran all the way up here, going around the front of the house to the plaza side and then down the path to the kitchen door, where I dived in through Gordo's doggy door. They couldn't have seen me do that. Soldiers searched all the streets and alleys around the house until Gonzalo got up and chased them off. That's about it."

"You're not leaving anything out?" Pedro asked skeptically.

"Only that one of the musket balls grazed my leg." Carlos pulled his pants leg up and he and Pedro examined the injury, a red welt beaded with blood. It had scarcely bled at all.

"You'll live," Pedro said.

"That's a relief," Carlos replied. "What have you heard about the incident?"

"Oh, a more dramatic story. The two soldiers said they'd been at a friend's house. They were heading back to the barracks when they saw a black dog that didn't look like an ordinary dog. They both fired at the dog, and they swear their musket balls went right through its body. It started to run, and they gave chase. It dashed up the path past your house and into the plaza, where it vanished into thin air."

"I guess that's not bad. I got away, and they can't figure out how."

"Or not so good. Now some people are saying it's witchcraft. So Governor Peralta, Vice Governor Cabrera, Major Cortés, and the two priests, Father Benedicto and Father Dorantes, are having a meeting. It's supposed to be a secret, but everyone knows about it."

"Everyone?"

"Sure. The governor and vice governor and the rest don't think their servants have ears. They talk business while the servants serve them breakfast. So everyone knows about this secret meeting. And it won't be long before we'll hear what happened at it."

The kitchen door opened and Inéz let herself in. She gave Carlos a searching look and said, "According to María, you spent the night prowling around after changing yourself into a dog. Now I heard that two soldiers fired their muskets at a dog, which somehow managed to run off. Was that dog you?"

"I confess it was," Carlos replied.

"Save your confessions for Father Benedicto. The story is that the musket balls passed through the dog's body. Was that some sorcery on your part?"

"No. One of the musket balls missed altogether; the other grazed my hind leg." He pulled up his pants leg to show her the wound. "As you can see, it's not much more than a scratch."

Inéz put her hands on her hips and glared at him. "I hope you learned something useful on this little misadventure of yours."

"I learned a few things, mainly that searching in the thickly settled part of the Barrio de Analco along the river is not going to pay off. I think the thief has a lair farther south, possibly near the south irrigation ditch."

"The *Acequia Madre*? There aren't many houses near it."

"That assumes that the thief lives in a house. She may have some other sort of hiding place."

"Hiding place? What sort—?" Inéz gave him a questioning look. "You must have something in mind," she said sharply.

"I want to walk the banks of the *Acequia Madre* to see if I can spot anything."

"That's not a great idea. You'll be very conspicuous," Inéz said. "People will wonder what a *hidalgo* is doing wandering around in that part of town."

"Perhaps I can ask the Town Council to commission me to inspect the banks of the *Acequia Madre*. It's not been done yet this spring, and I'm sure they'll be glad to appoint me to do a chore, and do it for free, that even the men hired to repair the *acequias* don't want to do."

"Maybe you should have them appoint me to assist you," Pedro suggested. "My presence will satisfy anyone who's curious. A *hidalgo* like you can't be expected to crawl around the banks getting his fine clothes dirty. That's a job for the likes of me, or Orfeo."

"Do you have time to help me?"

Before Pedro could answer, Inéz spoke up. "Pedro, please do it. You can keep Carlos from doing something stupid."

Carlos was affronted by Inéz's choice of words. "Me, do something stupid?"

"Yes, your running around last night as a black dog was stupid. You should have changed yourself into a big white dog or a little brown one, any sort of dog other than the kind that everyone is looking for."

He sighed. "I guess you're right. That wasn't very smart."

Carlos's admission led Inéz to adopt a softer tone. Leaning over and giving him a kiss on the cheek, she said, "I couldn't stand it if anything truly bad happened to you. Please be more careful."

Don Carlos and Pedro went in search of Horatio Padilla, who was the head of the four-man Town Council, and found him at work at the town's offices in the Palace of the Governors. Don Carlos did not bother with preliminaries. "I can tell you're busy with important matters," he said. "I hope you can take quick action on a request of mine."

"I'm always glad to be of service to one of Santa Fe's leading citizens," Padilla replied.

"It's come to my attention that the *Acequia Madre* may require repairs after a long winter. If you will authorize me to do so, with the assistance of my friend Pedro Gallegos, I will undertake to inspect the *acequia* from the point at which it separates from the Santa Fe River to the place at which it rejoins it. If we find any breaches in the ditch's walls, we will report them. I am, of course, willing to make the inspection free of charge as a service to the town."

Don Carlos could tell that his promise to make the inspection free of charge ensured the success of his appeal. Padilla took out a piece of paper that was embossed with the town's seal and wrote a brief note authorizing Carlos to inspect the *acequia*.

With the authorization in hand, Don Carlos and Pedro walked across the plaza and south to the Pecos Road, which they followed until it reached the south irrigation ditch. "Which way should we go first, east or west?" Carlos asked.

"There are almost no houses near the ditch west of the Pecos Road," Pedro said. "If I wanted to hide, I would find a place like that, isolated from houses."

Don Carlos went along with Pedro's suggestion. For the next two hours they walked slowly beside the irrigation ditch, giving careful attention to its banks. Two property owners noticed them, and Don Carlos stopped to tell them what he and Pedro were doing and to show them the authorization they had received from the head of the Town Council. The men recognized the official seal on it and didn't question Don Carlos's authority.

Carlos and Pedro found nothing that might suggest a thief's hideout along the *acequia* west of the Pecos Road, though they did find one spot in which the ditch's banks had partly collapsed, and they recorded that location to report to the Town Council. Retracing their steps to the Pecos Road, they stopped. The noon hour had long since passed, and neither of them had eaten since breakfast. "Let's go home," Carlos suggested, "you to yours and me to mine, and have something to eat. You may also have some chores to do around the stable. I'll send Orfeo over to help. We can come back here around four o'clock and finish our inspection before sundown." Pedro agreed and they headed off to their respective homes.

Carlos had been home only long enough to send Orfeo to Pedro's and to have a light meal when he heard a knock at the seldom-used front door. He went down the hallway, opened the door, and found a mestizo man standing there. The man said, "I work for the members of the Holy Office. Brother Gustavo told me to ask you to come to the priests' rooms to speak with him. He asks that you do this as soon as possible."

Don Carlos considered Gustavo's invitation a nuisance, but he thought it best to respond to it at once. "Would he be able to see me immediately?" he asked. "I have a little time right now."

The manservant indicated that now would be good, and the two of them headed off across the plaza to the rear of the chapel where resident priests and brothers were housed. Just inside the door to the priest's quarters was a room where visitors could be greeted without intruding on the privacy of the residents. Brother Gustavo was in the room reading a book, the title of which Don Carlos couldn't see. With greater politeness than he had displayed during their exchange on market day, Brother Gustavo stood up and greeted Don Carlos. "How good of you to come so promptly, Don Alfonso. I hope I am not interrupting your day's business."

"No. This is a convenient time. I was helping an old friend complete a job we'd agreed to do for the Town Council, but we were taking the mid-afternoon hours off and planning to resume our task later in the day."

"I will not require much of your time, Don Alfonso. I have been thinking about your comment on market day that there are no secrets in a town of this size. As you know, the mission of the Holy Office is to seek out cases of hidden Jews, blasphemers, practitioners of black magic, and the like. I wondered whether you had any particular secrets in mind when you said what you did."

"No, I didn't have specific secrets in mind. I was merely making a general observation that in a town this size, news spreads like wildfire. For example, even before today's supposedly secret meeting of the town's leaders took place, word was circulating that it was being held."

"Yes, I see. But I am asking if you know of any individuals the tribunal should question?"

Carlos was aware that the Inquisition was particularly interested in *Conversos*, Jews (and their descendants) who had been forced to accept Catholicism to avoid being driven out of Spain. A person from that background who was said to be observing Jewish customs, such as lighting candles on the Sabbath or bathing on Friday afternoon in preparation for the Sabbath, was apt to be investigated for continuing to follow Jewish practices.

With this in mind, and wanting to appear helpful, Carlos said to Gustavo, "A year ago I would have directed your attention to an old woman who lived south of the river. Her name was Rosario Serra. She raised chickens and sold eggs for a living. I often bought eggs from her. One evening late last fall, when I found I needed eggs for the morning and none of my servants was home, I went to Rosario's place. While she was getting the eggs for me, I looked around the room and noticed a picture that was turned face to the wall. I asked her about it, and she said it was a picture of the Savior, and that on Friday evenings she turned it to face the wall in honor of a grandmother who had always done the same. Whether she was observing a Jewish practice or only honoring the memory of her grandmother, I couldn't say. But Rosario died about six months ago."

"What about living individuals who might fall into categories of interest to the Holy Office?" Gustavo asked. "There's the case of the man who called himself Leandro the Magician."

"He, like Rosario, is dead. Many people, including myself, found him charming and were shocked that he turned out to be a kidnapper and a murderer. He was not a practicing Catholic, but I'm unaware of his having done anything blasphemous. It's possible that his magic had some element of sorcery mixed into it, but I don't know enough about the subject to say if that means he had traffic with demons."

"What about his two women associates?"

"Mara Mata and Selena Torrez?" Don Carlos felt the conversation had reached dangerous ground, since the two dancers still lived in Santa Fe. He kept his answer brief and framed it with great care. "They were not charged with any crime or even accused of culpability by the panel that investigated the kidnapping-murder case. Like Leandro, they were not practicing Catholics, but they did not display any disrespect toward the True Faith. I would never have thought to bring them to your attention."

"Were they, are they, immoral women?" Brother Gustavo asked.

"You mean were they prostitutes?"

Gustavo nodded.

"Not to my knowledge. Their house was near mine, and I never observed any indication that assignations took place there."

Brother Gustavo seemed about to pursue the topic further, but he checked himself and said, "I have one more question then. What do you know about a man named José Lugo?"

"José and I have had a long association that dates back to a time when I saved him from being hanged for a murder he had not committed."

"Is it true that he is studying to be a medicine man? That's been reported to me."

"That's true. Like many full-blooded Pueblo Indians, he has been baptized and has taken a Christian name. He attends Mass with some regularity, but he also retains an attachment to the traditions of his Native heritage."

"I realize that as an Indian he is outside the jurisdiction of the Holy Office," Brother Gustavo said. "But I find it distressing that a baptized Catholic

Indian persists in his attachment to pagan beliefs. What is your opinion on this matter?"

"Brother Gustavo, I am a Catholic layman, not a theologian, but I know that after the reconquest of New Mexico, the Spanish authorities tried to avoid antagonizing our Indian neighbors and made no attempt to eliminate their spiritual practices. Personally, I am ignorant as to what José's studies to become a medicine man entail, because those studies are esoteric in nature, not to be discussed with a non-Indian such as myself."

"I'm told that you've often accompanied Lugo on his visits to Tesuque Pueblo."

Carlos's mind came to an abrupt standstill. So Gustavo has been inquiring about me, he thought, recognizing that there had been a subtle shift away from the matter of what information he might provide about others to what he might reveal about himself. Carefully, without changing the manner in which he had answered Gustavo's previous questions, Carlos replied, "Yes, I have accompanied José on several of his visits to Tesuque Pueblo. I have done so in part because I enjoy taking long rides into the countryside surrounding Santa Fe, but also because I view myself as José's protector. Since he cannot under Spanish law carry firearms, I go with him to help defend him in case he's attacked by Native raiders, a possibility that's not theoretical. He and I were threatened with attack by a small Indian war party about two hours' ride from Santa Fe only a few weeks ago."

"I heard about that," Gustavo replied. "You were fortunate to escape unharmed."

Seeing a chance to take control of the conversation, Carlos changed its direction. "May I perhaps express some of my concerns?" he said in a more forceful tone, and went on without waiting for an answer. "Recently Santa Fe has experienced major changes, beginning with the arrival of a new vice governor and more than two hundred new settlers three months ago. Even more recently, the arrival of a contingent of forty soldiers nearly doubled the size of the Presidio garrison. We were told it was for our protection against hostile Indians, although in my observation the occasional Indian raids at some distance from Santa Fe have not been as disruptive to normal life as the presence of the soldiers and the quartering of some of them in people's homes.

"Then there was the matter of a thief who repeatedly broke into the houses of the wealthy while they slept and pilfered a few items, resulting—for protection, again—in soldiers being stationed around the homes of the town's wealthier citizens.

108 ———————

"Finally, there is the Holy Office's proclamation of a forty-day period of grace, which is presented as a time of safety in which heretical thoughts and actions, or even using spells and incantations for benign purposes, can be confessed and repented, and one will suffer only an ordinary penance. This was offered as yet another form of protection, this one against a threat to every *soul* in Santa Fe. But people are worried about being unjustly accused of wrongdoing, and about what might happen to them if they are accused. Frankly," he went on, his exasperation at the situation getting the better of him, "I believe that subjecting Santa Fe to an inquisition, far from having a positive effect, is making our whole town unwell."

Brother Gustavo stared at him for a long moment as if disbelieving what he had just heard. Then he exploded. "If the threat of exposing witchcraft and heresy makes Santa Fe unwell," he shouted, "then it is indeed in need of purgation by the Inquisition!" He stood up and began to pace around in the small room. Don Carlos, fearing he had gone too far, watched him closely. The sheet-lightning flashes in Gustavo's aura were shooting through it rapidly.

"I can see that you need to understand the absolute necessity of bringing what is hidden and what is evil into the light of day," Gustavo said angrily. He continued pacing, the muscles of his face moving as if he was in inner debate with himself. Finally he spoke. "Ordinarily I would not bring up my own experience in this matter," he said, "but in this instance it is appropriate." He lowered his voice. "I speak in the utmost confidence, of course," he added.

He stopped pacing and sat down. He directed his words to Carlos but he was not looking at him. "In my youth," he said, "shortly before I joined the Franciscan Order, I was possessed by a demon. It was a female demon who came to me in the night and lay with me, and it mixed its being with mine." He paused, as if at a repellent memory, and then went on quickly. "I cannot tell you what an unspeakable horror this was. I tried to run from it. I fled to Mexico City and became a Franciscan, hoping a life of prayer and sacrifice would end this possession. It was to no avail."

He paused again, and Don Carlos saw that the sheet-lightning bursts in his aura were quieting down. "I suffered in silence for a long time, knowing that I was damned even though I was an obedient son of the Church. Finally I found the courage to confess these assaults to my superior, Father Aurelio Abascal, the head of the Holy Office in New Spain. He performed an exorcism—a very powerful exorcism—and the demon left me. I emerged from my ordeal strengthened. If I had been a mere foot soldier in the army of the Church before, now I became a warrior against the power of evil, aflame to purify all the souls I encountered. My fervent desire is to flush out men's hidden sins, to purify them, to burn away their attachment to false beliefs and magical practices, and to bring them to recognize and repudiate the demons that dwell within them. Though Father Dorantes is my superior here, he is by nature an administrator. In regard to the real work of the Holy Inquisition, I am its flaming heart!"

Now Brother Gustavo fixed his eyes on Carlos. "Despite your present inability to recognize the terrible dangers the Inquisition is here to combat, I would like you on my side in this endeavor, because I see that there is fire in you also, and because your concern for the well-being of your community parallels mine. Although you are young, you have held an official position in the office of the governor, and you have the bearing of a man accustomed to leadership. Working together, we can accomplish great things! But if you see the Inquisition as your enemy and try to subvert it, the illness from which Santa Fe is suffering will be made worse."

Don Carlos held Gustavo's gaze briefly and then looked away. "I fear," he said, "you overestimate my influence in Santa Fe. I no longer serve as the governor's secretary, and the humble house that I occupy—I'm assuming you've seen it—does not suggest a high social position."

"Nevertheless," Gustavo insisted, "many people with whom I've spoken indicate that they have great respect for you."

Don Carlos was silent for several moments. "Thank you for your generous praise," he said at last. "And for your frankness. I may say that I had suspected that you, more than Father Dorantes, were the heart, as you say, of the Inquisition here. And it is true that we both feel the distress in the town, and we both wish to heal it. I confess I have no real method, whereas you do. All I can do is try to alleviate disturbances or solve problems where they occur. But, as you said, I am hopeful that our efforts are not, and will not be, at cross purposes."

"Then I can count on your cooperation?" Brother Gustavo asked. There was only one possible answer to this, and Don Carlos agreed.

Carlos suddenly felt tired, almost deflated, as if his will had been sapped. "You must excuse me, Brother Gustavo," he said. "Although our conversation has been very informative, I realize that time has passed and I must leave for my appointment." And, indeed, when Carlos stepped out into the street, he saw by the light that it was late afternoon. He forced himself through his fatigue to walk quickly toward the river. By the time he had reached Pedro's stable, his mind had cleared and he felt nearly his old self again.

Pedro joined Don Carlos, and together they crossed the river and walked south to the *Acequia Madre*. They decided to follow the irrigation ditch east to where it joined the river.

Neither bank of the *Acequia Madre* was more than two feet high. Pedro and Don Carlos soon concluded that the thief's hideout couldn't be on the irrigation ditch. When they reached the beginning of the *acequia* at the Santa Fe River, they scrambled across on stones that were barely submerged. On the north bank of the river they stood and consulted. "Perhaps we're on the wrong track altogether," Pedro said.

Don Carlos wasn't quite ready to give up. "What about that thick patch of brushy shrubs and cottonwood trees up ahead?"

"I suppose something could be hidden in there," Pedro replied. "Those chamisa bushes are almost six feet tall and the underbrush is dense."

Carlos and Pedro approached the tall chamisa bushes and walked along their edge. Pedro stopped and pointed to a place where a small opening in the brush was visible. "That opening," Pedro said, "is so low and narrow that no person could squeeze through."

"But a dog could," Don Carlos said thoughtfully. "Pedro," he continued, "maybe this is the entrance to a path that leads to a hidden retreat. I'm going to stay here, hide, and keep watch. I may be here half the night, and if you stay, María will worry. Go home. I'll report to you later."

Pedro agreed and retraced his steps back along the *acequia*. Don Carlos found a place among some boulders where he hoped he wouldn't be noticed if the thief in dog form emerged from the thicket.

Not long after nightfall Don Carlos saw a black dog scrabble out of the opening in the brush. It was carrying a cloth bag in its mouth. Without looking around the dog trotted off toward town. Don Carlos made no attempt to stop her. After twenty minutes had passed and the dog hadn't returned, Don Carlos took off his boots and clothes, changed himself into a medium-sized dog, and wiggled into the narrow, low tunnel through the brush. About fifty feet later, the tunnel ended and he came to an open space. He saw the thief's hideaway ahead.

At some point in the past, a one-room hut with adobe walls had stood in the open area. One wall had long ago collapsed, and one end of the roof had fallen in with it, leaving a structure that resembled a lean-to. Don Carlos in dog form peered through the low doorway into the darkness inside. Using his brujo vision, he could see a hearth on the intact wall of the hut. An iron pot and ashes and stubs of wood in the hearth indicated that it had been used. And there on the floor, next to a thin sleeping mat and some blankets, was a sight that revealed the motive behind the thief's crimes. Carlos's heart went out to her, and he resolved more firmly than ever to protect her from the authorities. He backed out, returned to the tunnel, and made several trips dragging his boots and clothes back to the lean-to. There he changed to human form, dressed, and waited.

Hours passed. He dozed a bit and awoke refreshed. He realized that he had been waiting all night. At dawn he finally heard a noise in the brush outside the lean-to. He pressed himself into a corner to the left of the entrance and hoped that she would be completely inside before she sensed his presence.

A sack of what seemed to be vegetables and meat scraps was thrust into the lean-to by unseen hands. Good, he thought, the odor would disguise his man smell. The girl, or perhaps she was a very young woman, ducked sideways through the low doorway with her back turned to him. Once she was inside, he moved swiftly to block the exit.

She cried in terror and cringed against the adobe wall that was farthest from him. "Can we talk?" he said.

In the dim light of early dawn, he could see that she was wearing what appeared to be a dress of some soft, dark material. She seemed to be groping for something to use as a weapon.

"Don't fight me!" he commanded her. "I'm stronger and have more powers than you can imagine."

"How did you get in here?" she asked.

"I changed myself into a dog to get through the thicket," he said, trusting that the truth of his words would be both evident and shocking enough to eliminate any further defensive sparring on her part. He was taking a risk, he knew; but such was his sympathy for her that he was moved to reveal himself as a shape-shifter. "We are two of a kind," he said. "I can also change myself into a cougar or a coyote, but I'm not going to do any of those things. I'm here to help you."

"I'll bet there's a reward you hope to collect for catching me."

"I don't want money."

A long silence followed. Finally she spoke. "Then what do you want?"

"First, sit back and face me with your hands in your lap the same way I'm holding mine." Once she'd done so, he said, "Let me introduce myself. I am known to most people in Santa Fe as Don Alfonso Cabeza de Vaca, but I am also a brujo with a secret name, Carlos Buenaventura. I am taking a risk in revealing my secret to you. I hope you'll reciprocate by keeping my name a secret and telling me yours."

There was long silence. "My name is Dolores," she said at last.

"Ah, yes, which means sorrows. Please tell me how you came to be a shape-shifter. Does it have something to do with your name?"

"No!" she exclaimed.

"If you want," Don Carlos replied. "I will go first and tell you how I became skilled at transformations. Long ago I trained with a master sorcerer, Don Serafino Romero. After many fruitless attempts, I finally learned to change myself into birds of prey, mainly hawks and owls. Did you have a teacher?"

"Not a person."

"How then?"

"I'm not ready to tell you."

"I have some idea why you stole these objects," he said, gesturing to a corner of the lean-to where, spread out on a linen napkin, there was a place setting made up of the items—a plate, a soup bowl, a goblet, and four pieces of silverware—that she had taken from rich people's houses. "All you lack is a cup and saucer. I suppose you were going to acquire them eventually."

"You know nothing of my reasons," she snapped.

"You took those things because you desire to have beauty in your life."

Dolores responded by putting her hands to her face and silently sobbing, her body racked by the effort not to cry. She rocked back and forth and asked in a muffled voice, "How did you know?"

"You have made a small corner of your home into a beautiful place, taking a few fine, expensive items from the houses of people who have a surplus of such material things. That tells me that your soul hungers for beauty."

She dropped her hands from her face and said contemptuously, "I live by stealing. Food, clothing, everything!"

"If you let me, I can do better by you."

"Don't torment me with lies and false promises!" she said angrily.

"As a shape-shifter you have a rare talent. I also sense that you have a yearning for love, which you expressed when you tenderly kissed those rich young women."

He felt her mood soften a little. "What do you want? What are you going to do with me?"

"If you will return the items you stole, I will see that you are safe."

"How can I return anything without being caught? Soldiers are guarding all the houses these things came from."

"I'm confident you can do it with my help," he said, and he went on to tell her his plan.

"It might work," she said. "But it would mean I would have to show my face in daylight without the scarf I use to cover it. I'm not like you. You are a *hidalgo*, and you're a handsome man. I'm not only poor, but I'm ugly. 'Uglier than a dog,' they used to tell me, until I believed it so deeply that I found that I'd become one. Eventually, I learned how to change back into a girl and then return to being a dog when that was to my advantage. My mother was an Indian, and she knew, and she kept my secret. But after my mother died, my father, who was a mestizo, found out what I could do and became frightened. In February, when I had just turned fifteen, he took me to the outskirts of Santa Fe and abandoned me. All he left me was one change of clothing and a blanket. I've lived on my own ever since."

"Ah!" said Don Carlos, understanding how deep pain and distress of soul had been her teacher in the technique of transformations. "As a brujo," he told her, "I can see very well in this dim light. Yes, you have a crippled arm and one eye that doesn't open fully, and some scars. But what you are inside is more important than external appearances, and you mustn't give up on that. I have friends who will aid us."

Sometimes Don Carlos's plans went better than at other times. This morning everything went precisely as he'd hoped. He and Dolores carefully wrapped the items she'd stolen in a thin blanket. With a little help from Dolores, he made it out of her lean-to and through the narrow tunnel in the chamisa bushes. He put his arm around her, hiding her crippled arm against his side. Together they walked down a rarely used path and hurried along the river to Pedro's stable. María answered the door, and with an intuition born of her warm spirit, she immediately understood who Dolores was and welcomed her.

Pedro came in from the stable, and Don Carlos gave him and María a brief description of his plan. María went to find clothing for Dolores that would make her appear to be an old woman, and gave her a long scarf to cover her head and the scarred side of her face. Once Dolores was dressed in her disguise all four of them walked to the northwest edge of the plaza. Although it was not a Saturday market day and still early in the morning, a few tradespeople and farmers were setting out wares they hoped to sell. Down the street to the west, three very sleepy soldiers, who had probably been on duty since midnight, stood guard outside the Presidio's gates.

María spread out a blanket in front of the Palace of the Governors near the chapel. Dolores, keeping her head tucked down and her face hidden as much as possible, tried to help. They set out a few trade goods on the blanket and settled down as if to wait for customers. Pedro took a position in the street at the far corner of the Palace of the Governors, midway between their blanket and the soldiers who were on guard duty.

Don Carlos slipped into the entryway of the building diagonally across the street from where Pedro was standing and, making certain that no one could see him, took off his clothes and changed himself into a black dog.

As a black dog he then stepped out into the street and barked loudly at the soldiers, who were a good hundred feet farther to the west. Before they were able to react, he turned and charged along the western edge of the plaza. "He went that way!" Pedro shouted to the soldiers, waving excitedly and pointing in the direction of the building's southern corner, around which Don Carlos, the black dog, had disappeared. "Quick! He'll get away!" Pedro cried.

The soldiers ran after the dog. The few people who were on the plaza turned to watch the unfolding drama, but all they saw was an ordinary black dog being pursued around the building by three soldiers.

With everyone's attention focused on the soldiers chasing the dog, María and Dolores stood up and entered the chapel carrying two bags. Pedro meanwhile strolled casually down the street toward the chapel. A moment later a black dog came charging past the Presidio, turned the corner, and ducked into the entryway of the building where Don Carlos had left his clothes — only to emerge soon thereafter, fully dressed, as Don Alfonso Cabeza de Vaca, a local real estate investor and a respected *hidalgo*.

The soldiers, panting from their exertions, reached the spot where Don Carlos had joined Pedro. "That damn dog got away!" Pedro told them. "The last we saw he was running that way." He pointed to the street that led north from the plaza. "You'll never catch him now. He probably wasn't the one everyone's hunting anyway."

As Pedro was talking with the soldiers, María and Dolores came out of the chapel, looking for all the world like two devout women who'd been to the chapel to pray.

Several hours later Inéz knocked on the kitchen door of Pedro and

María's apartment. Pedro got up to let her in and invited her over to the table where Don Carlos was drinking coffee with María and Dolores. "Alfonso," she said excitedly, "I went to your house to tell you about an amazing thing that happened today. Orfeo said I would find you here."

"I'm just having a cup of coffee with two old friends and a new one whose name is Dolores," Carlos replied. "Pull up a chair, have some coffee, and tell us the news."

Inéz greeted Dolores politely and sat down. Then she launched into her story. "This morning Father Benedicto went into the chapel to see that everything was in order. As he approached the front of the chapel, he saw that all the items that had been stolen recently were set out on the altar as though for a meal. Everything was there! No one has any idea how it all got there."

"I wouldn't say that no one knows," Pedro said.

Inéz eyed the four conspirators and demanded an explanation, which they gave her in great detail. "But now," she asked when they were finished, "what's to become of Dolores?"

María answered her question. "I will need help after the baby is born if I want to keep working for Señora Trigales. Pedro and I had talked about this, but we couldn't afford to hire a servant. So we've asked Dolores to stay with us. She can sleep in the extra room and help with the baby."

Dolores raised her hand, the one that wasn't deformed, and said, "I want to thank all of you. I can't believe my good luck. But it's only fair to warn you that I'll probably be a lot of trouble."

"Not at all," María said. "You'll be a help to me."

"That's not what I meant," Dolores replied. "It's just that I may find it difficult to get over my habit of stealing things, and that could cause you a lot of trouble."

"Not if we keep busy returning them," Carlos declared.

"Won't that be trouble enough?" Dolores asked, and everyone broke out into laughter.

Pedro, ever the voice of realism, spoke up. "I can tell that my old boss thinks that returning the stolen items will bring peace back to Santa Fe. Somehow I doubt that will be the case."

11

Witchcraft

*P*edro was right. The return of the stolen items didn't make things better. Father Dorantes, in particular, wasn't content to let matters rest. "The thief wasn't caught," he argued to a meeting of town officials. "What's more, a number of things suggest that witchcraft is being practiced in Santa Fe—the sightings of a human burglar who seems to disappear and be replaced by a black dog, a black dog that musket shots can't harm, and a black dog running away from the vicinity of the chapel where the stolen goods are mysteriously returned. We need to find out who's responsible for this." Father Dorantes's words were picked up and went into circulation in town. These murmurings of witchcraft increased the unease that had settled over the town since the deployment of troops outside the houses of the wealthy residents.

To make matters worse, the night after the items had been returned, a dreadful event occurred in the Barrio de Analco. About midnight an Indian family was awakened by agonized cries made by the family's dog. The father rushed outside with a heavy staff to see what was going on and found his dog lying dead a few feet from his doorstep. He looked down the path to the south and saw what he believed to be a very large wolf trotting away.

Carlos heard these details and more the next morning from Pedro, who knew many people in the Barrio de Analco. "First thing this morning," Pedro said, "Sancho Ibarra told me that he had seen a large wolf in the Barrio. He said his best friend, Lorenzo Simito, heard what sounded like a dogfight, went outside, and saw the wolf kill a neighbor's dog. The wolf broke the dog's back, snarled at Lorenzo, and then turned around and went off in an unhurried way."

Carlos believed he knew what had happened. "How many dogs in all were killed?"

"Three that I know of."

"Were they all black dogs?"

"Yes, and they all belonged to Indian families. No mestizo's dog was killed, not even when their families lived right next door to Indians who lost dogs."

"One last question, Pedro. Did Father Dorantes start visiting Indian families with black dogs yesterday, using the list the sexton compiled?"

"Yes, and all the families whose dogs were killed were visited by Dorantes, Father Benedicto, and another Franciscan named Brother Gustavo."

This seemed to confirm what Don Carlos suspected. The wolf in question was, he believed, a normal wolf that Brother Gustavo had taken possession of through sorcery. Using the wolf as a weapon, he had killed dogs belonging to Indian families. His motives were less clear. Was he simply trying to stir things up, or was he perhaps trying to flush a brujo named Carlos Buenaventura out of hiding?

"How are Barrio residents reacting?" he asked Pedro.

"The Indian families are very alarmed. They believe in witches, and they feel powerless because they can't own firearms. The last I heard they'd formed a group to speak to the head of the Town Council. They want either to be allowed to arm themselves or to have some of their mestizo neighbors patrol the Barrio. At the very least, they're not going to let their dogs out at night."

"I doubt that any of the authorities will allow Santa Fe's Indian population to own firearms. Night patrols by mestizo soldiers might be a solution. But are people blaming Dorantes and the inquisitors?"

"I don't think so, at least not directly," Pedro replied. "But everyone is talking of witchcraft, and they're saying the animal that killed the dogs is a werewolf."

All the talk of witchcraft made Carlos uneasy, and he wished it would stop. But when an hour later he said as much to Inéz, she urged him to get more involved in town affairs.

"How would that help?" Carlos asked rather irritably.

"Well, it wouldn't stop the talk, but it would put you in a position where you might have more influence in response to it. Anyway, wishing it would stop won't make the talk go away. Dorantes is aware of it, and I'll bet that right now he's busy compiling a list of persons he intends to investigate for witchcraft."

"You're probably right," he said with a sigh. "I'd be curious to know whose names are on the list."

"Yours might be," Inéz suggested.

"Yes," he agreed, "though I rather doubt it. Brother Gustavo called me in for an informal interview the afternoon I found Dolores's hideout. I believe he thinks I'm on his side."

118 ————

"What?" Inéz exclaimed. "How —? You haven't mentioned that until now!"

"Too much has happened," Carlos said, not wanting to go into it. "He and I agreed that we were both interested in the well-being of the town."

Inéz looked at him dubiously. "Well, all the more reason for you to take a more visible role in town affairs."

"So what do you suggest I do?"

"Ariel Padilla told to me the other day that her father is worried about who will take the vacancy on the Town Council caused by Francisco Morales's death. A few people are promoting the name of Manuel Contreras."

"But he's a troublemaker and a bad neighbor!" Carlos protested. "He's always trying to expand his property by claiming that the boundaries between his place and his neighbors' are not accurate."

"All the more reason for you to offer yourself to Horatio Padilla as a candidate. Ariel says her father knows that one of the remaining counselors, Arsenio Berdugo, definitely favors Manuel Contreras, and that the other, Alonso Miranda, is weak and would go along. But if your name came up, especially after you and Pedro surveyed the *Acequia Madre* for free, Horatio could persuade Miranda to support you for the empty seat."

"All right. I'll go see Horatio and will become a government official once again, much as I was happy to have that phase of my life end."

"This needn't be permanent," Inéz said. "A counselor's term runs for a year, and you'd be filling a vacancy only until next January's elections."

Don Carlos walked from the Beltráns' to Horatio Padilla's office in the Palace of the Governors. He didn't feel wholehearted about taking a municipal post, but Inéz's argument that it would reinforce his good standing in town made sense. As he entered the building and started down the hall toward Padilla's office, he felt his mood lift when he saw that Ariel was sitting at a small table next to the office door, reading a book. She looked up and gave him a brilliant smile. "Good morning, Señorita Padilla," he said, using a formal address even though they were on a first-name basis.

"The arrival of Don Alfonso Cabeza de Vaca has brightened my day," she replied with equal formality. "What can I do for you?"

"What sort of services do you offer?" he asked, shifting to a flirtatious tone.

"It depends on who's asking," she replied. "My usual purpose in being here at this time of day is to stamp and sign tax receipts that taxpayers want my father to notarize. Needless to say, this is a dull activity, though it passes the time. Since I doubt that you're here with tax receipts and my father is engaged with a client, I am willing to devote myself to exchanging witty remarks with you. Or do you have an alternative suggestion?"

He sat down on the bench opposite her. "Let me inquire," he said, "what book you're reading."

"This book? I'm embarrassed to be caught reading a silly romance, Lope de Vega's *La Dorotea*. I'm afraid you'll assume that I'm a frivolous woman, despite my best efforts to be taken seriously."

"Ariel, you don't strike me as the least bit frivolous, and if reading *La Dorotea* makes one silly, then count me in that number. A few years ago I was courting a woman and she and I and our friends passed the time reading Lope de Vega's novels to each other. Reading literature is much to your credit."

"My widowed father, having no idea what to do with a daughter, settled on teaching me to read, write, and calculate—to what end I don't know."

"Some parents," Carlos suggested, "want their daughters to be educated so that after they marry they'll be more interesting partners and good mothers."

"Alas, I lack any prospect for marriage, but perhaps I could become a governess to someone else's children," she said with a sigh, indicating that she didn't find the prospect the least bit appealing.

"Don't forget that Marco Cabrera has expressed an interest in getting to know you better. Perhaps we can get together and fence next Sunday afternoon."

"Probably nothing will come of that," she replied. "But thank you for trying to be encouraging. And now that the stolen items have been returned, may I have the thief's scarf back, as you promised?" When he didn't immediately respond, she asked, "What's the matter? Has it been lost?"

"Not lost exactly."

"If not lost, then what?"

"Ariel, please trust me to try to make good on my promise. I need to talk about the scarf with the person who has it in her possession."

Ariel's eyes widened. "You found the thief who lost it, didn't you? That's wonderful! Can I meet her?"

Before Carlos could reply the door to Horatio Padilla's office opened and a client left. Horatio put his head out the door and said, "Good morning, Don Alfonso. Please come in, if you're here to see me."

Carlos stood up, as did Ariel. "My office hours are over," she announced, "so I'll be leaving now. Please come back some day to discuss novels and to report on that other subject of mutual interest. You owe me an explanation, I trust you'd agree."

Ariel's father looked mildly puzzled by his daughter's reference to another topic of mutual interest. Don Carlos entered Padilla's office and sought to distract him by complimenting him on Ariel's upbringing. "I can see that you've given Ariel an excellent education," he said.

"I've tried to do so," Padilla replied. "She's very intelligent and picked up everything I offered her with exceptional quickness. If the practice of law were open to women, she would make a first-rate attorney."

Carlos nodded in agreement and changed the topic to the matter of the vacant seat on the Town Council. Padilla was pleased to hear that Carlos was willing to fill the position. "I'm sure," Padilla said, "I can persuade the other council members to appoint you. Your duties won't be onerous. Most of the major business—setting a tax rate, establishing the annual budget, and hiring men to maintain the roads, fences, and irrigation ditches—has already been completed."

"Will the council be involved in this nasty affair of a wolf killing three black dogs belonging to Indians in the Barrio?"

Horatio's face clouded with concern. "We are involved already," he replied. "Earlier today I was visited by a group led by Sancho Ibarra. The Barrio's Indian residents are angry and fearful. They want protection. I've assured them that the council will deputize some of their mestizo neighbors to patrol the Barrio at night. They much preferred that to the idea of having Presidio soldiers in their neighborhood after dark."

"That sounds like an excellent idea," Carlos said. "If I can be of any help, let me know. I believe many of our Indian neighbors have a good opinion of me ever since I saved José Lugo from being hanged."

"I had forgotten that," Horatio remarked in a thoughtful way. "I will keep it in mind. It's another reason why you'll be a valuable member of the council." On that note, they shook hands, and Carlos went on his way.

The next order of business, as Carlos saw it, was to figure out what to do about Dolores's scarf. He'd promised it back to Ariel before he knew that he would find Dolores, and by now María may have returned it to her. Would she be willing to give it up?

He arrived at the Gallegos stable and knocked on the door to the apartment. Pedro came to the door and gestured for Carlos to come in. "We have a surprise for you," he said. He then called out to María, who was in the next room. "María, Don Alfonso has come by to visit us."

María entered the room, followed by Dolores—a barely recognizable Dolores. "Since you last saw her," María announced, "we've spent quite a while on Dolores's appearance. She needed a bath, and new clothes. Ana Lugo, who's about Dolores's size, has loaned her some things until we can buy some of her own. What do you think?"

Dolores's transformation from dirty waif to a clean, fresh-faced young woman was astonishing. Ana's clothes, a muslin blouse and ankle-length skirt, suited her well. The sleeves of the blouse covered her crippled arm down to her wrist. She had scrubbed her face with soap and water until her tawny skin fairly glowed, and her jet black hair, washed and combed, hung smooth to the level of her jaw and fell over the outside edge of her damaged eye, partly hiding it. "Dolores!" Don Carlos exclaimed. "You are indeed beautiful!" A sweet, shy smile was her only response.

"Indeed she is," María agreed, "but she is still anxious about going out in daylight without her face hidden by her scarf."

"We will take things slowly," Carlos said. "However," he added, "there is the matter of that scarf, which she lost outside Ariel Padilla's bedroom window. Ariel let me have the scarf on the condition that I would return it to her. Now that it has found its way back to its owner, I don't know what to do."

At Carlos's mention of the scarf, Dolores's face contracted in worry. After a long pause, she said, "That scarf was my mother's. It's the only thing I have of hers."

"What should we do?" Don Carlos asked, genuinely perplexed.

Another long silence ensued as Pedro, Carlos, and María looked questioningly at each other. Finally, Dolores spoke. "Is it true that this woman Ariel didn't want me caught?"

"That's what she told me," Carlos replied.

"And," Dolores went on, "she kept it a secret that she had found the scarf?"

"Yes."

"If she had given it to the authorities," Dolores said, half to herself, "I would never have gotten it back."

"Not likely," Carlos agreed.

Another long silence followed. Dolores seemed deep in thought. When she did speak, she said, "If this woman Ariel didn't want me caught and tried to protect me, then she won't betray me now. I want Don Alfonso to take me to her to decide what to do about the scarf."

"That's brave of you, Dolores," Carlos said. Turning to Pedro and María, he asked, "Who shall we say Dolores is?"

"I've thought about that," María replied. "She is an orphaned country girl who wound up in the household of her cousin, who mistreated her so badly that she ran away. We're keeping where she came from a secret."

"And that's why," Don Carlos added, "we're not saying what her last name was."

"She can be Dolores Gallegos for the town records," María declared, hugging Dolores to her side. Dolores rewarded her with a grateful look.

Don Carlos and Dolores then set out for the Padilla residence, hoping to find Ariel home alone. To ease Dolores's anxiety about being seen in the daytime, María had loaned her a long shawl with which to cover her head and the side of her face. As they passed the Palace of the Governors, Dolores, who at Carlos's suggestion had taken his arm, nervously tightened her grip, but once beyond the government offices she relaxed. Ariel answered their knock. When Carlos asked, "May we come in?" she stepped aside and gestured toward an adjacent room.

To Carlos's surprise, before he could speak, Dolores reached under her shawl and brought out her precious scarf. "This belonged to my mother. It's the only thing of hers that I have. Thank you for not turning it over to the authorities."

Ariel immediately grasped the situation and impulsively stepped forward and gave Dolores a hug. "I'm so glad you're safe!" Ariel exclaimed, pulling back enough to look directly into Dolores's eyes.

"Ladies, ladies," Don Carlos said. "Allow me to introduce you by name—Ariel, this is Dolores; Dolores, this is Ariel Padilla."

Another hug followed. Then they stepped apart. "You are so much prettier than I realized that night," Ariel declared.

"You are every bit as beautiful as you looked to me in the dark. I hope my kissing you didn't frighten you. I just wanted—"

"It didn't frighten me. It was sweet."

"But what do we do about this?" Dolores asked, holding out the scarf. "Must you really take it back?"

"No, definitely no! I intended to be its caretaker only. It's yours, and yours alone."

Don Carlos was feeling better all the time. "I hope you both know that we are now bound together in a secret society whose members are the only ones who know the origins of this scarf."

"Pedro and María Gallegos also know," Dolores said. "I'm going to be living with them and helping María with housework and her baby, once it's born."

"That's very good," Ariel said. "And before we part for now, let me assure you that your secrets are safe with me."

More friendly words were exchanged and promises made to meet again soon. After Dolores and Don Carlos left the Padilla house, Don Carlos asked, "Would it be all right if we made one more stop before going back to the Gallegos's? I'd like my friend Inéz to see how nice you look. She lives nearby with Cristina and Javier Beltrán, for whom she works as their head cook and as a hostess for their parties."

Dolores was willing. When they knocked at the kitchen door, Inéz's assistant, Rita, answered and said, "Señora Recalde has just left to visit her friends, Pedro and María Gallegos. She went out the front door. If you hurry, you can catch up with her." So Carlos and Dolores circled around the house and reached its far corner at the same time as Inéz.

"Sweetheart!" Carlos exclaimed.

Inéz gave him a light kiss on the cheek and then turned to Dolores. "How pretty you look! I'm so glad that you are safe now with Pedro and María. I was just on my way to see them. Shall we go together?"

Their route to Pedro's stable took them past the west end of the Palace of the Governors. Carlos looked down the street and saw a crowd gathered outside the chapel on the Palace's southeast corner. "Let's walk over there," Carlos proposed, "and see what has drawn the crowd."

Dolores looked nervous at this suggestion, so he said, "Why don't the two of you keep going and wait for me on the veranda of my house? Once I've learned what this is all about, I'll join you." Inéz took Dolores's arm and they went off together.

Don Carlos reached the back of the crowd and overheard the word "Inquisition" repeated several times. He was tall enough to see over everyone's heads. The cause of the murmurs seemed to be something Father Dorantes was nailing to one of the chapel's doors. "What's going on?" Don Carlos asked a young farmer he knew who was standing nearby.

"Father Dorantes just read a proclamation. The Holy Office wants to arrest a mestizo woman who ran away from them in El Paso del Norte. They think she came here, and they think she's a witch. They're offering a reward for information that leads to her arrest."

"What's this woman's name?"

"Manuela is her first name. I didn't catch the rest."

Don Carlos had a bad feeling that this Manuela was the old shape-shifter who had approached him on Saturday market day. He edged forward in the crowd. It was composed almost entirely of common people who yielded instantly to a *hidalgo*. When he reached the front row, he saw that Father Dorantes had finished nailing up the proclamation and was standing to one side, speaking with Brother Inocente, the youngest member of the Inquisition tribunal. Don Carlos was now close enough to the posted document to be able to read it.

May 22, 1706, the Villa of Santa Fe in the Province of New Mexico.

By Order of the Holy Office:

Be it known to all that the Holy Office seeks the arrest of one Manuela Maldonado, a mestizo, previously a resident of Santa Fe but more recently of El Paso del Norte, from which she fled northward to avoid questioning with regard to cases of witchcraft about which she may have knowledge. A reward of fifteen pesos is offered for information leading to the accused's arrest.

All persons are put on notice that failure to cooperate with this investigation, either by withholding information or by harboring the accused, will be cause for severe penalties, including the loss of property and possible loss of life.

Damn, Carlos thought. He didn't want to be involved, but he felt it would be unwise not to report what he knew of Manuela in the event that Dorantes somehow learned that he'd met her. In any case, he reasoned that the little he knew could not, as far as he could see, contribute to her capture. The only thing he would hold back was that Manuela had told him she had once been a shape-shifter.

He walked over to Father Dorantes and said, "Father Dorantes, a word, perhaps."

Dorantes turned around. "Don Alfonso," he said. "What can I do for you?"

Carlos pointed to the proclamation nailed to the door. "This must be the woman you told us about at the Trigales's dinner party, the one who escaped from you and Brother Gustavo in El Paso del Norte."

Father Dorantes looked slightly annoyed, as if Carlos had been indiscreet in bringing up that conversation. "Yes," he said shortly.

"I feel obliged to report," Carlos said, "that I encountered an old woman, unknown to me, at last Saturday's market. She said her name was Manuela."

"No last name?"

"None that she mentioned."

"Did you ask her where she lived?"

"Yes. All she said was that she didn't live in Santa Fe."

"What was the nature of your interaction with her?"

"I was selling some semi-precious stones that the previous residents of my house had left in a storage area. Given my status as a *hidalgo*, I would not usually engage in such ordinary commerce; however, I had a secret purpose. I thought perhaps I would be able to identify the thief who had been stealing pieces of silver and china from the houses of my friends. It seemed to me possible that a thief of that sort would be attracted by crystals and other beautiful stones. Unfortunately, I had no luck.

"As I was beginning to pack up," Carlos continued, "an old woman approached me. She asked to look at some fire opals. I had many of them, and since I wanted to get rid of the stones rather than profit from their sale, I offered her several. The name she gave me, Manuela, came up in the course of our exchange."

"Is that all you know?"

"Yes," Carlos replied. "But given the strong warning of the proclamation, I thought I should report it."

"And you don't believe that the old woman's interest in your opals suggested that she was the thief?"

"No. Since she was old and very hunched over, I thought it was unlikely. I was looking for someone young and agile. I am only mentioning her, as I said, because she told me her name was Manuela."

"Your concern is appreciated," Father Dorantes replied. "If you should see her again, perhaps you could find out where she is staying."

Don Carlos, feeling himself dismissed, nodded goodbye, turned away, and made his way through the crowd. As he reached its edge, Brother Gustavo, who had been hovering nearby during the exchange between Dorantes and Carlos, caught up with him and grasped him by the arm. A wave of pain shot through his arm and numbed his whole left side. Carlos reflexively pulled away. "I injured my arm yesterday," he said, attempting to explain, "and it's painful to the touch."

Brother Gustavo hastily removed his hand and apologized. Then he went on, "I overheard what you said to Father Dorantes. I am most interested that you have spoken to this woman called Manuela. Perhaps there is something more you can tell me?"

Brother Gustavo's eagerness was not lost on Don Carlos. The hunt is on, he said to himself. Then he replied, "I can't add anything to what I just told Father Dorantes, but I am curious about one thing. The proclamation said she was wanted for fleeing to avoid questioning in regard to cases of witchcraft in El Paso del Norte. It doesn't say she was suspected of being a witch herself. But from what Father Dorantes told me about her escape from you there, it would seem that you are both certain she is a witch."

"Without question!" Gustavo said forcefully. "She escaped by means of sorcery, to which I was a witness. She is what is called a shape-shifter. She turned herself into a bat and flew out a window."

"Did you know she was a witch before that point?"

"Not that she was a shape-shifter, but, as I told you, we knew she had used potions and spells. Turning herself into a bat confirmed that she is a witch. She is extremely powerful. In El Paso del Norte I could not hold on to her even though she is an old woman. What's more," Gustavo added, eyeing Don Carlos intensely, "being physically close to her brought back the memory of my being possessed by that female demon, that succubus. I find it hard now to separate the two in my mind. So you can understand why her capture is of such great importance to me. I expect there are others, as well, who do the Devil's work, and we will flush them out. The Evil One often gains access to souls through the desires of the flesh. For this reason we will be looking for anyone who deals in love potions and the like."

Carlos felt the need to escape. Murmuring a few conventional words, he excused himself and hurried away. The man is obsessed, a fanatic, he thought. He resolved to do what he could to keep Manuela out of Gustavo's grasp.

As he approached the veranda of his house, where Inéz and Dolores were waiting for him, Carlos resolutely shut the preceding scene out of his mind. He greeted Inéz and Dolores and told them that nothing important was happening on the plaza—merely the posting of a notice—and he kept up with a light conversation as they walked along the path that led to Pedro's stable. Once inside the Gallegos's apartment, he made an effort to be as entertaining as possible, both to deflect questions and to distract himself from thinking further about Gustavo. "I would like to turn this gathering into a party," he proposed. "We have much to celebrate—the presence of Dolores, the solution to the black dog mystery, and Inéz restored to health.

Let's have some wine, and I will regale you with a story from one of my previous lives."

"Perhaps you should explain to Dolores," Pedro suggested, "about your previous lives."

Don Carlos turned to Dolores. "Many years ago I received training in how to be reborn with an awareness of my previous lives. I have accomplished that five times. That, along with my skill as a shape-shifter, is an essential element of my secret identity. I must ask you again never to speak of these facts outside of this small circle of intimate friends. As you surely realize, it would be dangerous if this became known to Father Dorantes or Brother Gustavo."

Dolores nodded solemnly. "I have had my own experience with living a secret life. I won't betray yours."

That being settled, Don Carlos began to speak in a storyteller's voice. "In my third life," he said, "almost a hundred years ago, I was a Mayan Indian. Acting on instructions from my mentor in the Brujo's Way, Don Serafino Romero, I set out on a quest to find a jewel called Montezuma's Emerald. In the course of my journey I learned that Montezuma, the last of the Aztec emperors, had possessed an emerald of wondrous powers. He had entrusted the emerald to his favorite mistress, and after his death it had passed from her to a series of virgin girls of Indian descent. After many years of searching, I eventually traced it to Chichicastenango, a village in the mountains of Guatemala, and there I encountered Don Malvolio, an evil sorcerer who had long been my mentor's enemy."

Don Carlos's narrative took nearly an hour to complete, and he held his audience's rapt attention as he described every step in his adventure: the many obstacles he faced and overcame in trying to find the emerald, and then the complications that arose from his having to deal directly with Don Malvolio, who in that life was both a high-ranking Spanish government official and an agent of the Inquisition. He was also, as a sorcerer, in pursuit of the emerald.

The climax of the story was a battle between Malvolio and Carlos that resulted in Malvolio's death, after which Carlos found himself sorely tempted to seize the emerald for himself. Should he take it and use its powers to do good, or should he leave it undisturbed in the keeping of Alejandra, the little Mayan girl who he believed was the emerald's protector?

"But," Carlos now asked his audience directly, "was the emerald really concealed in a doll that never left Alejandra's hands, or had my belief in the existence of the stone and its powers just convinced me it was there?"

"I don't know," said Dolores said, looking worried at the possibility.

"I don't know either, but what did you *do*?" Inéz demanded.

"I don't rule the world, so I must have decided not to take it," Carlos said with a laugh.

"Or you took it, and it didn't work!" Pedro added with a bigger laugh.

"What sort of a low-life do you think I am?" Carlos asked in a playfully aggrieved tone. "Of course I didn't try to take it. And as to whether or not it was actually in Alejandra's possession, we will never know."

12

Friendships

*S*unday started badly. As was his custom, Don Carlos dressed in his Sunday best and headed to the Beltráns', intending to meet Inéz and escort her to Mass. But halfway across the plaza he could see that something was wrong. Up ahead, a crowd had gathered outside the chapel in the Palace of the Governors. Carlos was puzzled because no one in the crowd was trying to enter the chapel. He made his way to the outer edge of the gathering. Two things quickly became apparent. Everyone was carefully keeping his distance from the doors of the chapel, and the doors were tightly closed, although by this time on a Sunday morning they were usually wide open. The crowd was composed almost entirely of mestizos and Indians. Gazing over their heads, he saw that they were intently watching the scene unfolding before them. Father Dorantes was holding a crucifix in front of him and his two Franciscan companions were swinging censers from which clouds of incense were rising. Dorantes was chanting in Latin. Carlos's Jesuit education enabled him to understand that it was some sort of rite to drive away evil.

Only when Don Carlos edged through the crowd a bit farther did he begin to understand. He saw that the notice from the Inquisition that Dorantes had posted yesterday was no longer on the chapel door. Edging a bit farther forward, he could see that Dorantes's attention was focused on the ground in front of the door. A shrine of sorts had been set up there. It consisted of six candles that had burned down to their stubs, sprigs of spring herbs and flowers, and, in the middle of these items, a pile of ashes, which Carlos assumed were the remains of the Holy Office's notice. The mood of the crowd was solemn in the extreme. The way everyone except the three Franciscans stayed far back from the chapel doors indicated to Don Carlos that the assembled men and women were fearful.

Within a few minutes of Carlos's arrival Dorantes brought the ceremony to its conclusion. He stopped chanting in Latin and said something in Spanish to Brother Inocente, the third member of the Inquisition tribunal. The young Franciscan produced a small brush from his robe and, an expression of strong distaste on his face, stepped forward and began sweeping the candle stubs, herbs, and ashes from the makeshift shrine into a bag.

Once every vestige of the shrine had been swept into the bag, Father Dorantes took it from his associate and raised it in the air. In a loud voice he announced, "See! These objects, which were employed in a pagan, idolatrous rite, have been stripped of their power."

Don Carlos, whose brujo vision enabled him to see the aura that surrounded the bag containing the shrine's remnants, could tell that Father Dorantes had no idea what he was dealing with. Despite the disruption they had undergone in the process of being swept into the bag, the objects within still radiated a strong aura. Whoever had set up the shrine had power, no matter what Father Dorantes believed.

Father Dorantes now turned toward the crowd and held the crucifix above his head. He shouted a command, "Kneel!" Everyone, including Don Carlos, fell to their knees. Dorantes, gazing above the heads of the kneeling crowd, called out, "Be assured that whoever was responsible for this abomination against the Holy Office will be severely punished. And now may Almighty God bless you, the Father, the Son, and the Holy Spirit."

There was a flurry of hands as people crossed themselves. Then Dorantes gestured to his two companions, who opened the chapel's front doors. After doing so they turned aside and followed Father Dorantes along a path that went around to the back of the Palace of the Governors.

Don Carlos stood up and continued on his way to the Beltráns' house. He found Inéz and the Beltráns—Javier, Cristina, and Elena—waiting for him in the front *sala*. He gave them a quick summary of what he'd just seen and heard, including Father Dorantes's warning that whoever was responsible for tearing down and burning the Holy Office's notice and building a pagan shrine would be severely punished.

"That's frightening," Inéz said. "He'll punish someone, a scapegoat if he can't find the person actually responsible."

"I'm afraid you're right," Carlos agreed.

"Do we have to go to Mass today?" Elena asked. "I don't want to."

"We must, today of all days," Javier said. "Father Dorantes will be watching closely, and anyone who stays away will be suspect."

"I intend to go for that very reason," Carlos declared. "The Franciscans opened the chapel doors. Mass will be said."

The five of them set out for the chapel in a subdued mood. They arrived to find that a new notice from the Holy Office, a duplicate of the original, had been posted on the chapel door. Three soldiers were stationed nearby, and Carlos assumed that a round-the-clock military guard would protect the notice from being torn down again.

Mass was said by the parish's senior priest, Father Benedicto. Father Dorantes and the other two inquisitors were nowhere in evidence. The Mass itself was briefer than usual. Carlos paid little attention, being intent on formulating a plan to be put into effect after Mass.

As the worshippers filed out, Carlos whispered to Inéz, "Would you be able to come to my place after lunch today during siesta? I'll invite Ariel Padilla and Marco Cabrera to join us."

"I can do that. What do you have in mind?"

"I think this is a time when friends should gather. Look around. People are already drifting away instead of staying to talk." He scanned the thinning crowd and saw Ariel and her father a few yards away. "Hurry," he said. "The Padillas are starting to leave."

Luckily, Horatio Padilla looked back toward the chapel and Carlos was able to wave to him and indicate that he wanted to talk. Carlos then said to Inéz, "Please join the Padillas. I'll be right there. I want to catch up with Marco, who is also leaving."

In a few quick strides, Carlos came up beside Marco, who had paused momentarily to speak with Nicolas Archuleta. "Good morning, gentlemen," Carlos said. "Nicolas, if I may, I would like to steal Marco and take him to speak with the Padillas."

"Please do," Nicolas replied. "Marco was only checking to be sure I had heard about a meeting that starts in half an hour."

Carlos took Marco by the elbow and steered him toward where Inéz and the Padillas were standing. "What's this meeting?" he asked.

"You can imagine," Marco said. "Governor Peralta has called it to discuss this morning's incident."

"Will it last long?"

"An hour at most."

There was more that could be said, but Carlos was focused on his social objective. Once he and Marco had reached Inéz and the Padillas and had exchanged greetings, Carlos said to Ariel, "If your father is willing to forgo the pleasure of your company during siesta today, I hope you'll join Inéz and me, and Marco, if he will come, at my house for dessert." Marco nodded his assent.

"That sounds pleasant, Ariel," her father said. "You might take some of the dessert you made last night, just so you leave some for me."

Ariel smiled at her father. Carlos could see that they had a loving relationship. "Thank you, Father," she replied. "Fortunately, I made a lot of *crema de chocolate*." Turning to Carlos, she asked, "What time should I arrive?"

"Marco has a meeting that's about to start. He can come by for you and Inéz as soon as the meeting is over, and the three of you can walk to my place together."

Turning to Marco, Inéz said. "Lunch at the Beltráns' will be over by one o'clock, and I will be free afterward. Come by then. I'll bring almond tarts as my contribution to the table."

"Two desserts!" Carlos exclaimed. "At this rate we will all end up as fat as Gordo."

After exchanging a few more pleasantries, the little group broke up, its members heading to separate destinations—Marco to his meeting, the Padillas to their home, and Carlos and Inéz to the Beltrán place. "Did you come up with this idea on the spur of the moment?" Inéz asked.

"During Mass it struck me that I can't do much in regard to the general state of affairs in town. Even though I'm quite sure I know who was responsible for the wolf killing the dogs of Indian families, there's nothing I can do about it."

Inéz gave him a searching look. "How did you find out?"

"I put two and two together. You remember that at Chupadera Mesa, we overheard Don Malvolio say that an assistant of his named Gustavo had visited Santa Fe in February, and that Gustavo had taken possession of a wolf then. I believe Gustavo controlled the wolf that attacked the dogs of Indian families. The man has great powers, some that I don't fully understand. The only good news is that, according to Manuela, he can't read auras."

"How did all of that lead you to invite us for dessert?" Inéz inquired.

"One thing that I can do is gather friends to enjoy each other's company."

"So," Inéz commented, "you hope a social occasion will be an antidote to bad times?"

"Exactly," he replied.

As it turned out, Carlos's three guests didn't arrive until close to two o'clock. Marco apologized, explaining, "The meeting ran longer than I expected."

"So did lunch," Inéz said. "The whole Trigales clan, Raul, Bianca, and the children, dropped in as Rita and I were serving dessert. They were so full of questions and comments about the destruction of the Holy Office's notices that I didn't think I could leave. It was a good thing that Marco didn't come over with Ariel until a few minutes ago."

"Let's start with dessert," Carlos suggested. "Waiting an extra hour has made me even more eager to sample what you've brought." He began to pass out plates before he remembered that he didn't have four of the same design. He'd had four originally, but one had been broken. Trying to disguise the deficiencies in his supply of dishes, he gave Ariel and Inéz plates in one design and himself and Marco plates in another.

Inéz wasn't fooled. "I can see," she announced, "what I can give you for your birthday, assuming your pursuit of a bachelor's life will allow you to tolerate having at least six plates of the same design."

He was tempted to say that he was ready to abandon his life as a bachelor if she would agree to marry him, but she anticipated his response and gave him warning look.

"I always look forward to my birthday," he replied diplomatically.

Ariel looked at Carlos and Inéz appraisingly. "I thought the two of you were engaged. Excuse my nosiness, but it seemed to me that more was unsaid than said just now."

"Cristina has led people to believe that we're engaged," Inéz replied, "on the grounds that I wear a ring Alfonso gave me. I consider it a friendship ring."

Reaching over and putting her hand on Inéz's, Ariel said, "I'm embarrassed by having pried into your relationship, which is a lovely one. I apologize for being rude, and Marco will certainly conclude that I have no manners whatsoever, very unappealing."

"On the contrary," Marco spoke up. "I find you very appealing." He flushed, and Ariel reddened too. "Oh, my!" he said. "Now it's my turn to cause embarrassment. Sorry."

"Don't apologize," Ariel replied. "I'm happy to accept your compliment."

"Dessert time," Inéz announced, passing out plates on which she'd put equal portions of *crema de chocolate* and almond tarts. Gordo, who had been watching intently as she distributed dessert, sat up and begged. "When did he learn that trick?" Inéz asked Carlos.

"My lodgers, the three soldiers who sleep here, have been training him."

Addressing Gordo, Inéz told him, "I don't care how cute you are, you shouldn't be allowed to beg at the table."

"I am reproached," Carlos commented, "for another of my bachelor ways."

"Are the soldiers a problem for you?" Inéz asked, steering the conversation away from Carlos's bachelorhood.

"No. I like the three of them, and they're only around for a few hours. They usually come in a little before bedtime. We exchange a few stories about our day. Then they go to bed, and they leave early in the morning."

"Speaking for myself only," Ariel declared, "I find the combination of soldiers guarding our houses and the presence of the Franciscan inquisitors most unpleasant. And this business of these poor dogs being slaughtered by a wolf is truly appalling. I saw the looks on the faces of the Indians who came to speak with my father this morning. They want protection from witches, but neither the extra soldiers nor the presence of the Franciscans makes them feel safer."

"What I heard at the meeting I just attended won't help matters," Marco said.

"Can you tell us what happened?" Carlos asked.

"Yes, I'd like to. I'm assuming that I can count on all of you to keep what I'll say to yourselves." They all murmured that they would respect his wish.

Marco went on. "The meeting was tense. Major Cortés and Father Dorantes wanted to respond aggressively to this morning's destruction of the Inquisition's notice. Father Benedicto and, I'm proud to say, my father, counseled moderation and patience. Unfortunately, the governor wants to do something, anything, so he went along with an idea proposed by Dorantes."

"What was Dorantes's proposal?" Inéz asked.

"He wants to hire informers. There will be at least two of them, a mestizo and a Pueblo Indian, and Dorantes already seems to have particular men in mind. They'll be paid to produce names of people thought to practice witchcraft and sorcery."

"That's terrible!" Inéz exclaimed. "It's an invitation to bear false witness against their neighbors."

"Inéz is right," Carlos agreed. "No good can come of that."

"Father Benedicto and my father made the same point," Marco said. "And we've all heard that in the past people accused of heresy or witchcraft were usually assumed to be guilty by the very fact of having been accused."

"This seems to be another example of something that we can't do anything about," Inéz said, looking meaningfully at Carlos.

Carlos smiled at her. "So we must have more recourse to the antidote. Here's to friendship!" he said, lifting a spoon laden with *crema de chocolate*. Laughter ensued, and they engaged in playful conversation for the rest of the afternoon.

Monday and Tuesday passed quickly without any new troubles coming to the surface. Nevertheless, Carlos was relieved to get away from the worries of Santa Fe on Wednesday for a picnic with Inéz, Elena, and Santiago at the spot he and Inéz called their Sacred Pool. Soon they were settled at the edge of the pool and began spreading out a feast. Inéz and Elena had prepared most of the dishes, but Carlos contributed some corn bread and Santiago surprised everyone by opening a box of dates. "My aunt likes to import exotic foods," he explained, "and these are very good."

They were nearly done eating when Inéz announced, "I hope everyone will excuse me after lunch. I want to see if I can locate an old friend who lives up the canyon from the pool."

Elena brightened. "Is this that skunk you call Elvira?" she asked.

"Yes. I'd forgotten that I'd told you about her."

"Just a little bit. Do you think I could meet her?"

Inéz smiled, "I think we'd better tell Santiago a little bit too, though not so much that he'll report us to Father Dorantes."

"There's not the slightest chance that I would do that," Santiago said seriously.

"Then," Inéz said, "Santiago should know that Elvira and I seem to be able to communicate. She gives me advice involving matters of love. I suppose you must think I am crazy," she added, giving Santiago a slightly concerned look.

"You needn't worry," Santiago replied. "My aunt Josefina has been telling me about Pueblo Indians who worked on the Mendoza estates or lived nearby. They had many stories about animals. From what she told me, I don't find it far-fetched to learn that you can communicate with them."

"How interesting," Carlos said, wanting to know more about what Doña Josefina had said.

"If Elena and I go off in search of Elvira," Inéz said, "that will break up the party and leave you two on your own. Is that a good idea, Alfonso?"

Carlos turned to Santiago. "If you're interested in Pueblo Indians, perhaps you'd like to see a sacred site of theirs that's on the cliff above us."

"Yes, I would," Santiago replied. "My aunt has told me that Indians had sacred sites in the canyon east of her house. I've been hoping to see one of them."

While Inéz and Elena went off up the canyon, Carlos and Santiago began to climb to the cliff that overlooked the pool. The slope was steep, but Carlos knew the easiest route. In about half an hour they reached the ledge. Carlos led Santiago to the back wall, where there was a crevice in which many clear quartz crystals were visible. "Over the years," Carlos said, "Pueblo Indian medicine men have come here. They fasted, chanted sacred songs, and perhaps ingested mind-altering plants — all in order to contact the spirits of their ancestors, or possibly to have a vision that would reveal what they should be seeking in their own life."

Santiago was silent for a few moments. Finally he spoke. "I would like to have a vision like that," he said. "At present, what I should make of my life is very unclear to me."

Santiago's openness touched Carlos. He pointed to one perfectly shaped quartz crystal in the crevice that had broken away from its matrix, "Pick up that loose crystal, and let's take it to that shallow alcove over there. There's room for both of us to sit in it. If you're willing, I would be glad to have you tell me about the lack of clarity you just mentioned."

They moved over to the alcove and sat down facing toward the dramatic vista of mountains, sky, and clouds that was spread out to the west. Carlos waited for Santiago to tell him more.

"You may not know," Santiago said at last, "that I am much younger than my brothers. I am only eighteen, while they are twenty-six and twenty-eight. We have three sisters who were born between them and me. My brothers are very masculine and aggressive. They love the thought of following in the footsteps of our late father, who died fighting in the war over the Spanish succession."

"I'm sorry to hear that," Carlos said. "For which side did he fight?"

"In support of Archduke Charles, the Habsburg claimant." Carlos noted to himself that the Mendozas were aligned with the same faction that Governor Peralta favored.

"If your brothers wanted to follow in your father's footsteps," Carlos asked, "why are they here? The conflict over the Spanish succession has engaged all the great powers on one side or the other, and large armies in the tens of thousands have fought in nearly every part of western Europe."

"My brothers did take up arms, along with our father," Santiago replied. "My mother would not let me join them because at the time I was not yet sixteen. In addition, my sisters had recently married, and without me at home she would have been alone. After our father died in battle in 1704, my brothers came home, and when my father's estate was examined by the lawyers, it was found that the war had hurt our businesses so badly that there was little income, and most of the family's fortune had been spent as dowries for my three sisters. It was a great relief when we received a letter from Aunt Josefina inviting us to come here, with the expectation that one of us would be named heir to her fortune. She has many properties, and her large land-holdings in Santa Fe are the least of them. She also owns silver mines in New Spain and a highly productive vineyard near Jerez, Spain."

"Do you get a sense that she favors one of you over the other two?

"Under normal circumstances the main heir would be Antonio, my eldest brother, or in default of him the next in line by age, Julio. Both of them have complete confidence in their superiority, and I am so far behind in age and accomplishment that I scarcely count. Certainly my brothers are of that opinion."

"Even if that's true," Carlos said, "you'll probably end up with a nice legacy, a larger estate than most Spaniards can expect. That seems rather straightforward to me."

"Perhaps," Santiago replied. "But what I've observed since we arrived here is that Aunt Josefina doesn't especially like Antonio and Julio, particularly their attitudes toward Pueblo Indians, whom they consider little better than dirt. My aunt has spoken sharply to them on several occasions for disparaging remarks they have made about Indians. 'They are fine people,' she says, 'worthy of our respect, and in no way inferior to us.' My brothers just laugh and seem not to realize how offensive their remarks are to her."

An idea had come to Don Carlos as Santiago had told his story. "I have a suggestion," he said, "but first turn around and look at the back wall of this alcove. See the hand that a long-ago Pueblo seeker painted there?" Santiago nodded. "That man and many others like him have sat here and waited for a sign or a vision. I want you to move up to the front of the ledge and sit there in complete silence, holding that crystal you found. I'm going to wrap this leather bag I brought along around your left wrist. There's a red-tailed hawk who lives nearby. He often visits this ledge, and if you see him flying toward you, hold out the arm that's covered with the bag. He may well land on your wrist."

Santiago looked astonished. "A hawk?" he said. "I'm not sure—"

"I know this hawk well," Carlos assured him. "He will not attack you."

They moved to the front of the ledge and Santiago sat down, holding the crystal in one hand while Carlos secured the leather bag around his left wrist. "You need to sit in silence by yourself," Carlos told him. "I'm going to go off now, but I won't be far away."

Don Carlos made his way along the ledge until he was well out of sight of Santiago, and then he disrobed and transformed himself into a red-tailed hawk. He was pleased with the way things were working out. When Inéz had proposed this destination for the picnic, he had no idea that he would be able to get away and practice his brujo skills. In no time he was airborne, soaring with the updrafts on the face of the cliff. He circled, dived, soared again, and let a gust of wind carry him in a straight line across the face of the cliff. He felt, as always, released into the full powers of his being. But today he knew he had another task to perform, and he headed back toward the ledge where Santiago was sitting, waiting for a hawk to visit him.

On the way, Don Carlos intentionally flew over the area near the pool, where he saw Inéz and Elena lying on their backs on the grass. Elvira was crouched near Inéz's ear, whispering about matters important to women. Elena was playing with five baby skunks, who were climbing all over her. Elena didn't notice his passing flight, but Inéz looked up and saw him. She favored him with a happy smile. He veered off away from the site of Elvira's den and flew directly back toward where Santiago was waiting.

Santiago saw the hawk-Carlos coming and raised his arm straight out from his body as Don Carlos had told him to do. Skillfully, Don Carlos in hawk form landed gently on Santiago's left wrist. Young man and hawk studied each other in silence. Santiago was transfixed. Then he murmured, "Beautiful...beautiful."

The hawk-Carlos opened his wings to their full span, a sight that few humans except falconers ever see that close to them. Then, closing his wings, he turned around and faced the open country to the west. With seemingly no effort, he lifted off his perch on Santiago's wrist and with a few quick beats of his wings soared out over the canyon and turned to the north, where he had left his clothes.

Once he had landed, Don Carlos returned to human form and dressed. He quickly hiked back to the place where Santiago was still sitting. "From the look on your face," Don Carlos said, "I believe you had a visit from my friend the hawk."

Santiago told Don Carlos about the hawk's visit. "Having him sit on my wrist, looking at me—it was indescribable! He was like a being from another world. When he looked at me I felt as if he spoke to me, though there were no words."

"That was the hawk's gift to you, I'm sure," Carlos told him. "But now it's time for us to get back to our friends. Let's look for another crystal to take to Elena."

With the two crystals in Carlos's leather bag, he and Santiago climbed down the face of the cliff and found Inéz and Elena barefoot, having taken off their boots, and wading in a shallow part of the pool.

Both women climbed out of the pool and dried off their feet with a towel that Inéz had brought along. "How was your visit with Elvira?" Carlos asked.

"Very satisfactory," Inéz replied.

"Did Elvira have anything to tell you?"

"Yes, private messages just for me."

"Secrets, then?" Carlos said.

Elena couldn't stand it. "Can't we tell Alfonso and Santiago about the baby skunks? Does that have to be a secret too?"

"Go ahead," Inéz told her.

"It was the most adorable thing!" Elena began. "There were five babies. While Elvira chattered in Inéz's ear, the babies climbed all over me. They let me hold them, too. They smelled faintly of skunk, but so faintly that it wasn't unpleasant."

"That sounds magical," Santiago said.

"It was!" Elena agreed. "But what about you two? How was your visit to the sacred site?"

Inéz spoke in a warning tone. "We have to be careful. If word of our interest in a site used by medicine men got back to Father Dorantes, we might be arrested and questioned by the Inquisition."

Carlos and Inéz's two young friends looked momentarily somber at the thought. Then Carlos said, "What we have here are stories we can share with each other, but they must remain secret from everyone else. If we all agree to that, then Santiago can tell about his adventure."

Santiago had a slow, deliberate way of speaking that Carlos felt was unusual in a young man. "We climbed up to a broad ledge in the cliff, and once we were there Don Alfonso showed me a crevice in which we found many quartz crystals. I brought one back for Elena.

"Then we moved to a shallow alcove at the back of the ledge where a hand had been painted long ago by an Indian on a vision quest. We sat there and talked for a while. Then Don Alfonso told me to sit near the front of the ledge and to be prepared if a hawk swooped down and landed on my wrist. He went away so I could have this experience alone.

"I don't know how long I sat there, but while I waited for the hawk, I began to feel a strange sort of calm. I was confident that I could meet the hawk without fear. Then, just as Don Alfonso had said, I saw a hawk flying directly at me. I raised my arm, which Don Alfonso had wrapped in leather, and the hawk landed on my wrist. We sat there looking at each other. I either thought or said the words, 'Beautiful, beautiful.' It spread its wings wide open, as though it understood me. Then it flew off, and a few minutes later Alfonso returned and we came back here."

"Amazing!" Elena exclaimed breathlessly.

"It certainly was," Inéz agreed. "But I think it's time for us to pack up and start back for Santa Fe. Just remember that the most important things that happened today must remain secrets. All anyone needs to know is that we had a wonderful ride and picnic."

"I would like to tell my Aunt Josefina that Alfonso and I visited a Pueblo Indian site," Santiago said. "Would it be all right if I described the crystals and the painted hand?"

"I should think so," Carlos replied, "given what you told me about her attitude toward Pueblo peoples and their spiritual ways."

In a state of general contentment, they gathered their things, mounted their horses, and started off for Santa Fe. A perfect day, Don Carlos thought. If only I could always manage to make things turn out so well!

They rode south at a leisurely pace. When they were less than half an hour from Santa Fe they heard the sound of horses approaching from behind them. Carlos turned in the saddle and saw a squad of eight cavalrymen coming toward them at a fast trot. Ominously, two of the soldiers had bloody bandages on their upper bodies, and the eight mounted men were followed by two horses that were saddled but had no riders.

The cavalrymen passed Don Carlos and his friends with barely a nod of recognition. Carlos, curious to know what was going on, spurred Eagle into a canter and quickly caught up with the troops. One young private, whom he'd met through his lodgers, was in the rear, ponying one of the riderless horses. "What's going on, Private?" Don Carlos asked.

"We were on a scouting mission when we were attacked by a large war party. There were fifteen or twenty of them, and they took us by surprise. We fought them off, but two of our men were killed and two were wounded. We're hurrying back to Santa Fe to report the incident to Major Cortés."

Thanking his informant for this news, Carlos slowed Eagle to a walk to let his three companions catch up with him. On hearing Carlos's report Santiago said, "Does it mean war?" Carlos thought it probably did.

By the time Carlos's small party reached Santa Fe, the Presidio was a beehive of activity. Cavalrymen and their horses were milling around on the parade ground. Noncommissioned officers were shouting directions. Wranglers were pulling supply wagons out of sheds and inspecting their condition. A crowd of civilians with anxious expressions on their faces had gathered to watch.

It was nearly nightfall, and Don Carlos assumed it would be at least twenty-four hours before a punitive expedition could be organized. He suggested that Inéz, Elena, and Santiago go to their respective homes. "I'll stay here and see if I can learn anything more," he told them.

He found his young lodgers and talked with them, but they didn't know anything more than he did. Don Carlos decided that there was nothing to be gained by hanging around any longer. He went home, had a quiet dinner with Orfeo and Gordo, and went to bed early.

13

Secrets

Thursday morning Carlos paid a brief visit to Pedro, who always seemed to know what was happening before anyone else, to see if he knew anything about the expected military response to the attack on the soldiers. Pedro had no information, so Carlos returned home, where he found a note on the kitchen table asking him to call on Doña Josefina in an hour. Since he had a little time, he decided to stop first to see Inéz. As he crossed the plaza, he saw his three lodgers—Alejandro, Gonzalo, and Luis—standing guard in front of the chapel doors. "I'm surprised you're not at the Presidio preparing to march off," he said.

"We're probably going to be left behind to protect Santa Fe," Gonzalo replied.

"Nothing's going to happen today anyway," Luis put in. "It's going to take a while to get everything organized, and Major Cortés wants to recruit Indian and mestizo auxiliaries to come along."

"A lot of men from the Barrio de Analco have already volunteered," Alejandro added.

"They're volunteering to go along?" Don Carlos asked, rather surprised, given the Barrio residents' general distrust of Presidio soldiers.

"They're probably bored with town life and want some excitement," Luis said.

"That's not it at all," Gonzalo asserted. "What they want is to get away from those Franciscans from the Holy Office."

"Hush!" Alejandro said sharply. "You can get in trouble saying things like that. The real problem is that a lot of people in the Barrio are poor and don't have enough food for themselves and their families. If they join the expedition they will at least be paid and get regular meals."

Feeling the need to be on his way, Don Carlos excused himself and went on to the Beltrán residence. He knocked on the kitchen door, let himself in, and found Inéz at work. She looked up and said, "I'm glad, as always, to see you, but I'm very busy. Is there something important we need to talk about, or can it wait?"

"I didn't have anything important to say," he replied. "I just stopped by on my way to my next appointment. I can come back at a more convenient time."

Just then, Rita, Inéz's assistant, came in the kitchen. "Sorry to interrupt," she said. "I'll come back when you're not in the middle of something."

"Don't go," Inéz told her. "You and I have very little time to finish preparations for lunch. Don Alfonso was about to leave — although," she said, turning to him, "I don't know where he's headed next."

"I'm off to Doña Josefina's, summoned by a message her Indian servant delivered to my house this morning when I wasn't home. Orfeo left it lying on the kitchen table. I have no idea what she wants to discuss."

"If she were fifty years younger," Inéz said with a smile, "I would suspect her of trying to seduce you."

"I expect she would," he replied with a laugh.

"You'd better go," Inéz said. "Doña Josefina is waiting for you."

Carlos walked up the hill to the Mendoza house. The Indian woman servant who had given Don Carlos a note on an earlier occasion answered the door and looked surprised to see him. "Doña Josefina is not here," she said. "She expected you to meet her at Señor Archibeque's house. She left by carriage some time ago."

"Doña Josefina didn't mention a location in her letter to me."

"It was not in the letter. I gave your manservant the instructions on where to meet by word of mouth."

Orfeo had been gone when Carlos found the letter. "Unfortunately," Don Carlos said, "the message didn't get relayed to me."

"Then you must hurry. Doña Josefina doesn't like to be kept waiting."

It was at least a mile to Juan Archibeque's house. Don Carlos took a shortcut through the fields east of the plaza, crossed the river, and walked quickly up Canyon Road. Fifteen minutes later he saw the Archibeque house ahead. By then he'd had a chance to think through the situation.

Doña Josefina had unwittingly put him in an awkward position by summoning him to a house he had avoided visiting ever since Mara Mata and Selena Torrez had moved there to become governesses for Juan Archibeque's children. Carlos's relationship with Mara and Selena was complicated, and unresolved currents ran beneath it. He liked them both; he considered them friends, up to a point — that point having to do with their long involvement with Leandro the Magician, who had kidnapped the Trigales children and had been revealed to be an apprentice of Carlos's old enemy, Don Malvolio.

In addition, Mara and Selena, who were half sisters, were Malvolio's daughters by two different women. As far as Carlos knew, they had had little contact with their father and considered him secretive and not particularly likeable. But some question remained in Carlos's mind as to how much they knew about their father's obsessive search for a brujo named Carlos Buenaventura. What complicated matters further was their habitual flirtatiousness. Mara, in particular, was skilled in the art of erotic enchantment, and Carlos had all too nearly succumbed. After Leandro's terrible death and the rescue of the Trigales children, Carlos had thought it wise to keep his distance from Mara and Selena, particularly since Inéz had been ill and any visit would have been made without her. Inéz, for her part, also liked Mara and Selena up to a point—that point being Carlos's susceptibility to Mara. Inéz had not asked him to stay away from them, but he knew she would have preferred it. And now here he was, approaching Archibeque's (and Mara and Selena's) doorstep.

The house itself, which was not large, had a plain adobe exterior and only a few narrow windows. A handsome carriage that obviously had brought Doña Josefina stood waiting in the road, a black servant sitting in the driver's seat. He returned Don Carlos's greeting.

Mara opened the door as he raised his hand to knock. He'd thought he was prepared to meet her, but the actuality of seeing her disturbed him. He had a visceral memory of their last dance together, when he had nearly lost himself in her violet eyes. Now, in the doorway, she held his gaze again. "It's been a long time," she murmured in the soft-voiced way she had.

Selena, taller and tawny-skinned, moved forward from where she'd been standing in back of Mara. "You've been bad to neglect us," she said as she stepped past Mara. She lifted her face and kissed him on the mouth. "Inéz would not like that," she said smilingly, "but she's not here."

"Inéz does visit us here," Mara announced.

"Shh!" Selena hissed. "My sister seems incapable of keeping a secret."

Carlos was nonplussed. "Inéz comes here?" he asked incredulously. "Why?"

Mara and Selena looked at each other and smiled in a way that reminded him of a similarly conspiratorial smile that had passed between Inéz, Elena, and Ariel when he had asked them where they went on the Monday morning excursions they took together. "It's a secret," Inéz had said, laughing.

Carlos looked back and forth between Mara and Selena, who were clearly enjoying his bewilderment. "I know that Inéz and two of her friends are in the habit of going off to some secret location for some mysterious activity on Monday mornings, but here—? Why?" he repeated.

"And mysterious it will remain," Selena declared, "until they're ready to tell you why they come here. But Doña Josefina is waiting for you in the *sala*. Mara and I have to get back to work, though keeping an eye on those little charmers"—she gestured toward an open doorway ahead, where three little girls were clustered together, watching him with big eyes—"is no trouble most of the time."

He entered the room to which he had been directed and found Doña Josefina seated. She was dressed, as was her custom, in black. He went up to her and kissed her extended hand. He started to apologize for being later than he'd expected. "I went to your house first, not realizing…" he began, but she waved him off with a hand.

"That's not important," she said. She directed him to sit in a chair next to her and went on immediately. "Santiago tells me that yesterday you took him to a ledge high on a cliff where Indians mined for crystals. Why was that?"

"I thought he would benefit from having an experience in which he was not overshadowed by his older brothers, and he, like you, had expressed an interest in Pueblo Indian life."

"Good," she replied. She stood up. "Let's take a walk together," she said and started for the door. Turning left in the hallway and opening the front door before he could reach it to open it for her, she beckoned to her black manservant and walked past the front of the house toward a path that led up the canyon. "Mabruke will follow us at a respectful distance," she announced, "so he can carry me back, if I fall down. I'm sure you could do so, if needed," she added with a wry smile, "but carrying me is more suitable work for a servant than for a *hidalgo*."

"Mabruke is an African name, isn't it?" Carlos asked.

"Yes. How did you know?"

"A boyhood friend of mine, my best friend at the time, was an African named Mabruke." What he didn't say was that Mabruke had been his friend a hundred and fifty years earlier during his second life as a *brujo*, when he had lived in Buenaventura, a port city on the west coast of New Granada (present-day Colombia).

"You seem to know a lot about many things," Doña Josefina observed, adding, "That's good for my purposes."

Carlos said nothing, waiting to see if she was going to explain what her purposes were.

They had gone only a short distance when she spoke again. "I asked to meet here because in my home I can't be sure our conversations won't be overheard. The walls of my house seem to have ears, and not all listen with a friendly intent."

After a short pause, during which she stopped and stood silent, she resumed walking and said, "I've told you that I invited my nephews to come to Santa Fe so that I could consider them as possible heirs to my fortune. The better I've gotten to know them, the less I like the older two, particularly Antonio, the eldest. He is arrogant and prone to outbursts of temper if he doesn't get his way. I dislike his attitude toward Indians. He's made it plain that he considers them dirty, stupid, lazy, and ignorant. This morning he and Julio were all afire to join Cortés's punitive expedition. I hope they do; it will be a relief to have them out of the house."

She stopped speaking and stood still again. "I could say more about my nephews, but discussing them is not my only reason for bringing you here. When I was a young woman, I sometimes wanted to be alone, and I took walks across the fields and up this canyon. My husband did not approve, saying that it was unsafe to do so. One day I met two Tewa men from Tesuque coming down the path. Recalling my husband's warnings, I was afraid, but I had the presence of mind to speak to them in a friendly way, and to ask them what they had in the pots they were carrying.

"My speaking to them seemed to surprise them, and they responded that they had been to a place not far from there that in their language they called *pik'ondiwe*, meaning where red pigment is found. I realized that this was the source of the red-colored paint they used to decorate their bodies and moccasins, and I told them that I had seen Pueblo dancers on the plaza the previous year and thought their costumes were beautiful. They smiled and went on their way. I found the spot they'd visited and dug up a handful of the red soil.

"I want to try," she went on, "to locate *pik'ondiwe* today, but everything has changed so much in fifty years that I'm not sure I can find it."

Carlos looked up and scanned the path ahead of them as far as he could see. "I believe there's a trail ahead that may lead to it," he said. His brujo vision had enabled him to see a faint trail leading up to a place on their left that had a bright aura. In his experience, such a luminous aura usually indicated a power spot of some sort.

Doña Josefina peered in the direction he was pointing and said, "I don't see any trail."

He didn't feel safe telling her how he'd noticed it, so he said, "Let's walk forward a bit. I think we'll be able to see where the trail splits off from the path we're on and goes up the slope."

Some twenty paces farther on they came to the trail Don Carlos had spotted. Doña Josefina looked around and then called Mabruke to come over. "This does seem familiar. I want to follow it up to its end," she announced. "The two of you can help me."

The trail led up a gradual incline, and with Carlos and Mabruke helping her, Doña Josefina slowly made her way up the slope until it leveled out at a flat spot a hundred yards farther on. For the last twenty feet or so, the soil of the path and the surrounding slope was distinctly reddish, and at the end of the trail the earth was very dark red. There were clear signs that the dark-red part of the hillside had been excavated. To Don Carlos's surprise, Doña Josefina stepped forward and went down on her knees in front of the excavation site. "This is it!" she exclaimed. "I thought I would never see it again."

Next she asked Mabruke to hand her a pot and a trowel he'd brought along, and she bent down and filled the pot with the dark-red soil. In the process she got the red pigment on her hands. She examined them and said, "I don't care, but everyone in my household would wonder what this old woman had been up to. Do you, Don Alfonso, possibly have a handkerchief I could borrow?"

He had one in his coat pocket and passed it to her. She wiped the dirt off her hands, but a good deal of the color remained. She sat back on her hips, her legs to one side, apparently comfortable, and asked with a tentativeness that was different from her usual commanding way of speaking, "May we sit here a few minutes?"

Don Carlos and Mabruke settled down and sat cross-legged. Much more time passed than a few minutes. Don Carlos didn't mind. He enjoyed the chance to be quiet. Birds of many types flitted through the trees in the river valley below. They were vocal, and the tone of their songs was welcoming and soothing. He was surprised at how strong the positive energies of *pik'ondiwe* were, inducing in him a sense of calm awareness. He supposed that this was the result of hundreds of years of visits from Indians preparing for their ceremonies. What surprised him most of all was to find such a place so close to town.

After half an hour Doña Josefina stirred at last. He was impressed that she had been quiet for so long. "I'm ready to start back," she announced.

"Before we leave here," Don Carlos said, "You might notice that some incense has been burned just outside this excavated area." He pointed to a small pile of powdery ash. "There have been recent visitors." Doña Josefina indicated that this pleased her a great deal.

Once they'd made their way back to the main trail, she told Mabruke to walk on ahead to Juan Archibeque's house. "We'll be along soon," she assured him.

As Mabruke disappeared from sight up ahead, she continued the narrative that she'd broken off earlier. "A conflict has arisen in my house," she said. "My grandson's widow, Marta, is pressing me to draw up papers leaving all my property to Antonio at my death, with Julio as the next heir in case anything happens to Antonio. I have been putting her off, saying that I won't make a decision until one of my nephews marries and has a male heir. I told her, 'To designate as heir to my estate someone who himself has no heir is like standing with a foot on the bottom rung of a ladder that has no more rungs.'

"She didn't like my answer one bit and snapped at me, 'Having no designated heir makes it all too likely that your properties will be broken into small bits!' And with that she marched off."

"What alternative do you have?" Carlos asked.

"I've thought of something, but I wonder whether you have any suggestions."

"Would it be possible," he said, "for you to give a small legacy in your lifetime to each of your nephews, an equal amount to each, and watch to see who puts what you grant them to the best use?"

"It would be possible," she replied. "But I'm no youngster. I could die any day. Ah! Here is Monsieur L'Archevêque," she said, using Archibeque's French name. "Good afternoon, Jean," she called out.

Archibeque had been sitting on a bench on the side of his house toward the path. He waved a pipe on which he'd been puffing, stood up, and strode over to greet her, bending and kissing her proffered hand. He was a tall, thin, angular man with a long nose and hooded eyes. He looked to be in his mid-thirties.

Archibeque turned to Carlos and offered his hand for a firm handshake. "I am pleased to meet you, Don Alfonso. I have heard many good things about you from my children's governesses." From inside the house, Carlos could hear singing and laughter. Archibeque remarked contentedly, "Yes, those are my daughters with Mara and Selena. They are happy together."

Addressing Archibeque, Doña Josefina said, "Jean, I haven't asked Don Alfonso yet, but I would like him to show my youngest nephew, Santiago Mendoza, a place we located today that brought back memories of my youth."

"I can see your youthful spirit shining through," Archibeque ventured gallantly.

"Bah!" Josefina replied, though she didn't look displeased. "French-men are full of romantic nonsense that they deliver to women of any age."

Archibeque bowed slightly. "Don Alfonso is welcome to bring your nephew here any time. Is this place perhaps one that Indians visit now and then?"

"It could be," Doña Josefina said. "We saw signs that it had been visited recently."

"I have lived here for a dozen years," Archibeque replied, "and during those years I have occasionally seen Indian men and women go by my house headed up the canyon and returning many hours later. I always assumed that they went to a site that tribal people revere."

"That's most interesting," Doña Josefina declared. "We located a place where red pigment for body paint can be found. Perhaps Don Alfonso can locate more places that Indians visit. But now, Jean, you'll have to excuse us. I have a private matter that I need to speak with Don Alfonso about." Archibeque bowed to them both, moved back to sit on his bench, and lit his pipe again.

Doña Josefina led Carlos toward the road. "My next subject," she said, "is potentially dangerous and must be handled with the utmost discretion. May I count on you for that?"

"I will do everything in my power to earn your trust," Carlos replied.

"I am worried about Manuela Maldonado. These Franciscans, Father Dorantes and Brother Gustavo, will do her grave harm if they catch her."

"You know her?" Carlos asked in surprise.

"Yes. Forty years ago she entered my service, and eventually I grew to love her. My husband often took me to task, saying that I treated her more like a sister than a mestizo servant."

"Was she with you for a long time?" Carlos asked.

"Oh, yes. For fifteen years. She fled with us to El Paso del Norte during the Pueblo Revolt and lived with us there until I returned to Spain. So it had been twenty years since I last saw her."

"But you have seen her recently?"

"Yes. She came to me here a few weeks ago. At first I didn't recognize her. Then we fell into each other's arms and wept. So many years, so many losses." She was silent for a moment and when she went on she said, "I think it was she who tore down and burned the Holy Office's notice that named her as a wanted person. The more I've thought about it the more I think it must be so. It's the sort of thing she would do. She was always bold and reckless, and she regards these Franciscans as her enemies. She told me that she had somehow attracted the interest of the Inquisition in El Paso del Norte. She fled the town, but naturally she does not feel at all safe."

"Did she tell you how she was connected with a case of witchcraft mentioned in the Holy Office's proclamation?"

"No. She didn't say why the inquisitors were after her, and I didn't inquire."

"You didn't inquire," Carlos put in, "but I think you have your suspicions."

She glanced at him sharply. "You are very astute," she replied. "Yes, I have my suspicions. I know nothing about these things, but—tell me: Do you think a person who is a sorcerer can recognize that another person is a sorcerer?"

"You must have some reason for asking that," Carlos said.

"Yes," she replied. "Manuela said that when a Franciscan inquisitor came to her house in El Paso del Norte to arrest her, she saw that this person—none other than Father Dorantes's assistant, Brother Gustavo—was some sort of sorcerer. She was so shocked that instead of cooperating, as she should have done, she 'called on her powers,' as she put it, and escaped out the window. She fled north, and came here. When the Franciscans arrived in April, she was convinced that they had tracked her to Santa Fe."

"Hmmm," said Carlos thoughtfully, wondering about the wisdom of leading Doña Josefina to make more connections than she had already made. As usual, caution lost. "That story is consistent," he ventured, "with a story Father Dorantes told at a dinner party given for him by the Trigaleses. He spoke then of seeing with his own eyes an instance of sorcery. He said that he and Brother Gustavo had been sent to an old woman's house to arrest her. Brother Gustavo, who was more experienced in such matters, told Dorantes to wait outside. Dorantes soon heard sounds of a struggle, and then he saw a bat fly out a window. When he entered the house, there was no old woman, only a pile of clothes on the floor."

Doña Josefina looked at him with narrowed eyes. "Indeed," she said.

Carlos met her gaze. "Indeed," he repeated. "In fact, from what Manuela told me—as it happened, she spoke to me at Saturday market—I got the idea that she thought Brother Gustavo was more dangerous than Father Dorantes."

"So she has spoken to you. How interesting," Doña Josefina said. "I think," she went on, "we have established that we can trust each other."

Carlos nodded, wondering again if he should go further. "Do you think Father Dorantes and Brother Gustavo might have different objectives in bringing the Inquisition to Santa Fe?"

"I'm not sure what you mean," she replied.

"Did Manuela say anything about the Inquisition being in pursuit of a larger quarry, a sorcerer with greater powers than hers, whose whereabouts or identity she might know?"

"The inquisitors never had a chance to question her, so I can't see how she could know exactly what they wanted. But," she said, turning to him, "are you suggesting that Dorantes believes that there is a very powerful sorcerer in northern New Spain, someone so powerful that he must be"—here her lip curled slightly in irony—"in league with the Devil? Who knows, perhaps the Devil himself?"

"I don't know," Carlos said. "But if Dorantes sees himself as pursuing the Devil, that might explain the fervor which led him to bring the Inquisition to our small, remote town."

"That would make him a dangerous type of fanatic, one who believes he is serving a righteous cause. And yet—" she broke off.

"And yet?" Carlos prompted.

"And yet there is a kindness in him. It is apparent from time to time. But, in your opinion, is Brother Gustavo any different? Is he equally fanatical?"

"From something Brother Gustavo said to me, I believe he had an experience long ago that left him with a particular hatred of women like Manuela, who reminded him of a demonic seducer of young men."

Doña Josefina let out a bark of a laugh. "He's right about Manuela being a seducer of young men, though I don't know about the demonic part, and I hardly see her behavior as the worst of sins. Let me tell you a little more about her. When Manuela was about forty, she fell in love with a man named Amado Ugate. He was much younger than she was, only twenty, and a servant in a neighbor's household. It was something to behold!" She laughed heartily again. "They were like a young stallion and an older mare separated by a fence. After a lot of excitement the mare finally broke the fence and they ran off together.

"This caused a great fuss, and a woman who considered herself engaged to Amado accused Manuela of bewitching him with potions and spells. She might have, for all I know. I must say I was not pleased with her for running off, but they returned to town two weeks later, as full of themselves as before. I wanted Manuela back to attend to me, so we took Amado on as a field hand, and it worked well for as long as it lasted. When the potion, or whatever it was, wore off, Amado lost interest in Manuela and returned to his former employer. This would have been 1677 or 1678. Shortly after that came the Pueblo Revolt, and Manuela and I fled to the south. Amado was an Indian man, and he cast his lot with the rebels. After the reconquest he found a job with a local rancher. When she came back a few weeks ago, Manuela went looking for him and found him. I don't think the meeting went well. She told me that Amado is not quite right in the head. He can handle only the simplest chores, like mucking out stalls."

"Do you think she's staying in Santa Fe, or nearby?"

"I doubt it, although this incident of the Holy Office's proclamation being destroyed makes me wonder. It's possible she's gone to live with a cousin who works for an old friend of mine, Emilia Ceballos, who owns a ranch near Bernalillo. She has always had great sympathy for mestizo and Native people, and she would be more than glad to shelter Manuela in defiance of Dorantes."

"If I find myself anywhere near Bernalillo," Carlos said, "I may drop in on Señora Ceballos."

"I'm sure she would like to meet you," Doña Josefina replied. "Like Manuela, she has always enjoyed the company of handsome men. But now it's time for me to go home and see whether my nephews have managed to sign up for the punitive expedition. May we give you a ride back to the center of Santa Fe?"

"No, thank you. I have something I want to ask Selena. But I thank you for the offer and, even more so, for the rest of our conversation. I promise to explore the canyon soon with Santiago."

After watching Doña Josefina's carriage depart, Carlos walked back to Archibeque's house, noticing that the Frenchman had left his place on the bench and evidently gone inside. Carlos knocked on the door, and Selena opened it. "Hello, Alfonso," she said. "We're just about to have lunch. Would you like to join us?"

"I'd like to join you," he began, but she interrupted him.

"I don't believe you. If you really wanted to, you would simply say yes."

"What I want to do," he went on, "is to have a word with you privately."

Selena seemed pleased at this prospect. "Privately, just the two of us. I like that," she said. "But Mara will be deeply disappointed."

"If you'll let me get a word in edgewise," he replied, "I want to ask you a question."

"Please ask," she said, sitting down on the bench next to the front door and inviting him to join her by patting the seat next to her — very close to her, Carlos noticed. But he couldn't very well stand while she was sitting, so he sat down. She moved closer to him so that her arm touched his lightly.

"Before I get to my question," he said, shifting away from her a little, "I need to tell you something. The day before Leandro left town he told me a good deal about the man he called Master, who I know is your father. I was surprised that he was so forthcoming, since previously he had been extremely secretive about everything related to your father. He also admitted to me that his Master, your father, had sent the three of you on a mission to find a powerful brujo named Carlos Buenaventura."

Selena looked taken aback. "I'm surprised to have you bring up the subject of my father," she said. "I barely know him."

"But you did see him on various occasions, including the time, now about three years ago, when he brought Mara to join you and Leandro to become itinerant entertainers. Didn't he give you instructions then about what he hoped you'd do for him?"

She turned her head away from him and studied the ground for a moment before answering. "The topic of Leandro is painful to me," she said. Then turning back to him, she went on. "As for this brujo named Carlos, I know very little about him. My father thought he was an Indian and that we would be able to identify him by the powers he displayed. We thought we might have located him when we heard of a powerful magician in Nombre de Dios named Mateo Pizarro, but by the time we got there Pizarro was dead and he was, in any case, a mestizo. Leandro believed he had been killed by a more powerful sorcerer and supposed that man might be this Carlos. We continued our search northward and ended up in Santa Fe. But as far as we could tell, nobody in Santa Fe was an Indian with great powers, and we heard no rumors of hidden sorcerers."

"Yes," Carlos said, satisfied with what she had told him. "Now for my question: have you ever heard of or met one of your father's associates called Gustavo de Illueca?"

Selena looked blankly at him. "No. Why?"

"There is now a man in Santa Fe, a Franciscan brother and a member of the Inquisition, who knew Leandro and was also connected to your father. I believe he knew that Leandro was involved in the occult, and he knows about Leandro's role in the Trigales's children's kidnapping and your and Mara's exoneration. In other words, he knows about your relation to Leandro and your presence here in Santa Fe. I am telling you this to warn you; because of your ties to Leandro, he may attempt to go after you and Mara for witchcraft."

Selena ignored Carlos's warning as if she had not heard it and responded with anger to his earlier words. "You said this Brother Gustavo knew Leandro and was one of my father's associates, but he's a Franciscan and an inquisitor. That makes no sense. How do you know that this Gustavo knew Leandro and my father?"

"When I was trying to find Leandro and the Trigales children, I talked with a rancher and his wife who kept an inn just south of Albuquerque. They told me that Leandro had met twice at their place with a Franciscan brother named Gustavo. I'm assuming that this was more than coincidental."

Selena's anger, now mixed with fear, escalated. "There's something you're not telling me!" she said. "You know how Leandro died, don't you? Did this Gustavo have something to do with Leandro's death?" Something worse apparently occurred to her, and showed on her face. "Or did my father—?"

Carlos gently put his hand on hers. What, he wondered, could he safely tell her? "No, Gustavo had nothing to do with it," he said. "As you know, the Council of Inquiry concluded that Leandro had accomplices, and that they had a falling out over the distribution of the ransom money. The Trigales children testified that their kidnappers were gigantic monsters. I believe that Leandro's accomplices were these monsters, and that they killed him."

"Oh!" Selena interjected. "Leandro's potion—!"

"Yes," Carlos said. "When Inéz, José, and I reached the place where the groom and the governess had been killed, we found many huge footprints, even bigger than ones that Leandro could have made after ingesting his potion. His accomplices must have had access to a much stronger potion to become as large as they did—to become monsters. And, as you know, even Leandro's weaker potion tended to make him violent."

Selena looked as if she remembered only too well. "I'm sorry to upset you," Carlos said sincerely. "But I think it is important for you and Mara to know that Brother Gustavo has some knowledge about Leandro's activities, and he could be a danger to you."

"Thank you," she said, quickly recovering her composure. She stood up. "We will continue to keep to ourselves, as we've been doing ever since the kidnapping. And now I need to go inside for lunch or everyone will wonder what has happened to me. Mara and I don't keep secrets from each other. I will tell her what you've told me."

"I assumed you would," he replied, also standing up. For once, she didn't try to kiss him. They parted with a formal nod and she turned and went into the house. He went on his way down the path back to town.

14

Spirals

Instead of going directly home, Carlos walked over to Pedro's stable. He hadn't seen Dolores for many days and wondered how she was adjusting to her new life. "Not so good," Pedro said in answer to his question.

"What's the problem?"

"She won't say, except that she's not used to keeping the same hours as we do. When she was a scavenger, she went out at night and slept all day. She's in her room with the door closed."

Carlos didn't hesitate. He went to the door and knocked. "Dolores," he called, "may I come in?"

He heard a faint response. "No, I want to be left alone."

"Please."

There was silence for a few minutes; then he heard bare feet pad across the room. She opened the door a tiny bit and looked out at him mutely with tear-stained eyes. "Please let me in," Don Carlos repeated. "Would it help if I gave you a shoulder to cry on?"

"I don't know," she said, tearing up again and going back to throw herself face down on her bed.

She'd left the door ajar, so Carlos pushed it open and stepped into the room.

Don Carlos went over to the bed where Dolores was lying. She looked smaller than she had seemed when he first rescued her. He was sure that she had not lost weight, only spirit. What could be the problem? He sat on the bed and put his hand on her arm. "You must not blame yourself for feeling badly. There's been a big change in the way you live. Naturally that's hard."

"I'm afraid to be out in the daylight," she said. "Always before the night was my protector."

"But now you have a place with Pedro and María. You're safe with them."

She murmured something and did not sound convinced.

"May I tell you something about myself?"

"What?"

"You and I share the ability to transform ourselves. You seem to have done so nearly every night. I don't dare do that. I can't take a chance of doing transformations in Santa Fe where someone might notice it." She lifted her head a little and looked at him out of her good eye.

Don Carlos went on. "I find that when I am in Santa Fe I have to disguise myself to appear as ordinary as possible, and I begin to feel—not exactly weak, but cut off from my brujo power."

She raised herself on one elbow and half sat up.

"So," he continued, "what I need to do, and what you may need to do to feel better, is to get out in the country away from Santa Fe. If we feel like it, we can practice transformations."

"In the daylight?"

"If we're out of town and away from any inhabited place, we can safely practice transforming ourselves. What I have in mind is riding together to Rancho Rosón, a place south of here but not far away. I want to introduce you to a friend of mine, José Lugo, who's in charge of training horses there. José knows that I am a brujo and has seen me transform myself into owls of various types. We'll ride out to a mountain ridge to the west of the ranch and hike up some places where Indians have made pictures on the rocks. We can transform ourselves there without being observed."

She sat up fully. "I don't know how to ride a horse."

"I'm sure Pedro can find a gentle, safe horse for you. You might be a little sore tomorrow, but I think you'll feel so good otherwise that you won't mind."

"I don't know."

"Let's ask Pedro about loaning you a horse. And Dolores..."

"Yes?"

"If this works out as I think it will, you'll have to promise to go for rides in the country at least once a week."

Carlos returned to the kitchen, where Pedro and María were sitting at the table with concerned looks on their faces. Carlos told them, "Dolores and I are going to go for a ride to visit Rancho Rosón. We probably won't get back until late today. Do you have a horse she could ride?"

Dolores had followed him into the kitchen. "I've never ridden a horse," she said.

"Yes," María said, "but you've been helping Pedro feed them, and you're not afraid of them. Is there one you like best?"

Dolores considered this. "I like Dulce," she said.

"Whose horse is Dulce?" Carlos asked.

"She's ours, I guess," Pedro replied. "Her owner couldn't pay her board, so he gave her to me to settle his debt. I was going to sell her, but maybe not."

"So," Don Carlos said, "you won't mind if we borrow Dulce today. While I go home and have lunch, you can get Dulce ready for a trip to Rancho Rosón."

Carlos went home, ate some cornbread, saddled Eagle, and led him across the fields to Pedro's stable. Gordo followed along. "I guess I've been neglecting you," Carlos said to his little dog. "You can come along, if you want. We'll be taking a slow pace because Dolores has never ridden a horse before, so we won't go faster than a walk."

By the time Carlos arrived at Pedro's stable, Pedro had gotten Dulce ready. He boosted Dolores into the saddle, gave her a few basic instructions, and concluded with the words, "If she doesn't stop when you pull back on the reins, just say 'whoa,' and she'll halt."

Dolores looked very nervous. "I don't like being seen in town during the day," she said, and she tugged her scarf farther across the scarred side of her face.

María, who had been standing off to one side, stepped forward and told Dolores, "You'll be much too hot in that scarf. Give it to me and brush your hair forward to hide the side of your face," which Dolores did, despite an anxious expression. "Once you're out of town," María added, pulling a ribbon out of her apron pocket, "you can tie your hair back with this."

"Don't worry, Dolores," Don Carlos said, "We're not going to be in town for long." He mounted Eagle and led the way across a ford in the Santa

Fe River and headed south on the road to Bernalillo. "If it's all right with you," Carlos said, "let's ride along in silence, enjoying the day." Dolores didn't object.

The sights that surrounded them—the blue sky above, the mountains in the distance, and the trees on both sides of the road resplendent in green spring foliage—all contributed to the good mood that arose in Carlos. But it was feeling the motion of Eagle underneath his saddle that most strongly captured Carlos's attention. He felt at one with his horse. He could understand how some Native peoples, on encountering mounted Spaniards for the first time, could believe that the man and horse were a new type of animal, a man-beast. Carlos gave his full attention to experiencing Eagle's steady walk and was drawn deeper and deeper into a consciousness located in his body.

Lost in this inner space, Carlos for a time forgot about Gordo. At first the little dog had jogged happily along next to Eagle, occasionally stopping to sniff something at the edge of the road. Dolores, however, noticed that Gordo had gradually fallen behind and called, "Gordo isn't able to keep up!" Carlos looked back and saw that Gordo was lagging well behind.

"Stop here," Carlos said. "We'll let him catch up."

A few minutes passed as Gordo plodded along. Eventually he came up beside Don Carlos and Eagle and flopped down on the ground. Carlos dismounted, picked him up, and handed him to Dolores. "Hold Gordo while I remount," he said. He got back on Eagle, maneuvered over to Dolores, and took Gordo from her and held him with one hand and the reins with the other. "You can ride the remainder of the way to José's," he told his dog, "and rest up for the trip home."

When they arrived at Rancho Rosón, Carlos could see José and several vaqueros working horses in a large field. As Carlos and Dolores rode up to a hitching post next to the corral gate, José saw them and spurred his horse over to the fence at a canter. Carlos dismounted, put Gordo down, and helped Dolores off Dulce. She looked apprehensive at the approach of José, a strange man, but fortunately a distraction was provided when a dog burst out of the bunkhouse and came running toward them, barking loudly. Gordo, totally recovered, let out high-pitched yips in reply and dashed toward the oncoming dog. It was, Carlos recognized, Nana, the mother dog that Gordo had brought home a few weeks earlier.

"Clearly Gordo and Nana are pleased to see each other," Carlos said. "They need no introduction, but some are in order among us. Dolores, this is my friend I've told you about, José Lugo. And José, this is Dolores, who is living with Pedro and María and who is going to help them, especially María, once the baby arrives."

Formal greetings were exchanged between José and Dolores, and Don Carlos was pleased to see that the two of them seemed to like each other. José gave her a genuinely friendly smile, which Dolores returned, though Carlos noticed that she hid her crippled hand in the long sleeve of her blouse, and she tried to keep the scarred side of her face turned away from José.

"What brings you here?" José asked.

"We're just out for a ride," Carlos replied, "and I thought we would visit the spiral image on the rock that you showed me last month. Could you keep Gordo here to rest while we explore? He wanted to come along but couldn't make it the whole way on his own power."

"Gordo is a welcome guest," José said. "I wish I could go back to that place with you, but right now I have too much work to do. Perhaps we can have a longer visit when you stop here to pick up Gordo on your way home."

"We look forward to it," Carlos said.

After giving Eagle and Dulce a chance to drink at the water trough, Don Carlos and Dolores remounted and rode through the sparse vegetation of the flatlands for about two miles. Ahead of them they could see the green of willows and cottonwoods along the river, and beyond the trees the rocky basalt ridge that rose up abruptly for hundreds of feet above the valley floor. They forded the shallow river, rode through the flat expanse on the other side of it to the base of the ridge, and there put Eagle and Dulce on long tethers to graze.

Carlos led the way up the rough, rocky slope. They climbed through and over large, sharp-edged basalt boulders that looked as if they had broken off and tumbled down from the top of the plateau eons ago. The higher they climbed the more striking the vista of the valley below became. The junipers that grew thickly near the base thinned out, and scrub brush through which lizards rustled grew among the rocks. As they worked their way up the slope they sometimes dislodged loose stones that rattled down the cliff. But there were many other sounds: the buzz of insects, birds chirping, three crows cawing as they lifted out of a juniper, and a hawk's cry from high above.

Several times they came upon rock slabs with figures that had been pecked into their surfaces with stone tools. All manner of animals were shown, and deer, antelope, and many types of bird images were common-place. There were also human figures, hump-backed flute players and others with horns projecting from their heads. They stopped frequently to study the animals and symbols. Dolores didn't comment, but Carlos could see that she was taking it in with great interest. More than three-quarters of the way up the side of the ridge they came to the place Don Carlos was looking for. Breathing hard, he pointed to a large spiral with two thunderbirds directly above it that had been pecked into the flat face of a huge slab of basalt. "I'm very much drawn to this spiral image," Carlos said.

"What are those birds?" Dolores asked, also out of breath. "I've never seen any birds like that, unless they're supposed to be gigantic eagles."

"They could be eagles," Don Carlos replied. "But they're said to be thunderbirds, a legendary bird that causes thunder and powerful winds by beating its wings."

"I would love to be able to do that!" Dolores said. "To be that powerful, to move the wind!"

"Yes," Don Carlos agreed, his breathing returning to normal. "But what do you make of this spiral figure?"

Dolores was silent for several moments. Finally she said, "I don't know."

"Then what do you think the spiral lines might mean?"

"It could have something to do with water," she replied. "If you drop a pebble into a pond, it creates ripples in the form of circles. Then again, there are many snakes around here. Maybe the spiral represents a snake coiling around itself."

"I like both your ideas," he said. "Coiled snakes and ripples made by a pebble in a pond are found everywhere, which may explain why there are similar rock spirals in Spain. But another possibility is that it's a solstice symbol. I like that idea because I was born on the summer solstice."

"I don't see it as a sun," Dolores remarked. "I don't say you're wrong. I just don't see it."

"Well, it could also be a simple labyrinth, the kind that is a circular path that winds deeper until it leads you to the center. But I suppose there's no knowing for sure. Why don't we just sit down under the spiral figure and enjoy the sun?"

"Yes, let's," Dolores said, and they sat down, their backs against the rock face.

Many minutes passed. Don Carlos wasn't at all sure how many because he stopped thinking about time. Warmth radiated off the dark gray rock behind him, and the bright sunlight made the valley that stretched out below seem extremely clear. He felt the sort of calm strength that he usually associated with desert landscapes.

A small voice came from his right, where Dolores was seated. "Do you feel it?"

"What?"

"I feel as if warmth from the spiral is heating me up on the inside and now something is softly glowing inside me. Perhaps you were right to say this image has something to do with the sun."

The moment Dolores mentioned it he realized that he was feeling something similar. "I think what you're experiencing," he told Dolores, "is a gift of the power of this place."

"Look away from me," Dolores said, and he did as she asked. He heard a rustling sound and recognized that she was undressing. Then, in a shy, gentle way, the black dog into which she'd changed herself lay its head in his lap and closed its eyes in what he interpreted as an expression of great happiness. Very tentatively, he stroked the dog's head.

They sat together like that for fifteen minutes until the dog stirred, got up, went over to Dolores's clothes, which were in a neat pile, and gave Don Carlos a significant look. He understood what she wanted and looked away while she got dressed. Soon she said, "It's all right to look now."

When Don Carlos looked, he saw that her aura was exceptionally strong. "You are radiant," he said.

"Look at the spiral figure," she replied. He turned to look at the ancient image, and it seemed to him that the marks pecked into the dark surface of the stone, revealing a lighter layer beneath, were tiny particles burning white-hot. "As if," he murmured to himself, "the curving shape of the spiral was a path that was on fire—no," he corrected himself, "illuminated. The path to the center is illuminated." He saw it clearly, without entirely understanding what it meant.

After a long pause during which they were silent, Don Carlos said, "I think it's time to start down. We have to stop at Rancho Rosón before we head back to Santa Fe."

"I'm looking forward to that," she replied.

Don Carlos smiled at her. "You sound as though you're feeling more confident," he observed.

"Yes. I feel as if something that happened here changed me. But you didn't do a transformation like we'd planned."

"What happened for you was much more important. I promise I'll take you somewhere in the near future and change into an owl or hawk."

"I remember you said you could transform yourself into many animal forms. I don't believe I can change into anything except a dog."

"That's possible," he replied. "You have special reasons for being able to do that. But perhaps if you had strong reasons to take on a different animal form, you could do it."

They hiked down to the base of the ridge, collected Eagle and Dulce, and rode across the valley to Rancho Rosón.

Gordo saw them coming and dashed out to meet them, cavorting around happily. José had spotted them too, and he came out of the bunkhouse and waved. "I'm between mounts. This would be a good time to visit."

In the few minutes it took Carlos and Dolores to water their horses and tie them to the hitching post, José went into the bunkhouse. He returned with three mugs. "Flavored water," he said. To Carlos it tasted like chilled herb tea. "How did your day go?" José asked.

"Dolores is the one with the most interesting experience," Don Carlos said. "I'll let her tell you."

"Please do," José said, turning his attention to Dolores.

Dolores met his gaze easily. "We were sitting with our backs to the spiral image that has two thunderbirds above it," she began. "I started to feel very warm, not from the sun. It was more like it was coming from the spiral, which was behind me. It seemed to fill me and make my whole body feel soft. I felt happy, calm, and secure in a way I can't ever recall feeling before."

"Ah!" José exclaimed. "You were drawing power from the spiral figure."

"Do you think it might be a sun symbol, José?" Carlos asked.

"It might be."

"I would like to think Dolores was also being given power by the sun."

"I think the sun is Dolores's ally," José said seriously, "a very powerful ally."

"I would like to think so too," Dolores affirmed.

They continued to talk about their climb up the basalt rocks and the images they found on them. José told them that the images were known as *piedras marcadas*, marked stones, and that they were surely very old, because they had been there when the first Spaniards arrived in New Mexico, exactly how long ago he didn't know for sure.

"Almost two hundred years ago," Don Carlos said in a reflective tone, thinking that that was as far back as his first life as a brujo. A Spaniard, his master Don Serafino, had seen something in him, a young Indian man, and trained him to be a brujo. Did Don Serafino, Carlos wondered, see some invisible mark on him from even earlier lives? Musing, Carlos fell into a reverie, and he and his companions sat there in comfortable silence until the sun was low in the west and Don Carlos realized they needed to leave in order to get back to Santa Fe before dark. Dolores mounted Dulce with a boost from Carlos, but Gordo, sensing that Carlos expected him to come along, lay down to show that he didn't want to leave Nana. Carlos bent down and picked him up. Gordo put on a very sad face, but Carlos handed him to José, mounted Eagle, and took Gordo back from José.

"Please come again," José called, as Don Carlos and Dolores started north to Santa Fe.

Don Carlos carried Gordo for several miles, worried that he would run back to Rancho Rosón the first chance he got. Eventually Carlos decided it would be safe to put him down, and Gordo seemed content to run along beside Eagle and Dulce. When he began to tire, Dolores volunteered to dismount and lift Gordo up to Carlos. While she was dismounted, she noticed a patch of wildflowers next to the road. She went over and picked a poppy blossom. Although it had closed at sunset, she threaded the poppy into the ribbon next to her ear, a fleck of orange in her black hair. It was still there when they reached Pedro and María's place. María didn't remark on the flower, but Carlos knew she noticed it, because she studied it for a moment and smiled.

Pedro helped Dolores dismount and María led her and Dulce toward the stable. When Pedro turned back toward Carlos, he was all business. "The military expedition won't be ready to leave tomorrow. They're planning to head off the day after tomorrow, Saturday."

Carlos said, "Major Cortés must be upset that it's taking so long. It doesn't reflect well on his organizational skills. A column should have been moving north today, or at the latest tomorrow."

"I don't think it could be helped," Pedro replied. "It was a big war party that attacked the cavalrymen, and Cortés thinks there are even more Native raiders to the north. If he goes off with too few troops, he'll be risking a fight in which his men are outnumbered. Also," Pedro added, "I don't think he has a brief campaign in mind. He's putting together soldiers, auxiliaries, and supplies to last a while. He's going to take the fight into territory beyond the northernmost Spanish settlements."

Remembering Pedro's experience as a soldier, Carlos was inclined to think he was right, and that, moreover, Cortés's strategy was sound. "That makes sense," Carlos observed, turning Eagle as he prepared to leave. "And it's a bold move."

Once home, Carlos led Eagle to his corral. After putting hay out for him—Orfeo had already fed Inéz's Alegría and Pedro's Pepper—Carlos went in to see how Orfeo was doing. He found him sitting at the table, eating a solitary dinner and looking morose. Don Carlos ladled up a bowl of chili from the pot and sat down across from him. "Is something wrong?" Carlos asked.

Orfeo sighed. "Señor Díaz seems to think I'm spending too much time at his place, keeping Marisol from doing her chores. He was in a bad mood today and told me I ought to find something else to do."

"Maybe you need a project to keep you busy around here," Don Carlos said. "Let me see if I can come up with something."

"The horses could use a bigger corral," Orfeo suggested.

"Not a bad idea," Don Carlos replied, but before they could pursue the topic further, Carlos's lodgers arrived. "This was sure a bad day!" Gonzalo announced, plopping down in a chair and throwing his hat on the kitchen table.

Luis shrugged his shoulders and explained. "Major Cortés is in a worse mood than usual. He kicks his officers, they kick the sergeants, and the sergeants kick us."

"According to Pedro," Don Carlos said, "the punitive expedition isn't going to leave until day after tomorrow."

"Yes, first thing Saturday morning," Alejandro replied.

"Not quite first thing," Gonzalo put in. "There's going to be a special Mass early in the morning, followed by a procession around the plaza. The expedition won't leave until after that."

"Pedro seemed to think Cortés is planning for an extended campaign. Is that true?" Don Carlos asked.

"That's the way it looks," Alejandro replied. "The rumor is that the campaign will last a month or more, but no one knows anything for sure."

"Where military campaigns are concerned," Don Carlos observed, "you never know anything for sure. Expect the unexpected, as the old saying goes."

Don Carlos's statement seemed to remind Orfeo of something. "Don Alfonso, I forgot to tell you. A message came today that Governor Peralta wants to meet with the Town Council tomorrow morning. You're supposed to be at the Palace of the Governors at nine o'clock."

"Anything said about the purpose of the meeting?" Don Carlos asked.

"No," Orfeo replied, and returned to his bowl of chili.

"You're not in your usual good spirits," Luis observed. "Why are you down in the mouth?"

"I don't want to talk about it," Orfeo muttered.

"I'll bet it's love troubles," Gonzalo ventured. "Did you have an argument with that blonde girl?"

"That's none of your business," Orfeo snapped.

"Sorry," Gonzalo said, holding his hands up and trying to back off.

Luis volunteered sympathetically, "Women are a lot of trouble—always trouble, in my opinion."

"What would you know about that?" Gonzalo asked. "You've never had a girl friend."

"You don't need to have had a girl friend," Luis asserted, "to notice how much trouble it makes when a man falls in love."

"Not all women cause men trouble," Alejandro said. "My mother and father get along fine."

Don Carlos could see a long argument starting, so he excused himself to go to his room. Gordo, tired from the trip to Rancho Rosón, had already gotten up on the bed and was sound asleep.

15
Surprises

Saturday's ceremony in honor of the men departing on the expedition surprised Don Carlos by its solemnity and effectiveness. The event, actually a series of events, began at seven o'clock in the morning with a Mass for the soldiers who were to participate in the campaign. Their ranks had grown considerably during the two days of preparation. Initially Don Carlos had heard that only the forty cavalrymen who had recently arrived under Major Cortés's command were expected to ride north. But Cortés insisted that more troops were needed, and he selected twenty soldiers from the Presidio's regular garrison and recruited another forty men from Santa Fe, Indians and mestizos who had volunteered for service either as militiamen or as drovers, cooks, and servants. A number of Indians were expected to join the expedition as it passed by pueblos on its march northward to Taos and beyond. The final tally of those in the campaign would, by Carlos's count, come to about a hundred and forty men.

The number of soldiers and support personnel was so large that they barely fit in Santa Fe's small chapel. As a consequence, few civilians were permitted to attend the special Mass. In addition to the top provincial officials— Governor Peralta, Vice Governor Cabrera, and Attorney General Archuleta— only members of the Town Council, of which Don Carlos was one, were invited. The Mass was said by Father Benedicto. He gave the briefest of homilies, expressing gratitude to the men for risking their lives in defense of New Mexico. He prayed that the campaign would succeed and that, under God's protection, all the members of the expedition would return home safely.

At the end of Mass all the participants filed out. The soldiers returned to the Presidio and mounted their horses, which had been kept ready outside the garrison's stables. They rode out of the Presidio grounds and turned left toward the plaza, sixty mounted cavalrymen led by Major Cortés in a tight formation three abreast, followed by a less orderly group of forty town militia volunteers on foot. Waiting for them in the street in front of the chapel were two dozen members of lay confraternities, religious societies devoted to the town's well-being through prayer and service. They carried religious banners and were accompanied by a small corps of drummers, who took up a marching beat as soon as everyone was in line. Then the procession moved forward, entered the plaza, turned to the right, and commenced a march that would take it around the plaza three times.

A large crowd had assembled. Some of the people were probably there for the usual Saturday market day, but many had come solely to see the expedition off. Don Carlos, standing next to Inéz on the north side of the plaza, estimated that at least eight hundred people—men, women, and children— lined the edge of the plaza or stood in adjacent streets. As the procession moved into the plaza, applause, shouts of encouragement, and huzzahs went up on all sides.

Carlos and Inéz watched in silence as the procession made its first circuit of the plaza. As it began a second circuit, Carlos spoke. "You know I have no fondness for war," he said, "but there is something powerful and inspiring about this display of military might."

"I know," Inéz said. "It's exciting and seductive. One forgets about the blood and death."

As the procession was approaching Carlos and Inéz for the second time she asked, "Do they really have to do this? What did you learn at the meeting the governor called yesterday morning?"

"Governor Peralta made a good case that something ought to be done. It's not just that a cavalry patrol was attacked and two soldiers killed, which heaven knows is bad enough. But Native raiders have also attacked several ranches on the outskirts of Taos. The situation is becoming dangerous, and it will get worse if these war parties are not crushed."

"What tribe are the warriors from? I thought even Apaches, Utes, and Navajos come to Taos for the fall trade fair under a peace agreement. Why would any of them want to disrupt a source of trade where they can get horses and iron implements—and probably, illegal though it is, firearms?"

"These war parties seem to have an entirely different tribal affiliation. They're not from New Mexico."

"As I recall," Inéz commented, "you said the five warriors who threatened you and José didn't come from any tribe you recognized."

"No. And in fact the more I've thought about it, the more I'm sure that's true. Later I remembered that one member of the war party had called to the others. He was not speaking Apache, and José thought the symbols the young braves had painted on their bodies were different from those used by Utes and Navajos."

"So that's it?" Inéz asked. "Raiders from a tribe new to the area need to be killed off, unless they can be drawn into agreements like the ones that have been worked out with the other tribes?"

"There's more to it than that," Carlos replied. "The governor has his eye on imperial matters beyond New Mexico's borders. He believes that French traders are expanding westward across the Plains. Our neighbor Juan Archibeque was a French soldier who got lost and wandered into the hands of Spanish authorities. He's an example of how close French intrusions have drawn. If the French develop trade and military ties with this new tribe of Native raiders, Governor Peralta believes the consequences could be quite serious."

"But isn't this all rumor, speculation rather than fact?"

"Maybe not. Since José and I got back to Santa Fe a month ago, more facts have come to light. Several Spanish traders from Taos have reported that local Pueblo Indians say the raiders call themselves Numunu, which apparently means The People. Although every tribe calls itself something similar in its own language, this is one we haven't heard of until now."

"I still don't see what the French have to do with this."

"I was coming to that, Inéz. One of the traders told a story about a rancher and his vaqueros who pursued a war party that had stolen the rancher's cattle. They killed one of the raiders and found that he was wearing a medal inscribed in French."

"So? All sorts of goods are exchanged from tribe to tribe. Finding a medal with an inscription in French doesn't mean the warrior was allied with the French. The raider might have traded for it as a pretty object."

"Agreed, but I've saved the most worrisome information for last. The rancher was sure that one of the raiders who escaped was carrying a modern musket of French manufacture. If the French are trading modern firearms with these Numunu tribesmen, that's alarming."

"I'm still skeptical," Inéz said. "How would a New Mexico rancher know what a French-made musket looks like?"

"Apparently, this rancher arrived in New Mexico only this year. Previously he had served in the Spanish navy, and he had seen this type of musket when his ship captured a French privateer."

The procession had passed Carlos and Inéz for the third time and was continuing its march from the plaza past the chapel and the Presidio gates onto the road that would take it north to Taos. As the column of soldiers and auxiliaries passed the chapel, Father Benedicto made the sign of the Cross and sprinkled holy water on them. They were on their way, and the crowd on the plaza began to disperse. Don Carlos was surprised at himself for saying a silent prayer for the soldiers' safety.

"Why do they, most of them anyway, look so thrilled to be going off to war?" Inéz asked. "Don't they realize that there's a chance they'll die in combat?"

"The allure of danger, my love. In all my lives I've never marched off to war, but I understand the seductiveness of danger. And young men seem to have little awareness of their mortality."

"I noticed that Antonio and Julio Mendoza were very excited about joining the fight, and they made quite imposing figures in their splendid outfits and mounted on their very expensive horses."

"Yes," Carlos agreed. "But you'll also notice that they have no intention of sharing in the discomforts that are the lot of ordinary soldiers. They were accompanied by servants leading pack horses, doubtless carrying the brothers' personal necessities."

"Including their mirrors," Inéz said sarcastically. "And did you notice the small scene that played out as the expedition left? Juliana and Victoria Peralta had been smiling and waving handkerchiefs at Antonio and Julio every time they passed by, and as soon as the column left the plaza they began dabbing at their eyes with their handkerchiefs. Then when Santiago Mendoza, who didn't join the campaign, passed not ten feet from them, they turned their heads and studiously ignored him. Their contempt for him was all too obvious."

"Poor Santiago. He must be feeling despised for not going with his brothers. I'll have to see what I can do to bolster his spirits. But right now let's walk back to your home. I have something else to tell you about that happened yesterday that I don't want to speak of until we can talk without being overheard."

Halfway to the Beltrán house, Carlos and Inéz found themselves alone. "Tell me what this other topic is now," Inéz said. "I have to get to work making lunch as soon as I get home."

"After I left the meeting with the governor yesterday, I was in a hurry, and as I turned the corner of the chapel I literally bumped into Jesús Escobar, who was coming around the corner from the other direction. I almost knocked him down."

"Ah," Inéz said, "Jesús, the man who adores your stepfather, General Alvarez."

"A stepfather whom I loathe for a variety of reasons, not the least of which is cheating me out of my inheritance and exiling me to New Mexico."

"Without which you wouldn't have met me," Inéz reminded him, "which I hope you don't regret."

"Of course not! But that doesn't make his behavior toward me any more acceptable. Jesús, on the other hand, is eternally grateful to him. After the military reconquest of New Mexico my stepfather rescued Jesús, an Apache captive who had been enslaved by the Pueblo rebels, and gave him his freedom. He even helped him find employment as Father Benedicto's manservant. That was twelve years ago, but Jesús has not lost his loyalty to my stepfather. And because of his loyalty to my stepfather, Jesús feels a loyalty to me. Soon after I arrived in Santa Fe he asked how he could serve me. Since I like learning new languages, I told him he could teach me Apache. In the process, I have become something like his confidant.

"Well," Carlos went on, "to get back to what I wanted to tell you, when Jesús and I bumped into each other I saw that he looked upset, and I asked him why. He replied in Apache, clearly because he didn't want anyone to understand what he was telling me.

"Jesús told me the rectory is an unhappy place because of a serious disagreement between Father Dorantes and Brother Gustavo. Gustavo is angry because they have not yet captured Manuela or found the sorcerer named Carlos Buenaventura. Father Dorantes says they are unlikely to catch up with Manuela, and if the sorcerer Carlos is an Indian, as Brother Gustavo seems to think, he is outside the jurisdiction of the Holy Office. Father Dorantes does believe the black dog and the wolf indicate that someone locally is practicing witchcraft, but since no one has provided information about either case, they have no one to accuse. So Dorantes feels they might as well leave after the forty-day period of grace ends. When Dorantes said that, Jesús told me, Gustavo exploded and starting shouting at him. Jesús then heard Father Dorantes say, 'You have a week either to capture this Manuela woman or prove that she's still in the area,' he said. 'But if I were you I would focus on the black dog and the wolf.'"

Inéz and Carlos had arrived at the Beltráns' kitchen door. Inéz turned to Carlos and said, "I suppose the good news is that there's dissension between them. But if, as you believe, Brother Gustavo is involved in the wolf business—"

"He should go and interrogate himself," Carlos said drily.

Inéz went inside, and Carlos started back toward his place. He had taken only a dozen steps when he saw Santiago Mendoza headed up the hill to his aunt's house. "Santiago!" he called, loudly enough to get Santiago's attention. Santiago turned to see who had hailed him.

Carlos hurried over to where the young man was standing and said, "I see that your brothers have joined the expedition, and that you decided not to."

"That's right," Santiago replied. "My decision has caused a lot of trouble. My brothers are angry with me, and Juliana and Victoria won't even speak to me."

"How is your aunt taking this?" Carlos asked.

"She's annoyed with my brothers, and she told them to stop behaving like children. Then they accused me of remaining in Santa Fe in order to curry favor with her and cheat them out of their inheritances."

"She might have tried to keep the peace by giving them some reassurance about their inheritance," Carlos said.

"She did make a gesture of sorts," Santiago replied. "But it didn't please them. What she said was, 'I'll take care of you, assuming you manage not to get yourselves killed.'"

Carlos thought this was so typical of Doña Josefina that he could almost hear her saying it. He couldn't help himself. He burst out laughing.

Santiago, infected by Carlos's laughter, allowed himself a smile. "May they have all the adventures they deserve," he said, letting one side of his smile curl downward slightly.

Santiago's response led Carlos to decide to do something for him without delay. "Your aunt was glad to know that I showed you a Pueblo Indian sacred site. There's one much closer to here. Why don't I come by for you after lunch and we'll walk to the place together?"

Santiago agreed, and early Saturday afternoon Don Carlos, having changed out of the clothes he had worn to Mass into an outfit more suitable for a walk in the countryside, returned to the Mendoza house. Santiago was waiting for him, and together they walked down to and across the Santa Fe River to Canyon Road and along it to the small house where Juan Archibeque lived. They passed the house without eliciting any response from the inhabitants. Carlos supposed that Juan, Selena, Mara, and Juan's three daughters were resting during siesta.

It was only a short distance up the trail to the faint path that led to the deposit of red soil that Indians used for body paint. "The Indian name for this place is *pik'ondiwe*," Carlos told Santiago. "Your aunt learned about it fifty years ago when she met some Pueblo Indians on the lower trail who were returning from it. This encounter created a strong sympathy in her for Pueblo culture. I believe that the present governor's antipathy to Native people distresses her. She told me that there have been a few times in the past when Spanish officials had a positive view of Pueblo Indian customs. According to her, at least two governors invited Pueblo Indians to perform their sacred dances on the plaza."

"That seems unlikely today," Santiago said.

"It does indeed," Carlos replied. "But let's honor this sacred place by sitting here for a while without speaking."

When the two men became silent, insects and birds could be heard in the brush. Within the many rustling sounds, Don Carlos heard a single tone, almost like the murmur of a distant river. Ignoring the varied noises about them, he focused on the tone that seemed to underlie the other sounds. His concentration became very strong.

After about twenty minutes Don Carlos got up and, gesturing to Santiago to follow him, they retraced their steps back to the main trail and continued up the canyon on it. For a while it stayed close to the river, but eventually it took a course up the side of the nearby mountains. The route soon took them out of the dense brush of the canyon onto boulder-strewn slopes with relatively little vegetation. About a mile into the hike Don Carlos found what he'd been looking for, an outline of a deer pecked into the face of a rock. He pointed it out to Santiago. "I have no way of knowing for sure, but I feel that this figure is very old—certainly from a time before the Spanish came."

Santiago studied it. "The deer seems to be in motion. It's very alive."

Continuing on their way, they saw more images—animals large and small, birds of many types, and also abstract designs. "Why did the Indians make these images?" Santiago asked. "It must have taken a lot of time when they could have been hunting or going about daily tasks."

"I don't think any Spaniard can answer your question, Santiago. Perhaps the people who created these images had a way of knowing that we have lost."

Santiago's response surprised Don Carlos. "Do you think," he asked, "that if we sit here near this image of an eagle, an eagle would visit us?"

Don Carlos replied. "I doubt that an eagle would approach the two of us, but if you sit here alone you might see one. But don't expect it to land on your arm as the hawk did at the ledge. Eagles have learned to be very cautious around humans."

"It would be thrilling to see one," Santiago said.

"We have plenty of time," Don Carlos said. "Sit down next to the image of the eagle. I'll hike farther up the trail. Once I'm well out of sight, be as still as a rock. Who knows?"

Don Carlos climbed up the slope and around a bend, where he changed himself into a golden eagle with a wingspan of nearly seven feet. Launching into the air above the canyon, he couldn't contain his exuberance and let out a high-pitched *kee-kee-kya*. Turning, he let updrafts along the mountain slope carry him above the trail. Having decided not to fly too close to Santiago, he coasted a hundred feet above the young man's position, making a single pass that carried him around another bend in the mountainside. Gaining yet more altitude, he circled up out of sight and then returned to the spot where he'd left his clothes. He landed, changed to his human form, dressed, and walked back to where Santiago was leaning against a boulder next to the trail. "Any luck?" he asked. "I thought I heard an eagle's cry, though only one."

"Yes, an eagle flew by, fairly high but just over my head. What an enormous bird!"

"I should warn you that you may not always be so lucky."

"I think," Santiago replied with a searching look, "I won't be so lucky unless you are along."

"Then we'll just have to take more hikes together," Carlos said. "Now let's head back to Santa Fe before our friends think we've been spirited off by Indians."

When they reached the Archibeque house, they found all its occupants in the courtyard in front of it. Juan was seated on his bench, smoking his pipe. Mara and Selena, in plain, loose-fitting, high-necked dresses with long sleeves, were playing an active game with Juan's children, four of them singing and dancing around in a circle while the remaining player stood blindfolded in the middle. As Carlos and Santiago watched, the song ended, the singers stopped in place and stood motionless, and the blindfolded player, who happened to be the littlest girl, lurched toward the spot where she thought one of her playmates was standing. She walked straight past Mara, who had to grab her to keep her from bumping into a tree. This occasioned a good deal of giggling and laughter.

Noticing Carlos and Santiago, the three little girls ran into the house, went to a window, and peered out over the sill. "They've been taught not to let strange men approach them," Mara said.

"But I'm not entirely a stranger," Carlos protested. "They saw me once before."

"You look different today," the eldest of the girls called out.

"You can't fool them," Selena said. "They can see that you've been on some sort of vision quest up the canyon."

"What clever girls," Carlos replied.

"We have to be very careful about men, especially handsome ones like the two of you," Selena said in her usual flirtatious way.

"Yes," Mara said. "We fall in love so easily, and then we always have our hearts broken."

"The truth is," Selena went on, "that we live a fairy-tale life here with Juan and his daughters. Of course, in a real fairy tale we would be two sisters who live deep in the woods, isolated from society, and we would know nothing of the greater world until two handsome men come and kiss us and awaken us from the spell that our evil stepmother put us under."

"The difference," Mara said, "is that we have a happy life here and don't need to know anything more about the pleasures of the world than we already know."

"Though we like being visited by handsome young men," Selena added, "and the two of you are always welcome here."

"You are both being silly," Juan commented. "These young men won't take you seriously unless you behave yourselves."

"Selena and I are being silly because we know both of them are already in love with other women," Mara said, putting on a sad face. "Alfonso is in love with Inéz, and Santiago with Elena."

Mention of Elena's name caused Santiago to flush with embarrassment. "Did I say something bad?" Mara asked.

"No," Santiago said, speaking for the first time, "I'm very fond of Elena, but I'm no prince. My older brothers have gone off to prove their courage in war, and I, as the youngest brother, have no real hope of inheriting an estate suitable to winning the heart of a rich merchant's daughter."

This statement startled Carlos. "It surprises me," he said, "that you seem to believe wealth is required to win a woman's heart."

"This is getting interesting," Selena commented, "not that we weren't enjoying ourselves before. But I've never heard two men discuss what is necessary to win a woman's heart."

"All you have to do to win Selena's," Mara said, "is to be a man."

"My sister is both naughty and getting us off the topic," Selena replied.

Don Carlos decided to take a chance and ask, "Santiago, suppose your aunt divided her fortune three ways among you and your brothers—giving her Spanish vineyards to one, her silver mines in northern New Spain to another, and her properties in and around Santa Fe to the third. If you could choose, which would you want to receive?"

Mara and Selena, to their credit, realized that this was a weighty question, and they dropped their teasing tone, waiting in silence for Santiago to answer.

With only the slightest hesitation, Santiago replied, "My choice, far and away my first choice, would be to stay here in Santa Fe."

"Good choice," Mara said.

"He's choosing with his heart rather than his head," Selena objected. "The other choices would make him richer."

"Are you saying," Mara countered, "that choosing love over wealth is not a good choice?"

"Choosing with his heart," Juan said, "is precisely what makes it a good choice."

Santiago was looking very embarrassed, and Carlos didn't think there was anything more to say. Trying to be diplomatic, he said, "Thank you for your advice, which I believe is excellent, but now we need to get back to town."

"You'd better come again soon," Selena said, "perhaps with Inéz and Elena, or if not that, at least Alfonso can bring Gordo. We miss that dear little dog."

"I will pass your invitation on to Gordo when I get home," Carlos replied. "I'm sure he'll be eager to visit you."

Carlos and Santiago wished everyone well and walked back to the Mendoza house together. "They're an unusual pair of women," Santiago said.

Carlos couldn't resist saying, "You don't know the half of it."

16
The Old Man

Carlos's Sunday began quietly. With the departure of the punitive expedition, his lodgers had moved back to the Presidio barracks, which now had plenty of space. Perhaps, Carlos thought when he woke up that morning at four o'clock, their absence accounted for the unusual silence in his house. Other than Gordo's soft snoring at the foot of the bed, the house was very still. No wind outside or mice in the larder—nothing to make noise.

Carlos got up and, after answering a call of nature, settled down to meditate. He soon dropped into a deeper quiet, an awareness of his heart beating and his slow in-and-out breaths. The worries and thoughts that did come flitted through his consciousness and quickly dissipated. The exhilarating feeling of taking eagle form yesterday afternoon filled his quiet awareness without disturbing it.

At seven o'clock he heard faint sounds of Orfeo pitching hay from the haystack into the corral. Carlos stood up, changed to his day clothes, went out to see how Orfeo was doing, and found that he'd completed most of his chores.

"You've accomplished a lot," Don Carlos observed, "and it's barely seven o'clock."

"I was restless all night," Orfeo replied. "I kept waking up almost every hour. By six I was so wide awake that I decided to get up and do my chores before breakfast."

"What's the matter?" Don Carlos asked. "It's not like you to sleep poorly."

"The usual problem. I was thinking about Marisol. It would help," he complained, "if I wasn't at such loose ends. When I'm idle, my mind wanders back to Marisol."

Clapping his young friend on the shoulder, Don Carlos said, "Love troubles can keep a man awake. I don't know what to do about Señor Díaz, but I have an idea for a big job that might occupy your mind and keep you from daydreaming."

"I would like that," Orfeo replied.

"Then let's go in, have breakfast, and while we're eating I'll tell you about it."

During breakfast Don Carlos told Orfeo about the idea he had been entertaining. "I'd like you to put your building skills to work expanding my house and enlarging the corral. More room for me, and more turnout for the horses.

"One serious deficiency of the house," Carlos went on, "is that it lacks a *sala*. The only social space is this small kitchen. I'd like to create a *sala* by knocking out the wall between the two rooms the soldiers were using. I poked around there last night after my three houseguests left, and it seems to me that the wall between them doesn't hold anything up. I think there was once a single room and then the owners decided to divide it into two."

"Removing that wall," Orfeo commented thoughtfully, "will be a dusty job."

"I guess so, though let me tell you the rest of my plan because it has two more parts. Part two would be to build a room in the place where the stalls are now located. Then in part three we'll construct a new stable and extend the corral perhaps thirty feet to the south."

Orfeo laughed. "All that should keep me busy for a while."

"I'll help when I can."

"What about materials?"

"We bought quite a lot of lumber and collected adobe bricks for the second wing of Dr. Velarde's house. I don't think he can afford to have that second wing built in the near future, so we can cart those materials over here. Also, some of the material from the wall between the two present rooms ought to be reusable."

"I'll start on postholes for the enlarged corral," Orfeo said. "I'll mark out a rough outline and you can check it over when you get back from church."

Carlos excused himself to get dressed for Mass. He put on his second-best outfit and headed for the Beltrán house. He found Inéz and the Beltráns in the *sala*, ready to leave with him. On the way to the chapel, Carlos asked Javier, "How was business yesterday during market day?"

"That's an odd thing, Don Alfonso," Javier replied. "There were more people than usual in town because of the departure ceremony for the expedition, but there was less business."

"How do you account for that?" Carlos inquired.

"Times are tight. People are holding onto whatever they have rather than trading for new goods."

As Carlos, Inéz, and the Beltráns entered the chapel, Carlos was surprised to see Doña Josefina seated toward the front of the chapel next to Governor Peralta and his wife. Usually only the governor and his wife were seated during Mass. The rest of the worshippers stood. Then again, Doña Josefina usually didn't attend Mass. Father Benedicto said Mass for her at her home.

Carlos began to understand the situation when he noticed that Santiago Mendoza was standing to his aunt's right, while the governor, his wife, and their two daughters were on her left. Apparently Doña Josefina was daring the Peralta twins to snub Santiago publicly in her presence. Carlos wished he had gotten to Mass sooner to see what had taken place, but he was fairly certain Doña Josefina's ploy had succeeded. When she turned to whisper something to her nephew, the look on her face was one of great satisfaction.

After Mass Carlos and the rest of his party joined Raul, Bianca, and their four children outside the chapel. As Anton did every time he saw Inéz, he took hold of her skirt and gazed up at her worshipfully. "I wonder whether he'll ever get over seeing you as his guardian angel," Carlos said to Inéz.

"I'm sure he will eventually," Inéz replied contentedly.

Just then Doña Josefina and Santiago emerged from the chapel. She smiled at Carlos and came over to him. "Don Alfonso, how nice to see you! I would appreciate being introduced to your friends."

Carlos first presented Inéz. "This is my friend Señora Inéz de Recalde," he began.

"Ah!" Doña Josefina said. "I am pleased to meet at last the woman who creates such splendid desserts, several of which she has generously contributed to dinner parties I've given."

Inéz murmured her thanks for Doña Josefina's kind words and said she was pleased to meet her.

Carlos turned next to the Trigales clan, introducing Raul, Bianca, and their children. "I am so pleased to meet you both, and these dear, brave children!" Doña Josefina exclaimed. Turning to the children, she added, "You had a terrible experience, but you were returned to your loving parents. A happy ending to a dreadful episode."

Raul spoke up. "Bianca and I will be forever grateful to you, Doña Mendoza, for helping to fund the ransom."

"A trifle, truly," she replied. "The lives of the rescued four are of incomparable value. But I see," she said, turning to Carlos, "that Don Alfonso has saved for last the three people whom my nephew is most eager for me to meet."

"Yes," Carlos replied. "Allow me to introduce Javier and Cristina Beltrán and their daughter Elena."

"I am delighted to make your acquaintance," Doña Josefina said, nodding to each in turn. Her attention then settled on Elena, to whom she said, "I have heard so much about you that our meeting seems long overdue."

Elena surprised Carlos by greeting this statement with a small curtsy followed by a simple "Thank you."

"There's much to say," Doña Josefina went on, "but allow this ancient woman to express a particular interest, which is a wish to watch my nephew fence with his friend, Señorita Beltrán. My father and husband were unable to curb most of my unladylike inclinations, but they did manage to prevent me from fencing. I am, for that reason, particularly interested in seeing a young woman fence."

"The real treat," Elena said, "would be to watch Inéz fence with Don Alfonso. Their bouts are extraordinary."

"I would be very interested in seeing them fence," Doña Josefina replied, "but don't think that will prevent me from insisting that you and Santiago demonstrate your skills too."

Carlos cleared his throat. "Surely that can be arranged. The Beltráns have a fine fencing strip that we've used with some regularity, usually on Wednesdays."

"Is it truly necessary to wait so long?" Doña Josefina said with a smile. "I'm a very old woman and may not live until Wednesday."

Taking the obvious cue, Javier broke in to say, "You would be most welcome to come by our house this afternoon, if you don't have a previous obligation."

"Usually," Doña Josefina replied, "Father Benedicto comes to my house on Sunday afternoon to say Mass for me, but since I attended Mass this morning, I won't need him to come today. I will inform him of that. If I may be so direct, what time would be best for you to receive me and Santiago?"

After a brief discussion they settled on a three o'clock appointment. Doña Josefina started to turn away, but then she looked over at Carlos and said, "I almost forgot to thank you for taking Santiago up the canyon yesterday. He reported that you had a splendid time; then this morning when Mabruke and I delivered some wine I'd promised Juan, he told us that you and Santiago had a most amusing exchange with those remarkable governesses of his, Mara and Selena."

Inéz gave Carlos a you-could-be-in-big-trouble look and said to him, "You didn't mention anything about seeing Mara and Selena yesterday."

"I haven't had a chance to tell you," he replied, feeling a bit defensive.

Santiago intervened to say, "The two sisters seemed very nice to me."

Elena shot him a look. "And also very attractive."

Carlos, in what he hoped was a soothing tone, said, "Santiago's heart belongs to you, Elena, as mine does to Inéz."

"Knowing Selena," Inéz retorted, "that won't stop her from flirting with both of you."

Doña Josefina sensed what was going on and came to the rescue by laughing. "Ah! Young love!" she exclaimed. "Why don't the four of you save the energy you've brought to verbal fencing to the actual matches this afternoon?"

Doña Josefina and Santiago went on their way, and Carlos escorted Inéz back to the Beltrán place, walking ahead of the others so they could have a private conversation. "I shouldn't have spoken so sharply to you about Mara and Selena," Inéz said, "but your having a private tête-a-tête with them and not telling me about it—"

Carlos broke in before she could finish. "For one thing, Inéz, it was anything but private. Juan and his three children were there. It was all very innocent."

"Humpf!" was her initial reply; then she added, "You'd better bring your best skills to our bout this afternoon. I might still be just angry enough to give you a tough test."

Initially, Carlos was mildly annoyed at Inéz's parting remark, but then he felt an upwelling of excitement about the possibility of a bout that truly tested his skills.

His walk felt exceptionally springy as went back to his house and put on his fencing outfit. As he started out the door, Gordo got up to come along. "Not such a good idea, old fellow," Carlos said. "Let's go to Pedro's and see if he'll take care of you this afternoon."

A short walk brought them to Pedro's place, where Pedro and Dolores were at work in the stable, cleaning stalls. "We're a little behind schedule," Pedro said. "We went out to get a look at the old man."

"What old man?" Carlos replied, puzzled.

Dolores spoke up. "A strange old man who arrived in town yesterday. Everyone has been talking about him."

"What's so special about an old man coming to town?" Carlos asked. "We have many old men in town."

"He's...different," Dolores said. "He stands out. He wears strange white clothes with lots of garters up the arms and legs. He has a funny kind of wagon that's painted in bright colors. Some people say it's like a Gypsy caravan."

"If he's a Gypsy, it's a bad time for him to be in Santa Fe," Carlos commented. "The inquisitors will be looking for anyone with Gypsy, Jewish, or Moorish connections."

"He seems to have anticipated that," Pedro replied. "Horatio Padilla told me that the old man came to him yesterday and presented papers signed by the Holy Office in Madrid certifying that the fellow's family history has been investigated back for many generations without finding the slightest hint of anything but pure Castilian blood. Padilla escorted him and his papers to Father Dorantes."

"Very interesting," Carlos said. "I'd like to hear more, but I'm on my way to an appointment with Doña Josefina."

Pedro shrugged. "The story of the old man can wait."

As Carlos walked across the plaza, he felt an unreasonable happiness. Smiling, he passed by the platform built by the Inquisition to punish any blasphemers, witches, or Jews secretly practicing their own religion in Santa Fe. He felt confident that as Don Alfonso Cabeza de Vaca he was safe. He also found himself pleased that his visit with Mara and Selena had aroused Inéz's jealousy, since it would make their upcoming fencing bout all the more intense.

He reached the north side of the plaza and the path that led to the Beltrán house. He heard children's laughter and looked down the street that led past the chapel to the Presidio. A small colorfully painted caravan had stopped in the middle of the street. Children were gathered around. A man in a strange white outfit and a white hat with a turkey feather was sitting on the driver's seat behind a white mule. It was impossible to tell his age at a distance. He was tossing some sort of treats wrapped in paper to the children. He threw them out one at a time and laughed as the children scrambled to grab them. Sometimes they caught them in the air, but at other times a treat fell to the ground and little bodies swarmed over where it had fallen until one child found it and held it triumphantly in the air. It was an amusing scene. Carlos might have stopped to watch, but he had to keep going to his appointment. As he began to walk away, the old man noticed him and, with a benign smile, lifted his hat in a gesture of greeting.

How odd, Carlos thought, without thinking about it too much. The old man and his caravan were certainly, as Dolores had said, strange.

Carlos continued on his way. As he neared the Beltráns' he stopped and looked around. The clouds had parted and the sun illuminated the place where he was standing and the town below. He noticed that a double rainbow hung in the showers over the Sangre de Cristo range to the east. He marveled at the beauty of it all. Even the Beltrán house, a large one-story adobe structure, suddenly appeared to him every bit as handsome as the mansions in the Mexico City neighborhood where he had grown up. He began to walk again, humming a *verso* about love that he and Orfeo had been singing a few days earlier. He reached the kitchen door, and before he could knock Rita opened it and greeted him. "Come in, Don Alfonso. You can go straight to the patio. The Señora will join you as soon as she's dressed."

Carlos walked through the kitchen, down the hallway, and into the patio. The sun was working its magic there too. The courtyard, with its verandas on the east and west sides, was lined with flowers. Near where he was standing a milkweed with orange blossoms was coming into bloom and a butterfly with variegated coloring, a mix of gold and black, had settled in to drink the flower's nectar.

Across the patio, he saw Doña Josefina, Santiago, and Elena sitting on a bench next to the fencing strip. A moment later Inéz arrived, a little breathless. She called a greeting to him and they approached each other to exchange a formal touching of cheek to cheek. He then moved to kiss Doña Josefina's hand and to say good afternoon to Elena and Santiago.

Inéz always looked good to Carlos, but she seemed especially glowing this afternoon. He beamed at her and, noticing his expression, she asked, "You're looking...I don't know what, something. Have you been drinking already today?"

"Not at all; just very happy to see all of you on such a glorious day in such a beautiful spot."

"Glorious? Beautiful? That's excessive even for you. I think you're a little drunk, not that it matters unless it gives me an advantage in our bout. Elena, Santiago! We need you to begin fencing."

The two young people moved onto the strip and began to fence. To Carlos's eye, both of them had improved considerably in the short time since they had begun fencing together. But they seemed distracted, as though their minds were elsewhere. Perhaps, he thought, they were feeling self-conscious under the scrutiny of Santiago's aunt. Carlos decided to intervene. "You are being lazy!" he shouted. "Fence with passion, as though something urgent, your lives or your love, depended on your every action."

Inéz took in his outburst with a surprised look on her face, but she said nothing.

Elena and Santiago resumed their bout with much greater intensity. They both attempted to take command, with the result that they sometimes became locked together at close quarters, panting from their exertions, their faces only inches apart. When they pushed away from each other, the electricity of their contact was not lost, and they went back to a sequence of thrust, parry, and riposte that repeatedly ended with Santiago crying "*Touché!*"

Each time this occurred Elena's determination increased until finally she broke through and scored a hit high on Santiago's chest. A triumphant grin flashed across her face and she cried, "You owe me a forfeit!"

"But we had no agreement on any stakes," Santiago protested.

"That being the case," Doña Josefina said, "you will have to leave it to me, as a disinterested observer, to decide on the nature of the forfeit. I'll announce it another day."

Something about the way Santiago's aunt spoke made Carlos confident that both the young combatants would be pleased. He stood up, bowed to her, and said to Elena and Santiago, "It's time for your instructors to test their mettle as fencers." He and Inéz moved to the fencing strip. When they had taken their positions, Carlos proposed that they begin with some lunge, parry, and riposte exercises, the type of schooling figures that all leading fencing academies incorporated into their training. Carlos was pleased to see that, even in the exercises, they were already fencing at a high level.

After barely ten minutes, Inéz said, "We're ready. *En garde!*"

They began their bout without having decided on any specific number of exchanges. The first five led to three hits for Carlos and two for Inéz. The second set of five produced four hits for him and one for her. During the third round, Carlos won all five exchanges. "It's time for me to provide you with more competition," Inéz said.

True to her word, she went on the attack with a fierce combination of speed and creativity. He retreated into a defensive mode to study her varied lines of attack. What followed was a series of exchanges that exceeded in skill any they'd had earlier. Carlos continued to score the most hits, though each came only after extended exchanges in which the advantage shifted back and forth repeatedly. He could only speak for himself, but he assumed that Inéz had also entered a state of mind rooted in total concentration and marked by extraordinary artistry—a fusion of body and mind so complete that he lost track of the score, the passage of time, and any sense that they were being watched by Santiago, Elena, and Doña Josefina.

Finally, Carlos made a proposal. "Let's have one last exchange before we tire too much. I want to attempt something that may surprise both of us. It will either be a magnificent success or a colossal failure."

"This is characteristic of Don Alfonso's approach to life," Inéz said in an aside directed at the three onlookers. "There's no middle ground with him."

"I would protest that," he replied, "but you seem to have made up your mind, and once you've done so, there's little room for change."

"I might surprise you on that score," she said. "Let's resume fencing with our swords rather than with words."

The final exchange followed the well-established pattern of the earlier part of the bout: Inéz launched a vigorous offense, only to find her every move blunted by Carlos's defense. Then he counterattacked with a powerful attack of his own, driving her back to the far end of the fencing strip. Although Carlos was enjoying these familiar strategies, he had it in mind to attempt a dramatic maneuver.

He waited for the right moment. It came when Inéz parried a skillfully executed attack of his and lunged forward in an attempt to exploit a possible opening. Carlos was beyond thinking; everything depended on being alive to opportunities in a way that went beyond thought. He adopted an unusual tactic of moving inside her attack, deflecting the left-handed Inéz's blade to her left, away from his body, he leaped forward, spun counterclockwise in a half turn, and tapped her right shoulder in a clear hit. "*Touché!*" he cried.

He half expected Inéz, whose sword arm was still extended past him to where he had been only seconds earlier, to accuse him of showing off. Instead, she simply commented, "I suppose that came out of your unusually high spirits."

"That's true," he agreed.

"Have you given this maneuver a name?"

"Flying lunge will have to do for now."

Lost in their conversation, Carlos and Inéz had all but forgotten that there were onlookers until Elena, Santiago, and Doña Josefina applauded and broke the spell. Turning to their three-person audience, Carlos took Inéz's free right hand in his and together they bowed. Doña Josefina said, "I've never before seen, or even imagined, such extraordinary fencing, and I'm impressed to learn that Inéz, a woman, can perform at such a high level. Would either of you be willing to say a few words about what's required to achieve such heights of skill?"

"Don Alfonso should speak for both of us," Inéz said, "since he clearly won the bout."

Don Carlos gathered his thoughts. "First," he began, "you must be willing to take instruction. Secondly, you must devote hours upon hours to practice. Third, you must pay attention to even the tiniest detail. Finally, you must practice some more." He paused and smiled at his audience. "Then," he added with a laugh, "if you live long enough, you may become good!"

"Well put," Doña Josefina said. "I know that Santiago usually comes here for fencing lessons on Wednesday afternoons. Do you suppose the three of you — Alfonso, Inéz, and Elena — could come to my house this Wednesday at two and join Santiago and me for refreshments?"

It was agreed, and soon Elena was showing Doña Josefina and Santiago to the door, leaving Carlos and Inéz alone in the patio. "That was a great success," Carlos declared.

"Yes," Inéz agreed, "Elena must be thrilled beyond belief at Doña Josefina's invitation."

"Do you have any special plans for your day off tomorrow?"

"Elena and I will go to visit Mara and Selena in the morning, as we've being doing on Mondays of late. What about you?"

"Orfeo and I are going to begin renovating my house. He's been bored ever since Fabio asked us to suspend work on the house Orfeo had been building for him. Also, Señor Ortíz has told him he doesn't want Orfeo coming around so often and interfering with Marisol's work."

"I doubt that Marisol's work is the problem," Inéz replied. "I'll bet that Marisol's grandfather thinks he might lose her to Orfeo, and he's not quite resigned to letting her go."

"True," Carlos said. "But the end result is that I've decided to keep Orfeo busy by enlarging my house and corral. Tomorrow we're going to start by tearing down the interior wall that separates the two rooms the soldiers were occupying. The goal is to create a single room so that I'll have a proper *sala* for entertaining guests rather than crowding everyone into the kitchen. Then we're going to build a new room where the stable is now, construct a new stable, and double the size of the corral. Orfeo measured the outlines of the new corral this morning and has started digging postholes."

"That all sounds good," Inéz said. "But if you're going to go to all that work, you really must add two new rooms, not just one."

"Two rooms? Why two? You seem very definite about that."

"I'll tell you later. Now I must get back to work." She kissed him lightly on the cheek and went off to her room to change from her fencing outfit. Carlos found his way out to the street. In so doing he realized that everyone at the Beltráns' treated him as a member of the household rather than a guest who needed to be shown around.

On a whim, he walked past his house and continued down the path to Pedro's stable. Their chores complete, Pedro and Dolores were sitting in the sun outside the stable doors. Gordo was napping at Pedro's side. "I'm pleased to see you enjoying the sun, Dolores," Carlos said.

"It's a nice day," Dolores replied happily.

"What she didn't mention," Pedro said, "is that the old man came by an hour ago."

"He's really funny!" Dolores burst out. "He has all sorts of strange animals in his wagon."

"What sort of animals?" Carlos asked.

"There are two monkeys dressed in little suits," Dolores said excitedly. "I got to shake hands with one of them. And there's a parrot, a big bird with bright green feathers. It talks!"

Pedro had been watching Dolores with an amused look on his face.

"The old man said his name was Pascal. He came by looking for a place to board his mule."

Carlos glanced into the stable's turnout and saw a white mule in one of the corrals. "It looks as though you've found a place for the mule. Where's the caravan?"

"Parked over at Roberto Barbon's inn, where Pascal is staying."

Before Pedro could say more, Dolores broke in. "He gave me a lump of dark sugar wrapped in a paper. There's something written on the paper, but I can't read it."

"I can't read it either," Pedro said. "I mean, I can pronounce it, but I can't understand it."

"May I see it?" Carlos asked.

"Dolores can get it for you. It's her treasure."

Dolores jumped up and went into the living quarters attached to the stable. She quickly returned and held a small scrap of paper with ragged edges out to Carlos. He recognized what was written on it was in Latin. He read the words out loud to his friends. "*Carpe diem.* That's Latin for Seize the day! Not a bad idea, don't you agree?"

Pedro and Dolores agreed. Carlos resolved to meet this Pascal fellow soon.

17

Frida

Soon didn't happen. Carlos became preoccupied with activities other than introducing himself to the old man who called himself Pascal. He saw him across the plaza and down streets that he passed as he went about his own business, but he never managed a face-to-face meeting with him. The old man, however, nearly always noticed Carlos, and when he did, he never failed to tip his hat to him.

After breakfast on Monday Don Carlos and Orfeo started removing the wall between the two small rooms on the south side of Carlos's house. It was dusty work. They started at the top of the wall to make sure that there was a beam to hold the ceiling up once the wall was removed. The wall had been constructed of adobe bricks and had been plastered and whitewashed afterward. Don Carlos was pleased that the dismantling process went quickly. After the top part of the wall was removed, the adobe blocks lower down proved to be quite loose.

Orfeo was already planning ahead and asked, "Shall we stack these adobe bricks along the east wall? When the time comes to use them for the new room you want to build where the stable is now, they'll be close at hand."

"That's a good plan, Orfeo. Right now the dust is getting thick. Let's step outside for a breath of fresh air."

About noon, while they were outside taking yet another break to let the dust settle, Carlos saw Inéz and Elena approaching from the plaza down the path to his kitchen door. They both waved gaily, and from the fact that they were wearing riding outfits and that Elena was leading her mare, Cottonwood, it was apparent that they were planning to go riding. "I've come by for Alegría," Inéz explained as she drew near.

"And Inéz told me about your construction project," Elena added. "We wanted to see it."

"Let us show you around," Carlos said. He led Inéz and Elena, with Cottonwood following behind, along the path to the east window of the room in which they had been working. "We've been removing the wall," he said, "between the two rooms that Pedro and María used to have. You probably don't want to go in there; the dust hasn't yet settled. But if you look through the window, you can see that there's now one room instead of two."

Inéz peered in the window. "That ought to make an adequate *sala*," she said.

"Now come along back here, please," Carlos said, continuing along the side of the house to where the stable was located. "We're going to build a small temporary shed in which to store tools and hay. Then we'll tear down this old stable and start building the room I propose to add on the south side of the *sala*."

"You really must add two rooms," Inéz said.

"Why do you seem so insistent that I need two new rooms?" Carlos asked. "One room for a cook or a couple of servants ought to be enough."

"No," Inéz insisted. "Your present bedroom is next to the kitchen. The cook should sleep there. You and Gordo ought to move into the new rooms south of the *sala*."

"He and I need only one room."

"You're never going to have guests, or let your groom sleep indoors rather than outside in the hayloft? You're not always going to have helpers like Diego, José, and Orfeo, who are young and willing to rough it."

"Perhaps you're right, as always," Carlos replied.

"Don't be sarcastic. All I'm saying is that if you're going to do this, you ought to do it with the long view. And on that count, you should build a four-stall stable that opens onto the corral."

"Ah, the corral," Carlos said, not wanting to argue with her. "You can see the stakes we've set out to mark the postholes Orfeo is digging."

"Good," was all Inéz had time to say before her horse, Alegría, spotted her and came trotting over to the fence. She nuzzled up to Inéz for a carrot and to be scratched on the nose. "I've missed you too, dear Alegría," Inéz said. "We'll have a nice long ride today."

"Is that wise, with all the Native raiders about?" Carlos asked.

"We're going to head south and visit José at Rancho Rosón. And Alegría and Cottonwood can outrun raiders. I'm not worried."

Orfeo had brought out Alegría's tack and was saddling her. "You seem," Carlos went on, "to have very firm opinions about my building project."

"Yes."

"Care to explain why?"

"No."

"But you seem to have been thinking about what I should do."

"Yes."

"I gather that's all I'm going to learn this morning, which is nothing?"

"Yes. But to change the topic, have you met Pascal, the old man in the strange outfit?"

"No, I've seen him around quite a bit but only at a distance. Have you?"

"Not yet," Inéz replied. "I haven't even seen him, but he seems to have made quite an impression on some people, including Dolores. On our way back from Juan Archibeque's house this morning, we stopped at Pedro and María's. María said that Pascal has moved his caravan to the Barrio near where the San Miguel Chapel once stood. She says he's going to offer free entertainment to the Barrio residents."

"What a nice idea!" Elena said. "The Barrio people haven't had much reason to laugh in the last month."

"You're right about that," Carlos agreed. "They're still upset about the wolf that killed their dogs."

Orfeo had finished saddling and bridling Alegría. Addressing Carlos, Inéz asked, "Would you give me a leg up?" Once he'd done so, she added, "María also told us that Pascal's mule is quite clever. Dolores is very enthusiastic about the tricks it can do. You'll have to ask her for the details, though more than likely you won't be able to stop her from telling you."

Inéz and Elena rode off to Rancho Rosón, and Orfeo and Don Carlos spent the early part of the afternoon clearing the future *sala* of debris. The adobe blocks they'd collected made a large pile near the window. "That will give us a good start on the new room we're going to build," Don Carlos remarked.

"Rooms, you mean," Orfeo replied. That made both men laugh at Inéz's instructions.

By mid-afternoon Carlos was ready for a different activity. "Orfeo," he said, "why don't you start on the postholes? And give some thought to what's the best location for this four-stall stable Inéz wants built."

"If I didn't know better," Orfeo said with a wry smile, "I would think she was your wife."

"Would that it were true," Don Carlos said as he turned away to go inside and clean up. He brushed off his work clothes and washed his hands and face in a basin of water on the kitchen counter.

Feeling at least partially clean, he walked across the fields to Pedro's stable. Gordo followed along. Dolores saw the two of them approaching and ran to greet them. Gordo stood on his hind legs a little unsteadily as Dolores scratched his ears and bent down to accept a kiss on her cheek. It occurred to Carlos that Dolores might have a special fondness for another creature with a damaged limb. "How are you today?" he asked her.

"The man in white came by for his mule this morning."

"Pascal?"

"Yes, that's what he calls himself. Don Alfonso, that mule is very smart. He can do tricks!"

Pedro, who had come out of the barn and was listening, chuckled and said, "Dolores has been very happy ever since meeting Pascal and his mule."

"I'm pleased to hear that," Carlos said. "Does this mule have a name?"

"Listo."

"Clever. So what clever things can Listo do?"

"When the old man says 'Up!' Listo stands up on his back legs. When Pascal says 'Bow!' he puts one leg out in front and kneels on the other, a perfect bow. But the best trick, the funniest, is when Pascal says 'Tail!' Listo turns in place really fast, as though he's trying to grab his tail in his mouth."

"That would be quite a sight," Don Carlos said. "Have you been to one of these shows that I'm told Pascal is giving?"

"Yes," Dolores replied. "When he came by this morning to fetch Listo, he invited me to go with him to the inn to get the caravan. He hitched Listo up and drove the caravan to the Barrio. The caravan is now on Pecos Road, across from the chapel's ruins. Once we were there, he unhitched Listo and tethered him to a stake, and a crowd began to gather.

"Pascal went into his caravan and opened up a panel in its side. It was like a window with curtains. Then a drum sounded and the curtains pulled back and we could see a small stage, at least that's what the woman standing next to me called it.

"The best was next. The old man's two monkeys came onto the stage. One was dressed as a man, the other as a woman. The man-monkey lay down and pretended to be asleep. The woman-monkey went over and kicked him in the side. He got up and walked away. Pascal's parrot came onto the stage and bumped into the man-monkey. Then the parrot made a cooing sound and said, plain as could be, 'Pretty Boy.' The man-monkey petted the parrot and seemed to try to kiss her. The woman-monkey saw this and ran over and kicked the man-monkey in the behind and knocked him down. Everyone laughed hard and the curtains closed."

"Was that it?"

"Yes. The caravan's panel closed and after that Pascal came out. He gave the children in the audience pieces of sugar wrapped in paper. I got another one with words on it that Pedro didn't understand." She pulled a piece of brown paper out of her pocket and handed it to Carlos. "*Caveat emptor*" was written on it in elegant script.

"*Caveat emptor* is Latin for Let the buyer beware," Carlos told her.

"What an odd message to give a girl. He's a strange fellow," Pedro commented.

Dolores was eager to say something more. She burst out, "Pascal is going to give another show late this afternoon. I want to go, but I'm supposed to cook dinner."

"What's for dinner?" Carlos asked.

"Chili and corn tortillas."

"Have you made the tortillas?"

"Yes," she replied. "And we soaked the beans last night and I cooked them this morning. But I've never made chili, and Pedro says he's too busy to help."

"I," Don Carlos announced, "am an expert chili-maker. Let's go in and I'll help. If we can get it done, you can go to the show."

They went inside and Don Carlos helped Dolores get the chili started. There were some beef scraps left from the previous night's dinner, so they chopped them into bits to add to the beans, along with some onions, dried tomatoes, dried chilis, cumin seeds, and dried oregano. Working mostly in silence, they spoke only when starting some new phase of the preparations, but finally Carlos asked, "What sort of man is Pascal?"

"Oh, he's the oldest man I've ever seen," Dolores replied. "His face has the deepest wrinkles, and his hands are all gnarled. But he's nice, and he's quick too."

"I hope to meet him soon," Carlos said.

"You could come with me to this afternoon's show," Dolores suggested.

"I will if I can, but first I'd better go home and see how Orfeo is doing on a project of ours. If I get done there I'll come back here, and we can walk together to see the show. If I don't make it, don't wait."

He gave Dolores a few final instructions for the chili and let himself out the door. He found Pedro in the stable, holding a mare while a farrier was replacing a shoe the horse had thrown that morning. "I can't find the shoe," Pedro grumbled. "It's probably out in the corral somewhere."

"I'm astonished at the changes in Dolores," Carlos said. "She seems genuinely happy. It's as if she's reverted to childhood."

"This is a strange thing to say," Pedro replied, "but I think it's the effect that the old man has had on her."

Carlos raised his eyebrows. "Pascal? How — ?"

"I don't know how," Pedro said. "But it seems to be a good thing. Just look at her — she's happy and she babbles like a child about him and his animals. He's given her something."

"The sweets — ?"

"I don't mean the lumps of sugar wrapped in pieces of paper with strange words on them. I mean — " Pedro made a frustrated face, and he gestured with his hands as if holding something large between them.

"Something invisible," Carlos supplied, understanding what Pedro was trying to express. Or, Carlos suddenly wondered, thinking of the sugar wrapped in paper inscribed with a saying in Latin, has Pascal worked a magic spell? This possibility opened a whole new line of thinking to Carlos. "Pedro," he said abruptly, "how do the residents of the Barrio feel about Pascal?"

Pedro shrugged. "They seem to like him. The children certainly do."

"You don't think—? Look, he's an entertainer, maybe a magician like Leandro. Is there any suspicion of him because of that?"

"Never occurred to me there might be. People in the Barrio didn't have much to do with Leandro. And he didn't kidnap any of their children. Are you saying they should be worried about Pascal?"

Carlos shook his head. "I don't think so. The important thing is that Dolores is feeling good. Please tell her that she and I will take another ride together soon."

"I'll tell her," Pedro said. The mare's shoe was back on, and Pedro turned away to lead her back to the corral.

Carlos went home to see how Orfeo was doing. His posthole-digging project hadn't progressed far. In the process of digging the third hole, he had hit an underground spring. He was up to his knees in muddy water when Carlos arrived. "I've heard," Carlos commented, "that this whole section of Santa Fe used to be a swamp. The water table must be close to the surface."

"Yes," Orfeo replied, "I'm barely down three feet and the water is already deep enough to dip a bucket in it. Another foot or two deeper and we can line it and have a well right outside the corral."

"Is there anything I could do to help?" Carlos asked.

"You could take the buckets of mud I've scooped out and dump them off in the field."

Carlos went to change his clothes, and soon he was lending a hand with the well project.

Half an hour later Inéz and Elena arrived back from their ride.

Inéz swung easily out of the saddle and landed lightly on her feet. "Alfonso," she said, "please help me get Alegría undressed and back in the corral. Elena and I are supposed to go back to Juan Archibeque's for tea and possibly some games with Mara, Selena, and the little girls. Indulging in so much physical activity after I've only recently escaped from my deathbed will probably leave me very sore tomorrow."

"Don't joke about your deathbed," Carlos said. "I gather you had a good ride."

"Yes, we made it all the way to Rancho Rosón, got a close look at the horses you and José rounded up, and had cold tea with him. I asked José about your visit there with Dolores. It seemed to me that she made a very favorable impression on him."

Once Alegría had been unsaddled and turned out in the corral, Inéz and Elena, leading Cottonwood, were ready to leave. Inéz kissed Carlos lightly on the cheek. "We're off for our next activity. I hope the rest of your day goes well."

After helping Orfeo for another half an hour, Carlos headed toward his house. As he reached the kitchen door, he heard a woman calling his name. It was Doña Josefina's servant, the Indian woman who usually delivered her mistress's messages. She came up to him and said, "Doña Josefina hopes that you will accompany me back to her hacienda to visit with her. Can you come now?"

He asked her to wait for him while he ducked into his house and put on clean clothes. Returning outside, he accompanied the servant across the plaza and up the slope toward the Mendoza residence. Feeling a wish to establish some sort of connection with the woman, he asked her, "Please tell me your name. I'd like to know it, since we often meet under these circumstances."

"Jacinta."

"Were you born in Santa Fe or in a pueblo?"

"I am originally from Isleta."

"Did you live there before the Pueblo Revolt?"

"Yes, my family fled south from Isleta to El Paso del Norte. I was just a little girl."

"How then did you come to be employed by Doña Josefina?"

"You ask many questions," she replied, indirectly reminding him that most Pueblo people viewed asking personal questions as impolite.

"I apologize," he said. "I'm a relative newcomer in New Mexico, and I am interested in learning about the history of the place where I now make my home."

"Doña Josefina speaks well of you," she replied in what seemed a conciliatory way.

When they arrived at the Mendoza hacienda, Jacinta showed him to the *sala*. Doña Josefina was waiting for him. They went through their now customary ritual greeting. He stepped to her side and kissed her hand. She motioned for him to sit in the chair opposite her.

Rather than starting by saying what she had on her mind, she asked, "Will you join me for hot chocolate and almond tarts?"

"I would enjoy that."

A rustling sound indicated that a servant had come to the door behind him. Doña Josefina looked in that direction and said, "Frida, please bring us the refreshments. We will eat in here." Then she turned to him and added, "Frida is, I believe, an unusual name. Do you know its origin?"

"Not it's origin, but I believe Frida means peace."

Doña Josefina gave a small sign of satisfaction. "Ah! I appreciate talking with a well-educated man. You may be amused to know that the name Frida was chosen in an ironic way. She has not brought much peace to anyone except me."

Frida soon returned with a tray. On it were two cups of steaming hot chocolate, a large plate with six almond tarts, two blue-patterned china dessert plates, and silver dessert forks. Frida placed one cup of hot chocolate and an empty plate in front of Don Carlos and did the same for Doña Josefina.

Carlos gestured toward his plate and smiled appreciatively. "I see," he said, "that you have brought plates from the Manila Galleon to our humble town."

"Over the years," Doña Josefina replied, "I have acquired many sets of dishes from Europe, but these imports from China are my favorites. I like to imagine a Spanish galleon sailing from the Philippines to the Pacific coast of New Spain. When I was younger I dreamed of making that voyage myself. Perhaps I should do it now. If I died on the trip, I would die doing something that made me happy."

Frida glanced inquiringly at him, and when he nodded she slipped a tart onto his plate and stepped back from the table. He was aware that she was an older woman with black hair and straight posture, but he hadn't looked at her closely. Now Doña Josefina directed his attention to Frida. "I believe," she said, "you know Frida by another name."

He turned to look at her. She was dressed in a white blouse and a long blue cotton skirt. She also wore a turquoise necklace and several turquoise bracelets, which seemed unusual for a servant. There was something about her.... Then, for the first time, he focused on her aura. She had a shape-shifter's aura. Could her other name be Manuela? It scarcely seemed possible. He ventured a guess. "Does her other name begin with an M?"

"Good for you!" Doña Josefina exclaimed softly. "The walls in my home have ears, and it's best to speak in riddles, though perhaps Frida will show you something she has in her pocket." Frida approached him, put her hand in her skirt pocket, and brought out an opal that Don Carlos had given her. He was astonished and a little apprehensive.

"Is it safe to have such a thing here?" he asked. The question wasn't about the opal, as he could tell both Doña Josefina and Frida understood, but about whether it was safe for Frida to be so openly in Santa Fe at a time when the inquisitors were intent on capturing her.

"Lean way over," Doña Josefina instructed him. Then she bent forward, as Frida did also, until their heads were almost touching. "She is safe here. As you can see, she doesn't much resemble the bent-over old hag that Father Dorantes and Brother Gustavo saw in El Paso del Norte. She tells me that neither of them can read auras, so they can't identify her that way. The only person in my household who might recognize her is my daughter-in-law, but she is an invalid who never leaves her bed, much less her room. They won't meet in the hallway."

"I have always appreciated disguises," Carlos said, pleased with how effective Doña Josefina's scheme appeared to be. The last place the inquisitors would think to look was in the home of one of Santa Fe's social leaders.

Doña Josefina straightened up, as did Carlos and Frida. "We must finish our hot chocolate before it gets cold," Doña Josefina said in a normal tone. "But I hope to meet with you again soon in a setting in which we can speak more freely. We can use that occasion to discuss what, if anything, we can do about this horrible Brother Gustavo." She then settled back in her chair and helped herself to another almond tart. "Unlike some old women I know," she said, "age has not diminished my appetite."

Frida left the room, and Carlos and Doña Josefina ate in silence. Once she had finished her tarts and hot chocolate, she announced, "That was all I wanted to accomplish for today; however, I hope we can walk up the canyon together the day after tomorrow. We can meet at Juan Archibeque's house around ten. Don't worry if you're a little late. I've been enjoying getting to know Selena Torrez. I find her quite interesting, and it seems that we both come originally from Seville, born there an unimaginable number of years apart."

Don Carlos by now understood that interviews with Doña Josefina could end abruptly, so when she stood up he knew it was time to leave. Thanking her for her hospitality, he left and was shown out by Mabruke. Frida was nowhere in sight.

Carlos decided to return to Pedro's place and see if Dolores had attended Pascal's afternoon show. He found Pedro and Dolores standing outside in the lane, and he inquired about the show. Dolores replied that she had been there, but she didn't want to talk about it. "Something happened that had to do with her hand," Pedro said. "It upset her."

"Wouldn't you be upset," she burst out, "if someone made you feel you're not good enough because you're crippled?"

At first she refused to say more, but Carlos persisted in urging her to tell them what Pascal's show had been like. Reluctantly, she complied. "It was a hand-puppet show on the caravan's little stage, a fairy-tale story about a pretty girl who was put under a spell by a witch. She fell asleep until a handsome prince came and kissed her. She woke up, they married, and lived happily ever after."

"What upset you about that?" Carlos asked.

"I don't want to talk about it," she replied, tears coming into her eyes. She turned and ran into the house.

Don Carlos followed her and spoke to her through the door to her room, which she'd slammed shut. "I don't see how any of that could have made you feel so bad. Please explain."

"Go away! I said I don't want to talk."

"You'll feel better if you tell me. Please let me in."

After a few moments she opened the door. Stepping aside to let him enter, she said, "I warned you I would be a lot of trouble."

"Dolores, what does that have to do with anything?

"I'm deformed. You and Pedro and María are all nice to me, but no one would ever want to marry me."

So that's it, Carlos thought, the puppet show about the pretty girl and the handsome prince. "Tell me more about the fairy tale and the hand puppets," Carlos coaxed.

Dolores hesitated, but finally she began. "I stayed after to talk with Pascal and asked if I could put on one of the puppets. He said I could, and he went in the caravan and brought out two. There was still a small crowd of people around us. 'Try on the princess puppet,' he said, and he put it on my good hand. 'The princess needs a prince,' he said, and reached for my crippled hand. I had forgotten about it, and let him take it. When he saw it, he said, 'You may have a more difficult time making the puppet prince move the way you want.' Then my hand seemed to me twice as crippled as before, and everyone was looking at it.

"I started to cry. I pulled the princess puppet off my hand and ran away."

"Did he try to console you or stop you from running off?"

"I guess he did try a little. He called after me, 'You'll do all right if you practice,' but I was too embarrassed to—" She stopped, hearing the sound of slow hoofbeats outside her bedroom window. She looked up and gasped, "Here he is! He's outside with Listo. I'm going to hide!" She ran to her bed, crawled under the covers, and pulled them over her head.

Outside, Pedro approached Pascal at the window of Dolores's room. "Is the young woman named Dolores home?" Pascal asked, "I want to speak with her and apologize for making her unhappy today."

"She's home," Pedro replied, "but she's not feeling too well."

"I'm afraid I'm at fault," Pascal said, "and I'd like to make amends. Would you do something for me? I have several extra hand puppets, and one of them is a princess puppet with black hair like Dolores's. She's a pretty young woman, and I'd like to make a gift of the puppet to her. Would you give it to her?"

"I'll see that she gets it," Pedro said.

"Also," Pascal went on, "tell her that Listo likes her very much. The other day when I asked Listo to perform tricks for her he did every one perfectly and right away. He's an old mule and isn't always so cooperative. I think he was showing off for her."

Pedro muttered something that Carlos didn't catch, and then he heard Pascal thanking Pedro for taking such good care of Listo and saying good night.

Don Carlos shook Dolores's bed gently and asked, "Hey! Did you hear Pascal say that you're a pretty young woman?"

He got a barely audible answer. "I don't believe him."

"Let's go out and see the princess puppet he gave you."

"Not yet," she said, lifting the blanket. "I need to heat up the chili. María will be home soon, and I want it ready for her when she gets here." She got up and went into the kitchen.

Carlos followed her and said, "It's all right if you want to wait until later to see the puppet. I just hope you'll learn to use it and make up a story to show the rest of us. I'll see you again soon. I want to take you to Tesuque Pueblo to meet the medicine man José is studying with."

"Will José be there?"

"He might be. I don't know."

She said nothing more, so he went outside. María had just come down the path, and Pedro was showing her the hand puppet. "The stitching on this puppet is very fine," she exclaimed, "and the cloth is expensive. And just look at the decorations! Smoky quartz for eyes, red silk thread for the mouth, and some kind of bone for the buttons on the princess's dress. It's a treasure!"

María asked to take the puppet to Dolores and went inside with it.

"María is a kind person, a good mother," Carlos said. "I'm sure she'll help Dolores sort things out. You're both good parents."

"I don't know about me," Pedro replied.

"You'll do fine," Carlos said. "What do you think of Pascal?'

Pedro took some time to consider the question. "I've been around you long enough," he said at last, "to recognize when someone has power."

Carlos was very interested. "What sort of power?"

"I don't know," Pedro replied. "But it makes me uncomfortable."

"He's certainly been good for Dolores," Carlos said thoughtfully.

"True," Pedro agreed. "But still—"

How big a problem was it, Carlos wondered, if Pedro sensed something about Pascal that might be troublesome? Don Carlos shook the doubt off. It was too vague to worry about. He went home and had a pleasant evening with Orfeo and Gordo.

Tuesday morning, after doing his meditation and having breakfast, he called on Inéz and told her about Manuela being in Doña Josefina's house and about Dolores's distress when Pascal called attention to her crippled hand. "Pascal coming by seemed to smooth things over," he said.

Carlos had been so focused on telling Inéz about Manuela and Dolores that he completely forgot to mention Pedro's comments about Pascal. He remembered them later, but he told himself they probably meant nothing.

18

Dreams

*W*ednesday morning something strange happened in Santa Fe.

The phenomenon first became evident toward sundown on Tuesday. Families were preparing dinner and wood smoke was rising from every home. That was normal, only on this night the smoke didn't dissipate into the atmosphere. Some odd atmospheric condition was blocking the smoke from rising beyond about fifty feet above the town. Glancing up, Carlos and his neighbors could see the smoke collected against what appeared to be a barrier of clear sky. Below that barrier, the air was hot and humid and the cloud of smoke was gradually growing denser. As the rays of the setting sun fell on the cloud, it turned a glorious golden color. It also seemed that fog was forming over the Santa Fe River, the irrigation ditches, and the swampier sections of town, and when the cloud of smoke from above joined the fog from below, Santa Fe was enveloped in a warm haze.

Don Carlos and Orfeo fed the horses and watched the dense haze develop. They agreed to have an early dinner and go to bed. "I feel lethargic, as though I didn't get enough sleep last night," Orfeo said.

They noticed that Gordo, instead of following his usual practice of begging at the dinner table, had already gone into Don Carlos's bedroom and climbed up on the bed to sleep. "I'm feeling a bit sleepy myself," Carlos said. "Gordo seems to be setting a good example. It reminds me of something my first mentor told me when I asked him how to conduct my life. He replied, 'When you work, just work; when you're hungry, eat; when you need to pee, go pee; and when you're sleepy, lie down and sleep.' Good advice that I'll follow tonight." Wishing Orfeo well, Carlos went to bed.

He fell asleep immediately. That wasn't unusual. He almost always fell asleep as soon as his head hit his pillow. What was unusual was that he had one dream after another, all of them vivid. One in particular stayed with him when he got up Wednesday morning.

The dream's location was a bedroom in Puebla, New Spain. The room was hot, and dark, and he was seated on a cushion holding a woman in his arms. They were engaged in Tantric meditation. Carlos was feeling intense activity in his crown chakra. He seemed to be breathing through an opening in the top of his head, his inhalations drawing energy from a vast space above him. He opened his eyes, and though the room was in darkness he saw that he was embracing a beautiful woman, Zoila Herrera. They were surrounded by a sphere of golden light, their individual auras having merged into one.

When, in the dream, they finally separated, Zoila sat back, her body covered with a sheen of sweat, as was his also. She looked at him lovingly and said, "It's about time you expanded your little house."

Even in the dream, Zoila's statement struck Carlos as a strange follow-up to their intense meditation together, but he replied, "I don't know quite why I'm doing it."

"Nonsense! You need a proper *sala* and two extra rooms."

"I don't see the need for two extra rooms," Carlos objected. "Even if the cook occupies my present bedroom, Gordo and I need only one bedroom, not two."

"Won't you need a room for guests?" Zoila asked. "And your wife will want a new bedroom to honor your new life together. That's two bedrooms."

"And just who is this wife to be?"

"You know very well who she is," Zoila said, and as suddenly as it had begun, the dream ended.

Don Carlos got up at four o'clock Wednesday morning, but instead of settling down to meditate, he went outside. The fog, mist, haze, whatever it was, still clung to Santa Fe. No breeze, not the slightest zephyr, had come up to blow it away. Taking a deep inhalation, Don Carlos noticed that the haze had a distinctive smell. The scent of wood smoke, of cedar and piñon pine, was dominant, but underlying the wood smell was another aroma, the fragrance of spices, cinnamon and cloves. The moon, only one day short of full, was orange behind the haze and cast a strange glow on the whole scene.

After his meditation, which put him serenely back into the loving state of his dream, he fed Gordo, helped Orfeo distribute hay and grain to the household's horses, and started a simple breakfast for the two of them. "I had a vivid dream last night," Orfeo announced. "In fact, I had the same dream over and over. It was a wonderful dream." He fell silent.

"And?" Don Carlos prompted him. "Surely you're going to tell me about it."

"It's a little personal," Orfeo replied.

"I won't pry, if you'd rather not talk about it."

"No, I can tell you about it in general. I was holding Marisol in my arms. She had her head on my shoulder, and it felt like she was melting into me, and I could smell her hair, which smelled of spices."

"There's a scent of spices in the air this morning," Don Carlos said. "It's lovely that you incorporated it into your dream."

"Yes," Orfeo replied, lost in thought.

Don Carlos wondered how widespread dreaming had been in Santa Fe last night. He was particularly curious to know if Inéz had had a dream. He called to Gordo and they set out for the Beltrán house. They made their way across the plaza in a haze that reminded him of fog he'd seen in London during his fourth lifetime. Very strange to encounter it in Santa Fe. As he'd hoped, Inéz was already in the kitchen, starting breakfast preparations. "How are you, sweetheart?" he inquired after he'd let himself in the door.

"I'm fine, happy, although outdoors it looks as though Santa Fe has ascended into the clouds."

"I'm wondering whether you had any dreams last night."

"Yes, I did. How about you?"

"I was hoping you'd go first," he said.

"As you wish. I dreamed I was fourteen and making *rosquillas* with my mother. My father was either asleep or not home, which meant I had her to myself." She sighed. "It was a precious moment. I loved her so much, and when she died I was devastated. And of course after her death came those unhappy events—my father giving me to Loreto Tiburcio to settle a gambling debt, and Loreto selling me to all those men. But my dream last night took me back to a time before all that unhappiness. It was lovely. Your turn."

"I had a dream about the time Zoila and I practiced Tantric meditation until our auras fused into a single golden aura, and I felt I was one with the universe. I've never again had an experience of that intensity, but the dream brought it back."

Inéz cast her eyes down and turned away from him.

"What's wrong?" he asked. "Surely you're not jealous of Zoila?"

"No, I'm just—regretful, I guess."

"I can't see why. That encounter with Zoila was what got me started on the Unknown Way and on my meditation practice."

"Yes, Carlos, and I know how important that is to you. What makes me feel regret is that I can't be your partner in Tantric practice, the sexual union part, because—because—you know why. Oh, I know how to be provocative and flaunt myself sexually, but believe me, that was always a heartless performance. I don't think I could open my heart in Tantric practice with you. I just couldn't do it. And the whole point of it is the opening of the heart and the spirit, isn't it? Carlos, I want to go with you on this journey, and I can't. And it's not natural for you to be celibate."

"I can be celibate, if need be," he said. "It doesn't require a partner to do the chakra meditation Zoila taught me. As for my past sexual adventures, I've told you that they were unimportant.

"But let me tell you the rest of my dream, the things Zoila said to me. She told me that the expansion of my house was long overdue—a point you made yesterday too. I complained that I didn't understand the necessity of adding a second room on the south side of the house, and she insisted, in almost the same words you used, that I'd need the second new room for guests."

Inéz eyed him speculatively. "What else did she say? What are you withholding?"

He hesitated, worried that Zoila's mention of a wife would upset Inéz. "Zoila told me that the larger of the two new bedrooms would be appropriate for welcoming my wife-to-be into my home."

"There you go again!" Inéz cried. "You want to get married, but I'm not cooperating. You know I don't even want to discuss it."

"That's why I was withholding that part of the dream," Carlos replied. "Still, I can't stop myself from hoping that we'll marry some day, under whatever conditions you want to impose."

"You would consider a celibate marriage?" she asked incredulously.

Carlos took a deep breath. "Yes, I would. With you."

"Well, I wouldn't let you do it," she said firmly. "It wouldn't be right." She lifted her face and looked at him. "But it's very generous of you to offer. Thank you. And it's not that I don't want to be your partner and share your life. I do. My strong opinions about your building project came from imagining the kind of house I would want to share with you. But right now the thought of any kind of sexual intimacy—I'd either leave my body, like I used to do when Loreto pimped me, or I would put on a provocative act like I used to do with you when I was trying to seduce you. Which, if I'd succeeded, might have been enjoyable for you, but it would have been mechanical and unfeeling for me."

"Dearest Inéz," he said, taking her hands. "We'll take this one step at a time. Remember our beautiful day at our Sacred Pool, when we played your fantasy princess game, and you were fourteen years old—the same age as in your lovely dream last night—and none of these bad things had happened to you. It was like we were both innocent and at the beginning of love, and a new way of being male and female was beginning to grow in us. That was only seven months ago! Let's give ourselves time for this growth to happen. I believe it will."

Inéz was about to reply when Elena burst into the room and announced, "I had the most amazing dream last night!"

"As it happens," Inéz replied, "Alfonso and I were just telling each other dreams we had last night."

"Oh!" Elena said. "I'm sorry for interrupting. I'll come back later." She turned to go.

"There's no need for you to leave, Elena," Carlos said. "We'd love to hear your dream."

"It's something I hardly dare to speak of," she replied, lowering her eyes.

"Then I'll leave and you can tell Inéz."

"Is that really necessary?" Inéz asked. "Alfonso and I are your friends. I suspect the dream involves Santiago."

"How did you guess?"

"Well, we had a wonderful time with you and Santiago just the other day, and the three of us are going to the Mendoza house this afternoon. Of course he's on your mind."

"Yes," Elena said, "but this was not anything I would dare to imagine."

"Please," Carlos said. "Don't hold out on us. What happened in your dream?"

"It wasn't a story," she replied, "so much as a single image." She paused and said breathlessly, "Santiago and I were kneeling in front of his aunt and she was blessing us."

"I don't believe that's beyond the realm of possibility," Inéz said. "By inviting us to have dessert with her this afternoon, she's already blessed your friendship. What happens next between you and Santiago and with Doña Josefina, only time will tell."

Carlos decided to excuse himself to let his two women friends talk privately. "I'll come by this afternoon a little before two and we can walk to Doña Josefina's together."

"Don't think," Inéz said, "I'm unaware that you also have an appointment to meet with her this morning at Mara and Selena's house. If I weren't an easy-going, tolerant person," she added in a light tone, "I would say that your many visits to the house of those entrancing sisters are highly suspect."

He laughed. "Not in the way you seem to imply. Doña Josefina has asked me to meet her there in order to discuss privately some matters involving her household. I promise to report fully on our conversation." Giving both Inéz and Elena a light kiss on the cheek, he left for home.

With Gordo tagging along, Carlos returned back across the plaza. It seemed to him that the dense haze that had gathered overnight was beginning to dissipate. Once home, he changed his clothes to something more suitable for a visit with Doña Josefina. Turning to Gordo, he said, "Why don't you come along to see Mara and Selena? They claim they've missed you."

After he had crossed the river to reach Canyon Road, Don Carlos saw Pascal's caravan parked a few yards down Pecos Road. Carlos supposed that Pascal had left it there last night rather than having Listo pull it back and forth between Barbon's inn and its present location. Pascal and Listo were nowhere in evidence. The haze that had enveloped Santa Fe was particularly dense in the area where the caravan was parked, and the aroma of spices was very strong. Don Carlos glanced around, but not seeing any obvious source for this, he continued his stroll up Canyon Road. Gordo jogged along at his side.

Juan Archibeque's house emerged suddenly from the haze. Doña Josefina's carriage was already there, but neither she nor Frida-Manuela was visible. With a wave to Mabruke, who was relaxing on the driver's seat, Carlos walked to the front door of the house and knocked. Mara greeted him. "Are you really Don Alfonso or a figment of my dream imagination?"

"I gather you've been dreaming," he replied.

"Come in. We're sitting around and discussing our dreams."

Mara escorted Carlos to the *sala*, which was crowded with Juan, Doña Josefina, Frida, Selena, and the three Archibeque girls. Only Doña Josefina and Juan were seated in chairs. The rest were sitting on cushions and benches. Juan started to rise to give his chair to Don Carlos, but he waved off the offer and sat on a cushion between Selena and the eldest of the little girls. One of the other girls pulled Gordo into her lap and scratched his ear. A look of bliss came over his face.

Doña Josefina brought him into the conversation. "We were having a splendid time," she said, "listening to the dreams the little girls had last night. They all dreamed much the same thing, which was that a man in funny white clothes came and entertained them by talking with a parrot that sat on his shoulder."

"Have they heard about the old man who arrived in Santa Fe last weekend?" Carlos asked. "He wears white clothes and has a parrot."

"Yes, I told them about this fellow, Pascal by name," Juan volunteered, "and they're eager to see him. I will try to have him bring his parrot here. We generally avoid town, all the more so now that Governor Peralta has taken it into his head that Frenchmen somehow threaten Santa Fe. It is absurd, of course, but one must be careful, and I am, as you know, a French exile in New Mexico."

"Did you perhaps have a dream too?" Carlos inquired.

A smile came on Juan's face. "Yes, I did, a very pleasant dream. I found myself on the banks of the Adour River in Bayonne, France, where I spent many happy hours fishing when I was a boy. The sun was warm and there was a mild breeze coming in from the Bay of Biscay. That was it, though it was more than enough."

Carlos felt he should recount his dream in response, but he knew he couldn't describe it in detail or even the feelings of bliss and serenity it had filled him with. So he told a condensed version of it. "My dream, like Juan's," he began, "was about a lovely memory from the past. I was in Puebla, New Spain to attend the wedding of my best boyhood friend. In the dream I was with the bride's half sister, Zoila, who was from Goa, a Portuguese city in India. Zoila's grandfather was a scholar of ancient Eastern wisdom, and in the dream Zoila was telling me about the Hindu belief that all beings are one. Being in her presence somehow made me experience that belief as a profound reality."

As if Carlos's words had cast a slight spell, for several moments no one spoke. Carlos felt that Doña Josefina was studying him. Was she seeing what he had left unsaid? Then she broke the silence. "Frida," she said, "also had a dream, which she told me about this morning. However, it's not suitable for the ears of little girls. Could they be excused?" The children looked disappointed, but they followed Selena and Mara out of the room without protest.

The girls' governesses soon returned. "We had to promise them extra bedtime stories and that we would take them to one of Pascal's shows," Selena reported. "We trust this was necessary."

"Definitely," Doña Josefina replied. "Now, Frida, tell your dream."

Everyone turned to Frida. Although she was nearly as old as Doña Josefina, her bright eyes and animated bearing seemed to belie her age. "My dream," she said, clearly enjoying herself, "was about an adventure I had many years ago, when I became enamored of a much younger man. In my dream we were entwined in bed"—she paused, and a variety of expressions played over her face—"and we made love all night long. Ah!" she said exuberantly, "a young man's ardor is a gift of the gods! The dream was so real"— she closed her eyes, as if seeing it again. Changing her tone, she added, "I was very disappointed when I woke up and found myself alone, and so much older!" This occasioned much appreciative laughter.

After the laughter had died down, Selena said, "Like Juan, both Mara and I dreamed of scenes that took place in our childhood, which in my case was in Seville and in Mara's near Mexico City. In Mara's dream, her mother, who was a dancer, was teaching her a beautiful dance, and Mara felt as if she were falling in love. She said she never wanted the dream to end. In my dream I was thirteen or fourteen and I was learning the dance that teaches young girls about the powers of a woman's body." Here she flashed her eyes at Carlos. "It was the same Moorish dance that Don Alfonso found so fascinating, the one in which the dancer bares her midriff so that the onlookers can see how the movement of the dance originates in her belly."

Doña Josefina clapped her hands. "I would love to see you do that dance some day. But now I need to take my turn. I had two dreams, and I woke up between them. But before I get to the dreams I must tell you about my marriage, which had been arranged by correspondence between my father and his old friend, Reynaldo Mendoza, while I was still a little girl.

"This is what happened: Reynaldo Mendoza, with his wife and young son, came to New Mexico around the time Santa Fe was established as a *villa* in 1610. As an original settler, Reynaldo received large land grants in and around Santa Fe. When Reynaldo's son, Marcelo, began to think of marrying, Reynaldo insisted on a Spanish-born wife for him and he asked my father for me, in accord with the earlier agreement between them. Less than two years later, when I was fifteen, Marcelo, who was then thirty, came to Seville to formally ask for my hand.

"You can imagine the scene: sherry in the family drawing room in Seville, myself, my parents, Marcelo, his aunt and uncle, as representatives of his family, and a lawyer. It would not be too much to say that I was intimidated, so much so that it seemed as though there was a wall of glass separating Marcelo and me, and though we could see each other, no real meeting occurred between us. He remained as much a stranger to me when he left the house as he had been when he arrived. Nevertheless, I agreed to marry him. It was an act of obedience to my parents, but also an act of will on behalf of my spirit, which was more than a little daunted by the prospect of marrying a man twice my age and going to live with him in a wild country that I could not even imagine. Or perhaps you could call it an act of faith. Nevertheless, I married him, and I came to live here.

"And this is what I dreamed: in the first dream I was in my parents' home in Seville, and I was alone. Then a door opened, and Marcelo came into the room. The scene reminded me of the first time I had seen him, but in the dream there were only the two of us, and he was not a stranger; it was as if he had returned to me from a long journey. I was flooded with joy. I wanted to reach out to him, to touch him, but the dream faded, and I woke up. And when I woke up, I could still feel his presence."

Doña Josefina paused briefly. Then she went on. "In the second dream I was a young married woman. Marcelo and I were on the deck of a ship that was taking us to New Spain. In my arms I was holding our two-month-old son. My heart was overflowing with the love I felt for my husband and our baby."

"If I had to describe the themes that seem common to our dreams," Juan said, "they would be love and happiness."

"I agree," Doña Josefina said. "And I've enjoyed hearing these dreams and I would enjoy hearing more. But, regrettably, I must leave to prepare for another engagement I have later this morning. Will you, Don Alfonso, see Frida and me out and ride back to the plaza with us?"

Selena stood up also and said smilingly to Carlos, "You always find a way to avoid my sister and me."

"That's not my intent," he replied. "I was pleased to hear your story about that Moorish dance. If you ever respond to Doña Josefina's wish that you demonstrate it for her, be sure to include Inéz and me in the party."

"Inéz will be there for certain," Mara said.

As Mabruke drove Doña Josefina, Carlos, and Frida back to the plaza, Gordo trotting along behind, Doña Josefina brought up the topic of the inquisitors. "Frida and I," she said, "talked at length on the way over here about Father Dorantes and Brother Gustavo. We concluded that not much could be done without endangering ourselves."

"I would love," Frida said in a spritely voice, "to fly into that pervert Gustavo's cell in bat form and scare the daylights out of him." She laughed in enjoyment of the thought. "He would think the Devil was after him!"

"I expect he would, and that would be dangerous," Carlos said, hoping to caution her but unable to reveal what Gustavo had told him about having been possessed by a female demon in his youth. It occurred to Carlos to wonder if Gustavo's strong animus against Manuela might have something to do with her delight in seducing young men, even though Gustavo had never encountered her until she was old. Did he somehow sense it in her, even if he could not read auras?

"I believe Brother Gustavo is much more of a threat than Father Dorantes," Carlos went on. "I think it is best if Manuela, as Frida, stays safely indoors."

They had reached the eastern edge of the plaza, and Mabruke stopped the carriage to let Carlos out. He bid the two women good day and, with Gordo, walked diagonally across the plaza to the lane leading to his house. At home he did some household chores, had a light lunch, and put on a dress shirt for his appointment at the Mendoza residence.

He had started back across the plaza when he was hailed by Marco Cabrera. Turning, he saw Marco approaching arm in arm with Ariel Padilla. They quickly covered the distance between them and Ariel explained, "We've been to visit Dolores at Pedro's stable. I wanted to see how she's doing and to introduce her to Marco."

"She strikes me," Marco said, "as a pleasant young woman, and clever too. She had a hand puppet, a princess puppet, given her by this old man in white, Pascal. She has been practicing with the puppet and did a little one-handed drama in which the princess told a story with many gestures of how she had once lived down a well but had been rescued by a handsome prince."

"Was this a story she dreamed last night?" Carlos asked.

"Yes," Ariel replied. "How did you know?"

"All of Santa Fe seems to have been dreaming last night."

"I also had a dream," Ariel said, "that's too personal to tell. But my opinion of dreams is changing."

"How's that?" Carlos inquired.

"I used to think they were insubstantial and meaningless, but Marco had a dream in which he was going for a promenade with me around the plaza, and since he acted on it, I now have to consider that dreams may be both substantial and meaningful."

"Enjoy your walk," Carlos said, and continued on his way.

By now he had concluded that everyone in Santa Fe had had dreams last night and that their dreams had been of love and happiness. But he had not reckoned with Brother Gustavo.

Carlos's path took him past the door to the priests' quarters, which, rather strangely, was open. He glanced inside and saw Brother Gustavo standing a few feet within. Carlos nodded to him and kept going. Moments later he heard Brother Gustavo rushing up behind him. He turned and saw Gustavo coming at him with an angry look on his face. The first words out of Gustavo's mouth were an accusation. "You promised to cooperate with me, but you've done nothing of the sort!"

"I'm sorry," Carlos replied. "I don't know what you're referring to."

"When we spoke about Tarascan Indians in Santa Fe you didn't mention Leonides Chamiso."

"That's correct," Carlos agreed. "I recall that I named several Tarascan Indians from Morelia, but I also said there were others."

"Are you aware that this Leonides is said to have an owl that occupies his barn during the day and flies out from it at night?"

"I've heard that," Carlos replied, feeling annoyed by the Franciscan's unpleasant manner. "And why is that important?"

"Has anyone ever seen the owl during the day? I haven't found anyone who has, and I suspect that this Leonides is a brujo who turns himself into an owl at night."

Don Carlos gave Brother Gustavo a skeptical look. "I've never noticed anything to indicate that Leonides dabbles in the black arts," he said, "but then I haven't had much to do with him."

"Have you never heard that he's a seducer of women?" Gustavo asked angrily.

Counseling himself to be careful in answering a question whose import he didn't understand, Carlos said, "I've heard that he's been married twice and that in those periods when he's been a widower, many women were objects of his attention."

Gustavo became visibly more upset. "I remember," he said, "a man in Morelia who had a reputation as a seducer of women. His name was Carlos Buenaventura; he was an Indian, and like this Leonides he was a handsome man, of almost exactly the same height, and about the same age as Leonides would have been then. I believe they are one and the same."

Hearing that Gustavo had known him in his previous life gave Carlos an unpleasant frisson. But maintaining an unperturbed demeanor, he asked, "Have you spoken with any of the other Tarascans in Santa Fe who might remember whether Leonides ever went by another name when he lived in Morelia?"

"No, but I intend to do so, and to see if there's really an owl in that barn."

"I thought the Holy Office," Carlos began cautiously, "had no jurisdiction over Indians."

"The rule on that is ambiguous," Brother Gustavo declared. "It may apply only to Indians who remain indigenous, living outside towns and not adopting any elements of Spanish culture. Leonides lives in Santa Fe and presents himself as a practicing Catholic."

Carlos thought it was worth trying to cast some doubt on Gustavo's assertions. "Even if he is this Carlos, being a seducer of women may be a sin, but it isn't heresy or blasphemy or witchcraft, and simply having an owl that lives in one's barn in a rural town like Santa Fe is not evidence of sorcery."

"Perhaps not. But there's more to it than that. Last night I had a nightmare in which the evil female spirit who long ago sought to seduce me and possess my soul came to me again. Her first possession of me happened in Morelia. I believe she is working through this Carlos, alias Leonides, here in Santa Fe, the same way she did in Morelia. I have been free of that possession all these years, and now I have been attacked again; that can't be purely coincidental."

"I'm confused, Brother Gustavo. The succubus who possessed you was a woman; Leonides is a man."

Ignoring Carlos's point, Gustavo went on. "There's something even worse," he said darkly. "The seducer I'm after, Carlos Buenaventura, was the cause of my mother's death."

"That's terrible!" Carlos exclaimed, worried that this might somehow be true. "How did this happen?"

"My parents," Gustavo replied, "did not have a happy marriage. My mother was hungry for love, and this villain seduced her. Then he tired of her and moved on to other conquests. My father found her weeping and tried to get her to tell him what was wrong. Of course, she did not tell him about her lover. Eventually, he learned the truth from neighbors. In a great rage, he accused her of being a whore and stabbed her to death."

Troubled by Gustavo's story, Carlos tried to remember such a woman. Gustavo had not offered her name and Carlos did not dare ask. He had pursued many women, married and unmarried, during his time in Morelia. He felt shamed by the thought. With considerable effort he returned his attention to Brother Gustavo and murmured, "I can understand your animosity toward this Carlos. I very much doubt that Leonides is the same man, despite superficial resemblances. But you must excuse me; I have an appointment for which I'm late."

Carlos continued his walk to the Beltráns' to meet with Inéz and Elena, but he was in a state of shock, scarcely aware of his steps. He had always thought he'd honored the motto that his mentor, Don Serafino Romero, had impressed on him during his training in the Brujo's Way nearly two centuries earlier. "The motto of brujos of our type," Don Serafino had repeatedly told him, "is *Do no harm.*"

With a flash of guilt, Carlos recalled what Zoila had said after he'd told her about this motto. She had asked him whether he had lived up to it, and when he'd replied that he'd never consciously injured anyone, she had observed quietly, "Surely such a handsome man and ardent lover as you has broken more than a few young women's hearts." He knew he probably had, but broken hearts were one thing, and behavior that led to the death of one of his mistresses was quite another.

Preoccupied with these thoughts, Carlos paid only the barest attention to his social duties. He met Inéz and Elena at the Beltráns' and walked with them to the Mendoza house, letting the two women do all the talking. Mabruke opened the door and showed them to the *sala,* where Doña Josefina and Santiago greeted them. Doña Josefina indicated a table covered with a linen cloth and set with the blue-patterned china dessert dishes and silver and invited them to be seated.

Still turning the situation with Brother Gustavo over in his mind, Carlos barely noticed when Frida entered the room, bearing a tray with chocolate cake and a large bowl of chocolate custard. "You are welcome to try both," Doña Josefina said. "One, the *natillas de chocolate*, is a special favorite of mine."

Inéz indicated to Frida that she would like the *natillas*. "Chocolate custard," Inéz said, taking a bite. "It's delicious. I must ask your cook for the recipe."

"That would be only fair as an exchange," Doña Josefina remarked, "because the other dessert, *tarte de chocolate*, is from a recipe you gave her."

"That rich chocolate cake is a treat that we beg Inéz to make often," Elena said, speaking for the first time. "I would like a piece of that, please."

Dessert was served to everyone, and the conversation continued without Carlos's participation. He didn't truly follow what was being said until Inéz addressed him rather sharply. "Alfonso, what's wrong with you? Doña Josefina asked you a question."

"Oh, sorry; I'm very sorry," he replied. "I'm not quite myself. I had a troubling conversation with Brother Gustavo on the way here and I can't seem to get it out of my mind."

"What was so upsetting?" Doña Josefina asked.

"He, possibly alone among Santa Fe residents," Carlos said, "had a bad dream last night. He believes a demonic seducer, a woman, wants to take possession of him and that Leonides Chamiso is behind it."

"He's crazy!" Inéz exclaimed.

"Obsessed is a better word for it," Doña Josefina put in. "But I don't see how Leonides comes into the picture. He has a reputation as a womanizer, but that's so well known that no one takes it too seriously."

"Brother Gustavo takes it seriously," Carlos said, "and I'm worried that Gustavo will cause a lot of mischief due to his obsession. But let's not dwell on an unpleasant topic. What was your question, Doña Josefina?"

"I asked where you studied fencing."

"My mentor in Mexico City was Don Ignacio de Tortuga."

"But you admit," Inéz said, "that in time your skills exceeded his."

"I honor him for laying the groundwork," Carlos replied.

"And what about you, Inéz?" Doña Josefina asked.

"I had a variety of teachers in Spain before coming to Mexico City. But in one way I am self-taught, or rather, I learned from fencing with my betters. I found that if I went to a fencing academy and challenged the students there, all of whom were men, they would fence at their best because none of them wanted to lose to a woman."

Doña Josefina seemed pleased. "Good for you," she said. Turning to Elena, she asked, "What inspired you to take up fencing?"

Elena reddened a little, perhaps remembering that her initial motive for learning to fence had been to attract the attention of Leandro the Magician. "Inéz was my inspiration. I had no idea that women fenced, but she offered to tutor me."

"And was it, perhaps," Doña Josefina asked, "the somewhat unconventional aspect of it, the fact that women rarely fence, that appealed to you?"

Elena hesitated before saying, "I admit that it did, but I wouldn't have you think of me as a rebel against conventional behavior."

"You needn't worry," Doña Josefina replied. "What I see in you is not a rebel but a spirited young woman, and I applaud that."

The conversation continued, but Carlos, while trying to listen for any remarks directed at him, did not follow all the details. Everything seemed to flow in a friendly way. Before Carlos, Inéz, and Elena left, Doña Josefina said that they would have to get together again soon. "Perhaps we can have an outing to Juan Archibeque's place for a demonstration by Mara and Selena of that Moorish dance."

After they were outside, Inéz looked at Carlos and asked, "Did you put her up to that idea of going to watch Mara and Selena dance?"

"Not at all," he protested. "That came out of the blue."

"Hmmpf!" was her clearly skeptical response.

Once they were back at the Beltráns' and had a chance to speak alone, Inéz asked, "What didn't you tell us about your encounter with Brother Gustavo? You seemed to be more upset than you would be on Leonides Chamiso's account alone."

"I was. According to Brother Gustavo, a fellow named Carlos Buenaventura, who lived in Morelia when Gustavo was a boy, seduced his mother and then abandoned her. Gustavo's father learned of the affair and stabbed his wife to death."

"Oh, God!" Inéz said. "And you believe you were the cause of the poor woman's death? I can understand why you were so upset and withdrawn."

"Yes," Carlos replied, "and it also explains why Brother Gustavo is so obsessed with tracking down this brujo Carlos, despite Father Dorantes's assertions that the Inquisition has no jurisdiction over Indians."

"Oh, Carlos," Inéz said. "What are you going to do?"

"I don't know."

19

Tesuque

During his usual pre-dawn meditation on Thursday Don Carlos was beset by doubt. He had always thought of himself as a good person. He was well aware that in all his lives he had used his brujo powers mainly to entertain himself, and that in his pursuit of pleasure he had regularly pursued women. But he'd always assumed that seduction was something enjoyed by both parties. Now he'd learned of terrible consequences in at least one such case, and what made it even worse was that he couldn't remember Gustavo's mother. It was no consolation that he probably would remember her if he knew her name. That might even make his shame at his thoughtless behavior worse. In any case, she had been killed in part because he had taken advantage of her desire to be loved. Troubling thoughts along those lines churned through his head for the two hours that he sat. He could barely force himself to sit still.

He was relieved when urgent knocking at the kitchen door gave him an excuse to get up. He went into the kitchen and opened the door to find Jacinta standing there. "Doña Josefina asks that you come at once," she said.

"Just a minute," he said, turning toward the bedroom.

"Please! Don't delay," she called after him. "This is urgent."

Sensing near panic in her voice and manner, Don Carlos hurried into his clothes and boots, stepped into the lane behind his house and began to walk toward the plaza ahead of Jacinta. "Please run," Jacinta urged him, giving him a light shove from behind.

Don Carlos broke into a run and soon was well ahead of her. Possible sources of the urgency came to mind, all of them related to Frida-Manuela. But what? When he reached the Mendoza house he was greeted at the door by Doña Mendoza herself, further evidence that something was seriously amiss. "Before I let you in where we might be overheard," she whispered, "I'm asking you to follow me to Frida's room. Usually we are both early risers, and she is supposed to bring me coffee around dawn. When she didn't come this morning, I went to her room. She was nowhere to be seen, but there was a bat on her bed. It's not dead, but it's twitching, obviously in distress."

"Do you think—?" Don Carlos began.

"Yes. I think she changed herself into a bat and then couldn't reverse the process."

"Why call me?" he asked.

She gave him a sharp look. "You know about auras and shape-shifters. I want to know if anything can be done. I'll take you to her room. Come inside. Hurry! The whole household will be up soon."

Don Carlos followed Doña Josefina through the house's main hallway to a narrow corridor that led to the servants' quarters. She opened a door, backed out of his way, and once he was inside quietly closed the door behind him.

The situation had changed from when Doña Josefina had first looked in. The bat had fallen off the bed and was lying on the floor. It seemed only half alive, alternately thrashing and then lying still. Carlos remembered the difficulty he'd had in his first attempts to change Inéz into a hawk, and then the even greater difficulty in changing her back to her human form. He feared he might find it even harder to transform Manuela, a woman he scarcely knew, from a bat to her human form.

But Doña Josefina had emphasized the need to do something, and to do it quickly. Doubt again clouded his mind as it occurred to him that trying to deal with Manuela's stalled transformation might do more harm than good.

Pushing away the doubt, he reached down and gently picked up the bat. It twitched weakly. He carried it to the bed, laid it down, and bent over it. He blew on it, which caused it to move its wings slightly; then he closed his eyes and conjured up an image of the healthy, vigorous Frida he had seen only one day earlier. Finally, with all the mental power at his command, he visualized her whole again.

He opened his eyes and saw that he had half succeeded. As in the first few times he'd tried to return Inéz from hawk or owl form to her normal body, his transformation of Manuela was incomplete. She had the head of a human, though it was very small, and where her arms should have been there were leathery bat wings, and below them was a tiny body and little legs.

Groaning inwardly, he closed his eyes and tried to visualize Manuela as a full-sized human being. This time he opened his eyes to find a naked old woman lying on the bed in front of him. But she was still not quite her old self; she was somehow precariously balanced between her human form and her bat form.

Manuela's eyelids fluttered open. In an extremely weak voice, she said, "Trapped."

"Yes," he said, agreeing with what he'd thought she meant. "You were trapped in a bat's body."

"Not…not that," she managed. "Gustavo," she went on, though it came out, "Goose tahvoo."

"Gustavo trapped you?" Don Carlos asked.

"Almost."

Don Carlos wanted to know more, but the effort to talk seemed to be too much and Manuela fainted.

He tiptoed over to the door and opened it a crack. Doña Josefina was right there. "I've done the best I could, but she's in a bad way," he said. "She's very weak and not completely coherent. For general consumption the story must be that something frightened her and she hit her head in trying to crawl under her bed."

"Why tell the story that way?" Doña Josefina asked.

"Just in case anyone looked in the room and noticed the bat but didn't see her."

"Very good," Doña Josefina replied. "Marta has been hovering around asking questions. Here she comes again."

Doña Josefina's granddaughter-in-law Marta, followed by Mabruke, had come down the hall as Don Carlos and Doña Josefina were speaking. Carlos stepped out and closed the bedroom door behind him before Marta could see inside. "What's going on?" Marta demanded. "I heard some noise here earlier and looked in Frida's room. She was nowhere to be seen, but there was a bat on her bed. I went to get Mabruke to deal with the bat. He was not dressed, so I had to wait for him."

"Ah!" Doña Josefina said, as though this was the first she'd heard about a bat. "That explains it. The bat must have given Frida a fright. When I came in to look for her, I found her unconscious under her bed. She must have crawled there to hide. But Don Alfonso reports that she's suffered some sort of shock that's left her weak and incoherent."

"Why is Don Alfonso here rather than Dr. Velarde?" Mata asked, regarding him with narrowed eyes.

"Dr. Velarde," he replied, "is out of town. Yesterday I happened to mention this to Doña Josefina. That is why she sent for me."

Persisting in her interrogation of Don Carlos, Marta said, "And do you have qualifications to deal with a situation of this sort, whatever it is?"

"Marta!" Doña Josefina hissed. "You are being rude, embarrassingly so."

Marta seemed to be preparing a tart retort, but before she could get it out, Don Carlos spoke in a reassuring way. "I'm not a physician," he said, "but in my travels I have often had to provide emergency aid to a companion."

"I appreciate your having come," Doña Josefina said. "What do you suggest we should do for Frida?"

"She needs to rest and to eat simple, warm food and drink lots of water. My advice would be to have Mabruke prop her up in bed and that you not let her sleep for more than half an hour at a time. She may have sustained a head injury when she fell out of bed. In similar cases I've observed, the injured person can lose consciousness permanently if not helped to stay alert."

"Mabruke and I will go in to see her immediately," Doña Josefina said. "I will stay by her side. I can't have a servant of mine dying due to neglect. Thank you for your help."

"I assure you," Carlos replied, "I was glad to come. Please keep me informed about her progress."

Doña Josefina opened the door just enough to allow herself and Mabruke to slip inside. Mabruke shut the door firmly behind them.

As he started down the hall to let himself out, Marta followed behind him. "You are part of the trouble that's come to this house," she snapped.

"Trouble?" he said, slowing down to let her catch up with him. "I wish the Mendoza house no trouble."

"Bah!" Marta shot back. "You're part of the conspiracy to cheat Antonio and Julio out of their rightful inheritance."

"Although it's none of my business," Carlos replied, "I was under the impression that nothing's been settled on that score."

"It will be soon," Marta said, "if I have anything to say about it. And this little incident may just give me the leverage to see that the right thing is done."

Puzzled by Marta's obvious threat, Carlos paused as he reached the large hall that served as the house's entryway. "I have no idea what you mean," he said.

"You will soon enough," she replied, and turned and strode off down the hall in the other direction.

Jacinta let him out the front door, and he walked through town to his house. Before going in he went around back to see if the horses had been fed yet. Orfeo was tossing hay into the corral for them. He looked up and said, "I saw something strange just now. That Franciscan, Brother Gustavo, was

216 ———————

headed across the field toward Pedro's stable. He had a musket in his hand and looked as though he intended to use it."

Don Carlos's immediate thought was that Dolores might be in danger. Had Brother Gustavo somehow figured out that she was a shape-shifter, and that she had escaped after the burglaries by changing herself into a black dog?

Breaking into a run, he dashed across the fields toward Pedro's stable. A short distance ahead Carlos could see Brother Gustavo pass Pedro's stable and cross the Galisteo Road ford of the Santa Fe River, which was just south of Pedro's place. Carlos's first reaction was relief that Gustavo's destination didn't involve Dolores; then he realized that Gustavo was headed directly for Leonides Chamiso's house.

Pedro had noticed Brother Gustavo passing his place, and he had stepped out to see where the Franciscan was going. He was still standing there when Carlos reached him. Pedro said, "Trouble's brewing. I heard the Franciscan muttering about shooting an owl."

"Not good," Carlos replied, and he hurried on toward the Galisteo Road ford.

Ahead of him he saw that Brother Gustavo had splashed through the ford and was advancing on Leonides's house, some forty feet away. He was shouting, "Leonides Chamiso! Come out! Show yourself!"

Leonides, obviously having heard the shouts, though perhaps not the exact words, came out the front door, followed by a large brown mastiff. A look of astonishment came on his face as he took in the spectacle of a brown-robed Franciscan shaking one fist at him and brandishing a musket in the other hand. "What's wrong?" he asked in a firm voice.

"You know very well what's wrong, you seducer!" Gustavo shouted. "You have set a succubus on me as I slept, the same demon temptress with which you plagued me in Morelia."

"What can this be about?" Leonides said, looking around at several neighbors who had begun to gather. "I don't remember you from Morelia," he added to Gustavo. "I don't recall us ever meeting before the day you came around to see my dog, the black dog that the wolf later killed."

"Liar!" Gustavo snarled, seeming to grow more incensed. He turned away from Leonides and looked in the direction of the barn, which was closer to the river. "I'm going to that barn to see if the owl is there."

"Of course she's there," Leonides said. "She comes back every day at dawn."

Gustavo stopped and gave Leonides a piercing look. "She! She!" he shouted. "You direct the actions of an owl at night and make it do mischief, tormenting and tempting innocents." He took several steps toward the barn. "That owl must die, if it's possible to kill it."

Don Carlos, having reached and crossed the river, arrived on the north side of Canyon Road, which ran past Leonides's barn and house. He had heard Brother Gustavo's accusation that Leonides manipulated the owl to do his will—exactly, Carlos realized, as Gustavo had manipulated a wolf to do his.

Leonides was a large man, taller by several inches than Brother Gustavo, and he moved forward with astonishing quickness to block Gustavo's advance on his barn. "You'll not harm my friend Rubia," he said, taking Gustavo's arm.

"Rubia! So that's her name, a blonde temptress," Gustavo replied, pulling his arm away and aiming the musket at Leonides. "I'll shoot you too, if you interfere." At that moment the huge brown body of Leonides's mastiff hurled through the air and crashed into Gustavo's chest, knocking him backwards so that he fell heavily against the side of the barn. Gustavo's musket, now pointed harmlessly toward the sky, discharged.

Don Carlos saw an owl fly out the loft window of the barn and head off across the fields south of the river at a great rate. "There!" Carlos shouted. "The commotion frightened the owl and it has fled."

Brother Gustavo was struggling to his feet and glaring at all the onlookers, including Carlos. But then he turned his attention fully to Leonides and pointed a finger at him accusingly. "You!" he said. "You've tried to hide by changing your name from Carlos Buenaventura, the scoundrel who brought great harm to my family in Morelia. But I've found you out."

"The man is crazy," an onlooker said. "I've known Leonides since we were boys together in Morelia, and his name has always been Leonides."

The expressions on the onlookers' faces varied from shocked to angry, and Leonides's mastiff was glowering at Gustavo, ready to attack him again at the slightest provocation. Don Carlos felt the timing was right to step in. He first addressed the small crowd that had gathered, all of them Indians or mestizos from the Barrio de Analco. "Friends," he said, "this is nothing but a case of mistaken identity, and fortunately no harm has been done. As a member of the Town Council, I will take responsibility for restoring peace."

He leaned over and whispered in Brother Gustavo's ear. "Help me out. No good can come of pursuing this any further. Let's leave before that dog attacks you again. I'll walk you back to the chapel, and you can tell me what triggered this incident."

Brother Gustavo seemed reluctant to let the matter drop, but Leonides's mastiff produced an exceedingly threatening growl accompanied by bared teeth, and Carlos took Gustavo's arm and bodily pulled him away. "Let's make our retreat as dignified as possible," Carlos suggested in a quiet voice. A motion off to his right caught his eye. It was Pascal, the old man in white. He'd apparently joined the crowd late in the incident. He tipped his hat respectfully to Carlos.

"So what's this about a female demon visiting you last night?" he asked Brother Gustavo as they walked back toward the center of town.

A shiver went through Brother Gustavo's body. "Early this morning," he said, "before dawn, a bat flew into my cell. It touched my body with its wings, which woke me up. I knew it was the same succubus that had tempted me with sexual thoughts and feelings years ago in Morelia, and I knew its intention was to take possession of me, body and soul. I leaped out of bed, grabbed a broom, and tried to hit it, but it evaded me. It was a demon!"

"But you did get rid of it," Carlos put in, hoping to calm Gustavo down.

"Yes," Gustavo said in a defeated tone. "After I was exhausted from flailing at it, it flew out the window."

"With all due respect, Brother Gustavo," Don Carlos ventured, "bats are common in Santa Fe. Indeed, I believe several live in the chapel's bell tower. When I sit on my veranda as night falls and look at the sky, I often see bats flying around in the vicinity of the chapel."

"This was no ordinary bat," Gustavo replied sourly.

Don Carlos, who knew the bat was, in fact, Manuela, went on with his inquiry. "What led you to go after an owl, given that your tormentor appeared to you in the form of a bat? I can't make sense of that."

"I believe that the same evil brujo, Carlos Buenaventura, is in back of all the examples of witchcraft that I've witnessed in Santa Fe—the thief who turns into a black dog, the destruction of the Holy Office's proclamation, and the dreams that have plagued me for two nights running."

"You didn't mention the wolf that killed black dogs," Carlos observed.

"Yes, that too," Gustavo said sharply.

After seeing Brother Gustavo to his quarters at the chapel, Don Carlos walked back to Pedro's stable.

He greeted Pedro in what he hoped was an offhand way. "That was quite a disturbance this morning, wouldn't you say?"

"Dolores saw the whole thing. Scared her out of her wits."

"Is she all right now?"

"No. She tried to change herself into a dog and run off, but couldn't manage it. That frightened her all the more."

"Where is she?

"She's hiding in her room."

"I think I should get her out of town, perhaps ride to Tesuque. I want her to meet Old Man Xenome."

"What if she won't go?" Pedro asked.

"I think I can convince her to come along. Why don't you saddle Dulce while I go home and get Eagle? I'll be right back."

Pedro looked skeptical, but he didn't say anything. Carlos returned to his house, saddled Eagle, and told Orfeo that he might spend the night at Tesuque. "Also," he went on, "I'll see if I can recruit José's cousins to help you with your building project here."

Those details settled, he walked Eagle to Pedro's stable. Pedro had Dulce ready to go. Handing Pedro Eagle's reins, Carlos said, "Let me go in the house and invite Dolores to join me for a ride."

Pedro, obviously still skeptical, shrugged his shoulders and grunted.

Dolores proved surprisingly easy to convince that getting out of town was a good alternative to hiding in her room. "I've been wanting you to meet José's mentor in the Shaman's Way," Don Carlos said, "and a ride to Tesuque will put some distance between us and Santa Fe."

"Will José be there?" Dolores asked.

"He tries to spend a day with Xenome every week. We might get lucky and find him there."

Ten minutes later they were on a path west of the plaza that connected with the road to Tesuque. Don Carlos could see the Beltrán house a little distance up the hill, and he wished he could take a detour and tell Inéz about the morning's events, but he didn't feel he could speak freely in Dolores's presence about the Frida-Manuela situation. He'd asked Pedro to have María tell Inéz that he was taking Dolores to Tesuque and might not be home until tomorrow. That would have to do for now.

Once they'd rounded a curve in the road north of Santa Fe and could no longer see the town, Don Carlos relaxed. It was a beautiful day in late May. From the freshness of the morning, he estimated that the afternoon temperature would be warm, but not hot. He looked over at Dolores, who was riding beside him, and said, "Pedro thinks you tried a transformation this morning and that it didn't succeed."

Dolores gave a little gasp. "I didn't realize Pedro knew."

"He's a quiet man, but very observant," Carlos replied. "Over the years we've been together, he's often noticed things that surprised me. Tell me what happened."

"Nothing happened. That upset me. I've always used transforming myself into a dog as a way to hide. Not being able to do it when I wanted to made me feel unsafe."

"I can understand that, Dolores. But tell me; was this the first time you've failed at a transformation?"

"No—but I haven't been doing it so often lately."

"Why not?"

"A while ago I began to feel sick after every time I transformed myself. I felt as though my body was full of holes and all my strength was leaking out. That made me reluctant to change myself to dog form."

"But when you and I visited the *piedras marcadas* and sat next to the rock with the spiral figure, you achieved a transformation quickly and easily, and on the trip home you seemed to be feeling very well. Was I wrong in those perceptions?"

"No, Don Alfonso, but I felt that your presence, and perhaps the power of the spiral image, helped me out."

"What about afterward? Were you feeling sick and I didn't notice?"

A long silence followed. Finally, she said, "No, but—that's kind of personal."

"You mean that you like José and meeting him made you feel good?"

"You see too much," she replied.

Don Carlos laughed. "I've learned a few things over six lifetimes. But I was asking those questions because Inéz also got sick after I helped her make many transformations. Her symptoms were like yours: fatigue and feeling as though her body was full of holes. She says that as exciting as she found it to fly around as an owl or hawk, she doesn't think it's good for her health."

Dolores was silent again for a long time. Then she said, "I always thought I was some sort of freak. It helps to be around people who have some idea of what I've felt."

"I'm sure you'll like Old Man Xenome for just that reason," Carlos replied.

The approach of the horses and their riders startled a large flock of great-tailed grackles that had been feeding in a marsh at the side of the road. They exploded into the air with a loud beating of wings. Once airborne, they didn't fly away but circled over the marsh at a safe distance from Carlos and Dolores. Don Carlos brought Eagle to a halt, and Dolores followed suit with Dulce, and they watched the virtuosity of the birds' flight.

The flock turned and twisted in the air in unison. One moment the birds would be in full silhouette, their combined shapes so closely aligned that they almost blacked out the sky behind them. Then, in a sudden shift, they turned so that every grackle's body was sideways to the human onlookers, so that what Don Carlos and Dolores saw was hundreds of narrow lines against a blue background. Back and forth, turning and twisting, but always in unison as though the hundreds of birds were of one body, one mind.

The grackles swooped down and landed all at once in the marsh. Don Carlos and Dolores rode on. An hour later they came to the turnoff for Tesuque Pueblo and followed the road to the Tewa Indian settlement there.

Having often visited the pueblo, Don Carlos steered them down a lane between adobe dwellings to the two-room homes where Ana and José Lugo's cousins, Lázaro and Rubén, lived. Rubén was sitting on the tiny porch in front of his house and stood to greet them. "Is everyone abandoning Santa Fe to move here?" he asked.

Don Carlos laughed. He'd already noticed that José's horse, Viva, was in Rubén's corral. "I hope you have room for a few more of us," he replied. "Rubén, this is Dolores Gallegos, a recent addition to Pedro and María's household."

"I heard they'd brought in a girl to help María once the baby's born."

"For someone who lives a long way from Santa Fe," Don Carlos observed, "you certainly know a lot."

"I also heard," Rubén replied, "that you're expanding your house. Lázaro and I will come by for a day next week to help you along. As for your question about room, if you and Dolores want to stay overnight, we can find space for you."

"I don't know how to thank you," Don Carlos said.

"There's no need to try," Rubén replied. "You know that. José is visiting with Old Man Xenome. I expect you will want to join them. You can head over there. I'll take care of your horses."

Don Carlos and Dolores found Old Man Xenome and José engaged in conversation in Xenome's one-room house. They were greeted warmly and invited to take seats on the floor, which was covered by a woven rug of many colors. Carlos introduced Old Man Xenome and Dolores to each other and then brought out a few small gifts.

Xenome picked up one of the cloth bags Carlos had placed in front of him, opened it slightly, and inhaled deeply. "This is excellent tobacco," he said. "You know how to make an old man happy. Thank you." He looked first at Carlos and then at Dolores. "Perhaps we should have a smoke together," he suggested.

"I don't know if Dolores has ever smoked tobacco," Carlos said.

"Never?" Xenome asked, an amused look on his face.

"Never," she replied.

"The first time is not always so easy," Xenome went on, smiling broadly. "Let's wait a while. We can talk first. Since we are friends, I will begin by asking about the subject that interests me most. Dolores, I can see that you're a true shape-shifter."

"That's a secret," she said, looking uneasy.

"Secrets are often necessary. They serve an important purpose. But you are among friends, and your secrets are safe with us. I have not met many shape-shifters, only two in my long life, and that's why I am asking about your secrets."

"I think I'm losing my ability to change into dog form," Dolores blurted out. "Just this morning I failed, and when I do manage, I don't feel well afterward."

"How did you originally learn to change your form?" Xenome asked.

"So many people told me I was as ugly as a dog that I became one."

Xenome gave Dolores a tender look and said, "Perhaps you are now seeing that they were wrong, and perhaps, having found a safe place to live with Pedro and María, you no longer need to take a dog's form."

"But I may need to," Dolores protested. "There are mean people around, and I could hide from them in dog form."

"True," Xenome agreed. "Sometimes a gain is also a loss; you've gained the knowledge that you are not ugly, but you may have lost a defense that depended on your believing you were. Please tell me more about the sickness that follows a transformation. Carlos's friend Inéz also got sick after many changes in form."

"It's hard to describe. It's like—my bones are dissolving," Dolores replied, making a helpless gesture.

"What do you think, Don Carlos?" Xenome asked. "You've changed form many, many times over many lifetimes. Yet you don't seem to have suffered as a result."

"I've only lately begun to wonder about that," Carlos said. "My original teacher in the Brujo's Way, Don Serafino, once remarked that I was unusual. Something about the way my body was constituted made it easy for me to do transformations once I'd learned the technique. I'm puzzled. I need to think more about this."

"José has to leave soon," Xenome said. "Perhaps it's time to smoke some of the tobacco you brought." He reached for a pipe and poured some tobacco in it from the bag Carlos had given him. Lighting the pipe with an ember from his hearth, he inhaled, exhaled, and smiled. "Very good."

"Dolores," he went on, "I'll pass the pipe around. For your first smoke it's best to draw smoke into your mouth and hold it there. In time, perhaps even today after several pulls on the pipe, you'll be able to take some smoke into your lungs without choking."

Xenome passed the pipe to Don Carlos, who took a deep inhalation. He gave it to José, who did likewise. José passed the pipe to Dolores, who tentatively drew on the pipe. She blew out the smoke and coughed.

The ritual of smoking together continued, with Xenome passing the pipe four times, "Once for each of the four directions," he said. Don Carlos primarily attended to his own feeling of heightened alertness that tobacco induced in him, and he was aware that Dolores was gaining confidence and taking deeper inhalations each time the pipe reached her.

After the pipe had made its final circuit, the four companions sat silently, each lost in thought. Xenome finally spoke to Dolores. "How are you experiencing the effects of our friend, *Tobaco*?"

"I feel stronger; everything is brighter."

"Yes, everything is brighter, and stronger is good," Xenome replied.

A longer period of silence followed until José announced that he had to leave in order to get back to Rancho Rosón before dark. He stood up and addressed Xenome. "Thank you for your teaching, Grandfather." Looking next at Dolores and then at Carlos, he added, "I'm glad to see you again, Dolores, and you too, Don Carlos. I also feel brighter and stronger."

José let himself out the door, and Xenome asked Don Carlos, "Are you planning to stay overnight?"

"I'd like to," Carlos said. "My original intention was to practice a transformation after nightfall, but what Dolores has told us about her transformations' aftereffects leads me to feel that we should simply sit outside and enjoy the full moon."

"I feel safe here, and happy too," Dolores said. "The smoking together helped. I would like to try a transformation to see what its aftereffects are when I feel safe."

Don Carlos expressed his doubts. "It's good you feel secure here, Dolores, but I'm not sure that will guarantee your feeling all right after you come back to human form."

A look of determination came onto Dolores's face. "I lived alone and under poor conditions for a long time. I'd like to learn to live with the aftereffects in case I ever need to change my form in the future."

"What do you think, Grandfather?" Carlos asked Xenome.

Xenome did not answer directly. He simply said, "In facing danger, the ability to change form might be a useful skill."

"I want to do it," Dolores repeated.

"I can't stop you," Don Carlos replied, "but we need to work a few things out in advance. For one thing, Dolores, perhaps you might want to stay here for a day or two after you return to human form."

"Yes. If I'm not feeling well, Grandfather Xenome can help me with healing chants. I'm sure María will understand if you tell her that I'll only be away for a few days."

Don Carlos went on. "Then I will also do a transformation. I want to become an owl and fly around at night. Once I'm in animal form I can usually communicate with other animals by forming words in my mind. But that doesn't always work. If I seem to be trying to communicate with you and you don't understand, bark twice."

"What do you suggest we do while in dog and owl form?" Dolores inquired.

"When the sun is about to set, I'll walk up the slope west of the pueblo to an overlook site. After dark I'll change into an owl, fly around for a while, return to the overlook, change back to my human form, and walk back here around dawn."

"But what about me?" Dolores asked.

"I think you should stay here with Grandfather Xenome."

"If we do things that way," Dolores objected, clearly disappointed with his proposal, "I won't get to see you in owl form."

"And neither will I," Xenome said. "True shape-shifters are so rare that I would like to get a good look at both of you."

"Then what I'll do," Carlos said, "is fly here after the full moon is at the highest point it will reach in tonight's sky. If you and Dolores sit on your front porch waiting, I will land on Grandfather's arm. By that time of night all your neighbors should be in bed and sound asleep."

Xenome laughed and said, "If they aren't and any of them see an owl swooping down on the pueblo, I'll have to spend the next week trying to convince them that the pueblo hasn't been haunted by a malign owl spirit."

"I'll keep an eye out for anyone wandering around at midnight and stay away if I spot someone."

Xenome offered them a light evening meal, after which they sat on the porch and waited for the sun to begin to set. Don Carlos was about to leave for the ledge where he intended to spend the early evening hours when Dolores announced, "I want to change to dog form while Don Carlos is still here."

Following a brief discussion, Don Carlos and Xenome agreed to turn their backs while Dolores attempted to become a dog. Having so recently seen that Manuela had been unable to fully control her transformations, Carlos was concerned that something might go wrong for Dolores. He needn't have worried. Minutes after he'd heard her undressing, a medium-sized black female dog stepped between him and Xenome and rubbed her head against his hand. He was startled to see that her front left paw was crippled and her left eye half-closed, just as Dolores's left hand and left eye were deformed.

Xenome undoubtedly observed the same phenomenon, but he made it clear that Dolores's deformities didn't matter to him. "What a fine dog," he said quietly, reaching over and stroking her on the head.

"Time for me to go," Don Carlos said, standing up. "Keep an eye out for a great horned owl, a really big one."

Old Man Xenome's one-room house was located on the far western edge of the pueblo. From Xenome's front porch Carlos could see a faint trail that led to a mountain slope on which there was a ledge overlooking the valley. The ledge had long been used for vision quests. An hour's hike, the last quarter of which took him up a steep, rocky path, brought him to the ledge in question. He settled down and waited.

Don Carlos had never before transformed himself into a great horned owl, and his usual practice the first time he changed into a new bird of prey was to listen for its call and, if possible, to observe its flight. He had seen many great horned owls in flight, so that posed no difficulties. But he hoped to hear one vocalizing. Finally, after nearly an hour's wait, he heard the characteristic five hoots of a great horned owl: *hoo hoohoo hoo hoo*. The voice was faint, clearly a long way off, but he undressed and prepared to transform himself if more such calls came.

He was in luck. Not just one but two great horned owls were in the vicinity, and as the next half hour passed, they moved closer to Don Carlos's position, and he could hear them distinctly. Satisfied, he concentrated intensely on the shape and size of a great horned owl and then took its form.

Pleased with his success, he took off and turned west from Tesuque Pueblo. Flying in a straight line with just enough beats of his wings to gain altitude, he soon reached a position level with the top of the ridge. After twenty minutes, he had gone as far to the west of the pueblo as he wanted to go. He began to circle, a maneuver he had always enjoyed. In the light of the full moon his owl vision perceived the terrain below—the mountain slopes, mesas, valleys, and rivers, and the trees, shrubs, and rocks—better than human eyes could see in daylight.

In a playful spirit he next practiced diving. Initially, he made shallow dives that ended well above the canyon floor. Each dive that followed was steeper and longer. Finally, he picked a big cottonwood with a dead limb that stood out from the rest of the tree. Slowing as much as he could, he coasted downward on a line of flight aimed directly at the limb. He carefully braked to a halt and settled on the branch.

The full moon was reaching its apogee in the night sky, the signal for him to begin his return journey. He launched into flight again and took a direct route back to Tesuque Pueblo. When he reached the pueblo's outskirts, he made a big circle to assess the situation. It was close to midnight, and everyone seemed to be asleep. As he neared Old Man Xenome's little house he saw the old medicine man seated on a bench on his front porch, smoking a pipe. Dolores in dog form was resting by his side.

Old Man Xenome saw his approach and stepped off the porch. He had wrapped a piece of leather around one arm, inviting Don Carlos to land there. With a deft dive and one beat of his wings, Don Carlos dropped down and gently closed his talons on Xenome's forearm. He addressed the old medicine man, asking whether he could understand him.

"Yes, I can," Xenome replied, mouthing the words as he said them, though Don Carlos understood them more in his head than through hearing the sounds.

Dolores in dog form had stood up and was eyeing Xenome and his owl guest with great interest. "Can you hear me?" Don Carlos asked her.

Receiving no answer, Don Carlos waited for Xenome to ask Dolores the same question, which he did, saying out loud, "Don Carlos is trying to speak to you. Can you hear him?"

Dolores responded with two soft barks, their agreed-upon signal for no.

Don Carlos addressed Old Man Xenome. "I can't seem to communicate with Dolores. It wouldn't be polite for us to talk at length without her being able to join in. I'll fly off and return in human form around dawn."

"It has been a privilege to meet you," Xenome said. As Carlos the owl spread his wings to lift off, Xenome moved his arm to help boost him into the air. Don Carlos returned to the vision-quest ledge, changed back to human form, dressed, and spent four hours quietly listening to the sounds and inhaling the smells of the surrounding night.

At dawn he hiked back to Xenome's house. The old medicine man was still seated on his porch, and Dolores in dog form was still lying by his side, but Don Carlos could see that this was an unhappy, anxious dog. "What's the matter?" Carlos asked before remembering that she could answer yes and no questions only. Intuitively, he knew the problem. "Have you tried to return to human form?"

A single bark indicated that the answer was yes.

Don Carlos bit his lip. The memory of his imperfect success with changing the bat back into Manuela was fresh in his memory. He took himself to task for letting Dolores attempt a transformation. The only comfort came from the thought that she had been determined to take on dog form, and that she had done so despite the doubts he had expressed.

"Let's move indoors," he suggested, "and have Dolores lie on the bed with a blanket over her. I'll try to help her return to human form, and if that succeeds the blanket will prevent us from seeing her naked."

Dolores went to Xenome's sleeping mat and lay down on her right side. Don Carlos was filled with compassion by the sight of her crippled left paw and half-closed eye. He put a blanket over her, leaving only her head uncovered. Closing his eyes, he concentrated on his image of Dolores and his intention to return her to human form.

Nothing happened.

Kneeling beside her, he addressed her urgently. "Dolores, I need you to help. I will count to three. At three, put all your effort into remembering your human form and believing that, as you have many times in the past, you can return to it. I will concentrate on the same thing." He paused, "One, two, three!"

Dolores's dog form twitched violently, but she remained a dog.

Suddenly it seemed to Don Carlos that he could feel Dolores's suffering in his whole body. The feeling flooded him, and his eyes filled with tears. He lay down behind the dog, put his arm around her body, and stroked her head. "Dear Dolores," he whispered in her ear. "We are with you in your suffering.

We love you." He placed his mouth next to her ear and kissed it.

He felt movement underneath the blanket. He'd closed his eyes as he kissed the dog; now he opened them and saw Dolores's face and the shape of her body under the blanket. "Thank you," she said. She lay without moving for several minutes. Finally she said again, "Thank you."

Don Carlos sat up and got off the sleeping mat. He went over to the corner where she'd left her clothes and brought them to her. He then moved away from her and joined Xenome in looking at the wall opposite the sleeping mat. "Xenome and I will turn our backs so you can get dressed," he told her.

Soon Dolores spoke. "I'm all right now; you may look."

They turned. There was Dolores, except she was different. Her left eye and left hand were no longer deformed. With a smile on his face, Old Man Xenome asked, "Dolores! What happened to your left hand?"

Dolores started to hide her hand as she usually did; then she noticed that it was perfectly formed. She put her hand to her face. "Is my eye all right too?" she asked.

"Yes," Xenome replied.

"It's like one of the fairy tales that Pascal's hand puppets performed," she said thoughtfully. "The prince kisses her and tells her he loves her, and she wakes up. That's what I feel like has happened to me."

Don Carlos was deeply pleased. Was it his sorcery, or was it something else? He didn't care which. Dolores and Old Man Xenome were clearly no less moved by the results. Still, he decided to stay with her at Tesuque all day Friday and overnight to watch over her.

As it turned out, his staying an extra twenty-four hours seemed to reinforce Dolores's healing. He and Dolores took long walks, talked, and rested, and Xenome taught them healing chants.

By Saturday morning, Don Carlos felt confident that all was well. Dolores had needed to rest a lot, but otherwise she seemed fine. After breakfast he excused himself to head home. "The forty-day period set by the Inquisition is ending," he said, "and I should get back to Santa Fe. It's all right," he said to Dolores, "if you want to stay a few more days with Grandfather Xenome. You can ride back to Santa Fe with Rubén and Lázaro when they come to town to help me with my building project."

"I'd like to stay," she said, "but" — this with a worried look — "will you explain to María and Pedro?"

"Of course, and I'll tell them that Xenome's healing chants restored your hand and eye to health."

"I will teach Dolores more healing chants," Xenome put in. "But there's no need for you to lie about how she was healed. Just say it was a miracle. Catholics are supposed to believe in miracles."

Don Carlos retrieved Eagle from Rubén and stopped by Xenome's house once more to say goodbye. Xenome got in the last word. "Thank you," he said, "for giving this old man a chance to witness things that brought back memories of his own youth — an animal transformation and a powerful example of healing."

Carlos started back for Santa Fe and, lacking any special reason to hurry, he rode along at a leisurely pace. It was Saturday, a market day, and most of the other riders he met on the road were headed to town to buy or trade. But when he was about half an hour from town he looked up from studying Eagle's ears and was surprised to see Inéz on Alegría riding toward him at a gallop. From the look on her face Carlos could tell that something was wrong.

Inéz pulled up beside them. It took a moment for her to catch her breath. "You must come quickly! Dorantes has announced an auto-da-fé to be held on the plaza today!"

Carlos was so jolted that his mind immediately leaped to stories of famous autos-da-fé he had heard of. "What?" he asked. "Are they going to burn somebody?"

Inéz looked horrified. "I don't think so. I don't know. Marco told me it's a public accusation and administration of punishment. By whipping, I think."

"Who is accused?" Carlos asked.

"We don't know their names. The rumor is that it's three mestizos, two men and a woman. Let's not waste time on speculation. Alegría is tired. Eagle seems to be fresh. You should ride ahead as fast as possible. I'll come along shortly and meet you at the plaza."

Eagle loved to gallop, so Carlos made it to Santa Fe quickly. He rode Eagle directly home, unsaddled him and turned him out in the corral, and then walked to the plaza to join the crowd there.

20

Puzzles

*T*he plaza was jammed to overflowing, but it was not a normal Saturday market scene. For one thing no business was being conducted. The crowd stood silent. On the north side of the plaza five chairs had been set up. They were occupied by Governor Peralta, Father Dorantes and his two fellow inquisitors, and Horatio Padilla, who represented the Town Council. Soldiers from the Presidio were holding the crowd back from the space between the five dignitaries and the platform, which was about fifty feet away.

Black storm clouds had gathered, and the humidity was oppressive. Don Carlos sensed that a storm was brewing that would bring heavy rain, thunder and lightning, and maybe even hail within an hour or less. He saw Marco Cabrera standing next to the five seated dignitaries. Don Carlos pushed through the crowd of Indians and mestizos, who made way for him to pass.

Tugging on Marco's sleeve, Don Carlos leaned close to his ear and whispered, "What has happened?"

Marco jumped; clearly his nerves were on edge. "You just got here?" He spoke so quietly that even their closest neighbors couldn't have heard his words. "Earlier this morning there was a Mass of Penitence in the chapel. After that three mestizos accused of various crimes by the Inquisition were brought out and led to the foot of the platform. The two men, Mariano Fuentes and Cipriano Rascón, were charged with blasphemy. Neither had repented. Father Dorantes ordered the soldiers to make Rascón mount the platform. He was given a final chance to admit to the charge of blasphemy and to repent. He remained obdurate, as they say, and was given forty lashes as punishment. He is one tough man and he did not cry out, though he could scarcely walk afterward. Two friends had to help him leave the plaza."

"I don't know much about him," Carlos said, "except that he's a day laborer."

"He was heard to curse God," Marco replied, "not once but many times, and I too would feel wronged, if not by God then by Fate, for the sorrows he's had to endure. He started out with a wife, a small house, a large pasture, and a flock of sheep. His wife died bearing an infant boy, who also died. Then a pack of coyotes attacked his flock of sheep and killed all but three of them. A year later he married again, less for love than for the two dozen sheep his second wife brought with her as a dowry. He hoped for a male heir, but his children were stillborn. His flock of sheep broke out of their pasture and drank some foul water that killed every one of them. Finally his wife died in her last childbirth. Rascón had acquired debts, and with no other way to pay them, he sold his house and land and became a day laborer who slept in barns owned by his employers."

"A terrible story," Carlos agreed. "Couldn't he have confessed to blasphemy to avoid the whip?"

"He refused. He shouted that he had nothing more to lose except his integrity, and he would be damned if he would repent of being angry at God."

"A kind of moral rigor," Carlos commented, "that demands a degree of respect."

"Indeed. But even if he had repented and asked for forgiveness, he would still have been whipped. Mariano Fuentes, the second man accused of blasphemy, denied his guilt. He claimed that an anonymous informer had accused him falsely, and he threatened that whoever had done so would pay for it. But when the man with the whip approached him, Fuentes lost his nerve, confessed, and begged for mercy. His confession did him some good, but only some. Father Dorantes announced that his sentence would be reduced to twenty lashes, which were administered just before you arrived."

"And the third case?"

"They are about to take it up. The accused is an old mestizo woman, Clementina Loera. She's over there. The charge against her is about to be read."

Carlos looked back to the platform and saw Clementina standing at the foot of it, supported by two soldiers. She looked exhausted and disoriented. The only thing Don Carlos knew about her was that she was a *curandera*, an herbalist who eked out a living selling herbal potions to people who were sick or to women who wanted to get pregnant or make a particular man fall in love with them.

"Where is Father Benedicto?" he asked Marco. "He's the senior priest. I can't believe that he would approve of such summary justice to someone who's a *curandera*, not a witch."

"Father Benedicto and my father, representing the province in his capacity as vice governor, are out of town. They have gone to the new town of Albuquerque to attend a ceremony officially recognizing it as having *villa*

232 —————

status under Spanish law. But in any case, members of the Holy Office tribunal have authority independent of both parish and secular officials."

Don Carlos groaned. "The forty-day period of grace has just ended. They struck fast."

"Yes," Marco said. "The Town Crier announced the news of the auto-da-fé this morning."

Don Carlos watched as two soldiers escorted Clementina up the stairs and onto the platform. They positioned her facing the post in the center, lifted her arms over her head, and bound her wrists to the post. She slumped down in place.

Dorantes rose from his chair, pulled a scroll from the sleeve of his robe, unrolled it, and read in a loud voice. "Be it known to all present that this person (gesturing toward his captive), Clementina Loera, has long practiced witchcraft. Upon her arrest last night and during her subsequent interrogation, she did not deny that she had employed heathen spells and potions for diverse purposes, but she persists in denying that she is a witch. Therefore she has been sentenced to be punished by the lash, but such is the merciful conduct of cases that come before the Holy Office that I, as its official representative in the province of New Mexico, am offering her a final chance to confess and repent with all of you as her witnesses. If she continues to deny the charge of witchcraft, as proven by the testimony of a reliable witness, she will receive the full measure of punishment, fifty lashes with a rawhide whip."

"Fifty lashes will kill her," Carlos whispered to Marco.

Dorantes then addressed Clementina and asked, "Will you, before these officers of the Holy Office and your neighbors, confess that you are a witch, and repent of that deadly sin?"

Clementina turned her head toward him as far as she could, and in a barely audible voice she said, "I am not a witch. I am a *curandera*."

Looking out over the crowded plaza, Father Dorantes declared, "You have all witnessed the accused's obstinacy. There is a lesson for all of you in her behavior. You find yourselves in a place where memories and even practices of bewitchment are common. Possibly you do not recognize that affecting the soul of another through magical means is not an innocent matter. If that magic is effective, it is because you have, perhaps unknowingly, called on the Evil One to assist you, and it is the Evil One, our enemy the Devil, who is working through you.

"If you confess and repent, the Church will give you penance and absolution. If, like this miserable woman you see here before you, you refuse, you will be handed over to the secular authority, which will execute your sentence. I hereby call on the guard to carry out his duty!" A burly man wearing a black mask and carrying a long whip positioned himself next to Clementina preparatory to administering the sentence.

Inéz arrived at Carlos's elbow and said, "This is ghastly! "Do something!"

"I wish I could. But what?"

"You've just been named to the Town Council," she said. "Doesn't that give you some authority over the use of the plaza?"

"I hardly think so," Carlos replied. "But I will go and speak to Governor Peralta."

"Isn't that risky?" Marco asked. "You could make a lot of trouble for yourself."

"There's some risk," he admitted, "but I can't let this play out without trying to do something."

Don Carlos made his way over to where the governor was seated. "Excellency," he whispered, bending over to speak in his ear. "Is this wise, a public humiliation of an old woman who practices a type of healing that our Indian and mestizo neighbors believe is benign?"

Peralta continued to look straight ahead. "Testimony from at least one witness," he replied, "indicated that she has used magic to do harm to several of her neighbors."

"With all due respect, Excellency," Carlos insisted, "even the devout Catholics among our neighbors have asked her to mix herb teas to help them sleep, calm an upset stomach, or relieve a headache. They're going to wonder about the veracity of an anonymous accusation."

The governor looked annoyed. After a pause, he at last said, "I cannot interfere. Civil officials have no power over the Holy Office in the matter of a church trial. Members of the Inquisition tribunal heard testimony that this woman buried a crow's feather on the walk of a woman she wanted to curse, and the woman soon became very sick. This is not a capital crime, but the tribunal determined that she should be whipped to demonstrate that such practices are the Devil's work and that they will not be tolerated."

Dorantes, standing a few feet away from them, was speaking again. "For a final time I urge you, Clementina Loera, to confess to the sin of witchcraft and ask for God's forgiveness. If you do not do so, the full penalty of fifty lashes will be administered." The masked executioner lashed the air with his whip in a menacing way and moved toward her.

Clementina twisted her face away from the post, her eyes wide with fear. "No! No!" she cried. "Don't whip me! I confess!"

"Do you truly repent of the sin of practicing witchcraft?" Dorantes demanded.

The sky, which had been growing darker, suddenly opened up. Rain poured down. Lightning struck a building that was under construction on the southeast corner of the plaza. Frightened cries came from the crowd in front of the construction site. The lightning ignited a stack of bark that had been stripped from trees to be used for the building's roof, and wind-driven smoke rolled out into the plaza. On all sides of the plaza many onlookers fled for safety. The horses of the Presidio soldiers who'd been assigned to guard duty stirred in alarm.

Don Carlos had been trying to come up with a way that he could intervene directly. Perhaps, he thought, the smoke, rain, and general confusion would offer an opening for him to dash onto the platform and cut Clementina down. But then what? He would undoubtedly be recognized. What would be a plausible next step in an impromptu rescue attempt?

The plaza was filling with smoke and sheets of rain, and the scene had become chaotic. The masked man raised his whip and prepared to strike Clementina. In a panicky voice she screamed, "I confess! Before God, I confess! Don't beat me!" Then her head fell forward, her body slumped, and she hung from the post by her wrists.

Don Carlos drew his dagger and ran to the platform. He took the stairs two at a time, reached Clementina, and began to cut her down. The masked executioner stepped forward as if to intervene. Don Carlos shouted, "Enough!" Faced with a *hidalgo* who held a dagger, the masked man shrank back.

As he gently lowered Clementina to the platform, Don Carlos could see that she was barely breathing. Turning on the executioner, he growled, "Stop threatening this woman. She has confessed!"

The rain stopped as suddenly as it had begun, and the storm moved away. Emboldened by Don Carlos's rush to the platform, other onlookers pushed through a break in the cordon of soldiers and moved forward. Those who did so first were mainly women. One mounted the platform and went over to where Clementina was lying. She stroked Clementina's brow and then, furious, turned on the masked man and shouted, "Murderer! She may die! Murderer!"

Father Dorantes had come to the bottom of the platform and tried to regain some control of the situation. "We had testimony," he said in a loud voice to the people gathered around, "that this witch put a hex on a neighbor that made the woman sick. From those facts the Holy Office's tribunal determined that Clementina Loera was doing the Devil's work."

"Bah!" the woman on the platform shot back, despite the best efforts of her companions below to shush her. "The heavens are weeping."

The crowd around the platform was growing and they were not in a friendly mood, though only the woman who'd shouted at Dorantes seemed sufficiently unintimidated to challenge him openly.

Don Carlos tried to think of something that would bring the affair to a conclusion and allow Clementina's friends to aid her. He descended the steps of the platform and stood next to Dorantes. "Father Dorantes," he said quietly, "the accused has confessed. Can't you give her absolution and allow the town authorities to take over? I see two of my colleagues on the Town Council over there, making us a majority of three."

"The accused has not yet received her punishment," Father Dorantes said.

"She will surely die if you have her whipped," Don Carlos replied. Then he lowered his voice so that none of the onlookers would hear him. "Besides," he added, "an act of compassion is more likely to produce respect for the Holy Office than exacting a punishment that kills her."

Dorantes hesitated. "Absolution without punishment is rare," he said, "but this is an unusual situation." He climbed halfway up the platform's steps and looked at the prone form of Clementina, who still had not regained consciousness, made the sign of the Cross in her direction, and pronounced words of absolution. With that done, he climbed back down, said to Carlos, "The situation is now in your hands," and walked away.

The woman who had shouted at Dorantes came down from the platform and spoke to Don Carlos. "You may remember me," she said. "I am Magdalena de Ogama. Like Leonides Chamiso, I am a Tarascan originally from Morelia. Señora Loera lives not far from me. She is a good woman and has helped many people."

"Would you take her into your home and try to help her recover?" Carlos asked.

"Yes," she replied. "But I have no way to move her."

Inéz had come to the bottom of the platform. "What a terrible day this is," she said, looking up at Clementina. "What now?"

Carlos saw Pedro and Orfeo standing at the edge of the crowd around the platform. He motioned for them to come forward. When they reached his side, Carlos spoke to Pedro, "Can you find a horse and cart to take Clementina to Señora Ogama's house?"

"Your neighbor Gilberto Barrera might loan us a horse and cart. I'll go see," Pedro replied. He turned and went off across the plaza.

Don Carlos climbed back up on the platform and knelt down by Clementina, whose dress was soaked by the rain, and covered her with his coat. "A *hidalgo's* coat to honor you in sickness. We pray for your return to health," he said, making the sign of the cross above her body.

Horatio Padilla had come over and had been listening. "I'm glad you did what you did, Alfonso. That was a terrible situation."

"Thank you," he said to Horatio, adding, "Señora Magdalena de Ogama has offered to take Señora Loera to her home and try to nurse her back to health. My friend Pedro Gallegos is bringing a horse and wagon to take her there."

"Ah!" Horatio said with an approving nod. "That is an excellent solution."

Inéz was tugging at his shirt sleeve. "As soon as you can finish your business here, we need to go to meet Doña Mendoza at Juan Archibeque's house."

It was the first Carlos had heard of this, and he was surprised at the urgency in Inéz's voice. But something in her manner told him that whatever was going on couldn't be discussed in public. Nevertheless, he protested. "I'm willing to go to see her, but neither of us is presentable after being caught in the rain."

"We can make a quick detour to the Beltráns' and stop long enough for me to put on a fresh dress. You don't look all that bedraggled."

"I need a coat," he replied. "Let me go to my house and get one." When she didn't try to stop him, he walked briskly to his house, got a coat from his bedroom, and started back to the plaza. He saw that Pedro had already arrived with Gilberto Barrera's horse and wagon. Orfeo helped Pedro load the still unconscious Clementina into the wagon. "Many thanks, old friend," Carlos said. Pedro and a small procession of Barrio residents who were Clementina's friends headed off, but not before several Indian and mestizo men and women spoke with Don Carlos and expressed their gratitude for his intervention.

Carlos and Inéz went to the Beltrán house, where Inéz put on a dry dress and redid her wet hair. Then they hurried over to Canyon Road and out to Juan Archibeque's place. "Do you know why Doña Josefina wants to see us?" Carlos asked as they went along.

"All I can tell you is that Doña Josefina's servant, Jacinta, came to the kitchen door this morning with a message asking you and me to meet her mistress at Juan Archibeque's house this afternoon. She'd been to your place with the same message, but Orfeo wasn't there, so she came to the Beltráns' to give me my message and to see if I knew where you were. She didn't explain further."

Carlos replied that it might concern Frida's situation, and he quickly filled Inéz in on the bat incident and on Doña Josefina's granddaughter-in-law's suspicions. "Marta," he said, "could be a source of trouble for all of us if she thinks that Doña Josefina has taken a witch into her household."

Marta's threats proved to be one of several subjects that Doña Josefina wanted to discuss. When Carlos and Inéz arrived at Juan Archibeque's house, they found Doña Josefina speaking with Mara and Selena. "You're here to talk with Doña Josefina," Selena said. "We'll step out of the room while the three of you talk. But we would like to speak to you later."

Carlos and Inéz sat down. "Don Alfonso," Doña Josefina began, "have you had an opportunity to tell Inéz about what happened to Frida?"

"Briefly, yes."

"I'm sorry to say that the situation in my household has taken a turn for the worse. I'm not referring so much to Frida's condition. On that score, the news is both good and bad. She's able to talk more and walk some, but she sleeps all day and stays awake all night. I remind myself that she's an old woman who may have exhausted herself with her little escapade as a bat. But that's not my primary concern. It's my granddaughter-in-law who's making trouble. She believes—quite rightly, as we all know—that Frida is my former maid, Manuela Maldonado, who is sought by the Inquisition. She is making threats to report this to the inquisitors. That would be bad for me, but also for Don Alfonso and anyone else who has helped Frida evade capture. I'm sure you can see how dangerous Marta might be."

"Indeed," Carlos murmured.

"That's dreadful!" Inéz cried. "How could she even think of such a thing—threatening to report her husband's grandmother to the Inquisition? I am speechless!"

Doña Josefina nodded her head. "You think such things are not done in a family. And, I agree, they should not be. But Marta was widowed young, and she stayed with me because she was expected to, and she is bitter. And, I might add, she was not my choice for my grandson's wife, for which I expect she has never forgiven me."

"Can anything be done," Carlos asked, "to keep Marta from carrying out her threat?"

"Fortunately," Dona Josefina replied, "she does not hold all the strong cards in this game. I have told her that if she goes to the inquisitors with her accusations, I will throw her out of my house, and that I have written a will that prevents her from getting even a peso from my estate."

"If the Holy Office became involved, wouldn't the inquisitors attempt to have such a will declared invalid?" Carlos asked.

"They would," Doña Josefina agreed. "But my new will excludes her from receiving anything from my estate if I am declared incompetent, which any action against me by the Holy Office would amount to. I have shown her a copy of this will, and another copy is safely in the hands of Horatio Padilla. I told her that it will be destroyed if she behaves herself."

"And she believes all that?" Carlos inquired.

"Oh, yes. She knows I can be ruthless if my interests call for it."

"So," Inéz commented, "you have a stalemate — you are holding her at bay for now, but she still might carry out her threats."

"Yes, she might convince herself that the Holy Office would invalidate the new will too, but she would be impoverished if it didn't, and I don't think she'd take that risk," Doña Josefina replied. "But I am hoping for a more permanent solution and am engaged in what you might call negotiations with her. I've promised to rewrite my will if she will provide a document in which she swears that none of her accusations are true. Were she to go back on that document, she would be guilty of perjury, having lied in a sworn, notarized statement."

"You seem to have thought this through quite thoroughly," Carlos said. "I don't see that you need our advice."

"Yes, my will is very specific with regard to Marta. But I have not yet decided on how to divide my estate among my nephews. And this is where your friend Elena Beltrán comes in."

"What can we tell you?" Inéz asked.

"I take your question, Inéz, as being an offer to give me frank answers. As a woman, and as someone who probably knows Elena better than Don Alfonso, what you say is of particular interest to me. Will you share your candid impressions of Señorita Beltrán?"

"Yes." Inéz paused to gather her thoughts. "She is an only child," she began, "indulged by her parents. She is headstrong, but she is also intelligent and serious. When I first met her I sensed that she was unhappy because her intelligence and seriousness were not appreciated by the other girls in her social group. I think she felt unattractive and lonely. But in the year I have known her she has blossomed. I think my friendship and the discipline of fencing have helped, but Santiago's genuine interest in her has been of great importance. He has brought out her strengths; she has always been responsible, but now she seems more mature. I believe she is ready for the lasting commitment of marriage, if that is what you're asking me."

Doña Josefina nodded. "I notice that you have not mentioned whether or not she is in love with Santiago. Perhaps you share my conviction that a good marriage depends more on the characters of the parties involved than on romantic sentiment. My own marriage, as you know, was an arranged marriage, and it was a very good one. My father knew his daughter, and my father-in-law-to-be knew his son, and between them they determined that the two of us were well suited. As his father's son, my husband had considerable responsibilities in Santa Fe; within a year of our marriage I had the duty of caring for a child, and soon thereafter the rather large challenge of life in what was quite literally a New World.

"Even as I am saying this, I am seeing that Santiago is in need of masculine responsibilities. Marriage, of course, would be one. But perhaps before we think of marriage, I should be putting him in charge of part of my Santa Fe properties. I am pleased, Don Alfonso, that you have introduced him to some elements of Pueblo culture. He is clearly interested and sympathetic, and I hope it is more than the interest of a dilettante. Do you think, Don Alfonso, that he would be a good manager of Indian workers?"

Carlos laughed. "I think that at the moment he wouldn't know where to start. But I also think that your idea of putting him in charge of something now, while you are here to guide him, is an excellent one. Santiago has good intentions, but he lacks confidence, and managerial skills are something he needs to learn. He is possibly less mature in that respect than Elena, but, like Elena, he is also responsible and serious."

"And I think Elena would develop into a good manager," Inéz put in.

"You mean," Doña Josefina asked, "that he may need a wife who can be a guiding hand?"

"If he does, I think she could provide it," Inéz said diplomatically.

Doña Josefina stood up, signaling that the conversation was over, thanked them both, and excused herself to go home. "Back to the hornet's nest," she said with a laugh. "Please tell Mara and Selena that I appreciated being allowed to use their *sala* for a rendezvous safe from prying eyes and ears."

After Doña Josefina left, Carlos and Inéz looked at each other questioningly. Carlos wanted to ask Inéz how she read Doña Josefina's intentions, but Mara and Selena came back before he had a chance. Both of them looked subdued. Addressing Selena, he asked, "You indicated earlier that you wanted to speak to us about something. What is it?"

"Pascal was here yesterday and gave a performance for Juan's girls, which, as you'll recall, we had promised them a few days ago," she replied. "The girls loved it, but Mara and I found the whole thing rather unsettling."

"He was very nice," Mara put in quickly, "and extremely clever in his use of hand puppets, and the children were enchanted by the two monkeys and the parrot."

"Don't be disingenuous, Mara," Selena said. "You had the same reaction I did. It was like seeing someone at a party who reminded you of someone else, but in many ways he was completely unlike the person he reminded you of."

"Now Selena is being evasive," Mara said. "What disturbed us was that he reminded us of our father."

Selena glared at Mara, and Mara stared back defiantly. "Yes, he did," Selena admitted at last. "But he's very unlike our father. For one thing, he's too old. And our father would never have wasted time playing with children and seeming to enjoy himself. Pascal laughs a lot, and his laughter seems genuine."

"What you mean," Mara came back, "is that he never played with either one of us—ever—even when we were little. And I can't remember him laughing. He never did in my presence."

"Not that we ever saw that much of him," Selena added. "He was always a stranger to us. And except for seeing that our talent as dancers might serve his purposes, he never took any interest in us."

"If he were your father," Carlos offered, "wouldn't he have recognized you?"

"He might pretend not to," Selena said, "if he's adopted a disguise. But I noticed that when Juan introduced us as Mara Mata and Selena Torrez, he looked surprised. He seemed to recognize our names, if not us. It's been only three years since we last saw him, so why wouldn't he recognize us?"

Carlos thought he knew the answer to that. If Pascal was indeed Malvolio, Malvolio would have believed that his daughters were dead, poisoned by Leandro. But Carlos was not sure how, or whether, to impart that information. Nor, if he was Malvolio, was Carlos sure that he wanted to unmask him. Temporizing, he said, "What you've told us is certainly very strange, and it must be upsetting to encounter someone who makes you think of your father, even if he's not."

"Yes, it is!" Mara said vehemently.

Selena reached out a hand and put it on Mara's arm. "If he doesn't want to be recognized, we won't recognize him. Since we usually avoid going to town, we should continue doing so. That way there's little chance that we'll run into him."

"That seems like a sensible solution," Inéz said.

Walking Inéz back to the Beltrán house, Carlos said, "We seem to have more puzzles and questions than answers."

"Is there any chance at all," Inéz asked, "that Pascal is their father, which would mean that he's Malvolio?"

Carlos, reviewing in his mind what Mara and Selena had said, drew a conclusion he did not quite want to admit to, and he did not quite answer Inéz's question. "Since we heard Malvolio tell Leandro that he was near death three months ago, I assumed that he would be dead by now."

"Yes," Inéz said, "but Leandro also said he was still searching for you to learn some secret he thought you possessed about how to extend his life."

"Not exactly extend his life," Carlos replied. "It was more how to reach a higher realm of being, to become like the angels."

"Hmmm," Inéz said. "Maybe the main lesson is that you should keep your distance from this Pascal."

"That's not so easy to do," Carlos said. "Santa Fe is a small town."

They'd reached the Beltrán house and entered the front hallway. "I'll be careful," he said, bending to kiss her on the cheek. "And I'll expect you to walk to Mass with me tomorrow morning."

"That's my dear Carlos," she said. "You don't let dangers, puzzles, or terrible events distract you from maintaining our routines. Yes, I will be glad to walk to Mass with you."

They exchanged another light kiss on the cheek and parted.

21

Revenge

*D*on Carlos woke up well before dawn on Sunday morning. As always, he got up to meditate. At the beginning of the two hours of his sitting and walking meditation, he could not quiet his mind. His world was shaken. War on its borders to the north; widespread upsets caused by the Inquisition in its midst; the threat of exposure of Manuela's presence in Doña Mendoza's house; and his troubled feelings at having learned that he might, more than twenty years ago, have caused the death of Gustavo's mother. He sat with it. Two hours later, the external situation was the same, but he was in a different relation to it. He felt calm and centered in his deep self.

He ate his breakfast slowly and reflectively, and then dressed in his second-best Sunday outfit. After a quick check on the horses to confirm that they were all right, he started walking toward the Beltráns' to meet Inéz for Mass. As he approached the chapel, he noticed that the area around it was not bustling with churchgoers, as would usually have been the case. Just before he turned to head for the Beltráns' house, he saw Marco Cabrera approaching down a street from the north. They met and shook hands. "Have you heard?" Marco asked.

"Heard what?"

"Heard about the first Mass of the day, the one for Indians."

"No. I just now left my house and you're the first person I've spoken to. What about the Indians' Mass?"

"No one came. Well, a few old women, perhaps a half dozen. Of late it's been quite crowded, but according to our cook, who went because I insisted she go, Father Dorantes was not pleased when he saw the nearly empty chapel."

"Perhaps," Carlos suggested, "the residents of the Barrio de Analco are angry at Father Dorantes and disinclined to attend a Mass he's saying."

"I believe you're right," Marco replied.

Carlos continued on his way to the Beltrán house, and from there he walked with Inéz back to the chapel. Apparently Father Benedicto had not yet returned from Albuquerque, since Father Dorantes said the Mass, and it also was rather poorly attended. Following the Mass, as he and Inéz waited for the small crowd to make its way out the door, Carlos noticed Pascal in the line in front of him. Inéz saw him too, and her hand tightened on his arm. Carlos leaned over and whispered in her ear, "It may not be as easy to avoid him as you'd hoped."

But no direct encounter followed. Pascal's purpose seemed to be to speak with Raul and Bianca Trigales, whom he approached outside the chapel. The Trigales children, who usually rushed over to greet Carlos and Inéz, stood with their eyes fixed on Pascal as the elder Trigaleses talked with him. "Why don't we take a stroll over to Pedro and María's place?" Carlos suggested. "I can bring you up to date on Dolores, and in any case, it will be good to see our friends."

"It will also get us away from here without having to introduce ourselves to Pascal," Inéz said, though at that very moment Pascal glanced at them, smiled, and tipped his hat in greeting.

"We can't avoid him forever," Carlos replied, nodding back to Pascal as he and Inéz started across the plaza.

"I suppose not," Inéz agreed. "But tell me about Dolores and your trip to Tesuque. So much has happen since you got back that you've never said a word about it."

"Dolores is well, and our trip was very good. I'll tell you about it when we get to Pedro and María's."

When they arrived at the Gallegos place, they found Pedro finishing the daily chore of cleaning out stalls and putting down fresh bedding for the horses. When Carlos greeted him with a pleasant "Good morning," he looked up with a grumpy expression.

"Nothing good about it," he replied. "But come on in."

They went to the kitchen that was attached to the stable and found María scrubbing the floor. She got up, set aside her brush, and wordlessly brought coffee to them at the table.

Carlos said without preamble, "Not many people attended either of today's masses. I think everyone is upset about yesterday's auto-da-fé."

Pedro snorted. "What María and I heard this morning is worse. People are saying that whoever informed on those three mestizos brought to the auto-da-fé should have something bad happen to him."

"Is it known who the informer was?" Carlos asked.

"People say it was Manuel Contreras's brother, Chico, who is a snake in the grass anyway. He's been feuding with Mariano Fuentes, and he thinks Clementina made a woman he liked fall in love with another man."

"So Chico was nursing grudges?" Carlos asked.

"Looks like it," Pedro said. "Then last night Chico got drunk at the tavern and was going on about some people having gotten what they'd deserved. He had a silver peso that he was playing with on the bar, and he was hinting that maybe it was his reward. After a while he staggered out of the tavern, got on his horse, and rode off."

Carlos raised an eyebrow. "A Judas?" he said.

"The men in the tavern seem to have thought so," Pedro replied. "Some of them mounted up and went after him. About an hour ago Contreras's horse came back alone and slightly lame."

"And Chico?" Carlos inquired.

"No Chico." Pedro replied. "We may never see him again."

"You think he might be dead?"

"Wouldn't surprise me. The men at the bar were drunk and very angry."

Carlos sighed. "Not good at all. Does anyone know the names of the men who went after him?"

"No one who's talking."

The four of them sat in silence for a while contemplating the implications of what Pedro had just told them. Finally Carlos remembered that Dolores had given him a message to pass on to Pedro and María. "Oh," he said abruptly. "I need to tell you why Dolores isn't back yet. We stayed at Tesuque longer than I'd planned. I didn't return until yesterday, and Dolores is going to stay for another couple of days."

His voice warmed as he recalled their visit. "We shared a pipe with Old Man Xenome and José, and Dolores felt courageous enough to attempt another transformation into a dog, even though the last one she tried here had failed, and that had frightened her. She succeeded in changing to dog form, but she was unable to change back. I had to help her, and by some miracle, when she returned to human form, her damaged eye and hand were healed."

María crossed herself. "A miracle!" she said breathlessly. It was as if the atmosphere in the room suddenly changed. Her face broke into a broad smile. "I'm so glad!" Then she asked, "Will she want to talk about it? It'll be hard not to notice."

"I'm sure you can mention it," Carlos replied. "Let her talk about it if she wants to."

After a little more conversation, during which María kept on smiling,

Carlos and Inéz wished their friends well and started back for the Beltrán house. "How are you spending the rest of the day?" she asked.

"After I get you back to your job, I'm going to fence with Marco. I want to hear what the governor has had to say about the auto-da-fé, and I'm sure Marco will be interested to hear that the man who informed against Clementina and the two mestizo men might have met a bad end."

"I could scarcely believe what Pedro told us about that just now. Vigilante justice is horrible!"

"So it is, but don't forget about the suffering of the people Contreras informed against. Clementina almost died, though I'm happy to report that she has regained consciousness and is expected to recover."

"That's good to hear! Still, it's incomprehensible to me that Contreras would inform on his neighbors because of petty grievances."

"And greed," Carlos said. "The Gospel story is that Judas betrayed Jesus for a reward in silver coins. Contreras bore grudges and received a silver peso for his services."

"I don't know enough to say, but the two stories don't seem the same to me."

"You're probably right," Carlos conceded. They had reached the door to the kitchen at the Beltrán house. Carlos said, "I guess you've got to get to work and I have my appointment to fence with Marco. What's happened in the past few days makes me feel a need to hone my skills at fencing." They exchanged a light kiss and went their separate ways.

After getting home Carlos had some lunch. Marco arrived half an hour later. He and Carlos changed into their fencing suits, walked to the Tiburcio place, and prepared to begin fencing. Determined to bring his skills back to the highest level, Carlos went on the offensive from the first, driving Marco back with ferocious attacks and winning point after point. Finally, Marco lowered his sword and said, "I've never seen you fence like this. You are a man possessed. I can't withstand your attacks."

"I should have explained," Carlos replied apologetically, "that I wanted to show you my best. But you've been doing better as our bout goes on, even without winning any exchanges. I congratulate you on rising to the challenge. Perhaps we've practiced enough for today. Let's sit, cool off, and talk."

Once they were seated at a small table in the shade of the veranda, Marco asked, "Would you like a report from behind the scenes?"

"I would."

"Governor Peralta was very upset by the auto-da-fé. Dorantes had assured him that it would simply be an edifying spectacle to frighten ordinary folk into abandoning any remaining ties they have with magic. But that poor woman being brought to death's door appalled him. If she dies, it will make things much worse; the residents of the Barrio are already angry about their dogs being slaughtered by a werewolf, and about the treatment Leonides Chamiso received at Brother Gustavo's hands."

"And now," Carlos added, "a mestizo named Chico Contreras flashed a silver peso at the tavern last night and seemed to suggest that he got it for informing. Some men followed him when he left, and this morning his horse came home without him. Pedro thinks he's been killed."

"Killed! That's shocking, Alfonso."

"Yes, it is, if it's true. And it wouldn't have happened without the work of the Inquisition. Do you think the governor is intending to do anything about the inquisitors?"

Marco replied, "He never sent for them in the first place, although once they were here they fit in well enough with his desire to achieve discipline and unity in town. Now he feels they are no longer helpful, but I doubt if he can get rid of them. What's more, they are no longer the biggest issue he has to deal with. Please keep this in confidence, but just this morning a courier arrived from Major Cortés with a report that the punitive expedition has encountered Native raiders that are more numerous and better armed than was previously thought. He has appealed to the governor to send reinforcements from the Presidio garrison."

"That's not good news," Carlos said. "And it will leave Santa Fe with almost no regular soldiers to defend its residents from attacks locally."

"Yes. But the greater threats seem to be east and north of us," Marco replied.

"Is the governor still convinced that the French are involved?"

"He is."

"Even so," Carlos said, "the immediate problem, if the governor sends reinforcements to Cortés, is the lack of soldiers to protect Santa Fe."

Marco laughed. "So we must defend Santa Fe ourselves!"

Carlos smiled, pushed back his chair, stood up, and flourished his sword in a dramatic gesture. "Then I must keep myself in top form as a fencer. Toward that end, you and I must continue our practice sessions."

Having decided this, the two friends went back to Carlos's house and changed from their fencing outfits. Marco soon departed for his parents' place. Orfeo had prepared a simple meal, and he and Carlos shared it amiably.

Several hours later Orfeo had gone off to bed and Carlos was about to do likewise when a knock came at the kitchen door. "Come in," he called.

It was Marco again. "Have you heard the latest?" he asked.

"No," Carlos said. "Tell me what's happened."

"Father Benedicto and my father have just returned from Albuquerque. About sunset, as they were nearing Santa Fe, they saw a grain sack in the middle of the road. They were curious about it, and they told my father's manservant to dismount and open the bag."

Marco was a little out of breath, so he paused in his account. "You told me," he went on, "you suspected that Father Dorantes's informant was a mestizo named Chico Contreras."

Carlos could see where this was leading. Prompting Marco, he said, "Was?"

"Yes, was. The bag contained Chico Contreras's head, cut off by some rough instrument, possibly a saw. But the even more grisly thing was that Contreras's tongue had been torn out and stuffed back in his mouth."

"Horrible!" Carlos exclaimed. "The whole situation is horrible."

"Agreed, and the governor is extremely upset and wants to meet with the Town Council. I've been rushing around notifying members. I've reached you last. Hurry, or you'll be late."

"A meeting right now?" Carlos said. "It's almost ten o'clock."

"Governor Peralta says the situation is too urgent to wait until tomorrow morning."

The unusual lateness of the hour contributed to the solemnity that Don Carlos could read in the faces of those present when he arrived at the Palace of the Governors. Governor Peralta acknowledged Carlos's arrival, and as soon as Carlos was seated the governor commenced proceedings. "This meeting," he began, "was called at my request after gaining the mayor's approval to hold an emergency session of the Town Council. Properly speaking, I am only an observer, though as governor of the province, I want to express my grave concerns about recent events. Before stating them, however, perhaps introductions are in order, especially for the benefit of Father Dorantes, who has agreed to meet with us.

"Father Dorantes is well known to you, but he may not know all the council members. Going around the table to my right is Horatio Padilla, who serves as mayor. Next is Alonso Miranda, the captain of the local militia. Next to him are Arsenio Berdugo and Don Alfonso Cabeza de Vaca. At the far end of the table is Mauricio Castillo, here in his capacity as sheriff."

The governor then launched into his remarks, beginning with a simple chronological list of untoward events that had occurred in the past forty-odd days. Don Carlos barely listened to what was said. Instead, he used the time to study the men in attendance. In his role as mayor, Horatio Padilla projected admirable gravitas and public-spiritedness. But Alonso Miranda, Carlos knew, used his position on the Town Council and as captain of the local militia in self-serving ways. The fourth councilor, Arsenio Berdugo, was associated with shady land dealings.

At last Governor Peralta reached the substance of his speech, and Carlos turned his full attention to him. "It behooves us," the governor was saying, "to speak frankly. I had high hopes when the inquisitors arrived in Santa Fe that they would inspire our neighbors to greater spiritual piety that would lead to renewed civic order. Instead, the past six weeks have brought little except grief and disorder to our beloved town. Among the most recent examples, I would include the abusive way of one of the inquisitors confronted a resident of the Barrio, the spectacle of the near death of an old woman during the auto-da-fé proceedings, and now the killing of Chico Contreras. Speaking with the utmost candor, I have concluded that the continued presence of representatives of the Holy Office in Santa Fe is not justified by any benefits they have brought, at least none known to me."

Father Dorantes was displeased. "With equal candor I must reply that I have previously pointed out certain facts that justify, indeed require, the presence of the tribunal in Santa Fe. There are simply too many examples of otherworldly activity—a thief who can change into a dog, the dog through which musket balls pass, the mysterious way stolen goods were returned, and the werewolf that attacks dogs belonging to Santa Fe's Indians. There is also the witch Manuela Maldonado, who has been seen in Santa Fe but not yet apprehended. Moreover, Brother Gustavo is convinced that a powerful sorcerer named Carlos Buenaventura is hiding in the Santa Fe area."

Don Carlos ventured, cautiously, to speak. "Brother Gustavo told me that this Buenaventura fellow is an Indian. Doesn't that put him outside the Inquisition's jurisdiction?"

"Perhaps," Dorantes replied, "but we won't know his status for certain until we apprehend him."

Despite Dorantes's insistence, the governor wasn't convinced of the usefulness of the tribunal's continued presence in Santa Fe. "If," he asked, "after six weeks in Santa Fe you haven't located this powerful sorcerer, is there any reason to believe that such a person is in our midst?"

"Brother Gustavo, who has a particular interest in this investigation," Dorantes replied, "has urged me to keep the tribunal here a little longer, and I have acceded to his request."

The governor lifted his head and stared hard at Dorantes as if to say, *Who's in charge here?* But Dorantes had evidently had the last word, and Peralta recognized it. He lowered his gaze, turned his head away, and impatiently muttered, "Yes, yes."

The governor then moved on to the atrocity of the beheading of Chico Contreras.

At the end of his account there was a great uproar. "I'll deputize a dozen men to find Chico Contreras's killers!" Sheriff Castillo cried. Alonso Miranda insisted that the search be led by members of the town militia, of which he was the captain. Arsenio Berdugo shouted that as a friend of Chico's brother Manuel, he, Arsenio, should play a leading role.

"Order! Order!" Horatio Padilla shouted, attempting to make himself heard over the din. "Let's display some basic decorum!"

Trying to refocus the discussion, Don Carlos asked, speaking loudly but in a conciliatory tone, "Can we make a decision about the most fruitful way to proceed?"

"My suggestion," Captain Miranda said, "is that we begin by interrogating the men who last saw Chico at the tavern and find out who followed him when he left."

"So far," Sheriff Castillo replied, "no one has admitted to having been there. Even the tavern owner, Roberto Barbon, says that he stepped out for a while before Contreras left, and he doesn't know for certain who was in the barroom while he was gone."

"Manuel Contreras will find out one way or the other who killed his brother," Berdugo asserted.

"I don't like the sound of that phrase about one way or the other," Horatio said. "If Manuel learns anything, he is obligated to report it to the proper authorities. One instance of vigilante justice is one too many."

Father Dorantes stood up abruptly. "This discussion," he declared, "has drifted far afield from matters that directly bear on the Holy Office's business in Santa Fe. It's very late. I will take my leave, wishing you success in your investigations, as I'm sure you wish us in ours."

Governor Peralta looked annoyed at Dorantes for having so brusquely brushed off the town's concerns, but he said nothing. Once the Franciscan had left, the men who remained wasted half an hour in inconclusive debate.

Finally Horatio Padilla attempted to pull everything together. "Captain Miranda," he said, "will be responsible for organizing ongoing nighttime militia patrols of the Barrio de Analco. Sheriff Castillo will question anyone known to regularly drink late at night at the tavern and try to find out who pursued Chico Contreras. The rest of us should speak with all our friends and neighbors and urge them to tell us anything they might know."

"Does that include," Marco asked, "following up on the Inquisition's pursuit of the sorcerer named Carlos Buenaventura?"

"I suppose so," Governor Peralta replied, "but I think they're chasing their own tails and are unwilling to admit that they've gotten nowhere."

"But they're not giving up," Carlos said.

"That's true, Don Alfonso," Governor Peralta replied. "And I wish they would leave. I can't force them to do so, but as far as I'm concerned they've worn out their welcome. In regard to other matters, effective as of this hour I intend to order Captain Posada to end the practice of having soldiers from the Presidio stand guard day and night at private homes. The return of the stolen goods convinces me that the thief has abandoned his mischief."

"Will you remove the guards on duty at the chapel doors too?" Sheriff Castillo asked.

The governor paused before he replied. "No, I suppose we ought to keep soldiers on guard there as a gesture of support for the Holy Office."

As he walked home, Carlos thought about the parts of the meeting that bothered him. Chief among these was Father Dorantes's statement that the inquisitors were still actively pursuing Carlos Buenaventura. Even though Gustavo had failed so far in his efforts along that line, Pascal—who might be Don Malvolio—was in Santa Fe. And if he *was* Malvolio, he might know that Don Alfonso was in reality Carlos Buenaventura, and he might reveal that fact to the inquisitors.

Carlos went home and to bed with these thoughts burrowing around in his head.

At breakfast Monday morning, he asked Orfeo, "How is the posthole project going?"

"I dug five. One had a lot of rocks right below the surface and took me longer to do than three of the others."

"What about the one that keeps filling up with water?"

"It's slow work, but I've gotten more than two feet below the water table. I've been lining the hole with stones. It's going to make a good shallow well for the house and the horses."

"That will be very useful," Don Carlos said. "See if you can finish it today. I'm going to take a ride to Rancho Rosón."

Once he arrived there, Carlos had a good talk with José and joined José and the four vaqueros who worked at the ranch for a simple family-style lunch of beef chili on tortillas. So amiable was the camaraderie that Carlos was reluctant to leave, and the disturbing news of the night before had completely left his mind.

When he returned to his house, he found Inéz and Elena out in the corral with Orfeo, who was up to his knees in water in the posthole.

While Carlos was unsaddling Eagle in the corral and Inéz and Elena were talking about the well, they heard hoofbeats and the sound of wheels crunching on the dirt lane. They looked up and saw Pascal's caravan and his mule approaching from the plaza at a stately pace. As the caravan reached the corral, it hit a bump in the lane and its back door sprang open. A monkey dressed as a soldier jumped out the door.

The monkey landed in the lane and looked around. Gordo saw the little creature and set out in hot pursuit. The monkey ran toward the plaza and then around the corner of the house. Orfeo, dripping wet from being in the posthole, dashed after Gordo and the monkey. Inéz shouted, "Your monkey has escaped!" and Pascal brought the caravan to a halt. He jumped down from the driver's seat and seemed uncertain as to which way to go.

Don Carlos, surveying the situation, guessed that the monkey would run all the way around the house and come down the side lane past the kitchen door.

Sure enough, as Carlos hurried up the lane, the monkey rounded the corner of the house, ran to Gordo's doggy door, and dived through it, followed closely by Gordo. A commotion, marked by loud barks from Gordo and insulting chatter from the monkey, ensued. Carlos went inside to find the monkey on the kitchen table, with Gordo standing right below and barking.

Pascal arrived at the door. "May I come in?" he asked. "I can catch that rascal of a monkey if you'll restrain your dog, who seems to like me even less than he likes Che."

It was true. Gordo had turned his attention from Che and was baring his teeth at Pascal. Carlos had never seen him be so aggressive toward a visitor to the house. "Gordo!" Carlos said sharply, as he moved to shoo Gordo back so that Pascal could reach the table. Che, meanwhile, seemed relieved to be captured and hopped onto Pascal's shoulder. Pascal attached a leash to Che's collar and went back out the door and into the lane.

Carlos followed and found Orfeo, Inéz, and Elena standing there with concerned looks on their faces. Che, who seemed glad to be back under Pascal's control, was holding onto his master's hat with one hand. "All's well that ends well, I suppose," Pascal said. "Allow me to introduce myself. My name is Pascal."

"So we've heard," Carlos replied. "I am Don Alfonso Cabeza de Vaca. These are my friends Señora Inéz de Recalde and Señorita Elena Beltrán. The young fellow with mud up to his knees is Orfeo Jiranza, normally my groom, but presently engaged in digging a well by the corral."

Addressing Elena, Pascal said, "Señorita Beltrán, it may interest you to know that this naughty monkey and I just gave a performance for the Trigales family that seemed to be especially well received by the household's children. Their father, your uncle, had an amazing story to tell about his children having been kidnapped and rescued earlier this year."

"Yes," Elena replied, "that was a terrible episode for all of us, the children in particular."

"What astonished me," Pascal said, "was that they were found in such a remote mountain area. According to your uncle, an Indian hunter stumbled onto the cave in which they were hidden."

"Yes," Elena said, "that's how I've heard the story."

"Anton, the youngest of the four," Pascal went on, "pulled me aside and whispered in my ear that he hadn't seen an old Indian, only an angel, a hawk named Redsy, and an owl named Hooter."

"Anton has a very active imagination," Don Carlos said drily.

"I could see that," Pascal replied. "But you must excuse me. I've promised some children from the Barrio that I would offer a performance for them in a little while." He returned to his caravan and drove off.

This brief exchange had given Don Carlos a chance to study Pascal at close range. He was, as reported, a very old man. His face was deeply lined and very pale. His aura was bright and intense, but it extended less than an inch away from his body. Carlos had never before seen an aura like Pascal's. Its closeness to his body seemed to indicate a lack of raw physical energy, but its brightness and intensity signified to Don Carlos that he was seeing the residue of what had once been enormous power.

Gordo popped out of his doggy door, still looking truculent. "Gordo certainly didn't like either Che or Pascal," Carlos commented, but no one, except possibly Inéz, grasped his point.

"I do believe," Elena said, "that Pascal is the oldest person I've ever seen."

"A hundred years old, at least," Orfeo said.

"He's either very old or someone who's lived a very hard life," Carlos suggested. "Have you and Elena seen enough of our building project?" he asked Inéz. "If so, I'll be glad to walk you home."

"We can find our way," Inéz said. "You need to get to work and so do I." Inéz leaned forward and kissed him on the cheek, and as she did so, she whispered in his ear, "He knows, doesn't he — knows who you are?" He nodded. "Take care," she said solemnly as she turned to go.

22

Allies?

 uesday, the first of June, 1706, was long remembered as a day on which a steady rain fell from sunrise to sunset. The weather seemed appropriate both to Don Carlos's mood and the general state of mind in Santa Fe. Carlos holed up in his house. In the morning he tried to read from his books on Christian and Hindu spirituality, but he found them too abstract. He turned to *Don Quixote*, one of his favorite books in Spanish literature, only to feel that stories about a foolish idealist echoed in a disconcerting way his own tendency to want things to be better than they were. He wanted to construct a benign world in which the sun shone, Inéz loved him, and he was contented with his life, but in the world in which he was actually living he felt threatened on all sides — by Dorantes and Gustavo, by Marta Mendoza, and possibly by Pascal.

Restless and depressed, he sought relief in physical activity. He roused Orfeo from his quarters in the stable loft and said, "I know it's raining, but we can still work indoors on the new big room we've created. Let's whitewash the three walls that won't be affected when we cut doorways into the south side." Once they got started, Don Carlos began to feel better and soon joined Orfeo in singing New Mexican folksongs. By dinnertime they'd almost finished whitewashing the walls, and in a pleasantly tired state they cooperated in making dinner.

But even during these periods of work and quiet domesticity, Carlos was dogged by a feeling that he should come up with something to improve the state of affairs in Santa Fe. He had begun to undress for bed when a plan began to crystallize in his mind. Instead of putting on his nightclothes, he donned his second-best breeches, a well-cut thigh-length coat, and his good shoes; satisfied with his appearance, he went out the door. The rain, which had continued through sunset, had at last stopped, but puddles of water had collected on the plaza, and he had to take a zigzag course around them as he walked to Governor Peralta's residence on the grounds of the Palace of the Governors.

Carlos had often been a guest there during the years that he had worked as Governor Villela's personal secretary, but he hadn't been in the governor's private quarters since Ignacio Peralta had become the province's chief executive. He went directly to the inner portal of the Palace of the Governors, the private door that social visitors were told to use. He knocked. A mestizo servant opened the door. Don Carlos addressed him in a formal way. "Please tell Governor Peralta that Don Alfonso Cabeza de Vaca wishes a private conversation with him on an urgent matter." The servant indicated that Carlos should come in and wait in the hallway.

Carlos was not at all sure the governor would agree to see him. Peralta liked protocol, and visiting him unannounced so late in the evening stretched propriety to the limit. But Carlos was counting on the governor being worried enough about recent events to overlook protocol, at least long enough to find out what Carlos had on his mind.

His gamble worked. The servant returned and asked Carlos to follow him to a library. In truth, it wasn't much of a library. Perhaps three dozen books were shelved on one wall. Carlos saw that they consisted in roughly equal numbers of books on religion, military subjects, and natural history. The governor hadn't yet come to the room, and while Carlos waited, idly scanning the books' titles, he wondered if Peralta had read any of them, or if their presence was mainly to impress visitors with the breadth of the governor's interests.

The rest of the room's décor was plain but attractive. Scarlet curtains covered the windows, a fine-looking cedar chest stood against one wall, and a pair of silver candlesticks on the chest reflected the soft golden light from candles in sconces.

The governor entered the room dressed handsomely in a coat of imported fabric and shoes with silver buckles. There were two chairs in the room. He sat down in one and indicated that Don Carlos should sit in the other. "You are welcome, Don Alfonso," he began, "but I am curious to know what business brings you here at this hour."

"I apologize for the lack of advance notice, for the hour, and for my choice to visit you in your private quarters, but we both know that almost nothing escapes notice in our beloved town, and I wanted to raise several topics that will be known only to us."

Don Carlos paused, and the governor said, "I appreciate discretion. Please continue."

"I don't need to repeat the description of recent events you provided to the Town Council only two nights ago. The discussion that followed your remarks made several things clear to me. Father Dorantes and his fellow inquisitors have no intention of leaving Santa Fe in the near future, and their continued presence will cause even more upheavals. Already their work has produced a vigilante killing. Other problems—widespread worries about food shortages and the fate of the military expedition—are not the inquisitors' fault, but these concerns, along with the inquisitors' actions, have undone the good feelings generated by your declaration of a festival day on the first of May. Instead of happily enjoying peace and well-being, the townsfolk are anxious about war and survival."

"I see much the same picture," the governor said, "and I'm wondering whether you have come here to suggest measures that might serve to reestablish peace and well-being."

"Yes, I've come to propose a plan for your consideration."

"Please go on."

"I believe it is time for a grand gesture to guide us into a new era, and that you are just the man to show the way. In the thirteen years since the Spanish reconquest of New Mexico, the new policies that supposedly apply to relations between Spaniards and our Pueblo neighbors have never been formalized. The grand gesture I propose is for you to call leaders of all twenty pueblos in New Mexico to meet with you in Santa Fe in late June, possibly on Saint John's Day. After a solemn Mass, you would issue a proclamation pledging New Mexico's government to honor the rights of our Indian friends—specifically, freedom from forced labor and from being required to supply foodstuffs to Spanish settlements, respect for their religious traditions, permanent titles to pueblo lands, and a system of cooperative trade based on the principle of fair value fixed by mutual agreement. Having issued and publicly signed this pledge, you would then urge the Pueblo leaders to endorse it. This would, naturally, be followed by a fiesta.

"You, of course, might want to offer a somewhat different list of measures, but the net result of such a proclamation would be to promote harmonious relations between Indians and Spaniards and thus the peace and prosperity of both—a dramatic act affirming the common interests of every segment of our diverse society.

"As I envision the plaza on such an occasion, it would be filled with color and joy, music and dancing, rather than the black clouds, thunder and lightning, and horror that we witnessed last Saturday. Additionally, for the festival to be truly festive, the government would surely have to open its grain reserves to assure that there is ample food for its guests and also relief from the food shortages that plague ordinary townspeople at present. I am not asking you to assign me any credit for my proposal, should you decide to act on part or all of it. It is enough, for now, to say how grateful I am to you for hearing me out."

The governor stood up, requiring Don Carlos to rise also. "In times like these," Peralta said, "I value every idea that's brought to my attention. Let me think about your proposal. If part or all of it is put into effect, you will have my sincere thanks."

The governor called for his manservant to return and show Don Carlos out. Don Carlos left rather buoyed up with the feeling that the meeting had gone better than he had expected. At least the governor had not rejected his proposals out of hand.

As he approached the corner of the Palace of the Governors where the town's chapel was located, he saw that three soldiers were guarding the Holy Office's notice. All three were leaning against the wall of the chapel near a torch that illuminated the doorway. They straightened up when they recognized Don Carlos, and he was pleased to see that the three were his friends and former lodgers, Alejandro, Gonzalo, and Luis. He hailed them. "You're out late at night."

"A soldier's work is never done," Luis replied.

"Besides," Gonzalo observed, "you're also up late."

"Have you heard anything about reinforcements being sent north?" Don Carlos asked.

"Yes," Alejandro said. "Twenty men have been told to be ready to leave tomorrow."

"Leaving only eighteen of us to share guard duty," Gonzalo complained.

"Is there no concern that this will make Santa Fe more vulnerable to raids by Native war parties?" Don Carlos asked. "Certainly many townspeople are going to be nervous when they hear about the latest attack, and then see more of the garrison ride off."

"The noncommissioned officers were told that the remaining garrison is large enough to protect the town," Luis replied. "Also, if there was a crisis, they would be aided by the local militia."

Don Carlos returned to the subject of the attack on the punitive expedition. "I heard about the last attack," he said, "but nothing about casualties."

"We haven't been officially informed," Alejandro said. "But we learned quite a bit about the battle, because the courier is one of our best friends. He told us our comrades were taken completely by surprise in an ambush."

Gonzalo broke in. "Major Cortés has a lot of experience with combat of the kind they have in Europe, where soldiers advance rank upon rank. These Indian raiders lay ambushes; they strike and then retreat."

"You asked about casualties," Alejandro went on. "Our friend the courier said that there were three fatalities on our side, and a dozen wounded. One of the young aristocrats had his horse killed and his arm broken when the horse fell on him."

"One of the Mendoza brothers?" Don Carlos asked.

"Yes."

"Do you suppose his aunt knows?"

"She does," Alejandro replied. "Our friend delivered a message to her."

"A most unhappy situation," Don Carlos commented. Wryly, he added, "But at least the Holy Office's proclamation is securely under your guard."

"A waste of time, if you ask me," Gonzalo said.

"Hush!" Alejandro whispered in alarm. "The inquisitors live right around the corner."

"Besides, it's our duty," Luis said resignedly.

Don Carlos could tell that one of their typical endless arguments was about to begin, so he wished them well and started off across the plaza. As he approached his house, he saw a light-colored mule tethered in front of it, and he could dimly make out that someone was sitting in the dark on the bench on the house's veranda. It was Pascal. Seeing no way to avoid speaking with him, Don Carlos headed for the veranda. As Carlos approached, Pascal called out, "Good evening, Don Alfonso."

"Good evening, Pascal. I trust you haven't been waiting long."

"Not long at all," Pascal replied. "I might have waited in the kitchen and talked with your manservant, but your dog remains highly suspicious of me. Even with me sitting here on the veranda he comes to the back corner of the house every five minutes or so and checks to see that I'm not up to mischief."

"Which raises the question," Carlos said, "of what brings you here at this hour."

"If you'll allow me to briefly delay giving you an answer," Pascal replied, "I want to say that everyone speaks very highly of you, and I was favorably impressed by your courage and effectiveness in rescuing that poor woman accused of witchcraft from further abuse, and in your preventing that angry Franciscan brother from harming the Indian man named Leonides."

"Thank you, but those were merely instances when someone had to step in," Carlos replied.

"Ah! But you were the one to do so. I applaud your boldness. Now as to my purpose. I've come to ask a favor that requires a measure of mutual trust."

Despite Pascal's friendly manner, Don Carlos's strong suspicion that Pascal was his old enemy made him very wary. "Are you sure we can trust each other?" he asked.

"From everything I've learned about you," Pascal replied, "I believe you are eminently trustworthy. But I admit that you might have grounds for distrusting me. However, what I need tonight won't require absolute trust on your part. I have several packages I'd like to deliver anonymously, and they're too heavy to handle by myself."

"Are you going to tell me what's in these packages?" Don Carlos asked.

"Certainly. I have come into possession of some of the ransom money that Raul Trigales paid for the release of his kidnapped children."

With that remark of Pascal's, any remaining doubts Don Carlos had about Pascal's identity vanished. He was unquestionably Malvolio. He was also sure that Malvolio knew who he, Don Carlos, was, which placed them on equal ground. Since Pascal avoided using Carlos's brujo name, Don Carlos reciprocated by not using Pascal's. Instead, he kept the focus on the kidnapped children. "The kidnappers did not return the children once the ransom had been paid," he said. "That was cruel. Had it not been for extraordinary luck, the children would have died in a cave in Los Organos."

Pascal replied, "I can't excuse what happened, and I am happier than you can imagine that an old Indian—or was it Anton's angel, hawk, and owl?—came to the rescue. What I would like your help with tonight is taking the bags of pesos in my possession and delivering them to the Trigales house." Don Carlos started to speak, but Pascal held his hand up and went on.

"I'm assuming that the front door of the house will be unlocked, and that no one will be awake to notice when we leave the bags just inside the door and depart as silently as we came."

"Why do you need my help?" Don Carlos asked.

"I have the contents of three of the four bags of pesos that were originally paid. They are too heavy for my old mule to carry by himself. I've divided them into four bags. If you would come along with a horse of yours, my mule and your horse could carry two bags apiece."

Don Carlos could scarcely believe that he was discussing these matters in such a calm tone of voice with his ancient enemy. But the potential danger of the situation had his brujo awareness at its sharpest, and he could see no sign of evil intent when he examined both Pascal's external manner and his aura. In that moment he realized that his attitude toward Malvolio had begun to change, almost imperceptibly, ever since the day several months earlier when he had overheard Malvolio acknowledge that he was near death and wanted to find Carlos, not to harm him, but to gain his help.

Pascal interpreted Don Carlos's momentary silence as requiring additional incentive. "I can understand why you're hesitating," he said, "but allow me to mention a few practical matters. If you were to try to have me arrested, I would certainly resist, and you are the only person in Santa Fe who could subdue me. But in doing so, you would reveal that you have secret powers that members of the Inquisition tribunal would be very interested in knowing about, to put it mildly."

"Are you threatening me?" Carlos asked, defensive again.

"I have no intention of doing so. If your secret powers become known," Pascal said, "it will only be because of something you do. So you see, oddly enough, in the matter of mutual trust, you're the only person I can trust with my secrets, and I am the only person you can trust with yours."

"The difference," Don Carlos observed, "is that I've done nothing of a criminal sort."

"True," Pascal replied, "though the inquisitors might think otherwise. But please leave all that aside. Will you help me return what's left of the ransom money?"

Suddenly, as if a gear shifted somewhere inside him, Carlos's remaining misgivings vanished and the lure of an adventure took their place. "What's your plan?" he asked, all hesitation gone.

"The bags of pesos are in my caravan, which is parked in front of the Fernandez place, which I believe you own. I depend on your knowledge of

Santa Fe to select the best route for transporting the bags from the Fernandez place to Raul Trigales's house."

Don Carlos knew exactly how he and Pascal should proceed. "There's a safe way to make the trip across fields that passes only a very few occupied houses."

"Excellent!" Pascal said. "Can we start right away?"

"Follow me around back," Carlos replied. "I'll get my horse out of the corral, and we can be on our way as soon as I tell Orfeo that I'm going out for a late-night ride."

Orfeo was puzzled, but he agreed to tell no one, not even Inéz, about his boss's curious nighttime activities. That settled, Don Carlos and Pascal led their respective mounts across fields south of the plaza to the Fernandez place, which was unoccupied now that the soldiers had moved out. Pascal climbed into the caravan. Then he pushed while Carlos pulled and they maneuvered four bags of pesos, one after the other, out the back door of the caravan.

Working together, they loaded two bags on Pascal's Listo and two on Carlos's Eagle. They then set out on a path that ran along the north side of the Santa Fe River. They soon came to a well-used path that connected the Galisteo Road south of the river with the road that continued northward as the Camino Real from Santa Fe to Tesuque and beyond. They passed three small houses, all dark, before coming at last to the Trigales place. The actual delivery, done in total silence, was remarkably simple. The family had left the front door unlocked, and it opened without an inordinate amount of squeaking. Pascal and Don Carlos unloaded Listo and Eagle and placed the bags of coins just inside the door. Closing it as quietly as possible, they began to retrace their steps.

They continued their return trip in complete silence. Only when their paths diverged did Pascal say, "Thank you for your help, and good night." Don Carlos waved a hand in farewell, but said nothing.

As he led Eagle up the path from the Santa Fe River to his house, he was lost in thought. Would their dark-of-night transfer of the ransom money to Raul Trigales's house arouse questions? Certainly Raul would be astonished to receive a large part of the money back and would wonder how it had been delivered, and by whom. How could such questions be headed off?

He and Eagle were nearly back to Carlos's house when he heard musket shots in the distance, followed by shouts. They seemed to be coming from the

Barrio de Analco on the south side of the river. "The wolf! The wolf!" a voice cried. "It's headed toward the plaza!"

At that moment, Eagle became agitated and threatened to bolt. Don Carlos tugged forcefully on his lead rope in an effort to bring the horse under control. Eagle's eyes showed white and he was closer to panic than Carlos had ever seen him. Carlos turned to look down the path toward the river, the direction from which the shouts were coming. He could see two or three torches held aloft. If the men holding them were pursuing a wolf, it was invisible in the darkness. Then, suddenly, he saw a black shape rapidly closing in on him.

His first thought was to get Eagle in the corral as quickly as possible and he reached for the corral gate, in the process turning his back to both Eagle and the wolf. Eagle swung around abruptly and bumped into Carlos with such force that he was knocked to the ground. When he looked up he saw the wolf's snout and open jaws inches from his throat.

He had no time to gather and launch a blast of invisible energy. Instinctively, he thrust his hands up at the wolf's chest, catching the animal in mid-lunge and pitching it over his head.

The wolf landed behind him as Carlos scrambled to his feet and turned to face it. When it leaped at him again, he grabbed the wolf's outstretched forepaw and slung it in the direction the animal's momentum was carrying it. The wolf crashed sideways to the ground, landing between Carlos and Eagle.

Suddenly Eagle became the aggressor. He charged forward, head down, teeth bared, ears pinned, snaking his head from side to side and hissing. The wolf shrank back. Eagle pulled up and lashed out with his forefeet. The wolf was doing its best to get away, twisting and rolling, but Eagle landed a solid blow to its ribs.

By now the men with the torches had reached them. Two of them, mestizos who had been on wolf-watch in the Barrio, arrived at Don Carlos's side just as the wolf got out from under Eagle's feet and tried to run away. One of the mestizos, a farmer named Anselmo Pacheco, leveled his musket and fired at the wolf, hitting it high on the shoulder. It yelped in pain but tried to keep going. Pacheco's companion, a man Don Carlos didn't know, aimed and shot the wolf behind the shoulder blade. It collapsed in a heap.

"Are you all right, Don Alfonso?" Pacheco asked.

Taking inventory of his condition, Don Carlos found that his coat was torn and that the wolf's teeth had gashed his shoulder. "Only some scratches," he replied, trying to minimize his injuries.

The two militiamen reloaded their muskets. "I want to see the beast close up," Pacheco said, "but not until I'm ready to defend myself if it's only unconscious." He called to the men carrying torches and asked them to come forward.

They all moved cautiously forward and Pacheco prodded the wolf's body with his boot. It did not respond. Pacheco's companions shook their heads. "It looks like an ordinary wolf," one said. "But when we saw it attack sheep and kill the sheep dog that tried to protect the flock, it seemed like a demonic beast. When we shot at it, it ran in this direction. Then, when it leaped at Don Alfonso, it seemed like something supernatural again."

Don Carlos was sure that this was not an ordinary wolf, but he didn't want to encourage talk of witchcraft, so he said, "If it were otherworldly and unnatural, your muskets couldn't have killed it."

"That's probably true," Pacheco conceded, looking down at the wolf's body and prodding it again with his toe. "Still, there was something supernatural about you, too. Not to mention your horse."

"Anselmo," Don Carlos replied, "you know that I'm a skilled fencer. Speed, deception, and muscle control are keys to success as a fencer. And Eagle is a brave and strong horse, a true warrior."

"No one disputes you, Don Alfonso," Pacheco said. "But you can't talk us out of being amazed."

"Please don't exaggerate what you saw," Don Carlos insisted. "The wolf attacked me, my horse intervened, and you arrived and shot the wolf, which is dead."

Orfeo, awakened by the musket shots, had come out to see what was going on. Gordo came along and approached the scene with his hackles up. Don Carlos turned to Orfeo and said, "Please put Eagle in the corral, and then bring some rope from the stable. We can tie the wolf's front and hind legs and slide a fence pole between them so that it can be carried off. I want to remove the carcass from where it's lying next to the corral. It's upsetting the horses."

Several fence poles were lying in a pile nearby. A militiaman gathered one up and brought it over to the wolf's body. Orfeo returned with two lengths of rope. The militiamen trussed the wolf's legs, inserted the pole between its fore- and hind legs, and picked it up. Flanked by the torchbearers, they headed back toward the Barrio. "Our neighbors are going to rejoice that the wolf is dead," Anselmo said. "Thank you for helping us."

"We all played a role," Don Carlos replied. "Now allow me to excuse myself. I want to get inside to treat the gash on my shoulder."

As Don Carlos started for his house, Orfeo asked, "What happened?"

"The wolf was running up the path from the Barrio. I was about to put Eagle in the corral, but he sensed the wolf's approach and spun around so fast that he knocked me down. Then the wolf was on me. I managed to throw it off and Eagle leaped in and struck it with his front hoofs. Fortunately, the two Barrio militiamen arrived and finished the wolf off with shots from their muskets."

"Will you be all right, Don Alfonso? Your shoulder is bleeding quite a bit."

"Don't worry, Orfeo. It looks worse that it is. You can come in and help patch me up."

Not waiting for anything more to be said, Don Carlos walked to his house and he and Orfeo went into the kitchen. After Carlos had taken off his coat and shirt, Orfeo washed the wound on his shoulder and bathed it in sherry. "It needs to be wrapped tightly to close it and stop the bleeding, Don Alfonso," Orfeo said worriedly. "Do you have a long piece of cloth I can use?"

Carlos looked resignedly at his torn and bloody shirt lying on the table. "My good shirt," he said. "Well, it's ruined. You can cut out the sleeve and tear a strip from the back."

Orfeo, with considerable skill, fashioned a bandage and tied it snugly. Carlos thanked him and sent him back to bed. After Orfeo had gone off Carlos put on a fresh shirt, sat down at the kitchen table, and drank what was left of the sherry. Gordo looked on sympathetically.

"The whole evening has been strange," Don Carlos said, speaking out loud to his dog. "First, I helped my longstanding adversary, Don Malvolio, alias Pascal, return ransom money anonymously to Raul Trigales. Then I was attacked by a wolf whose assault on me was almost certainly directed by Brother Gustavo, who was behind the wolf incident back in January. Now I am wondering what to do about the questions that will be asked when the ransom money is discovered in the morning." He pondered the problem for a while. Then he exclaimed, "Diego!" so loudly that Gordo jumped up in alarm from the place where he'd been dozing.

Don Carlos got up and hunted around for a piece of cheap paper he had used to make a cover for a book. He unfolded the paper, spread it out on the kitchen table, and, disguising his handwriting, he printed a message. Pleased with the result, he put on a fresh shirt, folded the paper, and headed for the door. Gordo got up to follow, and Don Carlos with a stern voice told his dog, "No, you must not come along. Stay!" At least, he thought, the three soldiers who'd lodged with him had taught Gordo one useful command.

He walked to the near edge of the plaza. Before he turned left to take the street that led to the Trigales place he glanced across the plaza. Over on its opposite side he could see only one soldier guarding the chapel door. It struck him as odd that one rather than three soldiers was on duty, but under the present circumstances that was a good thing; it meant fewer eyes to observe his movements.

When he reached the Trigales house it was as dark and quiet as it had been two hours earlier. His former groom and cook, Diego Campos, was the household's assistant cook, and Carlos knew from visiting him there that Diego slept in a tiny room on the back side of the house. He went to the window, found it open, and climbed into the room.

Diego was sound asleep and startled when Don Carlos placed his hand gently over Diego's mouth and whispered, "Diego. It's me, Don Alfonso. Don't make a sound."

In the nearly pitch-black darkness of the room, it was difficult to see Diego's face, but Don Carlos sensed that the young man's eyes were wide open, at first with fear, then surprise, and finally with puzzlement. "Get up and light a candle," Don Carlos told him, "so that we can see what we're doing."

Diego had always followed Don Carlos's instructions without protest or question. He got up, managed to light a candle, and looked at Carlos, waiting to hear what was next. "I need your help with a task that must remain absolutely secret. Guide me through the house to Señor Trigales's bedroom. Open the door enough to call to him softly that Don Alfonso has come by with a message that requires his immediate attention."

The two men tiptoed through the house to the corridor on which the family's bedrooms were located. Diego did as Don Carlos had instructed him, opening the door to the master bedroom and whispering, "Señor Trigales. It's Diego. Don Alfonso is here with an urgent message. Please come into the hallway."

Moments passed before Raul came to the door with a puzzled look on his face. He stepped into the hallway, closed the door behind him, took in the fact that both Diego and Don Carlos were standing there, and asked, "What's all this about?"

"Diego," Don Carlos said, turning to his young friend, "Can you find your way back to your bedroom without the candle? The business I have to conduct with Raul is best kept secret even from you. Please forget that you saw me here tonight."

Diego left the candle with Don Carlos and went off, feeling his way along the corridor. Don Carlos pulled the piece of paper out of his pocket and explained, "Tonight there was a lot of excitement in back of my place that left that marauding wolf dead. When I came inside, I found this note on my kitchen table. Let me read it to you: '*Tell Trigales that he'll find some of the ransom money in bags just inside the front door.*' I assume," Carlos went on, "this means the front door to your house."

"I'm astonished," Raul said. "Can it be?"

"Let's go look," Carlos replied.

They made their way by the flickering light of the candle to the front hall of the house. There were the four bags. Raul bent down, opened one, and reached inside. He pulled a handful of pesos out and stared at them. "How can this be?"

"I don't know," Carlos replied, regretting the necessity of having to lie in order to protect himself. "But I have a feeling that this should be kept a secret. With all the talk of witchcraft, someone would be certain to start a rumor that spirits were responsible."

Raul was a good man. "I suppose you're right," he agreed, "although as in previous events associated with the kidnapping of my children, I have the feeling that you know more than you're telling me."

Don Carlos put his hand on Raul's arm and said, "You cannot imagine how much I appreciate your willingness to keep my secrets. I only hope that some day I can reveal more of what happened tonight. For now, however, I suggest we move these bags to a hiding place in the house known only to you and Bianca."

The men moved the bags one by one to the family bedroom corridor, where they found Bianca standing in the hall with a candle in her hand. "What are you two up to in the middle of the night?" she asked. "Are the children all right? What is Don Alfonso doing here at this hour? And what's in the bags?"

"So many questions, dear," Raul murmured, leaning forward to give his wife a kiss on the cheek. "A few even have answers. The children are fine, sound asleep, I hope. Don Alfonso brought a note that told us to look for these bags in the front hallway, and the bags contain some of the ransom money, returned, it seems, by an unknown person. And Don Alfonso suggests that we keep this curious event secret so as to not add to the rumors of magic and witchcraft being practiced in Santa Fe."

After a brief discussion Raul and Bianca decided to hide the money in their bedroom. Carlos, having been thanked profusely, went off feeling satisfied and relieved.

Returning home by a route behind several buildings on the southwest corner of the plaza, Don Carlos checked on the horses in the corral in back of his house. They were calm and paid hardly any attention to him when he visited them. He walked around the house to the kitchen door. Looking across the plaza to the chapel on the north side, he could see the silhouettes of his three former lodgers on guard duty illuminated by the torch next to the chapel door. Whatever had taken two of them away from their assignment earlier was a puzzle that he supposed he could solve by talking with them in the morning. He checked the stars that had come out as the clouds above Santa Fe drifted away and decided that dawn was imminent. It had been a very long night.

23

Love

Gordo's excited barking woke Carlos with a start. Then he heard insistent knocking on the front door of his house. It took him a little time to collect his wits. The last thing he remembered was feeling very tired when he got home after visiting Raul. Though it had been close to the time that he usually got up to meditate, he had taken off his boots and lain down to take a brief nap. The light now streaming in the window indicated that it was well past sunrise. The knocking at the door came again and set Gordo off on another series of barks. Carlos swung his feet over the side of the bed, pulled his boots on, and got up to answer the door. His shoulder hurt, which reminded him that the wolf had bitten him. What a night! "I'm coming!" he shouted as he entered the narrow hallway that ran through the middle of the house. Gordo followed, growling. "Shussh!" Carlos said to his dog. "I don't think the wolf has returned. There's no need to be upset."

He opened the door to find two brown-robed Franciscans, Father Dorantes and Brother Inocente, standing there. "Good morning, Don Alfonso," Dorantes said. "I apologize if we have routed you out of bed."

"You have," Carlos replied. "I was sleeping late after a strenuous night. Would you like to come in?"

"If we may," Dorantes said. "We're investigating last night's incident with the wolf."

Carlos turned and led the way through the dimly lit hallway to the kitchen. "Word certainly gets around fast," he commented over his shoulder.

"Captain Miranda of the town militia came to our quarters at dawn to inform us that the wolf had been killed by his men."

They'd reached the kitchen, and Carlos gestured to chairs at the table. "Would you like to sit? I can make coffee."

"No, thank you," Dorantes said, as he and Brother Inocente sat down. "I'm curious," he said, looking around. "Doesn't this house have a *sala*?"

"The kitchen has served that purpose as long as I've lived here," Carlos replied. "Why do you ask?"

"If you'll pardon me for saying so, I'm mildly surprised that a *hidalgo* would live in such a small house."

Carlos was tempted to defend his way of life, but instead he answered agreeably, "It is unusual. In fact, I've just begun renovations that will result in my having a proper *sala* and two additional rooms, but surely that wasn't the topic you wished to discuss. What do you want to know about the wolf?"

Father Dorantes cleared his throat and spoke in an official manner. "As representatives of the Holy Office's tribunal, we would like to bring closure to the matter of this rampaging creature that some believe to have been a werewolf. Upon receiving Captain Miranda's report, we went immediately to the Barrio to talk with Anselmo Pacheco, one of the militiamen who fired the musket shots that killed the wolf." He paused and looked at Carlos questioningly.

"Yes," Carlos said. "I doubt that I can add much, if anything, to his report."

"Perhaps you can begin," Dorantes suggested, "by telling us how you happened to be out of your house at that hour."

"Ah!" Don Carlos replied. "The explanation is quite simple. I was getting a drink of water in the kitchen when I heard shots. I rushed outside to learn their source. My horse was upset, so I went to the corral to calm him. Just as I opened the gate to go in, the wolf attacked me."

"I see," Dorantes said, apparently satisfied by Carlos's answer. He then went on to say, "The circumstances described to us still left some doubt in our minds regarding the possible unnatural nature of the wolf. Pacheco and his companions seemed to believe that the beast displayed something akin to supernatural powers."

Carlos didn't want to give any credence to that opinion, so he said in a reasonable tone, "I wouldn't take such views seriously. Bear in mind that the Barrio's residents have lived in fear of this wolf for weeks, and its reputation has been greatly exaggerated by their superstitions. What I saw was an ordinary wolf that died when struck by two musket shots. A supernatural creature couldn't have been killed in such a normal way."

"Your point is well taken," Dorantes said, "but the militiamen were also in awe of your own abilities, which seemed to them unusual."

So much, Carlos thought to himself, for my efforts to dissuade Anselmo and his comrades from attributing unnatural powers to me. He laughed and replied, "I think they've not observed me fencing. If they had, they might have seen that my training as a fencer has given me very fast reactions. Even so, I was lucky to be able to fend off the wolf when it lunged at me, and to escape with nothing more than a torn coat and a gash on my shoulder. But the real credit ought to go to my horse, Eagle, who attacked the wolf and made it try to run away. At that point Anselmo and his companions arrived and dispatched the wolf with their muskets."

"So nothing you saw," Dorantes asked, "would lead you to believe this creature was anything more than an ordinary wolf?"

"Definitely not," Carlos replied. "And allow me to add that this seems to have solved one of the supposed mysteries that have kept you in Santa Fe."

"That's true," Dorantes conceded, pulling one side of his mouth down.

"Is that a problem?" Carlos asked. "I would think you'd be pleased to have this cleared up, along with the fact that whoever stole those pieces of china and silver has returned them and abandoned his criminal ways. The story that the thief turned himself into a black dog always struck me as preposterous."

Dorantes looked as though he was tempted to dispute Carlos's point, but he let it pass and said, "You may be right. Still, I find it frustrating that our inquiries have been so unproductive. We thought we were close to catching the witch known as Manuela Maldonado, and that she would lead us to the sorcerer named Carlos Buenaventura. Father Aurelio urged us to pursue him, but it now seems that he may never have been in Santa Fe."

Carlos decided to take a small risk by asking, "How does Brother Gustavo feel about this? He seemed convinced that Carlos Buenaventura was an Indian resident of the Barrio, and I notice he's not with you this morning."

"Brother Gustavo," Dorantes said, his lips tightening, "is not well today. He is in need of treatment, and we may have to leave to get him the help he needs."

"I'm sorry he's unwell," Carlos replied insincerely, very curious to know what Gustavo was suffering from. He probed a bit farther. "But as for leaving Santa Fe, what reason would you have to remain? The forty-day period of grace is over, and there are doubtless other towns or cities where you can pursue your inquiries."

Father Dorantes looked at Brother Inocente and said, "As it happens, Brother Inocente and I last night discussed what to do next. He has served on the tribunal for only a short time, and perhaps brings fresh eyes to the subject. He wondered, based on our experience in Santa Fe, whether it wouldn't be better to preach the love of God for all of His creatures than to threaten punishment the way the Inquisition has done. He observed that our founder, Saint Francis, preached a gospel of love."

"Am I correct in sensing," Carlos asked, "that preaching the love of God appeals to you?"

"It does. I've seen cases in which preaching eternal damnation opened people's eyes to the need to reform their ways, but I'm no longer sure that my own temperament is suited to that method."

"Thank you for being so forthright about your views," Carlos said.

"You are welcome," Dorantes replied. "Now if you'll excuse us," he went on, "I want to return to our quarters and write up the results of this morning's inquiries while they're still fresh in my mind. We may be leaving Santa Fe tomorrow."

"That soon?" Carlos said.

"Yes, Governor Peralta is sending a squad of soldiers with a proclamation to be delivered to the pueblos south of Santa Fe. They leave early tomorrow. We can travel with them for our protection."

"May your journey go well," Carlos said.

"Thank you, Don Alfonso. I wish you well also."

Carlos showed Father Dorantes and Brother Inocente to the door. Relieved of the necessity of being alert in their presence, he suddenly felt tired and aware that his wounded shoulder was hot and throbbing. He went outside to look for Orfeo, thinking to have him loosen the bandage to ease the throbbing. Orfeo was nowhere to be seen. Carlos quickly checked on the horses and then set off across the plaza. He was surprised to see his former lodgers still on guard duty by the chapel doors. He waved to them and went over to where they were stationed. "How is it that you're still here?" he asked. "I thought your eight-hour watch ran from ten to six."

"We're doing a double shift," Gonzalo replied. "We're replacing three of our comrades who left this morning with the contingent that's reinforcing the punitive expedition. They rode off an hour ago. We'll be done here at two this afternoon."

"It must be hard taking another shift right away," Don Carlos said. "Aren't you getting very tired?"

Alejandro shrugged and said, "We take turns resting against the wall. Finishing our shift at two will let us get some extra rest before we leave Santa Fe at dawn tomorrow morning."

"Where are you headed?" Don Carlos asked.

"Governor Peralta is sending a proclamation to every pueblo in New Mexico. We're supposed to deliver it to the pueblos south of Santa Fe."

"Have you been told its contents?" Don Carlos inquired.

"Not yet," Alejandro replied, "but I'm sure it will be explained to us before we go."

"Interesting," Don Carlos said. He knew he could find out more from Marco Cabrera. "By the way," he asked, "what was going on last night? You've probably heard about the wolf that attacked Eagle and me. Just before dawn I went out to see how Eagle was doing and I looked over this way. I saw only one of you standing guard. Did two of you leave your posts for a while?"

"Yes, we did," Alejandro said sheepishly. "We were pacing back and forth, trying to stay awake, when Father Benedicto's servant, Jesús, came running around the corner shouting, 'Come quickly! Brother Gustavo is having a fit!' Luis stayed here, and Gonzalo and I followed Jesús back to the priests' quarters. He opened the door to a small cell and there was Brother Gustavo, writhing on the floor and shouting, 'Let me go! Leave me alone!' The three of us tried to pin him down, but he fought us like a madman. Finally Gonzalo hit him hard in the ribs with the butt of his musket. That knocked the wind out of him long enough for us to pick him up and force him down on his cot."

Gonzalo picked up the narrative. "He tried to bite us and kept fighting. He was screaming and growling like a wild animal. After quite a struggle we managed to tie him down. He was foaming at the mouth. The man was out of his mind."

"Then," Alejandro put in, "Father Dorantes came and told us to leave. We don't know what happened next, but Jesús stopped by a half hour ago and said Brother Gustavo wasn't much better this morning."

"I wonder what set that off," Don Carlos said, feigning ignorance, though he had strong suspicions. Brother Gustavo, he was sure, had taken possession of the wolf and directed its actions. When the wolf was attacked by Eagle and shot to death by the militiamen, Brother Gustavo must have suffered the wolf's confusion and terror as if it had been happening to himself. Carlos almost felt sorry for him.

Having told Don Carlos their story, the three soldiers begged him for more details of his battle with the wolf, and he quickly sketched the event. He then continued on to the Beltrán place, where he found Inéz working in the kitchen. "I heard you had a busy night dispatching wolves," she said as he closed the door behind him.

"There was only one wolf and I didn't kill it," he replied. "And how did you hear all this so soon?"

"María got the news from several people who live in the Barrio, and she came over to tell me this morning. She'd heard that the wolf tore into your shoulder and thought I should know."

"Well, that's partly why I'm here. I think the wound may need attention." He took off his coat, unbuttoned his shirt, and slipped it off his left shoulder. The bandage Orfeo had put on was slightly bloody.

Inéz carefully unwrapped the bandage and inspected the injury. "At least it's not too deep, but I bet it bled a lot."

"Yes, and it made a mess of the coat and the shirt I was wearing."

"What did you do for the wound last night?"

"Orfeo washed it thoroughly and doused it with sherry, and then wrapped it up."

"Does it hurt to the touch?"

"Some," he said. "What's more bothersome is that it throbs."

"Hmmm," said Inéz. "I think I need to make it hurt more. Come over here to the table and take your arm completely out of your shirt. Better yet, take your shirt off."

Carlos expressed mild alarm. "What would anyone coming into the room think I was doing?"

Inéz looked amused and said, "Having a wolf bite thoroughly cleaned."

Carlos went to the table and sat down. As he removed his shirt Inéz brought a basin to the table. She told him, "Put your elbow in the basin. I'm going to pour hot water over the wound and wash it several times with soap." This she did, rinsing it thoroughly after each soaping. Finally she went to the kitchen counter, opened a small jar, and poured some oil onto a cloth.

"I'm making a poultice with oil from desert lavender," she said. "It's a good remedy for infections." She applied it to his wound and told him, "Hold this in place while I wash out your bandage."

Holding the poultice over his wound, Carlos said, sounding a bit surprised, "I believe that feels better. Now I can go on to the other things I have to tell you." He briefly recounted his lodgers' story about subduing Brother Gustavo, who had gone mad, and his, Carlos's, belief that Gustavo had been inhabiting the wolf's mind and thus had been unhinged by its death.

"I don't feel the least bit sorry for him," Inéz declared. Having washed the bandage, she poured hot water on it and wrung it out. "Here," she said as she rewrapped it. "The heat will draw the infection out."

Carlos stood up and carefully put on his shirt and coat, and then sat down again. Inéz sat down across from him. "Something else you may not know about," he said, "is that I made a late-night visit to the governor's residence and urged him to take measures to make peace with our Indian neighbors."

"Oh?" Inéz said. "Give me some details."

"The method would be relatively simple," he replied, "and should have been done years ago. I suggested that he invite the leaders of all the New Mexican pueblos to come to Santa Fe for a grand council at which he, as governor, would sign a document acknowledging the rights of tribal people—to their land, their work, and their religion. That's actually the post-Revolt policy, but it's never been put in writing."

"I wonder whether he'll agree."

"I just talked with my three former lodgers. They've been told to leave tomorrow morning to deliver a proclamation to the pueblos south of Santa Fe. They didn't know the proclamation's contents, but I'll bet it's something along the lines I suggested to Peralta. And what makes this even better news is that Father Dorantes and his fellow inquisitors will probably accompany the soldiers south."

Inéz's face lit up. "That's splendid news on both counts! How did you learn about Dorantes's plan?"

"He came by an hour ago, supposedly to complete his investigation of the werewolf stories. He seems persuaded that it couldn't have been a spirit animal if musket shots could kill it, and he said that Brother Gustavo was ill and they needed to get him to someone who could help him."

"Ill? I thought you said he'd gone mad."

"I suspect that Father Dorantes believes that Brother Gustavo is once again suffering from possession, and that they need to get him to a priest who's experienced with exorcisms."

"No one here could do it—Father Benedicto or even Dorantes?"

"I think it's a specialized procedure. Probably no priest north of Nombre de Dios has the skills to deal with someone as seriously afflicted as Brother Gustavo."

"I'll be glad to see them go."

"I will be too. But I must tell you about one more adventure I had last night. I hope you won't disapprove too strongly of what I did."

"What have you gotten yourself into now?"

"Last night when I returned home after speaking with the governor I found Pascal sitting on the veranda of my house. He asked me to help him."

Her eyebrows went up. Then she said, "Go on."

"He told me that he had come into possession of some of the ransom money that Raul paid."

"Holy Mother!" Inéz exclaimed. "You helped Malvolio! How could you?"

"He made the very good point that I was the only person he could trust with his secrets, because if I exposed him to the Inquisition, it would doubtless also expose who I am. And what reason could I have for not helping him anonymously get the money back to Raul?"

"Yes, but—" Inéz began. She paused and thought. Then she said, "What you're telling me helps me clarify something that happened about an hour ago."

"What was that?"

"Raul came by and repaid the thirty pesos I'd given him toward the ransom. When I asked him how he was able to do this, he simply said he'd recently had a bit of good luck."

"I suppose he'll try to repay me too, although I know that he didn't get the full sum back, only about three-quarters of it. I'm ignoring Pascal's part in this incident and treating it as a case of all's well that ends well."

"What makes you think the Carlos-and-Malvolio story has truly ended?"

"I don't know what might happen next, but I can tell you that we're both being very careful to call each other by our public names, Alfonso and Pascal. I find that reassuring."

"I don't, but you never take me into your confidence when anything truly important is at stake."

"Inéz! I could have kept my role in this a secret. I haven't. I've told you about it as soon as possible."

She seemed slightly mollified. She got up from the table. "Well, it's good news that Raul got most of his money back. And I have news, too. You and I are invited to accompany Javier and Cristina on a social visit to Doña Josefina. We are to be there at two o'clock. You'll need to get back here in your best clothes at least ten minutes ahead of time."

"Do you know what this is all about?"

"Do you really have to ask? Only a few days ago Doña Josefina asked us whether we thought Elena and Santiago would be a good match. This is the next step in that direction."

"But so soon?"

"Apparently something has caused her to move forward more quickly."

"Hmm," Carlos said. "Perhaps because one of the nephews has been wounded. Well, we'll find out. One more question. On my way here I remembered a fragment of a dream I had last night. Zoila appeared in it, fully dressed, I might add, and told me to ask you for your advice about my house renovation project. Are there any details you'd like to add to your suggestion that I build two new rooms?"

"Make the two additional rooms have windows that open on a small courtyard between them, where you can plant an herb garden. The new room on the east ought to be large; the one on the west can be small and have the stable attached to the south end of it. It can serve as the groom's room. You've made your grooms sleep in the hayloft for too long. Now it's time for you to be on your way. I have to get back to work."

Carlos returned home to find that Rubén and Lázaro had arrived from Tesuque. They were already helping Orfeo dig post holes for the expanded corral. "We'll have the posts in place in no time," Orfeo announced happily. "I'm teaching them some *versos* and they're teaching me some Pueblo chants. It makes the work go faster."

Don Carlos greeted his two Pueblo Indian friends with some of the few words he knew in their Tewa language, "*Woa'ah tamu*." They replied in kind. Then he asked, "I assume Dolores came back with you; how is she?"

Lázaro replied, "She rode to Santa Fe with us and seemed very glad to be back with Pedro and María. As for our work here," he went on, "do you have any idea where the new stable will go? We could throw up a four-stall stable in very little time, if we know where it's to go and have the lumber to use for it."

"Why don't I go negotiate with Raul Trigales for building materials while you keep digging postholes?" Carlos said. "As for where it should go, divide the area into a big room on the southeast side of the house, a smaller one on the southwest, and a courtyard between. The stable for the horses will be an extension on the back of the west room, which will be the groom's bedroom."

After asking only a few questions, the three helpers returned to their work, and Don Carlos left them to go to the Trigales place. He found Raul outside the warehouse in the back of the house, talking with several of his hired hands. He broke off that conversation and came over to speak with Carlos.

"I've begun repaying people money they gave me for the ransom," Raul said without preamble. "I can't tell you how good it feels to be able to do so. I can pay you most of your hundred and fifty pesos right now."

"Raul, I thank you," Carlos said, "but you didn't get all the money back, so you needn't rush to pay me anything. In any case, what I would prefer might be called payment in kind."

"What do you have in mind?" Raul asked.

"I'm starting major renovations on my house and property. Today Orfeo and two Pueblo Indian friends, Ana Lugo's cousins, are expanding the corral. The next order of business is to construct a new stable for the horses. Would you have beams and boards in your warehouse suitable for use in a stable? We could deduct the cost of those materials from the amount I gave you."

"I'd be happy to do so," Raul replied. "I'll have two of my men load those materials and deliver them to you this afternoon. Also, since there aren't any pressing jobs here right now, they can stay and work for you today and tomorrow."

"Excellent. I won't be around through mid-afternoon. I have an appointment to accompany Inéz, Javier, and Cristina to Doña Josefina's."

"I heard about that from Javier this morning. Do you think a marriage agreement for Elena and Santiago is being proposed? It scarcely seems possible after the way Señora Mendoza cooperated with Pilar Peralta's efforts to marginalize all of us in the merchant class."

"A lot of things have changed recently," Carlos replied. "But there's no knowing for certain. Meanwhile, thank you for the help you're giving me."

Don Carlos left Raul's place in a very good state of mind. His shoulder had stopped hurting. He and Inéz were in harmony. Dolores had returned to Santa Fe in good spirits. Dorantes and the other two inquisitors were leaving town tomorrow. Raul had gotten most of the ransom money back, and he was repaying Carlos by helping him with his building project. And now, possibly, a marriage was being considered between Elena and Santiago.

Carlos went home, gave his building crew a few more instructions based on Inéz's advice, had lunch, and dressed carefully to meet Inéz, Javier, and Cristina for their visit with Doña Josefina.

When he arrived at the Beltrán house he saw that, like him, Inéz, Javier, and Cristina were wearing their finest clothes. We are all, he thought, trying to make a good impression on Doña Josefina, on the assumption that her invitation has something to do with a possible marriage and family alliance between Santiago and Elena and the Mendozas and the Beltráns. In all his five previous lives, and this one too, Carlos had never before been a party to such negotiations. True, he had proposed marriage to Camila. But that was different. Then he was representing himself. If indeed Doña Josefina wanted to discuss Elena's future, that would place him more in the position of an uncle or guardian. He found that being in such a position rather pleased him.

Once at the Mendoza hacienda, the Beltráns, Carlos, and Inéz were shown into the *sala*. Carlos noticed that the room was more lavishly appointed than it had been on his previous visits. Two full-length portraits he'd never seen before had been hung on the walls. Silver candlesticks had been placed on an elegant Spanish chest, and a linen-covered table with five handsome chairs around it had been set with wine glasses and silk napkins. It was an impressive display of wealth.

Doña Josefina was seated at the table and was wearing a dress slightly more in the current fashion than was her usual custom. She rose and approached her guests. Directing her attention mainly to Javier and Cristina, she said, "I am pleased that you could accept my invitation on such short notice."

Javier and Cristina murmured their pleasure at being there and then, at Doña Josefina's invitation, everyone settled into chairs at the table. "You may know," she began without further preliminaries, "that I inherited a large vineyard and winery in the Jerez region south of Seville. My winery is located near the coast just outside of Sanlúcar de Barrameda, and its specialty is a dry sherry called Manzanilla. Allow me to offer you one of my favorite vintages."

At a signal from Doña Josefina. the Pueblo Indian servant Carlos knew as Jacinta entered the room and poured a very pale sherry into the glasses of Doña Josefina and her four guests. Doña Josefina lifted her glass and said, "To your good health."

"This is a very fine sherry," Carlos observed appreciatively. "I believe I can even taste a hint of sea air in it."

"Ah!" Doña Josefina said, smiling approvingly at Don Carlos. "Don Alfonso, you seem to have a very discriminating palate for someone so young— not yet twenty-two, I believe."

Carlos replied, "You flatter me. It's simply a matter of having grown up in Mexico City, the son of a man who loved wine, especially fine Spanish wines of all varieties."

"I've often thought," Doña Josefina remarked, "that there would be a good market for this sherry among New Mexico's best families, if it were easier to import it. Unfortunately, at present this war over the Spanish succession has all sides competing to disrupt each other's trade—or do you find it otherwise, Señor Beltrán?" she asked, turning to him.

Javier cleared his throat. "Please. I hope you will feel comfortable calling me Javier and my wife Cristina. As for your question, yes, some items that I would like to import from Europe are difficult to obtain right now. Oddly, it's easier to acquire spices from the Far East via the Manila Galleon than it is to import goods from the Habsburg states."

"Such a nuisance," Doña Josefina declared, "but not a unique circumstance. In my more than eighty years there has rarely been a time when two or more of the European powers were not at war. No matter. Life goes on, and my main concern now is with the future of my three estates—my winery in Sanlúcar, my silver mines in New Spain, and my properties in northern New Mexico.

"I have three grandnephews for whom I am responsible. I had hoped to put off any final decisions about the disposition of my properties until my older nephews, Antonio and Julio, returned from what I assumed would be a campaign of at least two or three months against hostile tribes north of here. But several days ago I learned that Julio was injured in a skirmish and that Antonio is bringing him back to Santa Fe to recover. I have told my granddaughter-in-law, Marta, that I intend to will my Sanlúcar winery to Antonio. His widowed mother lives in Cádiz, and as her eldest son, it is appropriate that he live nearby to look after her in her old age. Marta, who didn't want to come back to Santa Fe when I returned earlier this year, is fond of Antonio and will accompany him to Spain."

Carlos, who was listening intently to Doña Josefina's account, saw that she had found a way of deflecting Marta's threats, one that Marta doubtless found highly satisfactory. "Antonio is a most fortunate young man to receive such a legacy," he said approvingly.

"Yes," Doña Josefina replied. "But what I most want to discuss with you is what I hope to do for my youngest nephew, Santiago. He has told me that he is drawn to the idea of living permanently in New Mexico. He likes its vibrant mix of Spanish and Pueblo Indian societies. He has also, as we've all observed, become very fond of a neighbor, Elena Beltrán, who, it seems, is fond of him. So what I'd like to discuss with Javier and Cristina as Elena's parents, and Alfonso and Inéz as her friends, is the suitability of a union between the Mendoza and Beltrán families, as well as the suitability of Santiago and Elena for each other.

"To begin with," Doña Josefina said, "it strikes me that a union of our family interests has attractive material features. Joining the Beltrán trading business with Mendoza holdings that produce cattle, sheep, and coarse cloth and other trade items would seem an ideal match, a case in which one plus one adds up to more than two."

"I certainly agree that the material interests of the two families reinforce each other," Javier said. "Uniting them would be beneficial to both."

Carlos cleared his throat. "Doña Josefina, I'm wondering, may I raise a possibly awkward question?" He paused to see how she would respond.

"You should know by now, Don Alfonso," she replied, "that I appreciate directness. Ask your question. I'm curious to know what it is."

"Very well. During Governor Villela's term as governor, I never sensed that a social distinction was drawn between, how shall I put it, the families of top government officials and the families of merchants and businessmen. Since Governor Peralta assumed office..."

Doña Josefina held up her hand. "Excuse me for interrupting you, Don Alfonso, but I can see where you're headed, and I agree that your question is appropriate to the present circumstances. Let me explain. Upon my return to Santa Fe after fifteen years in exile, I did not want to give offense to the established social leaders of the town, and I deferred to the example set by the governor's wife in social affairs. But the distinction between high government officials and businessmen is not meaningful to me. And although it's true that my brother-in-law bore the title of marquis and his grandson, my grandnephew Antonio, inherited it on his father's death, you yourself once reminded me, Don Alfonso, that wealth is a great equalizer. So I do not regard Santiago as marrying beneath his social station if he chooses Elena to be his wife."

"I appreciate your clarification, Doña Josefina," Javier said. "And I appreciate Alfonso for having raised the question. I have only one reservation, which is that Elena and Santiago are both quite young."

Doña Josefina expressed amusement. "I should tell you that Elena's age is no obstacle from my perspective as a woman promised at fifteen to a man she'd never met. No, the stronger objection could be raised about Santiago, who is only a few months older than she is. If I should die suddenly, he would not have the experience to manage my properties. Of course, I hope to live a few years longer and during that time educate him to the task of running a large estate. But if I die before that process is complete, I would feel secure in knowing that he could turn to you, Javier, and draw on your experience with such practical matters."

"I have my own concern," Cristina said. "Elena certainly feels great affection for Santiago; she is, in fact, quite smitten with him. But I do not regard love alone as a sound basis for a lasting marriage."

"We are, I'm glad to see, in complete agreement about that," Doña Josefina said. "However, my hope would be that Santiago and Elena would agree to an engagement of at least six months, during which time we, as their elders, should educate them as to the serious practical dimension of marriage, and watch carefully to be sure that their romantic friendship has the potential to grow into a strong partnership."

"Very well put," Cristina replied. "So how do we proceed from here?"

"A first step," Doña Josefina went on, "is to consult the young people about their wishes. If, as I'm confident they will be, they are agreeable, then the marriage banns should be announced this coming Sunday. During the months to come, I will give Santiago increased responsibilities in managing the Mendoza properties in New Mexico. I hope you, Javier, will take him in hand too and acquaint him with how you conduct your business."

The conversation soon devolved into a general discussion of recent events—the skirmish with a Native war party in the north, the killing of the wolf, and the news that Brother Gustavo had been taken ill and that his fellow inquisitors intended to leave town the next day in the company of the soldiers bearing a proclamation to be delivered to pueblos in the south.

"A lot is happening all at once," Carlos remarked as he and Inéz walked back to the Beltráns' with Javier and Cristina.

"Hmmm," she murmured, apparently lost in thought.

"You didn't say a word during our discussion with Doña Josefina," he observed.

"I thought I had said it all when Doña Josefina asked me for my opinion of Elena a few days ago. I am very happy for her, and for both families," she said, glancing at Javier and Cristina.

Carlos smiled at them too, and it seemed to him they were all enveloped in a warm glow. "I'll stop by tomorrow morning," he told her as they parted at the door to the Beltrán place.

Clouds were piling up in the western sky, and as he walked toward his home he saw that all of Santa Fe except a small distant area was shadowed by the looming clouds. In that area a strong beam of light poured through a break in the clouds onto a spot across from the ruins of the San Miguel Chapel and onto Pascal's caravan, which was parked there.

As Don Carlos watched, the clouds shifted and the beam of light moved across the landscape. It progressed slowly from the Barrio de Analco, where he'd first noticed it, across the Santa Fe River, past a house on the north side of the river, up the path past the old Tiburcio place, and finally to the spot where Carlos was having new rooms added to his house.

The shaft of sunlight seemed to hover there as he walked across the plaza and down the lane to the back of his house. None of Don Carlos's work crew was in view. Apparently they were on their siesta break. Looking into the corral, Don Carlos, who had now been joined by Gordo, could see the sunlight reflecting off the water in the posthole that was going to become a well. Finally the clouds began to move again and closed above him, and the beam of light vanished.

Someone was calling him, "Don Alfonso! Don Alfonso!" It was Dolores. She was approaching across the field from Pedro's stable. Gordo ran over to her and licked her now-healed left hand, which caused her to laugh. "Did you see the sunbeam?" she asked.

"Yes; it was a lovely sight."

"It looked," she went on, "like I feel on the inside — full of light!"

"That's wonderful!" he replied as he put an arm around her shoulder and gave her a hug. "What's this in your hand?"

"It's another note that was wrapped around one of the sugar lumps Pascal hands out after performances. I went to one an hour ago and after it was over, he called to me. He reached out and took my hand, the one that used to be crippled. Then he said, 'What happened here?'

"I didn't know what to say, so I made up something about having gone to sleep and found it had healed when I woke up.

"Then he said the strangest thing. 'Someone must love you' — those were his exact words. He climbed into his caravan and when he came out, one of his monkeys was sitting on his shoulder with a lump of sugar wrapped in paper in its hand. 'Prospero wants to give this to you,' he said, and Prospero jumped down, came over to me, and handed the present to me. I didn't know what to say except Thank you, so I took it and walked away. But no one can read the message on the paper."

"Show me," Don Carlos said.

Dolores handed him the paper and he read the words *Amor vincit omnia.*

"It means Love conquers all," he told her.

"I like that," she said, beaming.

"It makes me feel good too," he replied.

24

Zoila

*D*olores stayed long enough to put Gordo through his paces, telling him in quick succession to roll over, catch his tail, beg, and bark. "You're a smart dog," she declared, giving him a pat on the head. Gordo wagged his tail enthusiastically, so Dolores bent down and gave him a hug. Then she excused herself. "I need to get home to help María with dinner."

About half an hour after Dolores went off, everyone else began to arrive. Orfeo returned first, saying that he'd been to see Marisol Díaz during the siesta period. Rubén and Lázaro came back next, explaining that they'd had lunch with their aunt Rosa Lugo, Ana and José Lugo's mother. "Aunt Rosa is upset," Rubén reported, "because the old man who has employed her for many years is moving in with his sister and won't need her any more. I hope Ana and José can help her out." Then Raul Trigales's hired hands, who turned out to be brothers named Tavio and Pablo Flores, arrived with two wagonloads of building materials. Finally, Pedro came by and offered to help for a few hours.

After introductions were made all around, Don Carlos realized that he had better suggest a division of labor. "Let's begin," he said, "by unloading the wagons in the lane on the west side of the house. The corral is nearly done;

Pedro and I can finish it by dinnertime. Tavio and Pablo can start tearing down the old stable; be careful to preserve the old stall divisions and doors for use in the new one. Orfeo, you've already measured out the space the groom's room will occupy. Work with Lázaro and Rubén, and see if you can construct the frame for a four-stall stable with a small room for storing hay and tools. You put the frame for Dr. Velarde's house together very quickly. With luck we might get this one up before we quit tonight."

The men tossed around a few ideas, but everyone was soon at work. It took Carlos and Pedro less than two hours to close the last gaps in the corral fence. They then joined Tavio and Pablo in tearing down the old stable. That work went quickly too. Meanwhile, Orfeo, Lázaro, and Rubén had made good progress on assembling the beams for the walls and roof of the new stable. Things would have gone more slowly had it not been that the beams Raul Trigales had supplied were already notched and ready to be fitted together.

Don Carlos called for a ten-minute break. Pedro had to leave and Orfeo needed to feed the horses, who were watching warily from the far corner of the new corral. The feeding chore done, Orfeo came back to the building site and said, "With six of us to lift the walls into place and secure them, we ought to have the stable's frame up in less than an hour."

"Let's get to it, then," Don Carlos replied.

A teamwork effort by the men, all of whom except Carlos were experienced with barn-raisings, lifted the frame and fitted its parts together in a sequence of quick maneuvers.

The six men stepped back to admire their handiwork. With a young man's energy, Orfeo suggested, "If everyone's willing to keep working, we can put the old stable's stall doors and walls in place before dinner. Even though the horses are spending the night out now, it will be good to have the stable more than half done."

No one complained about keeping going. These men were used to long hours and hard work. But Orfeo's mention of dinner reminded Don Carlos that he had nothing prepared to feed his helpers. He was about to excuse himself to start trying to put a meal together when María and Dolores arrived. "Pedro told us," María said, "that you probably needed help with dinner. If you'll show us what you have in the larder, we'll prepare something."

"Bless you," was the best a very relieved Don Carlos could think of to say. He led them into the kitchen and brought out all the vegetables he had on hand. María and Dolores looked at each other. "Doesn't your neighbor,

Gilberto Barrera, have some chickens?" María asked Carlos. "I could go next door and…"

"No, no," Carlos said. "I'll go."

He was back within minutes holding two freshly killed chickens by their feet. María and Dolores met him at the kitchen door, took them, and went to work plucking. "Chicken stew it is, then," María declared, as feathers flew. "Give us at least two hours," she added.

Two hours later María had a large stew ready to serve. Since Tavio and Pablo had excused themselves to go back to the Trigales place and eat dinner there, only Orfeo, Lázaro, and Rubén remained as Don Carlos's dinner guests. Seeing that there was plenty of food, Carlos invited María and Dolores to stay, but they demurred, saying that they had many chores to do at home.

Don Carlos poured wine and Orfeo set out bowls. A knock came at the kitchen door. Gordo ducked outside through his doggy door and began barking happily. Orfeo went to see who was there and found Don Carlos's former lodgers, Alejandro, Gonzalo, and Luis. "Oh!" Alejandro said apologetically. "We don't want to interrupt your meal. We just stopped by to tell you that we're leaving very early tomorrow morning, and we wanted to wish you well before we go."

It took some persuading, but Don Carlos finally got the three soldiers to agree to come in and share the chicken stew. "It sure will beat Presidio food," Gonzalo said as he accepted Carlos's offer. At that moment Carlos realized that he felt a great deal of affection for the three young men. He would miss seeing them around town once they left on their mission.

"Have you learned the contents of the message you're supposed to deliver?" he asked.

"It's a proclamation inviting the leaders of all the pueblos in New Mexico to come to Santa Fe for a special festival day late in June," Alejandro replied. "As a gesture of peace and friendship, Governor Peralta is promising to confirm certain rights of the Pueblo people."

"I like the sound of that," Carlos said. "Do you know which pueblos you're supposed to visit?"

"All of them south of Albuquerque, including Zuñi."

"Zuñi is far from any Spanish settlement," Don Carlos said. "And it's near an area frequented by Navajo tribesmen, many of them hostile."

"We're part of a squad of seven men," Alejandro said. "We ought to be able to defend ourselves. Oh—I also wanted to tell you that the three of us were assigned the southern pueblos because we'd traveled that part of the Camino Real with you last year."

"But several of the southern pueblos aren't anywhere close to the Camino Real," Don Carlos said.

Luis shrugged. "A soldier's life is never logical."

"That's true," Gonzalo put in. "It's surprising that Captain Posada didn't send us to the northern pueblos on routes we'd never been on before."

"Some of what we do is logical," Alejandro began.

Don Carlos, sensing that a new topic for debate — the illogic of army life — had emerged, forestalled him. "Please join us at the table," he said.

They all squeezed in around the kitchen table — closely watched by Gordo, who demonstrated the tricks the soldiers had taught him and was rewarded with many treats. At the end of the meal Orfeo brought out his guitar and sang a New Mexican folksong.

> De tus hermosos cabellos
> me darás para un cordón,
> y yo te daré ellos
> la vida y el corazón.

All three of the soldiers were from rural parts of New Mexico, and they also knew many traditional four-line *versos*; each soldier contributed at least one that he'd learned as a child. The simple melodies and romantic words created a mellow mood that stayed with Don Carlos long after Alejandro, Gonzalo, and Luis had gone back to the Presidio and Orfeo, Rubén, and Lázaro had gone to bed.

That night Don Carlos had three dreams, waking up after each.

The first dream seemed to be set in Puebla, south of Mexico City. The night air was hot and humid, and Carlos was seated on a firm cushion, meditating. He heard a soft knock at the door and the rustle of silk as Zoila slipped in from the hallway. She was wearing a long-sleeved blouse and loose-fitting trousers. She pulled a cushion over in front of him and settled down on it cross-legged. She sat silently for several minutes, studying him with a friendly expression. Finally she asked, "Which chakra was your attention focused on when I entered the room?"

"The third chakra, the one in front of my backbone just below my diaphragm."

"Tell me again what realm of life you associate with the third chakra."

"In my experience it's connected with the social world—family, house-holding, friendships, community."

"Good," she replied. After a period of silence she spoke again. "You have been careless about your life in the world."

He was astonished. "How can you say that? I'm more immersed in householding, friendships, and the social life of a community than I was in any previous life."

Conceding little to his defense of himself, Zoila said, "You have made a beginning by starting to build a proper *sala*. But you have neglected many other things, dismissing them as mere conventions, even though adapting to them would make your life more orderly. Before the month is out you must hire a cook and acquire a set of matching dishes, at least eight each of dinner plates and cups and saucers."

He was about to protest that he didn't see how such material things could be important to his pursuit of the Unknown Way, but Zoila's image disappeared abruptly.

Wide awake now, he reviewed Zoila's comments and felt slightly annoyed. It seemed that she was being critical of his bare-bones life, a way of living in which he had taken considerable pride. The Desert Fathers and Hindu holy men, he told himself, assigned no importance to conventional appearances and material comforts. Why should he?

It took Don Carlos an unusually long time to get back to sleep. Gordo seemed to sense that he was upset and came over and put a paw on his hand and gave him a solemn look. Gordo's concern softened Don Carlos's heart. He put his arm around his little dog and pulled him to his chest. Within minutes he was asleep.

Zoila now entered a second dream. This time she was wearing a beautiful silk outfit of an unusual design. An apricot-colored skirt flared out beneath a wide-sleeved tunic in the same color that came down almost to her knees. Blue flowers were embroidered on it. He wasn't sure where the dream was located, although it seemed to be the *sala* of a wealthy home.

Once again, Don Carlos was seated on a meditation cushion. Zoila gracefully sat down in front of him on a rolled-up rug. "What chakra were you focused on as I came into the room?" she asked.

"The fourth chakra, the heart chakra."

"What thoughts or emotions arose from that chakra?"

"A soft warmth. I would call it caring," he replied. "I was aware of the many friendships that have come into my life in Santa Fe—with José, Pedro,

María, and Dolores, to name a few of the most important, but above all with Inéz."

"You have changed your mind a great deal about this Inéz since we first talked a year ago."

"Yes, I scarcely knew her then. I was drawn to her as a splendid fencer and a provocative woman. That image prevented me from seeing more deeply into her character."

"But you continued to pursue her."

"Yes," he said, "It was the attraction of danger and sexual allure that drew me toward her. But over time our friendship has blossomed into something richer."

"And what are you going to do about her?" Zoila asked.

"Do? I can only wait to see where our friendship leads. She's made it plain that marriage cannot even be discussed, because her previous experiences of sexual intimacy involved nothing but degradation."

"Are you saying that joining with her in Tantric mediation is unthinkable?"

"Unthinkable? No, I think about it quite a lot."

"Carlos, Carlos. You know that the Tantric way encompasses chakra meditation, which you do on a regular basis. There's no reason why you can't teach Inéz chakra meditation."

"I could do that. But—it might be a parallel practice, but that doesn't address the issue of intimate touch, on which Inéz has set definite limits. She sees no way that we could become lovers."

"Carlos," Zoila said, seeming a bit impatient, "the two of you are already lovers. Isn't it true that you have often shared a bed with her?"

"Yes."

"Were both of you comfortable in doing so?"

"Yes."

He started to say more, but she cut him off. "Intimacy and love take many forms. Go back to your fourth chakra and explore your great love for Inéz."

Before Don Carlos could say anything or ask a question, Zoila was gone.

Awake again, Don Carlos puzzled about the mystery that his friendship with Inéz had become. How could he fully honor her feelings? He lay there thinking about the subject without coming to any great insights. His only thought was that he needed to draw on his practice of Watching to see what time brought.

Feeling tired, he turned over and fell asleep at once.

His third dream of the night was set in his Santa Fe home, only it was his house as it would be once his renovation project was complete. As the dream began he was meditating in the courtyard, surrounded by many fragrant flowering plants. Bright sunlight was pouring down, but the temperature was comfortable.

Zoila came around the back corner of his house, opened the courtyard's gate, and sat down next to him on a bench. She was wearing a white gown in the style of the ancient Greeks, with one shoulder exposed and a cord around her waist. She had a strong golden aura.

Her initial words surprised him. She picked up her foot, which was bare, and examined the bottom of it. "The lanes that lead to your house," she remarked, "have a lot of pebbles in them. It's a good thing that in my current state my feet scarcely touch the ground."

Don Carlos wanted to ask about her current state, as she had called it, but she immediately went on. "Which chakra was foremost in your consciousness before I arrived?"

"My fifth chakra, the throat chakra."

"To whom are you not expressing yourself?" she asked.

"I would like to talk more with Inéz about marriage."

"That's true, but it's not as though the topic never comes up. No, think again."

Don Carlos was perplexed. He had many secrets he didn't share with most people and a few secrets he shared with almost no one, but he didn't think that was what Zoila was asking about.

When he failed to answer, she prompted him. "Why haven't you spoken with Pascal about your past and present lives?"

"I'm not sure what his motive is in coming to Santa Fe. I don't trust him."

"Has he behaved in a threatening way?"

"No. Quite the opposite. He doesn't seem at all like the sorcerer who was my adversary through many lifetimes."

"Perhaps he is patiently waiting for you to take the first step." She stood up and held out her hand to him. He had assumed that she was a ghost and that her touch would be cold, but when he took her hand he felt warmth flooding through his body.

He stood up. Only then did he notice that he was wearing a white outfit not unlike Pascal's. Before he could reflect on this fact, Zoila took his arm and gently steered him out the courtyard gate to the fence of the corral. Eagle was there and came over and nuzzled his arm, nickering softly.

They moved away from the corral and walked slowly in the direction of the old Tiburcio place. Gesturing toward the house as they passed it, she asked, "Am I right in believing that this is where you had those erotically charged fencing bouts with Inéz?" He nodded.

They continued past the house and on toward the river. After a while Zoila inquired, "Do you remember our auras after the final time we did Tantric practice together?"

"Yes, both of us had strong golden auras that merged into one."

"Have you noticed our auras now?"

Don Carlos followed her suggestion and saw that they both had golden auras that merged into a single, even more intensely golden one. "The same," he said.

They had reached the Santa Fe River. He thought she might take the footbridge, but instead she led him into the water and playfully kicked a few splashes into the air. Each drop of water took on one of the colors of a rainbow. "I don't get to do magic often," she said, "and we don't really have time for foolishness today. But I'm very happy being with you."

"And I with you," he replied. He opened his mouth to ask a question, but she put her fingers over his lips and said, "There's no time for questions either. It is difficult for me to get away, especially in a form in which we can touch. Let's not waste our time together."

They were crossing the narrow field north of Canyon Road and about to reach the point at which it joined the southbound Pecos Road. Don Carlos saw Pascal's caravan ahead of them, parked on the west side of the Pecos Road across from the ruins of the San Miguel Chapel. Perhaps he tensed his grip on Zoila's arm, because she said, "You must go forward with this. Talking with Pascal is your major unfinished fifth-chakra business."

He stopped walking and burst out, "But you don't know my history with this man. He is a sorcerer whose secret name is Don Malvolio. Centuries ago he and my master were rivals to inherit the title of Great Magus. When my master, Don Serafino Romero, won the competition, Malvolio became embittered and sought to kill every brujo who had apprenticed to Don Serafino."

"What was the nature of the competition to be successor to the Great Magus?"

"Don Malvolio and Don Serafino, as the Great Magus's most advanced students, were told to master transformations. Don Serafino mastered a technique of complete transformation, the ability to change himself into an animal form."

"Just as you are able to do."

"Yes. Don Serafino taught me his method. But I suspect that the method can't be taught to someone unless that person has a natural aptitude for it."

"How did Don Malvolio fail?"

"He, too, achieved transformations, but only by ingesting a concoction that he formulated. His size changed and he temporarily became incredibly strong, but he did not fully transform into animal form."

"And how did you come into conflict with Don Malvolio?" Zoila asked. "You said you had a history with him."

"In my third life I thwarted him when he attempted to gain control of a gemstone known as Montezuma's Emerald, which had powers that could have given him control over the known world."

"And what happened as a result?"

"In my fifth life he managed to strike back at me with the aid of a dancer named Violeta Mata. She gave me drugged wine that left me in a stupor, and I was unable to prevent Malvolio from cutting my throat and killing me."

"Ah!" Zoila said. "I can understand why you're loath to have any dealings with Pascal. But he has come out of his caravan and is looking expectantly in your direction."

"Don't you mean our direction?" Don Carlos asked.

"No. He can't see me. But he can see you, and you must speak with him. This is unfinished business." She delivered these last two words with great force and pulled him forward to a spot no more than ten feet from where Pascal was standing.

Pascal tipped his hat and said, "I've been hoping you would come by to talk." There the dream ended.

Don Carlos slept soundly until his usual rising time. He got up, meditated for two hours, and then helped Orfeo fix breakfast for themselves and their overnight guests, Lázaro and Rubén. Looking up from his bowl of cornmeal, Lázaro said, "I'm sorry, Don Alfonso, but we need to return to Tesuque by nightfall. We'll have to leave here around mid-afternoon."

"I understand," Don Carlos replied. "You've been a huge help. But since you need to leave, perhaps we should concentrate on building and erecting the wood frame for the larger room we're adding. Raising it is easiest with lots of workers to do the heavy lifting."

Orfeo spoke up. "I've checked over the beams that Señor Trigales gave us, and there are enough to frame the larger room. We ought to be able to assemble them this morning and raise them into place before Lázaro and Rubén have to leave."

"Excellent!" Don Carlos replied. "The lighter and more time-consuming steps can be done by Orfeo and me later. Let's get started."

Shortly after the four men had moved outside and begun the day's work, Raul Trigales's hired hands arrived. Don Carlos asked them to start making door openings in the south side of the old house that would connect with the two new rooms. They at once launched into the dusty job of removing adobe blocks from the old house's wall.

The dreams Don Carlos had had the previous night remained a strong mental presence as he directed and assisted in the house renovation project. Zoila had set the agenda for the tasks he needed to undertake. He held in his mind's eye the first dream, in which she had said he must find a cook. Even though Orfeo sometimes helped with cooking, it had been up to Carlos to plan and prepare most of their meals. But there was a possible solution in that Rubén's and Lázaro's Aunt Rosa was about to lose her job. Having learned that Thursday was her day off, he excused himself and went to see her.

Rosa Lugo had a small, one-room house in the Barrio de Analco. Despite his long friendship with her son José and daughter Ana, Don Carlos had seldom visited her at her home. He went to the front door and knocked. Rosa, a tiny Pueblo Indian woman, answered his knock. A worried expression came on her face. "Good morning, Don Alfonso. Is everything all right with Ana and José?"

"They are both fine. I am here on my own account."

"Please come in," she said, inviting him into the room that served every purpose: cooking, eating, working, socializing, and sleeping.

"We have known each other for quite a while," Don Carlos began.

"Yes," she replied, "and I am very grateful for what you have done for my children. I do not forget that you saved José's life, and now you are helping him with his studies to be a medicine man. You have also been a good friend to Ana, both when she worked for your brother-in-law and now that she serves in Señor Trigales's household."

"I am honored by their friendship, and they are credits to their mother," Don Carlos said. "But I am here today because Lázaro and Rubén told me that you are soon to be out of a job. Ever since Pedro and María moved out, I have lacked a full-time cook. Would you consider taking a job as my cook?"

Her face expressed relief mixed with happiness. "I would be glad to.

But do you need me to start right away? It will be two weeks before my employer, Matías Villegas, goes to live with his sister. He is old and unwell. I feel I should stay to help him until he moves out."

"That fits well with my needs, Rosa. It will be at least two weeks before I have a room that you could occupy at my place."

Carlos's proposal obviously pleased Rosa and they agreed that she would start cooking for Don Carlos and Orfeo as soon as her job with Villegas was over. They would settle on details of her responsibilities at a later date.

Don Carlos was pleased by how well things had worked in regard to his need for a cook, but he also knew that the heart-chakra work Zoila said he needed to do with Inéz would not be so easy.

He left Rosa Lugo's house and headed directly for the Beltráns', where he expected to find Inéz beginning preparations for lunch. The cook situation had been straightforward: find an appropriate person for the job and offer it to her. But nothing was so straightforward with Inéz. He felt he needed to be much more indirect in approaching the topic of love with her. He had a plan. He only hoped that she would be receptive to what he was going to ask her to do.

He went to the kitchen door of the Beltran house and knocked. Rita and Inéz were engaged in preparing lunch. Both looked up, and Inéz waved him in. "Good morning," she said in a more formal way than was her custom. "How are your renovations going?"

"Very well, but I need your advice. Can you take half an hour off to visit the site?"

"Can't you see that we're busy?" she replied impatiently.

"Yes, I can," he said, "and I knew you'd be preparing lunch, but can't Rita handle that for a little while?"

"And why can't you just tell me what you want to know," she replied, "and I'll give you my answers here and now?"

"Please, Inéz. It's important that you see the situation. We're at a crucial point in our renovations. By late this afternoon we'll be farther along and you might not like what you'll see."

"All right," she said. "Let's make this quick." She tossed her apron aside and said to Rita, "Just keep rolling out tortillas. I'll be back soon."

Don Carlos held the door for Inéz, and they set out walking quickly to the plaza and then across it. To Carlos's great surprise, she said, "Marriage seems to be on everyone's mind this morning."

"I thought that was a topic we had agreed not to discuss."

"I'm not talking about us. I'm talking about Elena and Santiago. Javier and Cristina told Elena that Doña Josefina had proposed a union between her and Santiago, and he came over half an hour ago and formally asked her for her hand. This was done in the *sala*, in the presence of her parents. I watched from the hallway. It was the prettiest thing you ever saw!"

"Ah," Carlos said. "I am very happy for them."

"There's more," Inéz went on as they neared the south side of the plaza. "Last night Santiago's older brothers arrived back from the battlefields in the north. Apparently they had a conversation with their aunt, and—I have this from Jacinta, who stopped by for a recipe—this morning Doña Josefina made an appointment to see Ignacio and Pilar Peralta at the governor's residence early this afternoon."

Carlos was only mildly astonished. "She's going to propose that Antonio and Juliana and Julio and Victoria marry?"

"I'll be very surprised if she doesn't, and I'll be even more surprised if the Peraltas don't accept her proposal, and do so eagerly. Just think! One daughter, Juliana, married to a titled aristocrat who is to inherit a profitable winery in Spain, and the other twin, Victoria, married to the future owner of several rich silver mines in New Spain."

"Pilar Peralta's dream come true," Carlos said with a smile. "Next I suppose you're going to tell me that Marco Cabrera has proposed to Ariel Padilla."

"I think we might hear just that any day now."

"Hmm," he said. "You seem to know something I don't. If I had to bet, I would have said that Orfeo and Marisol are next in line for the altar."

"Perhaps so," she replied with a laugh. "But why not Diego and Ana, as long as we're marrying off all our friends and neighbors? Ana confided in me only yesterday that they've had serious discussions about getting married. The only issue seems to be when, not whether."

They had arrived at the building site. Don Carlos's five workers were busily engaged. Tavio and Pablo had cut a door through the old house's adobe wall where the large bedroom was going to be. They had moved over to the other side and were preparing to remove adobe bricks to open a door between the *sala* and the groom's room. Orfeo, Lázaro, and Rubén were making excellent progress on assembling the frame for the large bedroom. But they all stopped working and looked up when Don Carlos and Inéz arrived on the scene. Was this, he wondered, out of simple politeness, or because Inéz was such a beautiful sight to see? Probably a bit of both, he decided.

"So what urgent topic do you want to discuss?" she asked.

"I would like you to bring your woman's eye to bear on several things, mainly how many doors and windows to make and where to put them. The door Tavio and Pablo have cut between the *sala* and the master bedroom seems the logical way to move between those two rooms. As for windows in that room, I believe you suggested that they face into the courtyard, but wouldn't it be nice to have one overlooking the lane to the east that would catch the rays of the rising sun?"

Inéz studied the situation and said, "I'd been thinking about privacy, but I agree with you about greeting the rising sun. Add a window on the east side."

"What about the door between the *sala* and the groom's room? Any opinion on that?"

Again Inéz fell silent. "I don't like the groom's access to his room being through the *sala*," she said. "Picture a rainy day and a groom with muddy boots. Besides, you wouldn't want him coming through the *sala* while you're entertaining friends or holding a lunch or dinner party."

"What's the option then?" Don Carlos asked.

"Put the door to the groom's room on the west side of the house and extend the veranda to run just past it. The groom can enter from the veranda directly into his room. Also, you should make a door on the south side of his room that leads into the stable."

"We can do that, can't we, Orfeo?" Don Carlos asked his carpenter, who agreed that it was possible.

"One more thing," Inéz said. "There should be a door to the *sala* into the courtyard. Also, if I were to live here, an unlikely prospect I hasten to add, I would want a door from the master bedroom into the courtyard, and a small veranda with a bench next to the door where I could sit and enjoy the flowers and herbs in the garden."

"I look forward to that day," Carlos whispered playfully in her ear.

"Don't assume too much," she replied. "Now I must get back to work."

As they returned to the Beltrán house, Carlos told Inéz that he had hired Rosa Lugo to be his cook. She gave him a questioning look. "Did anything special happen to you last night or in your morning meditation?" she asked. "You seem highly motivated to deal with things that you've allowed to drift for months, like your need for a cook and for a larger house."

"Actually, yes," Carlos replied, "I've been wanting to tell you about three dreams I had last night. Each one had to do with a particular chakra, and Zoila appeared to tell me what each of them meant."

"I suppose she was naked again," Inéz said.

"No. She was fully clothed. Don't you want to hear anything about the dreams' contents?"

"Of course, but hurry. We're almost home."

"The very abbreviated version," he replied, "is that she told me I should be doing three things: hiring a cook, asking your advice on my house renovations, and going to talk with Pascal."

"Good Lord! Talk with Pascal!" she exclaimed. "You've already done the first two. Do you really think you should do the third?"

"Zoila seemed very sure that I should. She called it unfinished business, and whether it was truly Zoila or my inner convictions taking the form of a dream, I agree with her. Pascal has been unthreatening, and that seems consistent with what we heard him tell Leandro about wanting my help with a transformation he hoped to make."

"But we agree that you don't have the power he thinks you have."

"True enough."

"So won't he be furious with you when he learns you don't have the knowledge he desires?"

"Possibly."

"That answer," she said, "tells me that you're going to talk with him."

"Yes."

They had reached the kitchen door. "Oh, Carlos," she said. "At times you frighten me — or perhaps I'm frightened for myself, or for you — I don't know. These moments confuse me."

"I'll be careful," he promised.

"That's what you always say," she replied as she opened the door and went in. She closed it quietly behind her.

Carlos returned home, helped Orfeo prepare lunch for his work crew, and then joined them in raising the frame for the master bedroom. Lázaro and Rubén left to go home to Tesuque Pueblo, and Tavio and Pablo said they'd better get back to their regular jobs for Raul Trigales. Carlos's house, which had until then been noisy with activity, fell silent. Don Carlos told Orfeo, "Take a break; you've earned it. Go see Marisol. We can plan what to do next later this afternoon or this evening." Orfeo went off happily.

Don Carlos knew what he needed to do, and the sooner the better. He had no good reason to delay acting on Zoila's insistence that he had unfinished fifth-chakra business. He went to the kitchen door, telling Gordo not to come along. "You'll just get into a scrap with one of Pascal's monkeys."

Taking the same route that he and Zoila had followed in the dream, Don Carlos walked past the Tiburcio place, across the Santa Fe River, and on to the junction of Canyon Road and the Pecos Road. At that point he could see Pascal's caravan ahead, but the scene was different from what it had been in his dream. A dozen or more children were seated on the ground next to the caravan, expectantly waiting for a show to begin.

Shortly after Don Carlos arrived and sat down behind the children, along with three women who were most likely their mothers, Pascal opened the window in the side of the caravan that served as a stage. He looked out, and on seeing Carlos in the audience, he gave him a friendly smile. "I have a special show today," he announced. "My three animal companions—monkeys named Che and Prospero, and a very fine parrot named Polly—will enact a parable of sorts. See if you can figure out its meaning."

Pascal then placed a green crystal on one corner of the little stage and ducked out of sight. A moment later Che, dressed in a black outfit that resembled the uniforms of Spanish colonial officials, came on stage and began moving back and forth as though he was searching for something. His movements gradually became more agitated. A boy sitting in front of Carlos whispered to a companion, "He looks like he's getting upset."

The second monkey, Prospero, dressed like a farmer, came on the stage. He crouched down as though he didn't want Che to notice him, and then he began to creep up on the green crystal. Finally he grabbed it and started to run off with it, but Che saw him and jumped across the whole stage and began to wrestle with him, trying to snatch the green crystal. Just as it seemed that he was about to succeed, Pascal's parrot, Polly, came onto the stage and pecked Che hard on the back of his head. He fell down, unconscious or dead, and the curtain closed.

During an intermission of several minutes, the children in the audience whispered to each other in an animated way. Don Carlos was amused to see that they were trying to figure out a story that he knew first hand. It had taken place during his third life. Che (Malvolio) had been seeking to possess a gem, Montezuma's Emerald, with great powers, and Prospero (Carlos) had been doing his best to keep Malvolio from getting the emerald. As they fought each other, a Mayan woman whose granddaughter was the emerald's protector had rushed forward and cut Malvolio's throat.

Pascal's voice from offstage announced that the second act was about to begin. "It takes place many, many years after the first act."

Polly the parrot entered first. At her end of the stage she did a little

296 —————

dance, hopping up and down and turning in circles while opening her wings. "Pretty Polly! Pretty Polly!" she said. Prospero, dressed in brown trousers and a white shirt open at the collar, entered from the other side of the stage. Polly and he moved toward each other. Polly said, "Pretty boy! Pretty boy!" and pecked Prospero on the cheek, "Kiss! Kiss!" she said, and he responded by stroking her wing and kissing her beak. Then Che, dressed from head to toe in black, entered and crept toward the two lovers. He was carrying a small club.

The children in the crowd sensed that something bad was about to happen, and one who couldn't restrain himself shouted, "Look out!" But it was too late. The black-clad villain hit Prospero on the head, and Prospero fell down on his back with his feet in the air. Don Carlos, recalling how Violeta had taken him as a lover, then drugged his wine and watched as Don Malvolio slit his throat, knew that Prospero was dead. The curtain closed.

Pascal's voice came from back of the curtain. "Act Three follows immediately. It tells a story that hasn't happened yet and may never happen. Watch closely."

The curtain opened. Only the two monkeys, Che and Prospero, were on stage. They looked at each other and shook hands. Then they embraced and patted each other on the back. Finally they linked arms and danced a jig, each waving his free hand in the air. The dance continued for several minutes with amusing variations on popular New Mexican folk dances. At last they stopped, faced the audience, and bowed. The curtain closed, and then reopened. Che and Prospero had been joined by Polly. All three bowed, though in truth Polly's bow was more a matter of tilting her head. The audience's loud applause was accompanied by much laughter.

The curtain closed again. Soon thereafter Pascal emerged from the caravan with the three actors perched on his shoulders and arms. The children swarmed around him, and he rewarded several by telling them they could let Che, Prospero, and Polly sit on their shoulders. "I'll be back for them soon," he announced, "but first please allow me to speak to an old acquaintance who is in the audience today."

Pascal stepped away from the children and came over to Don Carlos. "I've been hoping you would come by to talk," he said, proffering his hand, which Carlos shook. "As you can see, I will be busy with the children for a while, but please come back. Would you be able to return in an hour or so?"

"Yes, I'll be back in an hour."

"Excellent," Pascal said, turning to rejoin the children and the three actors, who were the objects of great admiration. But over his shoulder, he added with a smile, "Perhaps it would be best if you brought the wine."

25

Pascal

As Carlos was heading home, Pedro intercepted him. "Good," Pedro said. "I don't have to walk all the way to your place."

"So what do you want to tell me?" Carlos asked.

"People are nervous about having practically the whole Presidio garrison away."

"I can understand that."

"You're beginning to sound a lot like me," Pedro observed.

"How so?"

"You're not as talkative as usual."

"I have a lot on my mind," Carlos replied, "including an appointment I just made to talk with Pascal."

Pedro looked at Carlos speculatively. "This is Pascal, the man Inéz says you believe is Don Malvolio."

"Yes."

"And why do you think this is a good idea?"

"It's a long story," Carlos said. "But first, you wanted to tell me something about people being nervous because there are so few soldiers in the garrison. I thought the town militia, led by Captain Miranda, was supposed to protect us."

"Hmmph!" Pedro snorted. "I don't have much faith in him. Apparently neither does Governor Peralta, since he asked Marco Cabrera to recruit auxiliaries to the militia from among his friends. Cabrera got wind of my military experience and asked if I would meet his recruits at the Presidio for musket practice. I wanted to ask you to help me."

"I'll help. When is this practice session to take place?"

"About ten minutes from now."

"Oh. Should I go home and get my musket?

"No need. Everyone will be issued muskets from the Presidio armory. That way all the auxiliaries will have the same arms and ammunition. Let's go."

Carlos and Pedro walked together to the Presidio. On the way over, Pedro allowed himself one more comment on the topic of Pascal. "If you ask me," he said, "meeting with your old adversary is just plain dumb."

"I didn't ask you," Carlos replied, "though you're probably right. But I also get the impression that he's come to town to talk with me and won't leave until he has."

Pedro grunted, but didn't comment further.

Once at the Presidio, Carlos and Pedro found that Marco had gathered nearly all the male members of the town's upper social ranks. A sergeant from the armory passed out two muskets apiece, plus musket balls and powder. No instruction in the use of a musket was necessary. Men of their social status all owned weapons. They all walked to the far northern part of the Presidio grounds and fired a few shots at wooden targets to familiarize themselves with the new muskets. The session then concluded with a brief speech from Marco Cabrera.

Knowing that he was already late for his appointment with Pascal, Carlos excused himself and walked to his house in order to drop off his muskets and ammunition. When he arrived home he found Orfeo in the kitchen. Don Carlos said to him, "I have an appointment that may keep me away all afternoon, but I hope you and I can lay the *sala's* tile floor tomorrow morning. Can you do the preparation for that this afternoon?"

"Yes," Orfeo replied. "I'll get to work right away."

Orfeo headed for the *sala*, and Carlos went into his bedroom and put the new muskets in a corner. He then chose a bottle of wine from his supply and made his way across the river to Pascal's caravan. He noticed that Pascal had a visitor, Juan Archibeque. They were seated on benches on either side of a rectangular table. For a moment he thought his first serious talk with Pascal would be diluted by the presence of Juan, but when Juan saw Carlos approaching, he stood up and shook Pascal's hand, saying, "I'm sure this will work out. I'll be on my way," and with a friendly nod in Carlos's direction, he left.

Before Carlos could say anything, Pascal volunteered some information. "Juan and I were talking about the disposition of my caravan and my animals when I leave Santa Fe, which will probably be quite soon. I have some French blood in me and that has made me particularly comfortable with

Juan. I also feel a certain affinity for him in that he and I are outsiders to this community."

Carlos sat down and opened the bottle of wine he'd brought, and Pascal passed two glasses to him. As soon as their glasses were full, Pascal proposed a toast, "To learning more."

"An admirable endeavor," Carlos replied.

One of Pascal's monkeys was sitting on the table to the right of Pascal, who now pointed to him and said, "While we were waiting for you to come by, Che and I played a game of chess." Carlos turned his attention to a chess board that was on the table between Che and Pascal. The black pieces were closest to Che, the white pieces nearer Pascal. From the arrangement of the pieces on the board, it looked to Carlos as if Che was winning.

"Che always wants to take the villain's roles in our plays," Pascal commented, "and I let him have the black pieces in our chess matches. Not unlike me, he likes to get his way."

"Do you also let him win?" Carlos asked.

Pascal looked amused. "What do you think?" he asked. He picked up the white king off the board and gave it to Che, who grabbed it and jumped out of Pascal's reach, waving the king in the air and voicing cries of triumph.

Pascal then turned his attention to Carlos and asked, "Are you wondering why I have come to Santa Fe?"

"Of course," Carlos replied, "but that refers to the present, and don't we have some old business we should discuss first, perhaps clearing the air?"

Not waiting for Carlos to explain further, Pascal said, "Ah, yes. I admit I killed you in your last life, but then in an earlier life you knocked me unconscious, thus enabling an old woman to slit my throat. My action merely evened the score."

"I am willing," Carlos replied, "to accept your point about each of us causing the other's death in a previous life. But your hostility to me didn't end there. More recently you sent your apprentice Leandro and your two daughters to find me for you. And when Leandro failed to identify me for certain, your treatment of him, your adopted son—letting whether he lived or died be decided by the flip of a coin, and then allowing him to be torn limb from limb by ogres—that was utterly despicable."

Pascal became animated. "So you were there!" he exclaimed. "I felt your presence, but couldn't quite credit it, even when the ogre I sent up the slope to search for you didn't return. But when I arrived in Santa Fe and learned that

300 ⎯⎯⎯⎯⎯⎯

the Trigales children had been rescued, I knew that the explanation had to be the intervention of a very powerful brujo."

Carlos wasn't about to let Pascal evade the topic of Leandro's death. "And what about Leandro?" he asked.

Something akin to sadness passed over Pascal's face. "I have done things in my many lives that an ordinary man might well regret, but allowing the ogres to kill Leandro is one of the few deeds I would take back if I could. I have always been prone to intemperate responses. I had counted on Leandro to track you down. His failure to do so annoyed me extremely, and my reaction was both arrogant and cruel."

Pascal's owning that he had been arrogant and cruel mollified Carlos somewhat. Still, there was one mistake Pascal had made that Carlos wanted to point out. "Leandro actually suggested that Don Alfonso Cabeza de Vaca was secretly Don Carlos Buenaventura, but you dismissed it out of hand. What changed your mind?"

"If you overheard my exchange with Leandro, you know that I assumed that you would be an Indian, just as you'd been the two times we'd met face to face. But after collecting the ransom money and dismissing the ogres I went back to Nombre de Dios, where you had killed my strongest apprentice, Mateo Pizarro. I spoke again with the Indian man who'd met you. The only name he recalled for you was an alias, Ricardo de Silva. But since my earlier conversation with him he'd remembered that the horse you'd boarded in Nombre de Dios was named Eagle. That was the final clue I needed."

"I'm surprised that you'd even heard of Eagle," Carlos said.

"Brother Gustavo apparently noticed him during one of his visits to Santa Fe, and happened to mention his name to me."

"And what about Brother Gustavo? He was obsessed with locating a brujo named Carlos because he wanted to do me harm, and you surely knew that when you set him on my trail."

"Ah!" Pascal sighed. "Sometimes one must rely on the means at hand. Yes, Gustavo had personal reasons for pursuing you, and I hoped that his hatred would achieve what Leandro's simple attempt to follow my instructions could not."

"Do you consider Gustavo your apprentice?"

"No. As the leader of the Inquisition in New Spain I couldn't let it be known that I had a personal knowledge of sorcery. Gustavo had an unusual ability to take possession of an animal's mind and manipulate its actions. I didn't have to teach him that, and I suspect it made him vulnerable to being possessed himself. I had to perform an exorcism on him, and after that I took him as a protégé. But I gave him no training in sorcerer's techniques."

"Very well," Carlos said, "but my question as to why you've come to Santa Fe is still on the table."

The word table seemed to set Che into motion. He leaned forward, grabbed several chess pieces, and bounded away with them, not stopping until he reached the caravan's steps. He accompanied this behavior with loud cries that brought Prospero, the other monkey, out of the caravan. The two of them faced off, and Prospero shook a finger at Che in a scolding way. "That word you used," Pascal said, "t-a-b-l-e, is part of an act that we sometimes do. We'll just have to wait for Che to realize that this is a different situation. Would you like a little more wine?"

Carlos had been taking very small sips of wine, wary lest his senses be dulled by alcohol, but the day was still warm and he was thirsty, so he held out his glass for more. "This is actually quite good wine for a country vintage," Pascal commented, filling his glass too.

Since Pascal seemed slow to address his question, Carlos decided to wait him out. Without truly relaxing, he sat in silence. It was, he observed, a lovely day. The sky was clear and a deep blue. He heard a hawk's cry in the distance and some laughter from children who were playing nearby in the Barrio. The sound of the Santa Fe River was faintly audible. Then a bright yellow butterfly of the cloudless sulfur variety flitted into view. It circled above Carlos and Pascal in the uneven pattern of flight that butterflies have before it settled down on Don Carlos's right shoulder. Pascal's face broke into a wide smile. "Ah!" he said. "How nice of Don Serafino to join us."

The butterfly, which was still moving its wings, touched Don Carlos on the neck, a touch from which he took a strange reassurance. But he couldn't resist saying, "I'm surprised by your welcoming tone. I thought you despised him for defeating you in the contest to be the Great Magus's principal successor."

"Yes," Pascal said "I devised a concoction that enabled me to achieve partial transformations, but Serafino achieved a more complete change of form than I did. It was, I must admit, brilliant, and I never learned precisely what his technique entailed. Even Serafino, I believed, had been unable to teach it to any of his apprentices except you. But when I first noticed the bruja known as Manuela Maldonado, I saw that she was a shape-shifter. Not quite the same as you, I know, but I hoped that she might somehow be able to lead me to you."

The yellow butterfly on Don Carlos's shoulder became agitated when Pascal mentioned Manuela. Not sure what this meant, or even if it meant anything, Don Carlos replied, "Manuela has, so far as I know, no connection whatsoever with Don Serafino, and, in any case, the powers of shape-shifters are quite limited."

Pascal gave Don Carlos a piercing look and said, "You mean quite limited compared with what you can do. But shape-shifters are exceedingly rare, so the fact that she's a shape-shifter of any sort suggests unusual powers."

"I suppose so," Don Carlos replied.

"And what about your young friend, Dolores? I saw at once that she is a shape-shifter, and if she was able to heal her injured hand and eye, that indicates impressive powers."

Don Carlos was alarmed that Dolores's name had entered the conversation. In an attempt to shift attention away from her, he said what he truly believed. "She has lost, or nearly lost, her ability to change from human to dog form. As for the healing you observed, I believe I was largely responsible for that."

Pascal sat in silence for a time. Finally he said, "That being the case, I believe you and I are the last of our kind, and even I am your inferior where transformations are concerned. I say the last of our kind, because both of my most advanced apprentices, Mateo Pizarro and Leandro de Luna, are dead, and I know of no living apprentice of Serafino other than you."

"Are you then prepared to tell me why you have sought me out?" Don Carlos asked.

"I intend to do so," Pascal replied, "but you might notice that Che and Pascal, though they've stopped fighting, are restless. I need to distract them with food or they'll start fighting again, and believe me when I say that will be disruptive." Pascal went inside the caravan and returned with two wooden bowls. Each contained a mixture of nuts and dried fruit. The monkeys eagerly grabbed the bowls from Pascal and retreated to separate positions, where they began to eat with gusto.

"I apologize for the interruption," Pascal said. "Now as to my purpose in seeking you out. Let me to tell you a story. You and I belong to different lineages among the Great Magus's successors. Serafino liked to call them the Sun and Moon moieties, with his attached to the sun and mine to the moon.

"As the originator of the Moon Moiety, I have taken diverse identities in my various lifetimes, and in all of them my aim has been to be in the first rank. In addition to being a powerful sorcerer in secret, I have been a leading scholar of ancient texts, a renowned alchemist, an advisor to kings and queens, a high-ranking Spanish colonial official, and, most recently, a priest who served the Holy Office as its Chief Inquisitor in New Spain. In all my lifetimes I have aligned myself with power and sought to accrue more power.

"By contrast, Serafino and his apprentices showed no interest in secular or material power. You are a good example. As far as I know, in your previous lives you have been content to live in humble circumstances among ordinary folk, either Indian or mestizo. Even in your present life, although you were born a Spaniard and inherited a title, you live in a house that's no larger than those occupied by most of the farmers, servants, and artisans in the Barrio de Analco.

"As I approach the end of my many sojourns on Earth—and don't look so skeptical, that's my belief—I've begun to wonder which of us made the better choice, I by seeking power or you by living modestly."

The two monkeys had finished their food and now began to hit the wooden bowls against the bench on which they were seated. A hint of impatience flashed across Pascal's face, and he hissed at them, "Stop it now! I mean it!" That got their attention and both of them crouched down, apparently not wanting to attract any further notice from him.

"The cost of the pursuit of power," Pascal went on, "is high in two respects. The first is that it hardens the heart. The second is that, once attained, power no longer satisfies. I find myself in that position, and my purpose in seeking you out is in my expectation that you will be able to help me in certain ways."

Pascal paused and looked questioningly at Don Carlos, who replied, "I can't tell you whether I'm willing or able to help you unless you specify what you'd like from me."

"A most reasonable observation," Pascal replied; then, as an impish look lifted his deeply lined face, he asked, "Would you like more wine?" Without his touching the wine bottle, it began to slide across the table toward Don Carlos.

"What sort of trick is this?" Don Carlos asked.

Pascal laughed. "Spoken like a true disciple of Serafino, who deplored magic of the sort he called tricks. But I've always enjoyed magic in all its varieties, even the kind that depended on spells, incantations, and the assistance of spirit allies."

Don Carlos had relaxed his vigilance ever so slightly during Pascal's account of the history of their lineages, but now he was on guard again. "And did moving the bottle," he asked, "require the aid of a demon ally?"

"Demon ally? Now that's a shift in vocabulary also worthy of Serafino. But no, I long ago learned to do such things without an ally's aid. Have you never turned to the old magic of spells and incantations?"

"I have," Don Carlos admitted, "but only on a very few occasions."

Pascal shrugged his shoulders. "I don't want to return to an old argument of mine with Serafino, which we've just replicated here. He always maintained that simple magic wasn't worthy of us as powerful sorcerers, and that it was inherently dangerous, all too easily turned to malign purposes. I suppose that since I was quite open to using sorcery for what he regarded as unworthy purposes, I saw no reason not to use ordinary magic to lay a curse or spell on my adversaries."

"Just your mention," Don Carlos commented, "of laying a curse or spell on your adversaries makes me wonder whether you intend to attempt that with me."

Pascal held up his hand. "I hadn't considered attempting anything of the sort. It's my belief that you have the power to deflect any such magic back on me."

Don Carlos felt the yellow butterfly on his shoulder stir restlessly at this turn in the conversation. Was the butterfly Serafino's presence, warning him to beware of Pascal's disclaimers? "Let's not put that to the test," he said.

"I have no intention of testing your powers in that way," Pascal replied, "but I did hope you would demonstrate them for me in various ways, the first and least important of which would be to join me in play." Noting Don Carlos's skeptical look, he quickly added, "I'm sure the word play sounds strange coming from my lips. Even I'm a bit surprised at finding play becoming such a central feature of my life. Surely you can see that I enjoy playing with children, something I never pursued in any other lifetime, nor in this one either until the past few months."

Don Carlos was about to deny that he had ever played at sorcery, but he knew that wasn't true. Many times in his past lives he had used his brujo powers mainly to entertain himself, to envelop a woman he wanted to seduce in his aura, to perform a transformation to please his friends, or to make a plant blossom out of season just for the pleasure of seeing its beauty. He suspected that all such uses of his powers would have been criticized by Don Serafino. He was, therefore, not entirely surprised when he found himself saying to Pascal, "What do you propose?"

"I think a few examples of our shared powers would be enough, and in honor of your old teacher, I suggest that we begin with something that will be good for the people of the Barrio de Analco."

"Such as?"

"Quite a few of the children's parents who are farmers have complained to me that though the drought of the last three years seems to have ended, the Santa Fe River's level is still too low to provide adequate water to irrigate everyone's fields. I've noticed that clouds have gathered over the canyon east of Santa Fe where the river has its origins. Do you suppose that you and I could cause a rainstorm in the canyon, one that results in a significant rain?"

Don Carlos indicated that he was willing to try, and the two sorcerers turned their attention to the east. Don Carlos had created storms in the past, though he couldn't say precisely how he had done so. It seemed a matter of deep wishing. Its success, he realized, may have been another example of something, like his full transformations, that he had a natural capacity to achieve.

Memories of Don Serafino came instantly to mind. It had taken many months of study to learn full transformations, and he well remembered his first success: a transformation into a hawk that occurred during a trip with Don Serafino into a wild mountainous region of New Granada. Only now did he recall that twice on that trip Don Serafino had said, "Carlito, the humidity is oppressive; please clear the air by making it rain." A downpour had followed soon, but Carlos had dismissed its arrival as mere coincidence. When he mentioned this to his master, Don Serafino had said, "Don't be so sure."

Focusing now on the clouds above the Santa Fe River Canyon, Don Carlos felt an intense wish to do something to help the farmers of Santa Fe's Barrio de Analco.

He and Pascal sat in total silence for half an hour. The clouds over the canyon to the east grew darker until flashes of lightning were visible and rolls of thunder could be heard. Sheets of rain poured down on the canyon. After fifteen minutes Pascal whispered, "Perhaps that's enough; we don't want to overdo it." The storm stopped shortly thereafter.

"I think Serafino approves," Pascal said. "Your friend, the yellow butterfly, has left your shoulder and is circling above your head. More magic, though this is a matter of a beautiful sight rather than a beneficial rain."

Don Carlos looked up and saw that the first butterfly had been joined by dozens of the same type that were arriving in a mass from the south. His rational mind quickly supplied an explanation—that butterflies of the cloudless sulfur variety, which usually migrated into the area in June, had begun to arrive in large numbers. But he again heard Don Serafino's voice saying, "Don't be so sure."

The mass of butterflies arranged themselves above Don Carlos's head into a column with a hollow center. For Don Carlos, seated below the column, it was like looking upward from the bottom of a well. He closed his eyes and turned his attention to his seventh chakra, the crown chakra at the top of his head. Of all the seven chakras this one had been the hardest to access. Even when he did manage to open it during meditation, the quiet pulse of energy he had felt when he'd reached it was so subtle that he often lost contact with it. But this time the energy pulse, the sensation of drawing energy into his body with every inhale and sending it out into the universe with every exhale, was extraordinarily strong. He felt a great calm, a sense that all was well, that he and the universe were one.

When he finally opened his eyes, he saw that the column of butterflies was withdrawing and forming into a single mass like a swirling globe above him. The sun was now low in the west and the rays of the light from the setting sun intensified the bright yellow of the mass of fluttering insects. Returning to his first thought, he again assumed that the butterflies' behavior was simply a natural phenomenon that arose from their migration northward. But was that all there was to it? As soon as the question entered his mind, he told himself to follow the advice he'd received from Don Serafino and from Zoila. Both of them had warned him not to allow rational explanations to limit his understanding of the world's magnificence.

Don Carlos looked over at Pascal, who broke the silence. "That was lovely, a truly magical sight. But I sensed that for you it was something more."

Speaking spontaneously from the heart, Carlos said, "One of my teachers, a Hindu adept, told me that the world is alive and that all life is seamlessly connected."

Pascal responded soberly. "That is also the philosophy of alchemists, whose views I attempted to apply for many years. But I was pursuing a theory, while you seem to have received that knowledge through direct experience."

"Sometimes," Don Carlos said.

Pascal looked to the west and said, "We have much to discuss and several more forms of sorcery that I want to explore with you, mainly those related to transformations, but I need to end this conversation to prepare for a fireworks display I'm going to put on tonight."

"Fireworks?" Don Carlos inquired.

"Haven't you heard? Today is Governor Peralta's birthday, and I've spread the word that as soon as darkness sets in there will be a fireworks display in his honor. I imported the materials from China on the Manila Galleon. I don't think anything quite like it has been seen in New Spain. Three big booms will announce its beginning. I hope all of Santa Fe's children will still be up to watch."

Don Carlos laughed. "I hadn't heard. You may be sure that I'm enough of a child at heart not to miss the fireworks."

"As for tomorrow," Pascal went on, "I've promised to have another kind of show for Santa Fe's children before lunch. Privately I'm calling its theme Illusions, but since children may not understand all the implications of that word, I've announced it as nearly the final performance of the Magic Theatre."

"Nearly the final performance?"

"I've told you I'm leaving soon, but not, I trust, before you and I can have a long talk about what I would like you to do for me. In addition to the Magic Theatre show in the morning, I have another commitment for tomorrow that may take most of the afternoon. Then the day after tomorrow is Saturday market, and I want to put on a show in the plaza. But I hope we can meet soon after that."

Feeling secure in the aftermath of his seventh-chakra experience with the butterflies and very curious to know what Pascal had in mind, Don Carlos agreed, adding, "The main difficulty will be finding a time. Like yourself, I have obligations during the next few days. Sunday morning I always accompany my friend Inéz to Mass, and Sunday afternoon I usually practice fencing with the governor's secretary, Marco Cabrera. Monday is Inéz's day off and we usually try to spend some time together. If we can't fit something into part of one of those days, I am free all of next Tuesday."

"I hope we can meet sooner than Tuesday," Pascal said, "but we'll have to see. I certainly can't compete for your attention with Señora Recalde, an exceedingly attractive woman, and is it true that she's also an exceptionally skilled fencer?"

"You are well informed," Carlos replied, not eager to have Pascal involved in any way with Inéz.

"Time for me to get to work," Pascal said, standing up and shaking Carlos's hand. "Thank you for coming by this afternoon."

"You're welcome," Don Carlos said. "Have a good evening."

"I expect to," Pascal replied. "I promise you that the fireworks will be quite spectacular, a combination of a Chinese art and a little European sorcery."

Carlos walked home and found Orfeo starting to make dinner. He looked up from a pot that was warming in the hearth and said, "I'm glad you've hired Rosa Lugo as our cook. I was getting tired of us having to cook and bored with the few dishes we knew how to make. I hope you don't take that as an insult."

"Not at all," Don Carlos replied with a laugh. "I've felt the same way."

They shared a simple meal, cleaned up afterward, and then took a couple of chairs, a bottle of wine, and glasses out to the future courtyard. It faced south, and they watched the stars come out after the last rays of the setting sun had faded. Gordo curled up next to them.

The evening air temperature was perfect, and the courtyard afforded a good view of the sky over the caravan from which he assumed Pascal would launch his fireworks display. Carlos told Orfeo what Pascal had told him about it. "This ought to be fun," Orfeo said.

"I'm looking forward to it too," Don Carlos replied, taking a sip of wine and reaching down to scratch Gordo's head.

A small bang from the area where Pascal's caravan was parked was followed by a faint trail of sparks that rose high into the night sky and then ended with a very loud "Boom!" Gordo, startled, leaped to his feet and almost caused Don Carlos to spill his wine.

"That's amazing!" Orfeo exclaimed.

"It certainly will get everyone's attention," Don Carlos agreed.

26

Risks

Two more loud booms followed in quick succession. Then there was a pause. Next a thin trail of sparks rose in the night, accompanied by a loud whistling sound and terminating in an explosion that showered sparks downward. Four similar projectiles followed, each whistling noisily and ending with a shower of bright white sparks.

Silence returned and the only light in the sky came from stars. Then a bright white trail of light shot high into the night air and burst into the shape of a dandelion's puffball. This was followed by a series of three more projectiles of the same sort in different colors, and then three of a different type fired off together, each of which exploded into three more parts that spun in place before they descended, emitting an eerie wail.

Another pause followed. Then a single projectile hurled into the sky, its trail thicker than any of the previous trails. As it reached its apogee and turned to begin falling it exploded in a ball of multi-colored lights. Burst after burst followed, each showering dazzling red, yellow, green, and blue stars. Just as they began to fade and it seemed nothing more could possibly happen, a loud boom rattled the beams of houses and the earth itself.

That concluded the display, and it was quite plain from the cheers and huzzahs that rose from every direction that the people of Santa Fe appreciated Pascal's efforts.

"Pascal told me," Don Carlos said to Orfeo, "that the fireworks came from China, where they are considered an art." To himself he observed that he'd never seen anything to match this spectacle, not even the fireworks display over the Thames when he was in London during his fourth life.

"It was astonishing," Orfeo replied. "Everyone will be talking about it, and it was a great way of honoring Governor Peralta's birthday."

"I agree," Don Carlos said. "I think I'll go to bed early tonight. We've a long day ahead laying the tile floor in the new *sala*."

Don Carlos slept a deep, dreamless sleep. He got up at his usual pre-dawn rising time and meditated. Although he had expected his mind to be full of thoughts in the aftermath of his long exchange with Pascal, his meditation was quiet. Instead of being apprehensive about what Pascal might want from him, he found that he was merely curious to learn what this might be.

Even these thoughts left his mind after breakfast once he and Orfeo began their project of laying the *sala*'s tile floor. Orfeo had prepared the surface and knew how to proceed efficiently, having laid a similar floor in Dr. Velarde's house.

Shortly before noon Don Carlos said, "Let's call it quits for now and have some lunch." As they were about to get up off their knees, Gordo, who'd been lying in a corner, leaped up, started barking, and ran out of the room toward the kitchen. Carlos stood up and followed, arriving in the kitchen just in time to see Gordo ducking out his doggy door. Carlos opened the door and found Mara, Selena, and Juan Archibeque's three daughters standing there. "May we come in for a little visit?" Selena asked.

"Please do," Carlos replied.

All five guests followed Carlos into the kitchen. Selena lined the girls up and said, "Don Alfonso, I would like to present Juan Archibeque's daughters."

"We have met, in a manner of speaking," Carlos said.

Mara corrected him. "They've seen you at their house, and they're quite fascinated by you, but they've never been properly introduced." She went on, "Don Alfonso, this is Danielle, Manon, and Nicole, in that order from eldest to youngest. Girls, this is Don Alfonso Cabeza de Vaca, about whom you've heard so much."

Nicole, no more than six years old by Carlos's estimate, spoke up. "Cabeza de Vaca, head of a cow, that's an odd name."

"No manners whatsoever!" Mara exclaimed. "Your father will be very disappointed that Selena and I have not taught you proper manners."

Nicole looked slightly chastened, but Carlos, who had gotten this reaction many times in the past, simply said, "Yes, it is. But I don't think you came to visit in order to hear about my name."

"That's right," Selena said. "We've just been to Pascal's show and we're now on our way to Doña Josefina's for lunch, but when I told them that we were passing by your house they wanted to stop and tell you about the show."

"Now that's interesting," Don Carlos replied. "I would very much like to hear about the show. But first, please sit down. And would you like some water? It's warm today and you must be thirsty."

Danielle said, "Please." And her little sisters nodded their heads.

Orfeo had been standing next to the barrel where they stored drinking water. He turned around, took five pottery mugs from a shelf, filled each with water, and passed them to Mara, Selena, and the three girls. This gave Carlos a chance to look at his visitors. Mara and Selena were conservatively dressed and decorous in manner. The teasing and flirting he'd come to expect from them in the past was not in evidence. He found that he rather missed it. It was the presence of the little girls, he thought; Mara and Selena were modeling proper behavior.

"Now tell me what the show was like," Carlos said.

"Pascal," Danielle began, "said that it was a play in three parts. Part One was called 'One Man or Two?' When the curtains opened, there was a big column in the middle of the stage. Right away a little man—actually, we knew it was a monkey—came out from behind the column. He was dressed in a white outfit from head to toe, and he had on a white mask. He did a little jig and then he hid behind the column again. Then another little man came out on the other side of column. He looked like the first one, except he was dressed all in black. He danced around and then he hid behind the column, and the little man in white came out again. They went back and forth like that five or six times, trading places faster and faster. Finally the curtain closed." She paused. She was evidently thinking about something. "It was definitely two monkeys," she declared.

"No," Manon insisted. "It was the same monkey. His front was in white and his back in black. All he had to do was turn around to look like a different monkey."

"I couldn't tell," Nicole announced.

"So what happened next?" Carlos asked.

Manon took up the story. "After a little while, the curtain opened again. Polly the Parrot was sitting on a nest—a very big, thick nest. It took up half the stage. She began flapping her wings and saying, 'Pretty Polly! Pretty Polly!' and nodding her head in the funniest way."

"Was that all?" Carlos prompted her.

"No," Manon replied. "After a minute or two she stood up. Her head almost hit the ceiling of the stage because she was standing on that big nest. She looked under herself and we could see that she'd been sitting on two eggs, one green and the other red. She sat down again."

"You forgot to say," little Nicole announced, "that when she saw the eggs she started clucking like a chicken. She sounded like a hen that has laid an egg! She sat down for just a moment and then stood up and looked under herself again. This time," Nicole said delightedly. "the eggs had hatched into two monkey heads, one black and one white."

"Monkey heads!" Carlos exclaimed. "Were they detached from the monkeys' bodies?"

Nicole's eyes widened at the thought.

"I think the rest of the monkeys were hidden under the nest," Danielle said. "So it *was* two monkeys, one in white, the other in black, in Part One."

"No," Manon said. "It could have been a single, two-sided monkey in Part One and two separate monkeys in Part Two, one wearing a black mask and the other a white mask."

"I don't know," Nicole announced with a shrug and a sigh.

"What about Part Three?" Carlos asked.

Danielle replied. "In Part Three there were definitely two monkeys. One had on a gold outfit and the other was dressed in red. The one in gold — we found out later his name was Che — was carrying a pack of little playing cards. He set them down in front of the other one, whose name was Prospero. Prospero took a card out of the deck and showed it to us without showing it to Che. It was the ace of clubs. Prospero put it back in the pack. Then Che spread the cards out on the stage and waved his hands over them. He picked out a card and showed it to us. It was the ace of clubs!

"Next Che gathered up the cards and invited Prospero to choose another. This time he drew the queen of hearts, showed it to us, and returned it to the deck. Che turned his back and Prospero stirred up the cards and spread them out across the stage. Che turned around, studied the cards, and picked out the queen of hearts.

"Now let me tell!" Manon said. "Then Che turned all the cards over and showed us that they were all queens of hearts! Next he passed the deck to Prospero. Then Prospero showed them to us one at a time, and all of them were aces of clubs!"

"It was quite a trick," Selena said seriously. "Neither Mara nor I understand how he did it."

The two women exchanged a glance. "Perhaps," Mara said, "you should tell Don Alfonso about Pascal's announcement before the show began."

Selena nodded. "He came out in front of the caravan and greeted everyone. Then he pointed to the caravan and said that it was a magic theatre, and that in it we would see things that might not be what they seemed. He went on about that for a while, which struck me as rather odd because creating illusions is what entertainers *do* — we should know," she added, casting a sideways look at Carlos — "and they don't usually make announcements about it. The more he talked, the more I felt that his remarks were aimed at *us* — Mara and me — and that strange 'Is he or isn't he?' feeling we'd gotten after the first time we saw him came back."

"Perhaps," Carlos suggested, "Pascal was saying, 'Don't try to find the answer, just enjoy the show.' And you must admit that you enjoyed the show, even though you still aren't sure who Pascal is."

"That's true," Selena replied as she stood up. "But we've dallied too long. As I said, Doña Josefina has invited us for lunch and we'll be late if we don't leave right now. I think the invitation is to make it plain to the town that both the two of us and Juan Archibeque's girls are socially acceptable. It's very kind of her." With that she and Mara shooed the girls toward the door, and all five of his guests gave Carlos friendly waves as they left the house.

Don Carlos was impatient to report his recent conversation with Pascal to Inéz, so after a quick lunch, he excused himself, headed for the Beltrán place, and knocked on the kitchen door.

Inéz greeted him and invited him in. Before he could say anything, she said, "I've been wondering what you've been up to."

"I had a talk with Pascal last night and a visit this noon from Mara, Selena, and the Archibeque girls, who stopped by after Pascal's show to tell me about it and then continued on to a luncheon appointment with Doña Josefina. Which part of my story do you want to hear first?"

"I already heard about Pascal's show. Diego and Ana took the Trigales children. They had a good time, although they couldn't agree whether the first act was performed by one monkey or two, and whether Polly the Parrot in the second act laid two eggs or two monkeys' heads. Or, for that matter, whether all the cards in the deck Che used in the third act were aces of clubs or queens of hearts."

"It was the same with the Archibeque girls. But it was clear that half the fun for them was being mystified."

"What about Mara and Selena?" Inéz asked.

"They couldn't tell how the tricks were done any more than the girls. But they did add that Pascal gave an introduction to the show in which he warned the audience that the things they were about to see might not be what they seemed. Selena said that it gave them the same odd 'Is he or isn't he?' feeling they had the first time they met him, and that they thought the introduction was directed at them."

"What do you think he meant?"

"Selena agreed with me when I suggested the message was for them to enjoy the show without trying to figure out who he is."

"How do they feel about that?"

"Neither of them seemed inclined to pursue the matter."

"Perhaps," Inéz said, "they'd rather not know, particularly if knowing that he is their father would stir up bad feelings. But tell me about your conversation with Pascal."

"For the most part I felt comfortable with him. He admitted to some regret about his role in Leandro's death and surprised me by speaking fondly of Don Serafino. But the most important thing he said was that he hoped I would help him in certain unspecified ways, and he invited me to join him in practicing sorcery."

Inéz's eyes opened wide. "And you did?" Before he could answer she went on. "Of course you did. The thunderstorm over the Santa Fe River canyon yesterday afternoon came out of nowhere. And I heard that a column of cloudless sulphur butterflies was seen in the Barrio de Analco. Did you and Pascal have anything to do with that?"

"I suppose so," Carlos replied. "Both things might have been entirely natural, although I admit I intended the thunderstorm."

Inéz looked dubious. "What if he's setting a trap for you, studying your brujo powers to do you harm when he asks you to help him, whatever that entails?"

"I'm trying to remain wary," Carlos protested.

"I've heard that before," Inéz replied tartly. "But let's not dwell on that. I have a special request that you can't deny, since you neglected me yesterday. Cristina has told me to take tomorrow morning off as soon as breakfast has been served. I want you to take me for a ride. Come by about eight o'clock with Alegría and we can ride somewhere nice, possibly even our Sacred Pool. I'll provide lunch."

"Bless Cristina!" Carlos said. "I'll see you then."

Only as he was crossing the plaza on his way home did it occur to Carlos to wonder whether there was more to Inéz's invitation than met the eye. But he was looking forward to finding out and went to bed that night in a very good mood.

His morning began in the usual way with meditation and breakfast. Orfeo, who also seemed to be in a good mood, joined him for breakfast, and Don Carlos told him about Inéz's plan for a picnic.

"That's a fine idea," Orfeo said. "You've been working too hard, Don Alfonso. A picnic will do you good." He helped Carlos wash and put away the breakfast dishes and then said, "I'll get Alegría and Eagle saddled and ready to go."

After he'd dressed for a ride, Don Carlos went to the corral and mounted Eagle. Orfeo handed him Alegría's lead rope and they started off toward the Beltrán house at a quiet walk. As they crossed the plaza, Carlos saw that most of the usual vendors had already set up for Saturday market. He was greeted by many smiles and calls of "Good morning." His neighbors were always friendly, but they seemed to be unusually so this morning. He wondered whether this had something to do with his role in dispatching the wolf. Don Alfonso the werewolf killer.

Inéz was waiting for him at the kitchen door. She looked particularly striking in her dark red riding outfit, which he hadn't seen her wear since she first came to Santa Fe and seemed intent on seducing him. He dismounted, and they exchanged a light kiss on the cheek. She had washed her hair in the fragrance that always set his head spinning. "What's going on?" he asked.

"Going on?" she replied. "We're going on an outing, and you're helping me pack lunch in your saddlebags."

"So you're not going to tell me why you're wearing your most arresting riding outfit and that perfume that always leaves me in a daze."

"You do love me, don't you?" she asked.

"You know I do, but that's not an explanation."

"Give me a leg up, please," she said, and after he'd boosted her into the saddle, she looked down at him and added, "Since you love me, my good mood ought to please you."

"It does."

"That being the case, mount up and we can be on our way to a picnic we'll both enjoy."

Inéz seemed very pleased with herself in a way that made Carlos feel she was keeping some delightful secret. Unable to think of how to get her to tell him, he decided to let it go and rode along happily at her side.

Eventually they turned off from the Camino Real onto the trail to their Sacred Pool. At the far end of the meadow that led to the pool they dismounted, put their horses on long tethers, and unloaded the lunch and picnic supplies Inéz had packed. These they brought to the edge of the pool, where Inéz spread out a blanket.

Once they'd arranged the picnic site, Inéz put her hands on her hips and said, "Here's what I propose. If you're going to display your brujo powers to Pascal, you need to bring them to full strength. I suggest that you climb up to the vision quest site and do whatever it takes to enhance your powers—transforming yourself into a hawk or meditating in the alcove that has the shaman's handprint on its back wall. I'll see if I can find Elvira and talk with her about this and that. After an hour or so we'll meet here, have lunch, and do our best to help me recapture my youthful self. Perhaps we can even play my favorite game, Princess for a Day."

"That all sounds good. As I always say, your wish is my command."

She gave him a meaningful look. "Please, Carlos. I said we'd play, but this play has a serious purpose, indeed several serious purposes, not the least of which is preparing you for a questionable encounter with Pascal."

Don Carlos climbed up to the ledge where Pueblo Indians had long gathered crystals and sought visions. He studied the site carefully and noticed that someone had visited it recently. Possibly this was José. There was no way of being certain. He had many options, but he decided to pursue his favorite, transforming himself into a hawk. He stripped down and changed himself into a bay-winged hawk. It was an unusual choice, since this type of hawk rarely visited northern New Mexico. It was also a type with unusual social habits, in that adult bay-winged hawks cooperated in groups of three to six in hunting and nesting. Although he was a solitary seeker today, his brujo intuition told him that this was an appropriate choice.

Launching into flight, he headed west toward Tesuque Pueblo. He planned a long flight to give Inéz plenty of time to visit with her skunk friend Elvira. In order to avoid intruding on their rendezvous he skirted the area where Elvira had her den. Turning north above the road to Taos, he was aided by a tailwind in coasting along above the road as far as the banks of the Rio Grande. Once at the river he followed its course northward until he reached the Rio Grande Gorge. Here he turned briefly east and then veered southward along the bold front of the Sangre de Cristo range. This put him on the final leg of a wide circuit above the largely uninhabited countryside. Throughout his flight, he had tested his skills at various maneuvers—coasting, soaring, and diving. Finally he arrived back at his starting point, the site that Old Man Xenome called Spirit Ledge. Here he changed back to human form, dressed, and climbed down the cliff.

Inéz was waiting for him. She had taken off her boots and was soaking her feet in the warmer part of their Sacred Pool. "My, what lovely feet you have, Princess," he said.

She laughed and replied, "Even the minimal training you gave me in reading auras is enough for me to see that yours has become very strong. You must have had a good flight."

"I did. But since I saw many edible small creatures without eating any, I've built up quite an appetite."

"That's fine," she replied, bringing her feet out of the water and drying them with a towel. They moved over to the picnic blanket, and while she unpacked lunch he opened the bottle of wine he'd brought. Inéz was an exceptional cook and the various little dishes she had prepared were delicious.

"You're being unusually quiet," she remarked after they had eaten their fill.

"I was waiting for the princess for a day to give me my marching orders."

"I would like you to take the princess in your arms and hold her close." As they lay down side by side and Carlos wrapped her in his arms, Inéz had an additional instruction. "Don't you dare fall asleep!"

They held each other for a long time, a timeless time. Gradually they began to breathe in unison and then their hearts beat to the same rhythm. Carlos gave himself completely to experiencing his heart chakra's energies, feeling immersed in his love for Inéz. He knew a deep contentment. Why seek anything more, he wondered.

Eventually, Inéz broke the silence. "We'd better start back."

"What's the hurry? This is very, very nice."

"Yes, it is. But there's a surprise waiting for you back in Santa Fe."

"What?"

"If I told you what it is, it wouldn't be a surprise," she said, and gave him a kiss.

So they gathered up their things, untethered their horses, mounted, and started back. The energy and compatibility they'd felt while in each other's arms carried over to Eagle and Alegría, who matched each other step for step. "They're a matched pair," Carlos observed. "Just like us." Inéz's only response was to laugh.

As they reached the northeastern outskirts of Santa Fe, Carlos could see smoke billowing up from somewhere that appeared to be just south of the plaza. He had a bad feeling. "It looks like a fire," he said, "and it seems to be coming from near my house." He spurred Eagle into a trot past the Presidio and into the plaza in front of the Palace of the Governors, from which point he could see that the smoke was indeed coming from near his house, but the house itself wasn't on fire.

Don Carlos had never given much attention to the small empty field between his house and the southern edge of the plaza. He wasn't even sure who owned it. But as he continued to trot across the plaza he could see a crowd of people in the field. They were congregated around four fire pits, each of which had a spit on it with meat being roasted over open flames. Probably, he thought, the fat dripping from the meat made the smoke dense and highly visible. But what was going on?

As he approached his house he slowed Eagle to a walk and was greeted with cheers and applause from all sides. Inéz, catching up with him, said, "Your friends and neighbors are throwing a party in honor of your service to our community."

"Service?"

"Yes, service, beginning with the time you rescued José from being hanged, to your essential role in rescuing the Trigales children, and now to your being instrumental in killing the wolf."

"But Inéz," he said to her in a whisper, "no one's supposed to know how we located the Trigales children, and I didn't kill the wolf; it was Eagle who stunned it and militiamen who shot it dead."

"No one knows the details of how the children were located," Inéz replied, "but everyone suspects that you had more to do with it than you'll admit. And if you can't accept a party in your honor, at least accept the fact that all of us needed an excuse to celebrate something—if nothing else, the departure of the inquisitors and the wolf's death. Raul Trigales had the idea first, and Javier Beltrán endorsed it. They gathered enough food from their storehouses to feed a big crowd. Then they asked around in the Barrio de Analco and found many people who wanted to help with a fiesta and offered to cook up large batches of chili and tortillas."

Don Carlos couldn't think what to say. "And there will be dancing too," Inéz added, gesturing toward two small bands that had struck up folk songs as soon as Don Carlos came into sight.

He saw Pedro and Orfeo standing near one of the fire pits and rode over to them. "You knew about this?" he said as he dismounted. Both Pedro and Orfeo grinned in a conspiratorial way, and Pedro replied, "It wouldn't have been a surprise if we'd told you."

"In fact," Orfeo said, "there's more to the surprise than you can see from here. Come along and see the corral."

"The corral? Have you changed it?"

"Not exactly. Please follow me."

Don Carlos accompanied Orfeo and Pedro down the lane, with Inéz still on Alegría following close behind. He soon saw that the exterior of the groom's room was complete, walls, roof, and door to the veranda. They continued past the new stable, where Inéz dismounted and handed Alegría's reins to Orfeo. Carlos walked around the new corral and was astonished to see that the large bedroom on the east side of the house was also complete. Pedro spoke up. "Everyone pitched in. This morning we had as many as three dozen men helping out. With that many hands everything went very fast. That's the way a house-raising ought to work. It's our gift, your neighbors' gift, to you."

"I don't know what to say," Don Carlos replied.

"Don't say anything then," Pedro said. "Come around front, have some food, mix with your neighbors, and maybe dance a few dances with Inéz. Orfeo can unsaddle Eagle and Alegría while you enjoy the day." And enjoy the day he did, sampling all of the various roast meats—lamb, goat, pork, and chicken—and dancing with Inéz. "This is a special party," he told her, "and it's not even my birthday."

The party was beginning to break up and the remaining meat was being wrapped up and handed out to guests to take home when Carlos noticed Pascal's caravan on the outer edge of the crowd. Several dozen people were moving in Pascal's direction. Carlos supposed that they wanted to thank him for the fireworks show he had put on. Pascal slowed Listo to a halt, and the people gathered around him. He chatted with them for a while. As he signaled Listo to move forward again, he spotted Carlos and Inéz and tipped his hat to them.

27

Revelations

Carlos walked Inéz back to the Beltrán house. As they crossed the plaza, many people came up to him and expressed their gratitude for his role in dispatching the wolf. He accepted these gestures, but he tried to downplay his part in the wolf's demise and to praise the militiamen who had defended the Barrio de Analco against the animal.

When they were finally out of anyone else's hearing, Carlos turned to Inéz and said, "I had no idea that my reputation had risen so high as a result of the wolf incident."

"Enjoy your fame," Inéz replied. "The good opinion of your neighbors is invaluable."

They reached the Beltrán house and went directly to its kitchen door. "I've had a lovely time with you today," Inéz said, "but now I need to get back to work."

"Isn't everyone well enough fed from the fiesta?" Carlos asked.

"Yes," Inéz replied, "but I'm sure they'll be hungry again later. Rita and I will need to prepare a light meal." Turning to go in, she added, "I hope you have a restful evening."

The evening passed amiably. Orfeo joined him for dinner, and after dinner he brought his guitar from the groom's quarters and they entertained themselves by singing *versos* until it was time for bed.

Sunday began in a quiet way. After meditating and having breakfast, Carlos spent most of the morning organizing his belongings to transfer them from his old bedroom to the new one. When he was done, he changed into his Sunday clothes and strode across the plaza and up the hill to the Beltráns' house. Inéz, having seen him coming, was waiting outside the front door. She said, "Elena and her parents have already left. They told me they would save a place for us in the chapel."

As expected, marriage banns for four couples present at Mass were announced with great formality at the end of Mass. Father Benedicto read the banns in the traditional words: "I publish the banns of marriage between Marco Escobar Cabrera and Ariel Graciana Padilla of this Parish. If any of you know cause or just impediment why these persons should not be joined together in Holy Matrimony, you are to declare it. This is the first time of acting."

Then, following the same wording, banns were read for three more couples:

Antonio Domínguez Mendoza and Juliana Evelina Peralta
Julio Montoya Mendoza and Victoria Milagros Peralta
Santiago Alconedo Mendoza and Elena Aurora Beltrán

After a slight pause Father Benedicto continued. "At the early Mass there was a first reading of banns for Diego Campos and Ana Lugo." Heads nodded in approval. Don Carlos felt a rush of warm feelings for his friends.

Following Mass, Carlos and Inéz made the rounds of the couples whose banns had been announced, starting with the two elder Mendoza brothers and the Peralta twins, then on to Santiago and Elena, and finally to Marco and Ariel. "Congratulations and great happiness to you," Carlos said to Marco and Ariel.

"You can tell by the smile on my face," Marco replied, "that this wonderful woman has already brought me great happiness by accepting my proposal of marriage."

Ariel added, "I regard this as a miracle that I never thought would happen to me, but Marco has rescued me from spinsterhood, and I will make sure that he never regrets it."

"I don't and won't, dearest," Marco said. Then, turning to Carlos, he said, "Could we substitute another activity for our usual after-Mass fencing practice?"

"Certainly," Carlos replied. "What did you have in mind?"

"Ariel and I would like to take a look at the Fernandez place, which I believe is now unoccupied. I'm hoping that you will agree to sell it to me so that my bride and I can have a proper home of our own."

Marco's proposal came as a complete surprise to Carlos. He mentally began assessing the financial aspect of the proposed transaction. Since he didn't have a tenant for the house, a lump sum from its sale was attractive. The money would pay for the remaining costs of his house renovation project and leave a small balance for other needs. But he was a bit worried that the house might not be large enough, especially if Marco and Ariel took in one or two servants. "It's a rather small house," he said. "Will it be sufficient for your needs?"

"We're a rather small family," Ariel said with a laugh. "But of course we want to visit it and see if it suits us. We hope it will. There aren't many vacant houses in good condition north of the river just now."

"What about the Tiburcio house?" Carlos asked. "Lucila Archuleta has had it fixed up."

"I inquired about that," Marco replied, "but she's found another buyer for it."

"Then you're certainly welcome to look at the Fernandez house," Carlos said. "The four of us can go over there right now."

The two couples walked to the Fernandez place. When they arrived, Carlos glanced around inside and decided that it might indeed be suitable as Marco and Ariel's first home. He had always rented it in furnished condition, and he told them that he would include the furniture in the sale price.

Carlos and Inéz left their friends to explore the Fernandez house more thoroughly. Inéz said that she needed to get home to serve lunch and then start dinner preparations. "What plans do you have for tomorrow? It's my day off. Perhaps we can ride out to Rancho Rosón. I haven't seen José for some time, and I would enjoy another trip on Alegría."

Carlos was pleased by the prospect, and they arranged to meet after Inéz's usual Monday session with Mara and Selena.

Carlos returned to his own house and had lunch. Then, feeling at loose ends, he saddled Eagle and went for a long ride south on the Galisteo Road. It was a route that he rarely took, and he and Eagle both enjoyed the novelty of a relatively unfamiliar landscape. By the time they got back to Santa Fe it was late afternoon. He unsaddled Eagle and turned to walk up the lane to his house's kitchen door.

He glanced ahead and saw Doña Josefina's black servant, Mabruke, hurrying toward him with a somber look on his face. Upon reaching Don Carlos, Mabruke, without any preliminaries, said, "Please come with me to Señora Mendoza's. It is a matter of the utmost urgency."

Don Carlos followed Mabruke to Doña Josefina's. They arrived at the main door of the house just in time to meet Father Benedicto leaving. "Don Alfonso," he said, "I'm glad you could come immediately. Our sister Frida is near death. I have given her the last rites, and she has lapsed into unconsciousness. But before she lost consciousness she asked specifically for you." Father Benedicto looked at Carlos with a slightly quizzical expression on his face, perhaps wondering why Frida had asked for Carlos.

Carlos said only, "Thank you, Father."

Doña Josefina was waiting for him in the corridor to Frida's room. "Her time has come. She never completely recovered from the bat incident ten days ago, and she's been failing for the past week. Earlier today she said, 'I'm near death.' She asked me to tell you that she would like you to stay with her through her final hours."

Don Carlos didn't know what to say. What did Frida expect of him? True, as Manuela Maldonado, she had been a shape-shifter, and he was the only person she knew in Santa Fe with the ability to change his form. But what did a brujo do under such circumstances? The situation had no precedent in his experience.

Doña Josefina showed him into Manuela's room. Curtains had been closed over the one window, and the light in the room was dim. Without thinking, Don Carlos went over to the window and pushed back the curtains. "Even if she is unconscious," he said, "let her have the last few hours of daylight."

Doña Josefina looked at him and nodded, and left him without saying anything more. Don Carlos stepped over to the bedside and took Manuela's hand. It was cool, but not cold. Her breath was coming at uneven intervals. He decided that the best thing he could do was to sit and meditate.

An hour later he got up and walked slowly around the room. Returning to his place by her side, he resumed his meditation. Another hour passed, and then another, and after each hour of meditation he repeated a slow walk around the room. The sun set and darkness was gathering in the room. During the next hour Don Carlos began to receive visitors, not living people, but friends who had died.

Don Serafino appeared first. His message was brief. "You have great powers. Use them wisely." Then he vanished.

Don Serafino's assistant, Sánchez, arrived about twenty minutes later. "Why," he asked, "didn't you ever ask me where I learned the trick of hurling blasts of invisible energy at an enemy?" Before Carlos could ask, Sánchez was gone.

He got up to stretch his legs. Even while walking around the room he maintained his slow breathing and his concentration. Shortly after he returned to his seated meditation, Violeta appeared. She was, he was surprised to see, dressed in black. "I am doing penance for my sins," she said, "specifically my betrayal of you, even though it was justified. The natural desire for revenge does not excuse betrayal."

Carlos was mystified by her reference to revenge, but he found that her repentance for betraying him dissolved his old anger. Her violet eyes looked at him with a mix of what he interpreted as sorrow and fondness. "You do not know the whole story," she said. "Ask Don Malvolio to tell you the truth." Then, like the other ghosts, she vanished.

A full hour passed. His chakra meditation was having a strong effect. His attention had moved from the first, second, and third chakras to the fourth, the heart chakra. He took another walk around the room, checked on Manuela, whose condition had not changed, and sat down. His fourth-chakra focus was still intense. About fifteen minutes later there was a knock at the door. He called out, "Come in." It was Inéz, carrying a candle. She entered, put the candle by the bedside, and sat down next to Carlos. Sensing his meditative quietness, she sat for a while without speaking.

Finally she said, "I heard that Manuela asked for you to sit with her."

"Yes."

"You realize that this could take some time."

"It may. But I don't have anything else that needs doing right now."

"Shall I bring you something to eat?"

"I feel as if this is a time for fasting, though you could bring me a pitcher of water. I've drunk the water in the glass on the little chest over there, and I'd like some more."

Inéz went off and returned with a pitcher, from which she filled the water glass. "Would you like to be alone?" she asked.

"There's no one I would rather be with than you, dear Inéz, but I haven't been entirely alone. I have been visited by a number of old friends—Don Serafino, Sánchez, and, though she isn't a friend exactly, Violeta."

"You can tell me about it later," Inéz said. "I think what's happening now is something you need to do on your own." She bent to give him a light kiss on the forehead and left the room.

Three hours passed without any more visitors. It was about two hours after midnight and the candle Inéz had brought had burned out. He went to the door and found Mabruke standing there. Don Carlos asked him if he could bring candles. Mabruke went off and soon came back with an oil lamp. "This will last longer," he said.

Don Carlos returned to his meditation. Over the hours that he had been meditating, his inner silence had grown deeper. All his senses were sharpened. Although Manuela's breathing was faint, he could hear it. Eventually he could hear her heartbeat too. She seemed completely at peace.

He lost track of time, but he believed it was close to dawn when another visitor came. His meditation had reached his sixth charka, the wisdom chakra in his forehead. He was following the pulse as blood flowed from both sides of his forehead to the sixth chakra in its center. Father Stefano, dressed in his Jesuit robes, appeared and looked at him benignly. "You have begun to take yourself and life seriously. I'm proud of you."

Don Carlos was floating on a feeling of joy that followed Father Stefano's words when Zoila came and sat at the foot of Manuela's bed. "You have a lot of work left to do," she told him. "By now you probably realize that you haven't always lived up to your motto, *Do no harm*. You have broken many hearts in your past lives. You need to find a new motto that better reflects what you are at last learning about how to live in the world." She reached over and caressed his cheek. "Don't look so dismayed by what I've said. You're a good person. Just do the best you can." And she was gone.

Several meditation periods later Don Carlos fell asleep. He awoke with a start. The oil lamp had gone out, but light from the sun, which had recently risen, came in from the window. He could see that Manuela's aura was very dim and growing more so, like an ember in a dying fire. He took her hand, quite cold now, and said out loud, "Go in peace." Then she was gone, and a faint trail of transparent white light rose from her chest and drifted out the window. He stayed with her body for another hour until Doña Josefina came into the room. They exchanged a few words. He expressed his condolences, and she thanked him for staying with Manuela to the end.

Then she said, "We'll have a brief burial service for her late tomorrow morning at the Mendoza family cemetery in back of my house. Please come, and ask Inéz to come, too."

As he crossed the plaza toward his house, he let his mind linger on the words his several ghostly visitors had communicated to him. In particular, he kept returning to what the penitent Violeta had said about asking Malvolio to tell him the truth. Without any conscious decision to do so, he found himself walking past his own house, across the river, and along Canyon Road to Pecos Road, where Pascal's caravan was parked. He knocked on the caravan's door. Pascal opened it at once, his eyes widening in surprise at seeing Carlos standing there.

Carlos dispensed with formalities. "I have just come from watching at a deathbed," he said. "In the course of my vigil I was visited by the spirits of several departed friends. Violeta was one of them. She was dressed in black, and she said she was doing penance for having betrayed me. She said that she, and not just you, had been motivated by revenge, and that I did not know the whole story. She told me to ask you to tell me the truth."

Pascal's eyes stayed wide throughout this recital. Then they grew more distant and thoughtful. "I see," he said at last. "So Violeta is doing penance! Who would have thought—! No matter," he went on, now turning his gaze to Carlos. "So you want to know the truth. I would invite you in, but my caravan is dark and crowded. Let's sit outside and talk."

Carlos backed down the caravan's steps. Pascal followed, and they moved to a bench and a table set up near the caravan and facing the ruins of the San Miguel chapel. "So your friend has departed," Pascal said, "and Violeta came to you and told you to ask me for the truth. Who would have thought—!" he said again. "Well, since you want to know…

"Let me sum up the background. As you know, you prevented me from gaining an object that would have given me great power, and you also contributed to my death. Therefore in subsequent lives I continued to search for you with the object of killing you in return. I knew you were a powerful brujo. I was, at the time of the Violeta incident, well past the middle years of my present life. I was then, as I was until recently, an official in the Holy Office, largely an administrator, but one whose responsibilities included receiving reports of alleged brujos, a situation that facilitated my search for you.

"Finding you was made easier by the fact that you had a reputation—as a powerful brujo, an adventurer, and a womanizer. Your reputation eventually extended even to the barrios of Mexico City, which is where I first heard your name spoken, and I was told that I would probably find you in Morelia. I changed my own identity, discarded my priestly clothes, and became, to all appearances, a Spaniard of the lower sort who lived on the outskirts of the law.

"Once in Morelia it didn't take me long to learn that you came and went at odd intervals, seemed well supplied with silver pesos but had no known means of livelihood, and were a well-known seducer. You were also said to be able to knock a man down without touching him, so for obvious reasons nobody dared to fight with you. But I talked with more than one husband or father who would have killed you if he could.

"When I learned that you had recently become the lover of the entrancing Violeta—who was as much a good businesswoman as she was a dancer—I knew I had found a way to get at you. I offered her a business proposition, which she was more than willing to accept because she also had a grievance against you. It seems you had not only seduced her younger sister, but you had caused the girl to fall so madly in love with you that when you abandoned her—consistent with your habit of suddenly disappearing—she hanged herself. Violeta agreed to what I proposed to do, and the very next night, after you had lost yourself in the luxury of her embraces, she gave you drugged wine.

"From my point of view it couldn't have been better. When you had drunk the wine, I came upon you unprepared and paralyzed. I struck you unconscious with a blow to the head so that you could not go into death with your consciousness intact, and then I hung you upside down and, in honorable revenge for Violeta's sister's death, I killed you by cutting your throat like a pig.

"It all would have been very satisfactory, except that your soul escaped. Naturally, I still wanted to finish you off, and I was sure that with a passion for life like yours you would reincarnate without delay. My mistake was in assuming that you would incarnate again as an Indian. I must say," Pascal added smiling, "I think your upper-class upbringing has noticeably improved your character."

The peaceful feeling that had come to Carlos during his long vigil and that had lingered through the beginning of Pascal's story had by now completely vanished. Carlos was aware of unaccustomed emotions roiling in him. He was on the verge of trembling with insult, and he had to consciously slow his breathing and will his face not to flush. Dimly he heard in his mind Brother Gustavo's accusation that his seduction of Gustavo's mother had led to her death. He had been upset when he first heard that accusation and feared that it might be true, but he had removed its sting by telling himself, "I don't remember her, and although it could have been her—there were so many—still, I don't remember." And now here was another woman, Violeta's sister, dead because she had loved him.

He had not intended harm, he thought; he had intended pleasure. He had never felt malice toward anyone except his stepfather, and he had not acted on that. But, he had to admit, when someone appealed to him to do something to put an end to a flagrant evil, he positively enjoyed vanquishing it. He could not help recalling his enjoyment of the fierce battle with the sorcerer Mateo Pizarro, Malvolio's most powerful apprentice. And just the day before yesterday Pascal had said that it had been on his recent return to the vicinity of Pizarro's death that he had found the last clue that Don Alfonso Cabeza de Vaca and Carlos Buenaventura were one and the same. A certain poetic justice there, Carlos thought wryly.

Pascal, who had not failed to notice Carlos's emotion, said, "I fear that my description of your past behavior has upset you, and you have not absorbed the truth I believe Violeta wanted you to know, which is that her betrayal of you, bad as it was, was not wanton treachery, but was motivated by a desire to avenge her sister's death, for which she held you responsible. But the truth she wanted you to know has also accused you, and one naturally is defensive against accusations. Perhaps you need some time to absorb what I've told you. I suggest we take a quiet walk up the canyon to allow your emotions to settle. After that, I have a confession of my own that I would like to lay before you."

Don Carlos recoiled inwardly. His curiosity about what Pascal's confession might entail was far outweighed by the feeling that he needed to get away by himself for a while. "I'm not quite ready for what you suggest," he told Pascal. "I want some time alone to sort through my friend's death and what you've just told me about Violeta. My friend's burial will be late Tuesday morning. Do you suppose we could meet again Tuesday afternoon?"

"That would be fine," Pascal replied. "The Archibeque girls asked me to come to their house Tuesday morning to answer some questions they have about how to manipulate hand puppets. I should be done there by noon. After that we will have time to talk."

Carlos walked back to his place. He didn't feel like resuming his usual routines, so he went to the Beltrán house to tell Inéz that Manuela had died and that he was going to take Eagle for a long ride in the country. In answer to her question as to when he'd be back, he said he didn't know. "My best guess," he said, "is that I'll probably stay away all day and overnight too, and return in time for the burial service on Tuesday."

"Is there anything besides Manuela's death on your mind?" she asked.

He hesitated. He was not entirely sure he wanted to repeat what Pascal had said. Finally he gave her a very brief summary of Pascal's revelations about Violeta. Inéz looked at him with sympathy. She intuited from his demeanor, even more than his words, that what he had learned from Pascal had damaged his self-esteem. "Yes," she said, "I can see why you might need some time alone. I think it's a very good idea. I'll see you at the burial service."

He spent the next twenty-four hours at the Sacred Pool, and though on the first day he made two excursions to the Spirit Ledge, he did not fly or do transformations of any sort. Ordinarily, simply being at these sites lifted his spirits, but this visit did little to restore him. If anything, when he awoke the next morning after a restless night, it seemed his mood had darkened. He tried to meditate, but he felt almost as if Pascal's words, like Violeta's drugged wine, had once more paralyzed him, and in his mind the genial Pascal began to seem less like his new persona and more like the old Malvolio. Malice, he thought. Was there malice in what Pascal told him? He could not doubt the penitent Violeta's appearance to him, and her telling him to ask Malvolio for the truth. But was there malice also in her, was her appearance as a penitent a lie?

Anger suddenly boiled over in him. His body demanded physical exertion and, getting up, he went to the cliff behind the pool and began to climb vigorously. When he reached the Spirit Ledge he stripped off his clothes, transformed himself into a turkey vulture, and took off into flight. He found an updraft and went higher and higher in wider and wider circles until he was out of sight of the Sacred Pool. He had no idea how long or how far he flew. At last, feeling spent, he coasted in a wide descent back to the Spirit Ledge. When he had transformed himself back to his human form and dressed, he felt like himself again, and his old reckless spirit had returned in force.

He arrived back in town with barely enough time to change into clothes suitable for a burial service, stop by the Beltráns' for Inéz, and walk with her to the Mendoza house. They were the last to arrive. Father Benedicto, Doña Josefina, her granddaughter-in-law, the three nephews and their fiancées, and the household's servants had formed a circle around an open grave. A somber yet peaceful silence prevailed. Manuela's body, wrapped in a plain linen sheet, had already been lowered into the grave.

The service was brief. Father Benedicto opened the proceedings with a prayer and read the burial service liturgy. Doña Josefina spoke next, saying simply that the deceased had been an old and trusted servant. After a short period of silence, Father Benedicto said a closing prayer. The mourners stepped forward to give Doña Josefina their condolences and then drifted off quietly in various directions.

Carlos walked Inéz back home. Once at her door, she asked, "Where are you going from here?"

"I'm going to locate Pascal and continue the conversation that we were having. He said he had something more he wanted to tell me."

"What was that?"

"I'm not sure," Carlos replied. "After he'd told me the story behind Violeta's actions, he added that he had a confession—that's the word he used—he wanted to make. I don't know what that's all I about. I'm curious to find out."

"I don't suppose it would do any good for me to urge you to be careful."

"Probably not," he agreed. And they both laughed.

Despite his curiosity Don Carlos took his time, strolling rather than hurrying to get to Juan Archibeque's house. He found Pascal and Juan seated on the bench outside the front door. They seemed to get along famously and were laughing heartily about something. As soon as he saw Carlos, Pascal stood up and excused himself to Juan. He approached Carlos and said, "I've finished tutoring Juan's daughters in the fine art of hand-puppet theatre. Now they're practicing some play they intend to put on for us tomorrow. Shall we begin our walk?"

Don Carlos and Pascal started up the trail into the Santa Fe River Canyon. As they walked along, Carlos was still strongly aware of his doubts as to whether Pascal was truly as benign as he appeared. He looked at him closely, trying to reconcile the evil person he had long believed Malvolio to be with the pleasant man next to whom he was walking. He deliberately let his eyes go out of focus and shifted to the broader and softer vision he used to see auras. What he saw was a black shadow behind Pascal's left shoulder, and another form, also dark but seeming to consist of particles, behind him on the right.

"There's something I must ask you," Carlos said. "Just now I saw a black shape behind your left shoulder. Are you aware of this shape?"

"Ah!" Pascal replied. "That's Death. He's lurking in hopes of catching me unawares. I know he's there, and sometimes, if I turn my head fast enough, I even catch a glimpse of him."

"And the black manifestation behind your right shoulder?"

"That's a collective spirit," Pascal said. "I call it Ghost, although it's actually a collection of bitter entities that are hungry for revenge. They are people I suppose I harmed in one way or another. When I was stronger, I could ignore them. They had no power. But now I'm almost constantly aware of their demand that I should feel guilty for having done them wrong."

"And do you?" Carlos inquired.

"Not at all," Pascal replied.

"Then," Carlos ventured, "do you harbor any lingering resentment, any desire to take revenge on me for my part in preventing you from gaining possession of Montezuma's Emerald a hundred and fifty years ago?"

Pascal laughed. "I think having cut your throat twenty-odd years ago was sufficient, though it took me a while to realize that. Also"—and here Pascal turned to look at him—"the world has changed. When you and I were both in pursuit of Montezuma's Emerald it was because we believed in it. We lived in a world in which a legend could compel belief. It was a world in which people who had heard the Legend did not doubt the *existence* of the Emerald and its powers. Many might have doubted that it would ever be found, but they did not doubt its power. At that time, a century and a half ago, you and I believed in its power enough to risk our lives to gain possession of it. But I must ask you, do you believe in that Legend now? Do you believe that such a stone exists and that it could confer such powers?"

Pascal paused for Carlos to answer. He had entertained his friends with the story not too many weeks ago. *Entertained his friends.* The phrase stood out in his mind. Now he wondered. Had the Legend become merely a story, an entertainment? Had the stone ceased being a mystery that shrouded great power? If not, then what?

Genuinely puzzled, Don Carlos said at last, "I don't know. At the time I was never sure that the little Mayan girl really had the Emerald hidden in her doll, but I did believe in its power. Do I still believe that it could give its possessor the power to rule the world by his thought—?" He broke off, having suddenly realized that he no longer believed it.

"Do you?" Pascal prompted.

"No," Carlos said decisively, surprising himself. "I don't think that's possible."

"My point exactly," Pascal said. "The world is changing. The old beliefs — which had the force of certainties — are gone, or going. I have lived long enough, through many lives, to have observed some of this upheaval. I was eight years old when Galileo was tried for heresy by the Inquisition, and as a young scholar I was very aware of the implications of his discoveries. Some of this, to be sure, was exciting, but my sense of the underlying mood was loss. What was lost was felt, and mourned. In the words of an English poet whose poems I admired, 'The new philosophy calls all in doubt; the element of fire is quite put out.'

"Today we think thoughts that were not possible two hundred years ago, and thoughts that were taken for granted as true then are increasingly impossible for us to believe now. My time as an alchemist has come to an end. The Ancient Mysteries, which were withdrawing even in the time of my earliest training as an alchemist, are now nothing more than words, to the extent that they are remembered at all."

"The Ancient Mysteries — ?" Carlos began.

"The Ancient Mysteries were what your master, Don Serafino, and I were to be initiated into by our master, the Great Magus. We were trained both in the Ancient Mysteries, which had to do with the journey of the soul, and alchemy, which had to do with affecting the material world by means of occult practices. I must confess I was more drawn to the practice of alchemy, and that is undoubtedly why when we were tested in our ability to do transformations, your master proved superior to me. So, having failed in this, I was not included in the last step of the initiation process into the Ancient Mysteries. I admit that my pride was severely stung, and my response was to vigorously pursue the study of alchemy with the intention of becoming the greatest of all alchemists, greater even than the Great Magus himself.

"But all of that is a long time ago, and as I said, that world is at its end. I do not know if I wish to be reborn into the world that is coming. My pursuit of power has become meaningless. Hence the change of my name and my demeanor and my becoming, like Leandro, a traveling entertainer. I no longer have anything but one wish — for some ultimate transformation that will rekindle in me the element of fire."

Don Carlos and Pascal had reached a point more than halfway up the mountain slope and had come to a boulder on which a figure had been pecked that seemed to represent a rising sun. "Perhaps this spot in close proximity to a sun symbol," Pascal said, "is a good place for me to tell you about an experience that underlies what I have just said. It is also the confession I promised you."

They sat down on the trail with their backs to the boulder with the sun symbol and looked out over the canyon. "Something quite strange happened," Pascal began, "after my unfortunate last meeting with Leandro. For all that I had told him I needed a large sum of money, what I had really hoped was that he would lead me to you. I knew that I was mortally ill and I thought that you, with your skill in transformations, might be able to transform me into a healthy state."

Carlos started to object, but Pascal cut him off. "It's not such a far-fetched idea, and I'm rather surprised it hadn't occurred to you. Your transformations change a human being into another type of being altogether. As Don Serafino demonstrated in transformations that I witnessed, it was not a matter of gross changes in one's human body, such as my potions produced, but something much more radical, more so even than transforming lead into gold. In any event, Leandro had failed to find you, or so I thought, and while he had brought me a large sum of money — the ransom money — I did not particularly like his treacherous method of obtaining it or, worse yet, his attempt to kill my daughters to protect them from the consequences of his crime. I rode away from that meeting, I may say, very highly annoyed.

"After I'd gone some distance from the site where Leandro had been killed, something impelled me to turn around and look behind me. I saw that there were only three ogres following me with the ransom money. The fourth, whom I had told to search the mesa above the road, had not returned. I debated — was it worth my time to backtrack and search for the missing ogre? Was it sufficiently important to learn why he had not returned? I do not like unanswered questions, and in the end I decided to go back. Soon I noticed that the quality of the air was different as we approached the site where I had met with Leandro, and the difference in the air increased as I drew closer. The air seemed to have a kind of sparkle, like a sparkling wine.

"I approached slowly and quietly, keeping my horse at a walk and the ogres behind me. We stopped at an elevated place in the road a little distance from the low-lying stretch where the meeting had taken place. From that higher vantage point I could see two men who appeared to be naked piling up a large heap of stones beside the road. I saw no sign of Leandro's body, which had been lying in bits and pieces in the road when I had left half an hour before. The sparkling quality of the air was very strong. The bodies of the two men — which, as I said, were naked — seemed to be sheathed in light. I was — and I assure you, this is not a word I use lightly — awestruck. I did not think I believed in angels, but that was what I thought these men must be.

"I decided to approach them. For some reason I thought it would be better to dismount and approach on foot, and as I dismounted my back was turned for a moment. When I looked for the men again, they were gone. I remounted and rode quickly down to the pile of stones and ordered the ogres to search the area, in which there were some large boulders but no real hiding places. There was nothing, only the fresh pile of stones and some blood in the road. And the sparkling in the air was gone. Had I observed angels? Had my allowing the ogres to kill Leandro been such an undeserved fate that two angels had come to bury him? Nothing in anything I believed could account for this — but I believed what I had seen. And it made me question everything.

"I was not, for all that I was a priest, a religious man. I performed ceremonies, and I was particularly good at exorcisms; I was an excellent administrator, but my interest was in the power of the Church as an institution and the role I could play in that. But if I had seen angels—! Suddenly it was not a transformative healing of my physical decline that I sought, but transformation into an angelic being. And if Carlos Buenaventura, the gifted apprentice of the gifted Don Serafino, could do what I saw Serafino do, then Carlos Buenaventura could do this for me."

Don Carlos knew perfectly well that the naked angelic beings covering Leandro's body with stones had been himself and Inéz, whom he had transformed into Iñigo the Basque warrior. They had been through numerous transformations in the hour or so before Pascal, as Don Malvolio, had come upon the scene. They had watched Leandro being dismembered, they had been afraid for their lives, and Inéz as Iñigo had killed an ogre. Their auras, when Don Malvolio saw them piling stones on Leandro's body, must have been extremely intense, making them appear to be angelic beings. But Carlos had been too busy to pay attention to those details at the time, and he didn't think that he had been raised to a higher level of being. And Inéz, in response to those many transformations once she got home, had been ill for months. But he had no intention of disclosing this to Pascal.

"I have never done such a thing," Don Carlos said, responding at last to what Pascal had said. "I believe I could transform you into another creature, something lower on the Chain of Being than man—for instance, some sort of hawk—but I don't know that I could transform you into something higher. So, even if I put you through a number of transformations, would it get you what you want? I don't know, and I rather doubt it."

Pascal laughed. "Just do your best," he said.

The words echoed in Carlos's mind. Then he remembered that they were the same as the last words that Zoila had spoken to him when she appeared to him at Manuela's deathbed. Should he take that to mean Zoila and Pascal were, in a sense, speaking as one?

"And why should I do this?" Carlos asked suddenly.

Pascal seemed momentarily stumped. Finally he replied, "Because you have the power."

Don Carlos was not sure if Pascal intended this as a statement or a question. "Well," he said at last, "let's try some transformations. Would you like to fly?"

"Indeed I would."

"I need to make some preparations," Carlos replied.

"Of course," Pascal said. "But could we do it as early as tomorrow? As I told you, Juan's daughters have invited me for a puppet-theatre performance tomorrow morning, and we could return to this place as soon as the performance is over."

Carlos agreed, and they began to walk back down the canyon. They parted at Pecos Road, where Pascal had left his caravan, and Carlos continued alone across the river, passing his own house, crossing the plaza, and heading for the Beltráns' as he turned Pascal's words over in his mind. "You have the power," Pascal had said. Was that a temptation, Carlos wondered, to use his power in a way that might prove unwise? And he had then, foolishly, rushed in with an offer to try some transformations on Pascal, which Pascal had eagerly accepted. Foolish or not, it was done. The problem now was how to go about it, while offering as much protection as possible to all concerned. The risks to Pascal he would do his best to explain to him. If there was any risk to himself in exposing his abilities to Pascal — well, possibly he could cover himself, too. He sighed. He would need Inéz's help, and he knew she wouldn't like it.

He found Inéz in the kitchen, in the thick of dinner preparations. "Not a good time," she said.

"I know," he replied. "But it's important."

She stopped what she was doing and looked at him, a shade of alarm on her face. "Rita," she said to her assistant, "I will be right back." She turned Carlos around and followed him out the door.

Quickly, he filled her in on his conversation with Pascal, ending with Pascal's wish to be transformed into an angelic being. "I told him I didn't know if I could do it, but I did offer to try. I asked him if he wanted to fly, and he said yes."

"Carlos!" Inéz exclaimed in shock. "Are you out of your mind? Transforming someone—and I should know—is a very intimate undertaking. Something of yourself enters into the exchange. I know this. You will make yourself vulnerable to him, even if you don't know it, and he is a very powerful sorcerer. He may even learn the secret of doing transformations from being transformed, for all I know. He could turn your power against you!"

"I know, I know," Carlos said. "You're right, I shouldn't have offered, but I did, and now I need to figure out a way to do it while protecting myself."

"Yes, but how can you do that?" Inéz cried.

Even while Inéz was fulminating, Carlos had begun to work out a plan. "Let me ask you this," he said. "If my life were threatened by an enemy, would you try to protect me?"

"Of course I would! I would risk my life, if necessary. But if that meant battling with Pascal—he has powers you and I know nothing about!"

"That's true," Carlos agreed. "But you won't need to match his powers to help me. Let me tell you what I have in mind." He then carefully set out his plan.

Inéz raised a number of questions, but in the end she agreed. The only thing she didn't like was the part that required her to be transformed into a falcon. "All those transformations we did when we rescued the Trigales children!" she protested. "They left me sick for months afterward."

"I know, Inéz. But in that case we made nearly twenty transformations in rapid succession over a very few days. I don't believe that undergoing just one change of form for a few hours will have the same bad effects on you."

"Carlos, for you, I will do it," she said.

They left it at that.

28

Flight

By Tuesday night Don Carlos felt very tired, having slept only briefly during his vigil at Manuela's bedside two nights earlier, and not having slept well the previous night at the Sacred Pool. Consequently he went to bed early, and he awoke refreshed on Wednesday morning about the time that he usually got up to meditate. He knew he had a good deal to accomplish before meeting Pascal later that morning. After his usual two hours of meditation, he joined Orfeo for breakfast. Then he saddled Eagle and left for Rancho Rosón, riding along at an easy trot that covered the distance quickly. Upon arriving at the ranch, he located José and explained what he hoped José would help him do. As soon as José could get Viva saddled and ready to go they were on the road back to Santa Fe.

They rode directly to Pedro's stable and found Pedro cleaning stalls. Carlos told him what he had in mind for later in the morning and the role he needed Pedro and his stable to play in it. Pedro, raising no objections, agreed, and told José where he could put his horse.

Carlos rode home and handed Eagle over to Orfeo to be unsaddled and turned out into the corral. He then walked to the Beltráns' and found Inéz working in the kitchen. "Lunch is about ready for later," she told him. "All Rita will have to do is heat the soup and serve it along with bread, cheese, and salad. I don't need to be back here until mid-afternoon."

Inéz and Carlos walked together across town back to Pedro's stable, where Pedro and José were waiting for them. Carlos went over his plan with them one last time. He reminded them that José had never undergone a transformation and had never flown. "I'll begin by transforming José," he said. "Then I'll transform Inéz, and she can coach José in his first attempt at flight."

"While you're practicing," he went on, "I'll go to Juan's place and meet Pascal there as planned. He and I will take the trail up the Santa Fe River Canyon. When we're far enough into the canyon to be out of sight of Santa Fe, I'll transform the two of us into some sort of raptor. By then, Inéz and José in falcon form should have arrived somewhere in the vicinity, doing their best imitation of two falcons circling above the canyon rim in search of a mid-day meal."

Don Carlos climbed into the stable loft with Inéz and José and effected the two transformations. So far, so good, he thought to himself as he left the stable, crossed the river, and took Canyon Road to Juan Archibeque's place. As he turned the last corner in the road that led to the house he could see Juan, Mara, and Selena sitting on the bench next to the front door. Pascal's caravan was parked beside the road and Listo the mule was nibbling on a small pile of hay next to the caravan. Pascal and Juan's daughters were nowhere in evidence.

Juan saw Don Carlos approaching and called to him. "We've been told to wait outside while the girls put the final preparations on a hand-puppet drama they intend to perform for us. I hear a great deal of laughter from inside the house. I hope that means they'll soon have their presentation ready for an audience."

A few minutes later Pascal poked his head out the door. He was grinning and had Polly on one shoulder, Prospero on the other, and was pulling Che along on a leash. "This rascal," he said, gesturing toward Che, "will disrupt the play if I don't keep a tight rein on him. The play, I'm told, is ready. Please come in."

By the time everyone got inside it, the small *sala* was quite crowded. Carlos, Mara, and Selena found seats on two benches and Pascal and Juan sat down in the only chairs. Facing them was a small stage with a wooden frame and a curtain surround below the stage. Carlos supposed that the Archibeque girls and their hand puppets were hiding behind the curtain.

His assumption proved correct when suddenly six hand puppets thrust up onto the stage. There were three pairs, a man and a woman in each. One pair was all green, a second was all yellow, and a third was red.

The green woman spoke first. "We are peaceful."

The yellow man spoke next. "We are wise."

The red man and woman shouted, "We are angry!"

Addressing the red couple, the yellow man remonstrated, "You would be happier if you were green and peaceful!"

"That's not our nature," the red man replied.

"But it's better to be happy than angry," the yellow woman said. "See how happy the green people are," she went on, pointing to them, and the green man and woman did a little dance.

"They're just pretending to be happy," the red man said. "No one's as happy as they're pretending to be."

"We're happy," the green man insisted.

"Liar!" the red man shouted. "If I punched you or kicked your wife, your mask of pretend happiness would fall off and we'd see the anger underneath it!" Carlos suspected that this rather complicated thought and sentence came from Danielle, the oldest of the girls.

With that, the red man rushed at the green woman and knocked her down and began kicking her. The green man yelled, "Stop!" and jumped on the red man and began hitting him, which caused the red woman to leap in and try to pull the green man off the red man.

Che became agitated and started screaming excitedly. "Che," Pascal whispered, "loves nothing better than a good fight."

"There's no such thing as a good fight," the yellow woman said, in what Carlos thought was probably an impromptu response. "I order everyone to start singing right now!" She began to sing a silly song: "Oh! I am so happy! I am so gay! I never felt like this on any other day! I'm just as happy as can be!"

The song didn't have an immediate effect, but by the third time through the fighting puppets had stopped pummeling each other and joined the yellow man and woman in singing. When the fourth round of the song ended, the two yellow puppets announced in unison, "You can't sing and be sad or angry at the same time. That's the meaning of this play." And the puppets withdrew from sight.

The audience applauded enthusiastically and Pascal called, "Come out, girls! Take a bow," which they did to more applause and many compliments.

Pascal stood up and handed Che to Selena, Prospero to Mara, and Polly to Juan and said, "Now you must excuse us. Don Alfonso and I are going to take a walk up the canyon. When we get back, I hope you'll have a show for us that includes Polly, Che, and Prospero as characters."

Carlos and Pascal left the house and started walking up the trail into the canyon. "Did the girls come up with that story all by themselves?" Carlos asked.

"They're very clever, and I'm sure parts of it were of their invention, but I believe the basic story, and the song, were something that Mara and Selena taught them. The girls and their governesses are all born entertainers."

Deciding to confront the issue directly, Carlos asked, "Tell me, Pascal, are you going to identify yourself to Mara and Selena as their father?"

"I'm quite sure they know," Pascal replied. "But we seem to have come to an unspoken agreement to say nothing about our blood relationship. I prefer it that way, and they seem to also. The past is past and, as you can see, I am living in the present in a way that's very different and that I enjoy very much."

"It's probably just as well to let go of the past," Carlos agreed. "If they think of you as their father, Mara, at least, will remember that she blames you for her mother's death. So the less said about your relationship, the better."

"I suppose you're right," Pascal said, "although I would like to assure her that I did not kill her mother. It was only a coincidence that I happened to be there when Violeta died. But I can't prove that, and simply saying so wouldn't serve any purpose."

They had been walking steadily uphill and had reached the boulder with the figure pecked on it that seemed to be a sun symbol. Stopping beneath the image, Don Carlos said, "This is where we spoke of undertaking what we called an experiment. Do you still want me to attempt to transform you into a raptor?"

"I very much hope you will," Pascal replied.

"Do you have any questions about the process, particularly about the risks it may entail?"

"I assume that when you mention risks, you are speaking from experiences you've had with transforming a person into an animal form?"

"Yes."

"What can go wrong?"

"At times," Don Carlos replied, "I've had trouble bringing about a complete transformation of another person on the first try. And sometimes people I have changed fully into animal form have experienced unpleasant effects once I've returned them to their original form."

"Such as?"

"Dizziness, disorientation, fever, extreme fatigue."

"Not that my knowing more matters one way or the other," Pascal said, "but I have always been fascinated with details. Do you have any thoughts about why people suffer these aftereffects?"

"I think it's a result of one's human body having been transformed into something that's totally alien—in size, weight, shape, and mind. The transition is a shock to one's whole being."

Pascal, undeterred by this information, asked, "So what kind of raptor are you going to attempt to transform me into?"

"The best choice would be a raptor with which you have some prior experience. What would that be?"

"I was a member of several royal courts, and as part of the king's entourage during hunts, I often handled falcons."

"Good. A falcon you will be, and I will join you as the same."

"Could you describe the process a bit? Once we are falcons, where will we fly, and will we be able to communicate?

"In my experience we should be able to communicate by exchanging thoughts. If that doesn't work, simply try to follow me wherever I go. As for our route, I thought we would start by flying up the canyon until you're clearly comfortable with flight; then we can ride updrafts until we're above the canyon's rim. From there we can fly northwest to the Rio Grande, which is magnificent when viewed from above. Finally, we can circle back on a course over Santa Fe and land here. How does that sound?"

340 ──────

"Good."

"Then if you'll squat down and bring images of falcons to mind, I will attempt to transform you."

"Why the imaging, and why should I squat down?"

"By squatting down you'll experience less disorientation when you suddenly find yourself five feet shorter than your human height. As for imaging, that may help the process along. One further detail. Once you've become a falcon, your clothes will be draped over you. I'll remove them, change myself into a falcon, and we'll be on our way."

The two men crouched down. Don Carlos didn't need to squat, but he decided to do so in order to provide an example for Pascal. Both men became silent. Don Carlos shifted his attention from normal human activities and thoughts to extending his sense of a larger self out into the wild environment of the canyon. He soon felt quiet and comfortable, although he sensed the presence of something besides nature. It was like a dark shadow. He decided that Pascal's hungry ghosts were hovering about. Time to act, he told himself. He imagined Pascal as a falcon, putting powerful mental energy into seeing Pascal in falcon form.

He heard a rustling to his left. Turning to look, he saw a falcon's head peeping out of Pascal's clothes. Don Carlos got up and quickly removed the clothes that surrounded the falcon. Then he just as quickly undressed and changed himself into a falcon. Concentrating his thoughts, he asked, "Can you perceive my words?"

"Yes!" Pascal replied emphatically.

"Then we're ready to fly," Don Carlos replied. "Test your wings while we're still here on the ground." After a few flaps of his own wings to demonstrate, Carlos went on. "Simply push off the trail into the canyon, flapping your wings strongly to get airborne. Follow me!"

With that instruction Don Carlos pushed off into the air above the canyon. He gave a few strong strokes of his wings and then banked to the left to see how Pascal was doing. Pascal had a small problem with coordination initially, but he quickly became adept.

Don Carlos set a course up the canyon, using occasional strokes of his wings to maintain altitude, but otherwise coasting. They soon reached a sharp escarpment on their right. Don Carlos veered into a tight turn and shouted to Pascal, who had fallen somewhat behind, "See if you can begin to fly in circles. There's a strong updraft here. Ride it upward."

Pascal didn't reply, but he seemed to understand. Soon the two falcons' flights took the form of a gyre, spiraling ever higher.

Once above the nearby peak, Don Carlos set a course to the northwest. About six miles later they reached the Rio Grande. Don Carlos thought this was far enough to go, since they had to make the return trip also, which would double the length of Pascal's first flight. He turned back and maneuvered into place next to Pascal and said, "Let's circle over the river for a few minutes. On a day when the sky is half clear and half cloudy, the reflection of the sky in the river can be quite absorbing."

For some time Don Carlos had been aware that three falcons were following in their wake about half a mile behind. The presence of falcons didn't surprise him; he was sure that the large female falcon was Inéz and that the smaller male was José. But he was puzzled to see a third falcon with them. Was this, he wondered, a lone falcon that had joined Inéz and José for companionship?

Pascal had noticed the falcons too, and he called out, "Why are we being shadowed by those three falcons? Are they a threat to us?"

"I don't believe falcons would attack us unless their nests were threatened. They're keeping a respectful distance and may simply be curious to see who we are, since we're newcomers to their territory. I wouldn't worry about them as long as we stick to our business."

Don Carlos had noticed something else. A large flock of blackbirds was visible at a low altitude below them. The blackbirds, perhaps a hundred in all, had moved along the same route as Carlos and Pascal. They would roost temporarily in a tree, making it appear to be an almost even mix of green leaves and fluttering black birds. Every time Carlos and Pascal got well ahead of them, the flock would lift off in unison and move to a tree closer to the falcons' new position. Don Carlos was fairly certain he knew what this was all about, but it wasn't until he and Pascal had begun their return flight that his suspicions were confirmed.

He and Pascal had been gradually drifting down to a lower altitude. Perhaps this was the result of Pascal becoming a bit tired, or it may have been occasioned by a mutual desire to see the landscape below from a closer vantage. The blackbirds' most recent migration from tree to tree had taken them to a huge cottonwood that was slightly ahead of the arc on which Carlos and Pascal were flying. When the two falcons were about to pass over the cottonwood, the blackbirds lifted off in a mass of beating black wings accompanied by harsh, creaky cries. They were flying straight toward Carlos and Pascal.

Instantly recognizing what was happening, Don Carlos called to Pascal, "Look out! We're about to be attacked by those blackbirds! Move forward as fast as you can."

But it wasn't fast enough, and although Don Carlos had thought the flock was preparing to attack both him and Pascal, it was soon obvious that Pascal was their primary target. As they caught up with him they dove down to peck at his head, back, and tail. No individual blow seemed particularly damaging, but the harassment was severe and it was distracting Pascal from his flight. Carlos thought this might become quite dangerous.

He veered to the right and approached the swarming blackbirds from the side. The outer edges of the flock shied away from him, but the inner group, the ones leading the attack on Pascal, remained undisturbed. Up close, the birds' black plumage and beady yellow eyes were an ominous sight that sent a shiver through Carlos's body. And as a result of his sortie, six blackbirds turned off to pursue him.

Out of the corner of his eye, he saw that the three falcons who had been shadowing him and Pascal were rapidly closing on the attacking blackbirds. Led by Inéz, they had gained altitude until they were above the swarm of blackbirds. Once directly over them, the falcons went into steep dives, aiming for the attackers that were closest to Pascal. The three brushed the upper band of attackers, frightening them into scattering.

As the falcons pulled up and returned to a position above the blackbirds, the attackers resumed their assault on Pascal. Apparently Inéz decided that stronger measures were called for. The falcons dived in among the swarm of blackbirds close to Pascal's tail and emerged from the ensuing melee with a blackbird held tightly in each falcon's talons. They quickly dropped their damaged prey and resumed their attack, plunging into the center of the blackbird flock and snatching more victims. Alarm spread among the blackbirds and they pulled away in a whirl of beating wings. But the falcons kept up their attack, following and picking off three more of the former aggressors.

The blackbirds being in full retreat, the falcons banked and flew off in another direction. Don Carlos would have liked to say something to Inéz, but he thought it was better to keep her identity secret, and she made no effort to speak with him. She and her two companions now resumed their former position half a mile away.

Don Carlos pulled up beside Pascal and asked, "Are you all right?"

"I seem to have lost a few feathers, but I'm still able to fly well enough.

Did you conjure up those falcons? If so, they're a magnificent expression of your brujo powers."

"Let's just say I had something to do with them, and that I was very glad to have them here."

Carlos was thoughtful on the rest of the flight back to the trail above the Santa Fe River Canyon. Pascal, following Don Carlos's instructions, landed successfully next to his clothes. Carlos dropped down beside to him, transformed himself to human form, and then did the same for Pascal. Carlos was relieved to see that only a few places on Pascal's body were bleeding, and those only slightly, from the wounds the blackbirds had caused. "Now," he said, "if you'll excuse me, I want to check on those falcons. There was something about them that I don't understand. I'll be back as soon as I can." With that, he resumed falcon form and took off.

He flew directly to Pedro's stable and into its hayloft. He found two falcons waiting for him. Changing to his human form, he picked up a towel left there for the purpose and wrapped it around himself for modesty's sake. Turning first to the smaller falcon, the male, he changed José back to being José. Then the two of them turned their backs while he returned Inéz to Inéz and waited for her to tell them she was dressed.

The first thing he asked her was, "Where's the third falcon?"

Inéz seemed pleased that he was so puzzled. "She went off to do her chores."

"Dolores?" he guessed.

"Yes. She saw us in the hayloft and asked Pedro what was going on. After he explained, she realized that you might be in danger, and she said she wanted to try to change herself into a falcon and come along with us. I think having a third falcon made our aerial attack all the more effective."

"Did she make it back to human form successfully?" Carlos asked.

"Yes, without any problems. She told us what Old Man Xenome said about transformations—that they work best when strong emotions are involved. She was motivated by a very strong emotion, her love for you."

Don Carlos nodded. "Thank you both for your intervention. It wasn't the one I thought might happen, but your improvisations were perfectly executed."

"I surprised myself a little," Inéz said. "When you came under attack, my Iñigo warrior self came to the fore. I was ready to slaughter that whole flock, if necessary. What was that all about?"

"I'll tell you later. Right now I'd better get back to Pascal. We'll talk more soon." He returned himself to falcon form and flew out the hayloft window and up the canyon trail to where Pascal was waiting for him. Once back in human form and dressed, he asked Pascal how he was feeling.

"Fairly well. After I dressed and stood up I had a mild attack of vertigo. I sat down and it went away. But I think I'll lean into the cliff wall as we walk down the trail. I'm not sure I'll be steady on my feet."

"And your experience of being a falcon and flying?"

"That was magnificent. Thank you. I want to do it again."

"Maybe wait a day or so to see how the aftereffects, if any, play out. And am I correct in assuming that the blackbirds were your hungry ghosts in bird form?"

"Yes. I heard a cacophony of voices shouting complaints about old grievances. I could scarcely hear myself think. Do you see them still hovering behind my shoulder?"

Carlos looked. "No. Death is still lurking to your left, but I don't see any shadows around your right shoulder. And now I think we should start back. The Archibeque household is going to put on a performance for us."

They found the Archibeque girls waiting for them, prepared to put on the performance as promised. It consisted of a reenactment of one of the skits that Pascal had taught Che, Prospero, and Polly. As far as Carlos could tell, the presentation was a flawless duplicate of the skit as it had been done under Pascal's direction. Pascal seemed delighted too. "You are swiftly mastering our repertoire," he said. "Even Che behaved himself, which is a great credit to your skill at handling him."

Don Carlos announced that he ought to be leaving. Everyone bid him farewell and urged him to return soon. Pascal stepped outside and said, "We have much to discuss."

"Yes," Carlos replied. "Can you come to my house tomorrow during siesta?" Pascal said he could, and Carlos then started down the path back to town.

29
Preparations

$\mathcal{D}$espite his impatience to visit Inéz the next morning, Carlos waited until she would be done with breakfast preparations before he walked over to see her at the Beltrán house.

Inéz saw him approaching, and she opened the door and invited him in.

"I want to thank you again," Carlos began, "for driving off those black-birds yesterday."

"You're welcome," she said. "But what were they?"

"Ghosts of people Pascal had wronged."

"Well, they certainly were pecking away at him with all the fury of angry souls."

"Yes," Carlos said. "But before we say more about that, tell me—did your adventure as a falcon leave you feeling ill?"

"No. In fact, I feel full of energy. I even had a strong dream. It was from that past life as Iñigo, the Basque warrior. Instead of dreaming, as I did before, that my house had been burned by raiders and that my family was gone, this time I saw the raiders approaching. I went after them, overcome with fury and ready to kill them for threatening my loved ones."

"Is that what you felt when you saw the blackbirds attacking me yesterday?" Carlos asked.

"Exactly. But what did Pascal say about our intervention?"

"He called the three falcons' attack a 'magnificent expression' of my brujo powers. I didn't bring your name or José's into it, but we all know that I didn't achieve that result solely by myself."

"Still," Inéz replied, "it wouldn't have been possible without your ability to transform José and me into falcons. What are you and Pascal going to do next?"

"He found the experience of flight exhilarating. He is coming over to my house during siesta to talk about it."

"I suppose you'll take him flying again."

"Yes. If he wants, I'll change him into an owl and we'll go out flying at night—not tonight, but some night later this week."

"So what will you do the rest of this morning?"

"Right now I'm going to Pedro's to see how Dolores is doing. I want to make sure her transformation didn't leave her feeling sick."

"Good. Elena and I have an appointment to fence this morning. Then Friday, Saturday, and Sunday many of our leading families—the Beltráns, Peraltas, Cabreras, and Mendozas—are hosting festive meals for the recently engaged couples in our circle and I'm supposed to help. I'm going to be very busy, but I hope you'll stop in and keep me up to date on what happens with Pascal."

"I definitely will," he said. He gave her a light kiss and let himself out the door.

As he was crossing the plaza on his way to Pedro's, Carlos saw Raul Trigales heading in the same general direction. Raul hailed him and said, "I was hoping to find you. I have a favor to ask."

"Anything I can do for you," Carlos replied, "I will."

"This morning Bianca reminded me that the rooms in our house that Diego and Ana now occupy are in separate wings, and neither room is large enough for the two of them. I'm thinking of cutting a door in the wall between Diego's room and the storeroom that's next to it. That would give the newlyweds a two-room apartment of their own. But since they hope to marry as soon as possible after the third reading of their banns next Sunday, this needs to happen fast."

"That sounds like a splendid wedding present, Raul. How I am involved?"

"I would like to borrow your carpenter to make the door frame. Orfeo has just made several such door frames for you. I know it will slow your project, but…"

"No 'buts' about it, Raul. Let's go to my place. I'll tell Orfeo he can start your job right away."

They found Orfeo putting the finishing touches on the door between the future master bedroom and the *sala*. After Don Carlos explained what Raul had in mind, Orfeo packed up his tools and went off with Raul. Carlos went in the opposite direction, walking across the fields to Pedro's stable. Pedro was repairing one of its front doors.

"I've come," Carlos said, "to see how Dolores is feeling."

"She's tired and a little pale, but she says she has no regrets. Why don't you go talk with her? She's in her room."

Don Carlos went in the Gallegos's apartment, knocked on Dolores's bedroom door, and asked if he could enter. She invited him in. He found her sitting in bed sewing. "I didn't feel like getting up," she explained, "but María gave me this coat to repair."

"Thank you for helping yesterday, Dolores. But what you did was risky. I didn't realize you could transform into anything other than a dog."

She paused before replying and then said, "I wasn't sure I could, but yesterday was an emergency. Also, Inéz helped me."

Don Carlos was surprised. "What did she do?"

"I'm not sure, but she and José were perched in the rafters when I told Pedro I intended to change myself into a falcon. Pedro left, and I undressed in one of the stalls. I looked up and saw Inéz watching me intently, and as my gaze met hers she spread her wings wide. She seemed to be inviting me to study a falcon's body before trying to change into one. Then I closed my eyes and imagined myself as a falcon. All at once I felt a jolt, as though I'd slammed into a wall, and warmth flooded into my arms, only now they were wings."

"You made a very fine falcon," Don Carlos assured her.

"Flying was exciting, but I don't want to try it ever again. I'm exhausted today."

"You've earned a good rest," Don Carlos replied. "Don't do anything that tires you until you feel better. You have to be ready to help María when the baby comes, which could be in six weeks or less."

"I think I'll be fine soon," Dolores said. They talked a bit more, and then Don Carlos went on his way and returned to his house. He occupied himself with clearing up construction debris in the house and patio and thinking about the kinds of plants he might put in the patio when work on the house was finished. When he was satisfied with the results of his morning's work he made himself lunch, cleaned up, and sat quietly in the kitchen.

It wasn't long before Pascal knocked at the kitchen door. Carlos called out, "Come in."

Pascal let himself in. Gordo, who had been napping in a corner of the room, instantly jumped to his feet and growled, teeth bared and hackles erect. Pascal said, "Your dog still doesn't like me."

Carlos laughed. "I suspect he associates you with his enemy, Che. Perhaps we should move our conversation outside. I've had a small courtyard built on the south side of the house. We can sit out there and have some wine." He stood, picked up some glasses and a wine bottle, and said, "Follow me."

Carlos led the way from the kitchen to the new *sala* and out a door into the courtyard. He steered Pascal toward a bench set against the wall of the new master bedroom. Carlos sat down on the bench and Pascal followed suit. After Carlos had poured wine for the two of them, Pascal held up his glass and said, "Let me propose a toast. To flying."

"So was it everything you'd hoped for?" Carlos asked.

"Indeed. But I trust you won't think me ungrateful if I add that, thrilling as it was, it took me only halfway to my ultimate objective."

"Which is…?"

Pascal threw his hands apart in an expansive gesture. "Access to higher realms!" he said in a dramatic voice. "What else is there? I have lived in Spain, in most of the rest of Europe, in the Far East! I have served the emperor, I have been in the courts of kings! I have the power to call up storms, or make men quake merely by looking at them! And what does it all matter? After a while it means nothing."

He paused and went on in a normal tone. "You probably don't think of yourself as a man of faith, but I sense that in some respects you are. Whereas in regard to myself, at my core I have always been a skeptic, a thinker rather than a believer. I didn't, as I told you, even believe in angels until I saw those two illuminated beings burying Leandro. That, in itself, transformed my thinking!"

After a period of silence he picked up a different thread of thought and spoke again. "I have devoted a great deal of time in many lives to attempting to create a potion that would bring about physical transformations in human bodies. These either failed miserably or, to the degree they did work, had disastrous results. They produced physical monsters when used on mentally limited men like those poor mestizos who became ogres, or moral monsters when used on men like my best apprentices, Mateo Pizarro and Leandro. The final encounter I had with Leandro, when he told me that he had killed my daughters to protect them, put an end to my work with potions.

"Also, as I have told you, I do not have much time left to live. And I believe that your assistance, your use of your brujo powers, is the only hope I have of achieving a transformation to a higher realm of being in my few remaining days."

Don Carlos studied him. He had initially dismissed Pascal's assertions that he did not have long to live, but it seemed to him now that Pascal's aura had grown weaker in the last few days, and the figure of Death hovering over his left shoulder had become darker. His suspicions of Pascal's motives had by now completely faded, and he was curious where their mutual inquiries might lead. "You'll have to tell me," he said, "why you think I can help. I've already said that I have no experience with transformations any more extraordinary than changing the two of us into falcons."

Pascal gave him a penetrating look. "My powers are not as strong as they once were, but I can see that you have achieved some mental and physical states that I have not. I also sense that you've achieved them in a way quite distinct from my own way of learning. I have always pursued intellectual inquiry into the occult. You seem, rather, to simply give yourself to other realms of being. I suspect that you believe that some sort of mystical union on a higher level is possible. Perhaps you have even achieved it."

Don Carlos remembered his experience of mystical union with the Divine in his Tantric meditations with Zoila, and he was impressed that Pascal had somehow been able to sense that. "Even if I believe that such union is possible," he replied, "it's not exactly the same thing as being transformed into a higher being, which is what you say you want."

"I understand. But in our remaining time together I would like you to transform me into more winged creatures. I'm not yet sure where that will lead, but I have an intuition that it will lead somewhere beyond ordinary existence."

Carlos was thoughtful for a moment. "What about Friday night?" he proposed.

"Night?"

"Yes. We've been falcons by day. Becoming owls by night will enable us to explore another way of being in another environment."

"Excellent, excellent!" Pascal replied with great satisfaction.

The next morning Carlos managed to have a brief conversation with Inéz before she became totally immersed in preparations for a dinner party the Beltráns were giving that evening. "What are you and Pascal going to do next?" she asked.

"Tonight we're going to change into owls and fly to that huge sycamore a few miles south of Rancho Rosón. There's a small pond nearby that animals of all types visit at night to drink. Pascal and I will just sit there and see what we can see."

Inéz looked at him thoughtfully. "I'm beginning to understand," she said. "That's the way you pursue knowledge. You put yourself in a place from which to watch quietly and then see what shows up."

"So," Carlos said with a laugh. "Pascal and I are like knights who set out on a quest, seeking something without having the slightest idea of what will present itself."

"Well, I thought the knights did have some idea," Inéz said.

"True enough," Carlos replied, "but expectations can get in the way of seeing what's really there."

Inéz smiled. "Then may your lack of expectations enable you to see something interesting."

That night, having gained Pedro's permission, Don Carlos and Pascal used the loft in his stable to effect their transformations into barn owls and to launch their flight to the giant sycamore tree. They flew first to the Rio Grande and then south along its course. The new moon hung dark above them. Still, ample light was cast by the abundance of stars that filled the clear night sky, and Pascal expressed astonishment at how well his owl vision enabled him to see the landscape below.

"When we descend," Don Carlos commented, "there will be much more to see." This was borne out over the next six hours as they sat in the giant syca-more and watched the procession of creatures — predators and prey, large and small — that came to the nearby pond to drink. Although nothing unusual happened, the normal, Don Carlos reflected to himself, was itself extraordinary.

The next morning, having spent the previous night as an owl, Carlos slept later than usual. When he finally awoke he knew, from the light streaming in his bedroom window, that the time when he usually meditated and had an early breakfast was long past. He heard some noises in the kitchen and, after getting dressed, he went to check. Pascal and Orfeo were clearing the table of breakfast dishes. Pascal said, a bit sheepishly, "I couldn't sleep after our adventures last night, so I came over to see if you were up, but you weren't. I went out to the stable and found Orfeo feeding your horses. He invited me to join him for breakfast."

Orfeo added, "Pascal has taught me the most interesting *verso*. It's unlike any other I've heard."

"How does it go?" Carlos asked.

The two men turned to each other and began a duet, Orfeo taking the tenor part and Pascal the bass.

Ninguno cante vitoria
aunque en el estribo esté;
que muchos en el estribo
se suelen quedar a pie.

"What does this mean?" Carlos asked. "The first two lines say 'Let no one sing victory, even if he's on horseback,' which seems to mean 'Don't count your chickens before they're hatched,' or maybe 'You're riding for a fall.' But the last two lines—'for many who start in the saddle, end up on foot'—are more ambiguous. If a soldier is unhorsed, he is usually injured, but here it might mean that he simply finds himself on foot."

"I thought it meant 'Pride goes before a fall,' or something like that," Orfeo said.

"I have a slightly different interpretation," Pascal said.

"I'd like to hear what that is," Orfeo replied, "but I'm late for my job at Señor Trigales's place." And he hurried out the door.

"Is that how you feel," Carlos asked Pascal, "pulled out of the saddle and now on foot?"

Pascal nodded. "That's part of it. I certainly don't hold any of the high positions I've had at one time or another. That's humbling in its way, and my present circumstances suggest that I no longer have anything about which to sing victory songs. You, by contrast, have done many things of which you could boast."

"My accomplishments, such as they are," Carlos replied, "have been modest at best."

"I don't want to argue with you on that point. Nevertheless, you have changed considerably in this lifetime," Pascal remarked. "Perhaps it's just a matter of your having been raised in an aristocratic Spanish family rather than the Indian or mestizo families you favored in the past. But several times in our conversations, you have surprised me with your command of knowledge an uneducated man would not have had."

"Blame it on my Jesuit tutors," Carlos replied with a laugh. "But our conversations have led me to see that I've made mistakes in the past, some of them with very bad consequences. That's left me in no mood to sing victory."

"There's no point in dwelling on past mistakes," Pascal replied. "We've both made them. Our present conduct is more important, and from what your friends and neighbors have told me, you are leading an exemplary life. You even appear to be carrying on a chaste relationship with Inéz, a great beauty. That's not like the old Don Carlos!"

Unable to think of an appropriate rejoinder, Carlos merely said, "You, too, seem quite different now from what I imagined in the past."

"You probably thought that the man known variously as Francisco,

Brother Placid, Prospero, Fausto, Maximón, and Aurelio did evil things just for the pleasure of causing pain and suffering. But I assure you, that was not the case. I will admit to having political opponents beheaded, ordering heretics to be burned at the stake, or simply driving rivals into exile and depriving them of their fortunes, but all of that was done in the interest of preserving or extending power. I acted against individuals who were a threat to factions within the state or the Church that I wanted to protect. I saw such action as a good that served not simply my own interests but the interests of the Spanish Crown or the Church."

Pascal stood up. "I could say more about this, but I have an appointment at Juan's to continue teaching Mara, Selena, and Juan's daughters the various skits that Che, Prospero, and Polly can perform. I must be on my way."

"Before you go," Carlos asked, "tell me how much time you think you have to accomplish the greater purpose you've mentioned to me?"

"Ten days; two weeks at most."

"There's a place I want to take you. Let me arrange to take you there, hopefully in hawk form, early next week. Monday, possibly Tuesday, would be good timing for our next adventure."

Carlos accompanied his guest to the door and watched as Pascal walked south toward the river. Carlos then turned and glanced toward the plaza. It was market day, and the plaza was already busy. As he idly scanned the crowd he noticed a change in its random movements; everyone seemed to be looking toward the northwest. Then he heard the thrumming of hoofbeats and saw the cavalry expedition returning on the Tesuque road. He watched the soldiers turn into the Presidio grounds. He set off across the plaza and went as far as the Presidio gates, hoping to obtain some information about the results of the expedition. The guards posted at the gates were uncommunicative, unusually so, Carlos thought, as if they had been ordered not to talk.

It was not until Sunday, as he was walking Inéz home from Mass, that he finally managed to corner a member of the expedition and ask him for a full report. This was Hector Sinoba, a sergeant he'd known for years. Sinoba looked weary. "We succeeded," he said, "in driving the raiders north of Taos, and we managed to kill quite a few. But we took some serious loses—five dead, and Major Cortés was one of them. These Indians, the Numunu"—he slowed down to pronounce the strange name correctly—"are fierce warriors and are skilled at hit-and-run attacks. Major Cortés went after an attacker and took an arrow in the heart."

"That is very bad news indeed," Carlos replied. "Who assumed command?"

"Do you remember Lieutenant Juan de Ulibarri? He is experienced in warfare with Native raiders, and he knew how to counter the Numunu tactics. He located their camps and took no prisoners—not warriors, boys or old men, or women and girls—and that ended their will to fight. We chased them far into the part of the northern plains known as Colorado.

Sergeant Sinoba brightened a little and said, "When we reached the Colorado River, something happened that would have made you proud to be a Spaniard. Lieutenant Ulibarri had us all gather around, and then he claimed the whole of Colorado for Spain. We threw our hats in the air and shouted, 'Long live the King! Long live the King!' Then we all let fly a volley of musket fire."

After Sinoba went on his way, Inéz asked Carlos, "How can they do that? How can they claim a huge tract of land that doesn't have a single Spanish inhabitant?"

"It's absurd, I agree," Carlos replied. "But Spain is an imperial power, and that's the way imperial powers prove that they're imperial powers."

"Hmmph!" Inéz said. "It's so because they say so? And I suppose people will kill each other over that. I really don't want to think about it, and I have work to do this afternoon. The Trigales family is giving a dinner tonight in honor of Diego and Ana. I've promised to contribute a dessert."

Monday morning, just as Carlos was about to leave his house, Mabruke came by. "Señora Mendoza hopes you will go to Señor Archibeque's later this morning," Mabruke told him.

When Don Carlos arrived at Juan Archibeque's half an hour later he found that he was not the only person to have been summoned. Santiago Mendoza, Marco Cabrera, and Pascal were already there. They were standing next to Pascal's caravan, talking with Juan Archibeque. To Carlos's questioning look, Juan said, "Doña Josefina has dispersed the men who reside at her house to diverse locations—Antonio and Julio to visit their fiancées at their home, and Santiago and Mabruke here. The explanation seems to be that she is holding a ladies-only affair, and she thought the three of you would be interesting company for Santiago, Mabruke, and me in a men-only gathering."

Some giggles from inside the house indicated that the female residents had not yet left, and moments later Mara, Selena, and Juan's daughters emerged, each of them carrying a bag. "Good morning, gentlemen," Selena said cheerily.

Carlos remembered Doña Josefina having said that she would like to see Mara and Selena do some of their Moorish dances. Putting two and two together, he said, "I see you have your costumes."

"He's too smart!" Mara declared.

"Don't give things away so easily!" Selena remonstrated. "My sister," she added, "can't seem to keep a secret. But," she went on, addressing Carlos, "since you've guessed our purpose, it's true that we have agreed to do a dance for Doña Josefina."

Carlos asked, "And will your students—Inéz, Elena, and Ariel—also demonstrate their skills?"

Mara raised an eyebrow and glanced at Selena. "I have nothing to say."

Selena was willing to be more forthcoming. "Inéz, Elena, and Ariel have learned the dance, but I don't know if they'll dance it today. I expect Elena and Ariel will demonstrate it privately some day to their husbands, which should make Santiago and Marco happy. I don't know if Alfonso, who hasn't yet persuaded Inéz to marry him, will be so lucky."

This comment seemed to amuse Mara and Selena enormously, and they and the girls left for the Mendoza hacienda full of laughter.

Once the women were out of hearing, Juan spoke. "We needn't be downcast," he said, "because we have not been admitted to Paradise. I'll serve wine and we can discuss the return of the punitive expedition."

Juan directed everyone to sit on two benches by the side of the house and distributed glasses and poured wine. Carlos asked, "Has anyone heard whether the expedition found any evidence of the French threat that Governor Peralta fears?"

"Not much," Juan replied. "A few weapons of French manufacture were captured, but that doesn't prove French support of these raids."

Pascal smiled at Juan. "My friend, you are French, and to you it must be agreeable to have a Frenchman on the Spanish throne. I will not dispute that with you. But what I see in this fact is an expansion of French power that will hasten the decline of the Spanish Empire, and I admit to having had a sentimental attachment to Spain's greatness. At least," he added, "to the idea of it. But now I am convinced that its foundations are being undermined and collapse will come."

Pascal's comments prompted a lengthy discussion on the subject of Spain's imperial power. Carlos joined his companions in drinking quite a lot of wine as the hours passed, but his mind was more on the invisible than the material world. Finally Carlos felt that he had had enough. "We can talk all we want about crisis, war, and decline, but it won't solve anything. What will be, will be. For ourselves, yes, we have a responsibility to support our militia and protect our town. But we also have a responsibility to stay connected to the source of our personal power" — here Carlos suddenly found that he had gone far out on a limb—"which is right here, in this beautiful landscape, in the mountains, in the natural world...." He trailed off, unsure of how to extricate himself from the line of thought he had begun.

"I have an idea," Santiago broke in. "Do you think you could attract a hawk that would fly over us?"

"There are many hawks in the canyon," Juan said. "But Alfonso has no influence over when they appear."

"You underestimate me," Carlos replied, grateful to be rescued. "I have often worked with hawks. And I believe Pascal has done so also. Let the two of us hike up the canyon. I'll bet we can find at least one cooperative hawk, and if one does appear, you'll never know for sure whether it's a real raptor or a figment of your wine-soaked imagination."

Carlos and Pascal left their companions behind and walked up the trail into the canyon. "Isn't this a bit risky?" Pascal asked.

"I don't think so," Carlos replied. "All they're going to see is two hawks flying overhead."

"Do we have to go far up the canyon to change into hawks?"

"No. Just around the first corner ahead. We'll accomplish two things at once. We'll entertain our friends, and we'll give you another experience of transformation."

Once they reached the spot, Don Carlos changed himself and Pascal into red-tailed hawks. They lifted off, flew high in the sky, coasted down the canyon, and circled three times over Juan, Mabruke, Marco, and Santiago. Then they turned back, flew up the canyon, returned to human form, dressed, and started walking back to Juan's house.

"That seemed to go well," Carlos said.

"I don't feel any ill effects at all, and you've whetted my appetite for a longer excursion."

"If it suits you, we can do it tomorrow. I've mentioned a special site I want to show you, and going tomorrow will give you a chance to rest up afterward for the even more important flight I want you to take with me on the solstice, which is a week from today."

"If I'm right about the time left to me," Pascal replied, "that's the outer limit of my remaining days in this life."

"We will move to an earlier date, if necessary," Carlos said. "Now we need to see what our companions have to say about the two hawks that circled overhead." As they expected, their four friends were amazed at the sudden appearance of two hawks. But he and Pascal only listened as the others discussed whether what they'd seen was a coincidence or the result of something Don Alfonso and Pascal had done. Unable to come to any firm conclusions, they had moved on to other topics when Mara, Selena, and Juan's daughters returned an hour later, to all appearances very pleased with themselves.

"Good afternoon, gentlemen," Selena said. "We trust you've had a good time."

"We got a little drunk and watched hawks fly over," Juan replied. "But, of course, our day is brighter now that you have returned."

Carlos and Pascal joined in the laughter and then excused themselves. As they walked back toward town, Carlos said, "Pascal, why don't you come by my place shortly after sunrise tomorrow morning? The flight I have in mind is best done early in the day. Come prepared to ride a few miles on horseback first."

Don Carlos would have preferred to transform himself and Pascal into hawks at Pedro's stable and leave from there. But Pedro had reported that his neighbors had complained about the birds of prey they'd seen flying out of his hayloft. "Anyone with chickens gets very nervous when falcons and owls are in the vicinity," Pedro said. "Use some other starting point, if you can."

"I think we won't need your barn again until next week," Carlos had replied.

Pascal came by promptly at sunrise on Tuesday. Carlos had Orfeo saddle Eagle for himself and Pepper for Pascal. "We're headed first to Rancho Rosón," Carlos told Pascal. "It's near the site I want to show you."

Neither man seemed inclined to talk, so they rode along in silence. When they turned off the road at the entrance to Rancho Rosón, Carlos said, "We'll say hello to my friend José and then continue to the ridge you can see to the west."

José was already at work in the main corral training a mare. He steered her over to the corral fence and greeted his two visitors. Don Carlos introduced him to Pascal and explained where they were headed. José, remembering the blackbird attack on Pascal, said, "I hope your visit to the *piedras marcadas* goes well."

Carlos and Pascal rode away from the ranch across a flat landscape with sparse vegetation. Pascal's only comment was, "Your friend José has some power, and it looked to me as though he has flown at least once in raptor form."

"José is studying to be a medicine man," Carlos replied. "To my knowledge he has flown only once and that was as a falcon."

"Then I may owe him a debt of gratitude, and I'm curious to know who the other two falcons were."

"Of course. But does it really matter? They were there when we needed them. Let me tell you what I have in mind for today." Carlos pointed to a dark mesa that rose abruptly from the flat valley ahead of them. "The surfaces of many of the boulders that have tumbled down the wall of that mesa are covered with figures pecked onto them by Native people. Many of the figures are animal forms; others are abstract or geometrical. But one figure near the top of the ridge has special power. That's the one I want to show you, and we can launch into flight from a ledge near it."

They reached the base of the slope, dismounted and put their mounts on long tethers, and began the steep, rocky climb. They made their way past many marked stones, and they stopped several times to admire the skill with which the animal figures had been rendered, many of them bounding forward as if in flight.

Near the top of the ridge they came to the great dark gray slab of rock that was their destination. On its face was a spiral figure, and two thunderbirds were pecked into the rock above it. "Let's sit here for a while," Carlos said. "I'm curious to know whether you experience the power of this place." Each of them sat down on a boulder a few feet opposite the spiral figure. Don Carlos opened himself to the image before him, from time to time turning his head and taking in the vast landscape that stretched out below them.

They sat in silence for the better part of an hour. At length, Pascal spoke. "This spiral image is a vortex of power that draws on both water and sun energies. It has a whirlpool form that captures the rays of the sun and pulls them into its center. I can feel the sun's rays pouring into it."

"Yes," Carlos said. "And I think that effect will be even stronger next Monday on the summer solstice. I want to return then and attempt to transform you into a thunderbird. It's said that every beat of the thunderbird's wings produces a roll of thunder. I can't predict what the thunder will do, but it might transport you into a realm beyond ordinary reality."

"To have the power to create thunder," Pascal mused. "I would like to experience that before I die."

"I ought to caution you," Carlos said, "that my effort to transform you into a mythical creature may fail miserably. You could end up as a crow."

Pascal laughed. "I appreciate the warning and also the lightness that you bring to matters of the utmost seriousness. Your lightness of spirit is, I believe, one of your strengths."

"Inéz, were she here, would probably say that it's also a source of folly."

"She is wise in her way, too," Pascal replied with another laugh.

"Then let's get to it," Carlos suggested. "I'll change you into a red-tailed hawk and take the same form. We can fly along the face of the escarpment to introduce ourselves to the power of this site, in anticipation of drawing on that power on the solstice next week."

Once Don Carlos had accomplished his and Pascal's transformation into red-tailed hawks, they launched into the air and explored the varieties of hawk flight. Several times Carlos repeated a maneuver he particularly enjoyed—making a steep dive and then reversing direction and letting the thermal currents across the face of the escarpment carry him upward until he was in position for another dive.

Coasting, circling, diving, riding thermals upward—Pascal tried them all without mishap. Don Carlos had had some concern that Pascal, who seemed to be showing his age more day by day, might tire quickly once airborne, but he seemed, if anything, to grow stronger.

Pascal was coasting along the steep face of the escarpment, a little too close to it, in Carlos's opinion, and he was about to call out, "Too close!" when a black wind swept in from Pascal's left and slammed him into the rock wall. Stunned, Pascal went tumbling into free fall.

Don Carlos dived after him, intending to try to grab Pascal's body in his talons and pull him out of his fall. He was closing swiftly on him when Pascal recovered and began to flap his wings. Barely fifty feet before he would have crashed to the ground, he pulled up and flew a relatively level course forward. Carlos caught up with him and stayed with him until Pascal was able to fly up to the ledge next to the spiral figure where they'd left their clothes.

Once they were back in human form, Pascal's first words were, "Death almost got me that time. He's moving in."

Carlos was relieved that Pascal had survived the incident, but he was worried that he might be hurt. "Did you break anything?" he asked.

"I don't think so. But my ribs are sore from crashing into the rock."

"Damn! Let's get back to Santa Fe as soon as possible so you can rest and heal for the flight I've planned for the solstice."

They dressed and made their way down the slope, found Eagle and

Pepper nibbling on the sparse desert grass, mounted, and started off for Rancho Rosón. When they reached the ranch's main buildings, they paused only long enough to tell one of the vaqueros—José was nowhere in sight— that they were on their way to Santa Fe. Once back to town, they went directly to Pascal's quarters at Barbon's inn. After helping Pascal and his aching ribs to dismount, Carlos said, "I'll get some healing salve from Inéz. I expect she has some. I'll bring it by later."

During the next several days, while Pascal was healing, Carlos turned his attention to making his old bedroom ready for Rosa Lugo so she could begin her duties as cook, and then to the larger task of preparing his reno- vated house for full occupancy. There was furniture to acquire—a bed for the master bedroom, a cot for the groom's quarters, rugs, benches, chests, and two chairs. Orfeo made the master bedroom's bed and several benches. Inéz came over briefly every afternoon after she'd served lunch and helped him shop for rugs and weavings. Saturday market proved to be an especially good source of such items. Not only were the regular merchants there, but a few new traders and Pueblo Indians were beginning to arrive in town in anticipa- tion of Peralta's grand conclave, now less than a week away.

On Sunday, as they left the chapel after Mass, Inéz turned to Carlos and said, "I've had Pedro deliver my birthday gift to you while we were at Mass. Although your birthday isn't until tomorrow, I sense from what you've told me that you're going to spend most of it taking Pascal to the *piedras marcadas* and attempting some bizarre transformation."

"Bizarre?"

"Yes, bizarre. Do you even know what a thunderbird looks like, except as a two-dimensional image? And can you transform Pascal into a mythical creature? It strikes me as very bizarre."

"Fair enough," Carlos replied. "But if it works you'll hear a lot of thun- der from the mountains west of Rancho Rosón."

"And how," Inéz asked, "do you know that thunderbirds don't eat men or hawks or whatever form you'll be in as Pascal is flying around producing rolls of thunder?"

"I don't know anything for sure about what will happen."

"Ever the adventurer. Well, let's walk to your house and see what your cook thinks of my gift to you."

It turned out that Rosa was favorably impressed. Inéz had made good on her promise to give him a full set of dinnerware. "Now you don't have to serve guests bachelor-style on mismatched dishes," Inéz said.

"Does this mean that my bachelor days are numbered?"

"Don't be silly. All it means is that you at last have a full set of dinnerware in a matched pattern."

"I am truly a fortunate man," he replied, feeling a great sense of contentment.

30

Beginnings

On each of his five lives as a brujo, Don Carlos had been born on the summer solstice. It was a day he particularly loved, not just because it was his birthday, but because it seemed to him that he could feel the momentousness of the sun's apparently standing still for three days, and then slowly starting to retrace its steps as it began again its journey southward.

Carlos was almost always full of energy on awakening, and he felt even better than usual when he awoke at dawn on his birthday, June 21, 1706. He was filled with the happy anticipation of a child, and he was looking forward to what he hoped would be a spectacular outcome of his plan to transform Pascal into a thunderbird.

He did a short period of meditation, watched from the east window of his new bedroom as the sun rose, enjoyed a breakfast cooked by Rosa, and took Gordo for a walk to Pedro's stable. All was well there. Dolores was fully recovered from her experience as a falcon. Pedro was satisfied with Carlos's solution to the neighbors' anxieties about their chickens when hawks or owls came flying out of Pedro's hayloft. "Pascal and I will leave as common ravens," Carlos told him.

Pleased with how his morning was going, he asked Dolores to look after Gordo for the rest of the day and walked to Roberto Barbon's inn, where Pascal had been staying. Barbon noticed Don Carlos's approach and stepped out the door to say that Pascal had just left for Juan Archibeque's. "He told me he was leaving today," Barbon said, "and gave me a few extra pesos for having taken good care of him." Barbon laughed uproariously. "I should have paid him for being such an excellent guest! He entertained my customers in the evening with stories of his travels." Barbon opened his eyes wide in amazement. "The man has been everywhere, from the Philippines to Jerusalem!"

Carlos arrived at Juan's house to find all its occupants seated in front of Pascal, who was standing up. He greeted Carlos and said, "I was just telling everyone that if a treat is given to one of our animal friends—Che, Polly, or Prospero—a similar treat must be given to the others. Not sharing treats equally puts the excluded parties into bad moods." Turning to Juan, he added, "I very much appreciate your willingness to take in my monkeys, my parrot, and my mule. I hope that the pleasure the animals will give your children will outweigh the nuisance of caring for them."

The little girls were nearly bouncing on the bench with excitement at the privilege of having the animals to care for, and Juan looked at them affectionately. Mara and Selena observed all of this with somewhat wry faces, knowing that the new arrangement would also entail more responsibility for them.

"Yes, yes," Pascal said, in response to Mara's and Selena's expressions. "I am very grateful to all of you. And now that Don Alfonso has arrived I am eager to be on my way. I dislike farewells, so I will make no speeches, other than to express again my thanks."

"Will you be coming back soon?" Danielle asked.

"I have been called to a new adventure!" Pascal said, lifting his voice dramatically. He added more soberly, "Probably I won't be back."

Manon, the middle daughter, gave him a sharp look and said, "You've told us you're sick. Are you about to die?"

He smiled at her directness. "It's true that I've been sick," Pascal replied. "But I've never felt better than right now, and I am quite looking forward to this adventure. Don Alfonso is going to accompany me out of town, where I will be met by another escort who will take me on my travels."

Nicole, the littlest girl, burst into tears, stood up, moved toward Pascal, and wrapped her arms around his leg, her head barely coming up to his hip. "I don't want you to go away," she cried.

Mara stepped over and disentangled Nicole from Pascal's leg. "We're all sad to see Pascal leave," she said to Nicole. "But Che, Polly, and Prospero are staying with us to make us feel better. And we've all had such a good time playing games, singing songs, and learning to help Che, Polly, and Prospero perform their skits."

"The pleasure has been mine," Pascal said, smiling.

With a suddenness that startled everyone, Che leapt off Juan's shoulder, where he'd been perched, and jumped up into Pascal's arms. He burrowed into the folds of Pascal's shirt and gripped the fabric tightly with his little hands. Pascal looked surprised and pleased. "Who would ever have thought," he said, "that this little rascal, who's been the most disobedient of my animal friends, wouldn't want to be left behind?"

He gently detached Che from his shirt and handed him to Selena. "I think Selena's Gypsy-Moorish background makes her the best match for Che's rambunctious spirit. And now, I wish you all good health and happiness, and Don Alfonso and I will be on our way."

Selena and Juan stood up, and the other little girls straggled to their feet. "Go with God," Juan said formally, and Mara and Selena echoed him. They all nodded to one another, and Carlos and Pascal turned to go.

Pascal and Carlos walked in silence down Canyon Road. After a while, without looking at Carlos, Pascal said, "I suspect you would have liked a more sentimental farewell scene, perhaps with me making a gesture of reconciliation toward my daughters."

Carlos glanced at him. This was perfectly true, but he did not feel like commenting on it.

Pascal returned his glance. "You are full of sympathy, and concerned with the feelings of others. That's very unlike the man you were in your past life. Perhaps you learned something when I thrust you so rudely out of it." He smiled.

Carlos had the feeling that he was being baited, and he did not like it.

"You have great powers," Pascal went on, "but you do not seem to have pursued power, at least not in this life. When we were both trying to gain possession of Montezuma's Emerald I assumed that you sought it, as I did, for the power it could bestow, but perhaps I was mistaken. The pursuit of power isolates one. It makes one untouchable and does not tend to develop one's capacity for sympathy. So I am rather surprised to find it in you, since your brujo power must necessarily isolate you, and make you, at least insofar as you are a brujo, untouchable."

Don Carlos found that he had fallen into walking in step with Pascal, and Pascal's words opened up his old question, which he thought had been resolved, as to whether or not brujos should marry. Pascal seemed to be offering a reason for a prohibition he had believed to come from Don Serafino but that he had not understood. And yet Pascal was also saying that he had observed in him, Carlos, a sympathy that seemed to be the opposite of untouchability or isolation.

"Help me with this, if you will," Carlos said, his earlier irritation with him having been dissipated by Pascal's last words. "Don Serafino seemed to say what you just implied, that brujos did not form attachments. I thought perhaps I had misunderstood him on that point, since I died before I finished my training with him. In this life I have been drawn to form attachments. Are you saying this is impossible, given my brujo powers?"

Pascal smiled at him. "Obviously, it is not impossible, since you are doing it," he replied. "I expect there will be difficulties, but since this is an unknown path to me I cannot say what they will be. I wish you well on your way."

When they reached Pedro's stable, they went directly to the hayloft and undressed. Don Carlos transformed first Pascal and then himself into ravens and they flew out the hayloft door. Though the sky had been clear earlier in the morning, it had since become overcast, and Don Carlos briefly worried that what he had planned to do might not work in the absence of bright sunlight. But the simple joy he felt in flying caused his concern to fall away, and he gave himself up to the experience of flight.

They landed on the ledge below the rock with a spiral and two thunderbirds pecked onto it. Don Carlos transformed Pascal and himself back into human form and they stood naked in the enveloping warmth of the day. "I think we both need to study these images of the thunderbirds," Carlos said. "A thunderbird is something I've never seen except in this two-dimensional figure, and it's a mythical creature at that; this will not be as easy as changing you into a falcon or an owl." He turned to the two boulders a few feet behind them. "I suggest that we sit there and open ourselves to the images."

Don Carlos, his eyes fixed on one of the images, went into deep meditation. His breath slowed and he felt himself becoming one with the bird. Finally, bringing himself back to a state halfway between deep meditation and normal consciousness, he spoke. "I believe I am ready," he said quietly, turning to Pascal, "Are you?"

Pascal nodded. "I am."

Don Carlos stood up, still facing the images. It was now late in the morning and the sun, hidden by overcast, was high in the sky to the north and slightly east of them. Carlos felt its heat on his bare back, and he drew on its energy as he began to attempt the transformation.

Nothing happened.

Don Carlos asked Pascal to stand up. Drawing his concentration deeper, he took Pascal by the arm and placed him between himself and the images. He noticed that Pascal was trembling slightly. "Assemble all your power and focus it on one of the thunderbirds," Don Carlos commanded. Together, they both gathered power and let power move through them. Suddenly Carlos felt as though he had been hit from behind and pitched forward, which brought him almost up against the back of a huge bird. The creature turned and spread its wings, knocking Carlos against the boulder he had been sitting on earlier. He quickly moved as far away as he could to avoid being struck by the thunderbird's wings as it launched into flight.

It took only a few strokes of his wings for Pascal, now in thunderbird form, to gain a hundred feet of altitude. From there he coasted a short distance along the face of the ridge before turning to head out over the vast landscape below. Carlos saw him give two powerful beats of his wings. Two rolls of thunder followed. Coasting back toward the face of the ridge, he gave two more vigorous beats of his wings. The thunder was louder this time. Pascal beat his wings once more, this time even more strongly. The thunder that followed was so resounding that it shook the ledge on which Don Carlos was standing.

Just then the cloud cover broke open and a shaft of sunlight fell on the spiral figure. It seemed to Carlos as though the spiral was pulling the light into its vortex, the way a whirlpool would pull objects into itself. Feeling as though he too were being drawn into it, Carlos took a step backward and steadied himself. He looked up to see the thunderbird heading directly toward the shaft of sunlight. Once in it, the bird angled its flight downward and glided, wings curved to slow its descent, toward the spiral figure, which was now brilliantly lit by the sun.

There was a muffled boom, similar to the thunder of the thunderbird's wings but seeming to come from a great distance. Suddenly the thunderbird was transformed—no longer a black bird with white-tipped wings, but a gigantic creature clothed in red flames, with reddish-gold scales on its body and long tail, all of it blazing. It descended slowly, wings curved, toward the ledge where Carlos was standing. He moved quickly to be out of its path as it gently landed below the spiral image.

The creature was so large that the very center of its body and its outspread flaming wings were at the level of Carlos's eyes. Transfixed, he saw that in the center of its body was the figure of Pascal dressed in his old-fashioned entertainer's outfit; that figure disappeared and was followed by a handsome, sharp-featured man in Franciscan robes; next came a figure of a high-ranking Spanish official. As each figure faded, it was replaced by another. After the high-ranking official's form disappeared, it was replaced by a monk with a tonsured head, then by an alchemist in a robe covered with strange symbols, next by a young courtier with a necklace indicating that he had great authority, next by a soldier in armor carrying a shield with a royal crest on it, then by a monk in Benedictine attire, and so on through a succession of figures until a young man dressed as a troubadour stood there with a lute in his hands. Finally, younger and younger versions of the young man followed until a naked infant sat in the midst of the flames. The infant, a boy, threw his head back and laughed, though the sound Don Carlos heard was more like a peal of thunder than an ordinary laugh. The beam of sunlight ended and the infant boy figure vanished.

As the figure disappeared, the great flaming body of the bird seemed to be consumed like straw. The flames gradually died down, leaving only a pile of embers on the ledge across from Don Carlos. Smoke arose from the embers until they slowly burned to ash.

Don Carlos sat still in a scene that seemed to lack sound of any sort. No birds, lizards, rustling of plants, or wind. Despite the heat of the late June day, Don Carlos felt a chill. But he didn't move, waiting to see what, if anything, would follow.

The first movement came from a light gust of wind. It was followed shortly by a stronger gust that stirred up the ashes where the giant bird had landed. By now Don Carlos was certain of what he'd seen. The figures within the flames were a succession of lives that Pascal had lived. The giant bird that had burst into flames was a thunderbird that had been transformed into a Phoenix.

As these thoughts passed through Don Carlos's mind, the wind grew stronger and stronger, and the ashes that were all that remained of Pascal in Phoenix form blew away on the wind currents. Eventually nothing was left but a bare ledge beneath a spiral vortex on an overcast day.

Knowing that according to the legend, the Phoenix is a creature that lives for five hundred years, is consumed by fire, and then rises from the ashes, Don Carlos half expected to see the final stage of the legend play out in front of his eyes. Eventually concluding that nothing more was going to happen, that no Pascal or Phoenix was going to appear, Carlos transformed himself into a raven and flew back to Pedro's stable, landed in the loft, changed to human form, got dressed, and climbed down from the hayloft to the stable's floor.

Lost in overwhelming emotions, he didn't notice Inéz standing in the shadows until she moved toward him. She threw her arms around him and murmured, "I'm so relieved that you're back; I was afraid for you."

Don Carlos replied, "Walk with me to my house. I'll tell you about what happened as best I can, but some of it was beyond belief." But as they walked slowly, arm in arm, across the fields between Pedro's stable and his house, he gradually returned to his ordinary mind and was able to describe what he'd seen in some detail.

"Did you bring about all those changes in Pascal with your brujo power?" she asked.

"They weren't all my doing," he replied, "certainly not Pascal's transformation from a thunderbird to a Phoenix. That was entirely his doing."

When they reached Carlos's house, Gordo, who'd apparently escaped from Dolores's care and gone home, trotted out to greet them. Everything was so ordinary, so familiar, so down to earth. Carlos told Inéz what he wanted. "I need you to come into my new bedroom and hold me in your arms."

She didn't object or even mention that the neighbors would talk. Instead, she followed him into his room and lay down next to him on the bed. Gordo jumped up and tried to wiggle in between them, but Inéz pushed him away. "You can stay on the bed," she told him, "but you can't come between us." Gordo understood and curled up behind Carlos's back.

"What's your strongest emotion at this moment?" she asked Carlos.

"Don't take this amiss," he replied, "but I feel terribly lonely."

"I understand," she said, pulling him closer. "It's as Pascal told you, that you and he were the last of your kind, and now there's only you."

"And I'm not exactly what I used to be either, though I hope that wherever I'm heading in this life, it's toward a better way of living in this world."

"In any case, it's over."

"What's over?"

"No more Don Malvolio, or Pascal as he called himself recently."

"I can't say that for sure. According to the legend of the Phoenix, this great creature lived for five hundred years, and then it burned to ashes, but it arose from the ashes a few days later to begin another life."

"So we might not be done with Pascal."

"I don't know, but why would he want to return from the exalted state he achieved today to being a mere mortal?"

"I don't know either, but right now I'm happy to be a mere mortal and to have you all to myself."

"Seize the day," Carlos said, trying to kiss her. "No matter how long one's life is, it's a good saying."

"Seriously, Carlos," she asked, pulling a bit away from him. "How long are you going to live?"

"My fondest wish, the deepest desire of my heart," he replied, "is to live with you, as your dearest companion, for a very, very long time."

Glossary of Names

Abascal, Aurelio: Chief Inquisitor
Alvarez, Joaquin: Don Carlos's stepbrother
Alvarez, Francesca: "Francie," Joaquin's wife
Alvarez, Rodrigo: Don Carlos's stepfather
Archibeque, Juan: French exile in Santa Fe
Archibeque, Danielle: Juan's daughter
Archibeque, Manon: Juan's daughter
Archibeque, Nicole: Juan's daughter
Archuleta, Nicholas: New Mexico's attorney general
Archuleta, Lucila: Nicholas's wife

Barbon, Roberto: Owns Santa Fe inn
Barrera, Gilberto: Don Carlos's next-door neighbor
Beltrán, Javier: Santa Fe merchant
Beltrán, Cristina: Javier's wife
Beltrán, Elena: their daughter
Benedicto: Father Murrieta, parish priest
Berdugo, Arsenio: member, Town Council

Cabeza de Vaca, Alfonso: Don Carlos's public name
Cabrera, Salvador: New Mexico's vice governor
Cabrera, Regina: Salvador's wife
Cabrera, Marco: their son, governor's secretary
Camacho, Sergeant Roque: cavalryman
Campos, Diego: Don Carlos's former groom
Castillo, Mauricio: Santa Fe sheriff
Ceballos, Emilia: Bernalillo ranch owner
Chacón, Estefan: Pueblo Indian
Chamiso, Leonides: Santa Fe resident, Indian
Contreras, Chico: informer
Contreras, Manuel: schemer, Town Council aspirant
Cortés, Major Tomé: Cavalry officer

de Illueca: *See* Illueca, Gustavo de
de Luna: *See* Luna, Leandro de
de Ogama: *See* Ogama, Magdalena de
de Recalde: *See* Recalde, Inéz de
de Rosas: *See* Rosas, Luis de
de Silva: *See* Silva, Ricardo de
de Tortuga: *See* Tortuga, Ignacio de
de Ulibarri: *See* Ulibarri, Juan de
de Vargas: *See* Vargas, Diego de
Díaz, Atilio and Caterina: Don Carlos's tenants
Díaz, Marisol: their granddaughter
Dolores: mestizo shape-shifter
Dorantes, Father Arturo: inquisitor

Escobar, Jesús: Apache manservant

Faustino, Clemente: Santa Fe farmer's son
Flores, Pablo and Tavio: hired hands
Frida: Manuela Maldonado's alias
Fuentes, Mariano: accused mestizo blasphemer

Gallegos, Pedro: runs stable for Raul Trigales
Gallegos, María: Pedro's wife
Gómez, Manuel: Indian farmer
Guzman, Alejandro: cavalryman

Herrera, Zoila: Don Carlos's meditation teacher

Ibarra, Sancho: Indian farmer
Illueca, Gustavo de: Franciscan inquisitor
Iñigo: Inéz's Basque ancestor
Inocente, Brother: Franciscan inquisitor

Jiranza, Orfeo: Don Carlos's handyman

L'Archevêque, Jean: Juan Archibeque's French name
Loera, Clementina: mestizo curandera
Lugo, Ana: Indian servant to Trigales family

Lugo, José: Ana's brother
Lugo, Rosa: Ana and José's mother
Lugo, Lázaro: Ana and José's cousin
Lugo, Rubén: Ana and José's cousin
Luna, Leandro de: magician, Malvolio's apprentice

Mabruke: Doña Josefina's black servant
Madrid, Luis: cavalryman
Maldonado, Manuela: mestizo shape-shifter
Malvolio: sorcerer
Mata, Mara: dancer and governess
Mata, Violeta: Mara's mother
Mendoza, Josefina: family's matriarch
Mendoza, Antonio: Josefina's nephew
Mendoza, Julio: Josefina's nephew
Mendoza, Santiago: Josefina's nephew
Mendoza, Marta: Josefina's granddaughter-in-law
Mendizábel, Bernardo: early New Mexican governor
Miranda, Alonso: Militia captain, town councilman
Montoya, Cristobal: mestizo farmer
Morales, Francisco: deceased town councilman
Murrieta, Father Benedicto: parish priest

Navarro, Gonzalo: cavalryman
Numunu: older name for the Comanches

Orgama, Magdalena de: Indian woman
Ortega brothers: furniture makers

Pacheco, Anselmo: mestizo militiaman
Padilla, Horatio: lawyer
Padilla, Ariel: his daughter
Pascal: itinerant entertainer
Peralta, Ignacio: currently governor
Peralta, Pilar: his wife
Peralta, Juliana and Victoria: their daughters
Piño, Rita: Inéz's Indian assistant
Pizarro, Mateo: sorcerer
Posada, Tito: Presidio cavalry captain

Posada, Margarita: his wife

Rascón, Cipriano: accused mestizo blasphemer
Recalde, Inéz de: Don Carlos's love interest
Romero, Serafino: Don Carlos's mentor
Rosas, Luis de: early New Mexican governor

Serra, Rosario: possible Jewish ancestry
Simito, Lorenzo: Indian farmer
Sinoba, Hector: cavalry sergeant
Suarez, Mateo: church sexton

Tiburcio, Loreto: Inéz's false father
Torrez, Selena: dancer and governess
Tortuga, Ignacio de: Don Carlos's fencing master
Trigales, Raul: Santa Fe merchant
Trigales, Bianca: his wife
Trigales, Anton: Raul and Bianca's son
Trigales, Carmela: Raul and Bianca's daughter
Trigales, Constanza: Raul and Bianca's daughter
Trigales, Cristofer: Raul and Bianca's son

Ugarte, Amado: Manuela Maldonado's lover
Ulibarri, Juan de: cavalry officer

Vargas, Diego de: first post-reconquest governor
Velarde, Fabio: Santa Fe physician
Velázquez, Diego: Spanish artist
Villegas, Matías: Rosa Lugo's employer
Villela, Juan: governor of New Mexico

Xenome: Tesuque Pueblo medicine man

Readers Guide

1. Don Carlos presents himself to the world as Don Alfonso Cabeza de Vaca, an upper-class Spaniard, and keeps his deepest identity, his brujo self, secret from all but a very few close friends. But is this so unusual— having a public identity and a private one that remains secret from nearly everyone?

2. Don Carlos's practice of transforming himself into hawks and owls is perhaps less pure fantasy than deep metaphor. According to Don Carlos, in order to change his form, he must have a deep understanding of the nature of another being. What quality does this require—an unusual degree of empathy with the "other," or what?

3. External forces disturb the peace of Santa Fe's residents in 1706—attacks by Native raiders (the Numunu, later known as Comanches), the threat of French imperial expansion westward from the Great Plains, and the arrival of agents of the Holy Inquisition seeking to root out sorcery and heresy. Did you tend to skip passages on these subjects, or did they add to the texture of the novel?

4. The *Glossary of Names* reinforces the fact that a great many individual characters appear in the novel. What did you learn from the variety of characters—their ethnic and class differences—about Santa Fe and Northern New Mexico in 1706? Of those individuals who received more than passing mention, which interested you most, and why?

5. Mundane daily matters—going to Mass, digging a well, socializing with friends, and the like—are intermixed with scenes of the extraordinary. Does this combination enrich the novel, or does it make it less coherent?

6. The topic of marriage often comes up between Don Carlos and Inéz. Do you find Inéz's reservations credible or admirable? What about Carlos's patience with her reluctance?

7. In the novel's final chapters Pascal says that the world he was born into—the late medieval world—is passing. The most dramatic signs of that transition are the fracture of Catholic unity caused by the Protestant schism and the replacement of the old science (alchemy, astrology, and magic) with the new (astronomy, chemistry, and the manipulation of the material world rather than the spiritual world). Do you see anything similar happening in the past fifty years due, for example, to the sexual revolution, the deep divide between religious extremism and secular values, and the rise of social media and information technology?

CPSIA information can be obtained
at www.ICGtesting.com
Printed in the USA
FFOW04n1121250915
17193FF